VAMPIRE HUNTER D

Other Vampire Hunter D books published by
Dark Horse Books and Digital Manga Publishing

VAMPIRE HUNTER D

VOLUME 11

PALE FALLEN ANGEL

PARTS ONE AND TWO

Written by

HIDEYUKI KIKUCHI

Illustrations by

YOSHITAKA AMANO

English translation by

KEVIN LEAHY

Dark Horse Books®

Milwaukie

Los Angeles

Cover art by Yoshitaka Amano

English translation by Kevin Leahy

Book design by Heidi Whitcomb

Published by
Dark Horse Books
a division of Dark Horse Comics
10956 SE Main Street
Milwaukie, OR 97222
darkhorse.com

Digital Manga Publishing
1487 West 178th Street, Suite 300
Gardena, CA 90248
dmpbooks.com

Library of Congress Cataloging-in-Publication Data

Kikuchi, Hideyuki, 1949-
  [Kyuketsuki hanta "D." English]
  Vampire hunter D / Hideyuki Kikuchi ; illustrated by Yoshitaka Amano ;
  translation by Kevin Leahy.
    v. cm.
  Translated from Japanese.
  ISBN 1-59582-012-4 (v.1)
  I. Amano, Yoshitaka. II. Leahy, Kevin. III. Title.
  PL832.I37K9813 2005
  895.6'36--dc22
                          2005004035

ISBN 978-1-59582-130-0

First Dark Horse Books Edition: October 2008
10 9 8 7 6 5 4 3 2 1

Printed in the United States of America

VAMPIRE HUNTER D

Pale Fallen Angel

PART ONE

Strange Traveling Companions

I

Though the moonlight should've been entirely impartial, the road alone seemed to stand out like a blue snake—it was surrounded by darkness. The leaves rustled restlessly. The wind was picking up.

The road was really a highway. A relatively high number of people and vehicles traveled it by day, but with the coming of night, it became a kingdom of the weird prowled by such famed creatures of the western Frontier as shape-shifting humanoids and matter-changing bugs.

Apparently an unfortunate traveler had invaded their domain tonight. Five or six bizarre silhouettes surrounded a tall figure in front of a carriage way station that sat by the side of the highway. The way station contained bolt-firing pistols, short spears, and longswords that might be used in an emergency, but the figure showed no sign of taking them in hand as he soaked in the hungry gazes of eyes aglow with a green phosphorescence.

What seemed to keep the fiendish forms from immediately pouncing on the man was the cruelty the Nobility had fostered in their creations—the desire to keep their prey in terror until the moment of death. But just then, the voice of the darkness turned that theory on its head as the man asked, "Why do you not come for me?"

By the sound of it, it wasn't the monsters who were waiting, but rather the traveler.

"Then I shall have to make it easier for you to approach. Come!"

With that last word, another light took hold in the darkness, streaking glows of crimson. In an instant, shadowy forms sprang at him from either side. One was an altered insect. Resembling a giant praying mantis, its body began to transform into something denser in midair, from organic to inorganic . . . to steel.

The light of the moon shot up from below. A body that was intended to repel any kind of attack split like a rotten vegetable, spraying an oily substance as it fell to the ground.

The bloodsucking moth-man who'd simultaneously pounced from the opposite side had phosphorescent flecks of gold flying from his wings as he was ripped right down the center. The scythe-like claws of the former and blood-siphoning proboscis of the latter had never managed to strike home.

"Come!"

In response to the traveler's second invitation, a thunder beast firmly planted all six of its paws on the ground as it turned its helmet-like head to the heavens.

Pale bolts of lightning struck the man. The air was ionized, and white smoke curled from the earth. Again and again, lightning struck.

The figure raised his right hand. In it, he grasped a black blade with an elegant curve. The sword had a sheen unlike any weapon local travelers, soldiers, or fighting men would ever carry, and from the instant he pulled it out till he held it aloft, it absorbed the lightning continuously. And even after he drove it deep into the thunder beast's chest, the creature likely never knew what had happened. Lightning crackled around the blade and, as if reading its wielder's mind, leapt from its tip to the thunder beast's face.

Spasms gripped the monster. Though it used the electrical discharge in the air rather than from its own body to shock its opponents, the creature didn't actually have any defense of its own against electricity.

With a pale glow still clinging to the sword, the man raised it high, and then brought it down in a stroke. Though his arms already seemed fully extended, the blade that split the thunder beast's head in two reached a foot further than it should have.

"Two to go—I wish I could tell you to attack me, but the one I've been waiting for has come. Away with you!"

And with that command from the man, the surviving creatures that'd been frozen in place as if awaiting their fate each gave a low growl and immediately vanished into the darkness to either side of the road. They were so incredibly fast that it almost looked as if they'd teleported away.

Flicking the gore from his blade with a single shake, the man slowly looked over his shoulder. At the far end of the highway that ran down from the north, the silhouette of a horse and rider had just come into view. Though the moonlight was bluish, the man on the steed seemed to be robed in a hue far deeper than the darkness. Beneath his wide-brimmed traveler's hat, a pair of oddly glowing eyes gazed ahead.

Stepping over the thunder beast corpse that lay at his feet, the man moved forward. A blue haze swirled in the middle of the darkness—at least, that was how it seemed. For the man was covered from the shoulders down by a cape the color of the deepest sea. The click that came from the vicinity of his hip was apparently his blade being returned to its sheath.

"Balazs?" the black rider asked from his mount's back.

"Indeed. How like the greatest Hunter of this day and age to be so punctual," the man said, although he didn't seem to consult a watch.

However, the rider had indeed appeared exactly at the appointed time.

"Though I must say," the man continued, "my body trembled the instant you approached. Otherwise I never would've let those last two creatures get away."

The rider had approached without the man on the ground even noticing his presence until the very last moment.

"From the time I turned onto the highway, you should've been able to detect me. I wasn't trying to go unnoticed," said the black rider.

With this remark, the man on the ground was made out to be a liar even though he knew all along whom he was dealing with—though it appeared he'd actually been paying the rider a compliment.

Which of them was right?

"State your business," said the figure in black.

"Will you not dismount at least? I have the most wonderful liquor."

There was no reply.

Not seeming to take any particular offense, the man continued, "Then I shall tell you. I wish you to see me to the village of Krauhausen."

The village was on the far edge of the Frontier—a hundred and twenty miles to the west. And it really was the edge, with an ominous chain of mountains miles high towering just beyond it.

"You're fully capable of going alone," said the rider.

"I'm afraid I can't do that," the figure in blue responded.

His hair was golden and flowing, and his ultramarine eyes possessed great beauty. The moonlight only added to his air of mystery, until it seemed that everything surrounding him was reduced to a blur. Everything save one person—the rider still up in the saddle.

"There is someone in the village who won't particularly welcome my arrival. As soon as I approach, I'm sure I shall be greeted with violence. Honestly, I don't believe I can make it on my own. I need your help, D."

"Tell me why you want me to accompany you. And don't say it's because you're not confident in your own abilities."

"*One reason* should already be clear to you. The other I cannot say. But the one who awaits me in the village is a Noble. I want you to destroy him. And that will have to suffice for now."

D said nothing as he gazed at his strange would-be employer. While it was certainly understandable that someone might want him to dispose of a Noble, refusing to disclose the reason was a grave breach of protocol. From the very start, D's attitude had been somewhat unusual. He turned his back.

"Please wait," the figure in blue—Balazs—called out. "I had no desire to expose the shameful actions of my own parents, but it's unavoidable. The name of the Noble who waits in Krauhausen is Vlad Balazs. He's my father."

The horse wheeled around once more.

"Do not ask me why I would have you execute my father," Balazs said in a hard tone. "I must see to it that he is destroyed. That is my sole purpose. I can't allow my power to be whittled away by needless opposition. Although it may be unheard-of for a Vampire Hunter to enter the employ of a Noble, I beg you to break with tradition. Will you not accept this assignment?"

There was no sound—even D couldn't help but fall silent at this explanation. For a vampire to seek assistance from someone whose very purpose was to destroy them, and furthermore to have as the target one's own parent, was not only completely unheard-of, it was truly bizarre. What thoughts flitted through the mind of the young Hunter of unearthly beauty?

Presently, D replied, "Okay."

He spoke from horseback to the other warrior.

"Many thanks," said the man clad in blue. "I haven't been out of my castle much. I thought it would be best to leave everything to your judgment for the duration of our journey."

"Fine."

"Splendid! Now, for your compensation—"

The figure he mentioned was exactly a hundred times the accepted rate.

"Here's an advance."

He pulled a small bag out of his cape and tossed it to D.

Catching it in his left hand, D didn't even look inside before saying, "Okay."

The coins were a precious metal worth a hundred times their weight in gold.

"While you're with me, I won't allow you to feed on humans. If you should happen to break this condition, I will destroy you on the spot."

"Understood," Balazs said flatly. Somehow, his voiced resembled that of the man in black. "Oh, I must be forgetting my manners not to have introduced myself properly. I am Byron Balazs, son of Vlad, the regulator of the western Frontier."

II

Viewed objectively, it really was a strange journey—although the term "earth-shattering" might've been more apropos. The employer traveling with the Vampire Hunter was one of the very bloodsucking Nobles he was supposed to destroy. Needless to say, Balazs could only act by night: This was what the baron said should be apparent to D. By day, he rode in a blue carriage drawn by a team of four horses, and his vehicle had been parked off in a nearby forest when he fought the monstrous creatures. Apparently the four cyborg horses had been told to comply with D's commands, and they followed him meekly.

However, it was plain for all to see that the vehicle belonged to the Nobility. As they went down the road by day, travelers and pedestrians stopped in their tracks with their eyes bugged. Many got off the road and hid. Some even readied their weapons. What's more, the young man who seemed to be acting as a guide possessed a heavenly beauty that no human could hope to equal no matter how they tried. And it was perfectly natural that this thought should pop into the heads of everyone along the road.

There goes a Noble and his servant.

There were some who served the Nobility that were still living, breathing humans. In many cases, it was a victim whose blood they'd stopped drinking just before the person was about to join their ranks—people who'd dropped off into a kind of hypnotic state highly open to suggestion. However, there were also those who retained their senses and still swore fealty from the bottom of their hearts—in a word, "traitors." D must've appeared to be one of the latter. But the people who thought that naturally had their expressions tinged with perplexity due to D's incredibly good looks.

Ordinarily, such a pair would travel back roads by day so that they wouldn't draw much attention and take to the highway by night. Or else they'd sleep somewhere deep in the woods by day and move solely in darkness. If one were to follow the Nobility's natural disposition, the latter option made more sense. However, D went right down the highway while the sun was shining, and stopped at night.

"Why don't we go when it's dark?" the baron asked on the third evening of their journey.

"Are you in a hurry?"

"No."

"Are you bored?"

"No," Balazs replied once more.

Undoubtedly the interior of the baron's carriage was furnished with amusements unimaginable by D. Although the Nobility's scientific prowess may not have unraveled the secrets of time, it had essentially mastered matters of space.

"In that case, deal with it."

"You're in charge. I don't mean to complain, but considering both our physiologies, wouldn't it be far less taxing for us to travel by night? It would also be that much easier for you to keep tabs on me."

Gently raising the brim of his traveler's hat, D looked at the baron.

Transfixed by that gaze, the vampiric Noble shuddered at the hue of the eyes that threatened to suck him in.

"Do you want me to keep tabs on you?" asked the Hunter.

A thin smile seemed to skim the baron's lips.

"No."

"I don't want you to get the impression that I trust you," D added in a voice like ice. "My job is getting you to the village of Krauhausen. And if I were a foe who knew you were coming, I'd choose to attack you by daylight."

"I see. That makes perfect sense," the baron remarked with a gorgeous grin. Though beautiful, his smile also bordered on ghastly. "Although you may not trust me, I have consummate faith in you, Vampire Hunter 'D.'"

He then added, "However—"

At that moment, the creak of what sounded like wooden wheels could be heard to the north of the woods where they traveled, coming from the highway. The roar of engines then came in due course—a number of them.

"There are five, counting the carriage," said the baron. "They're more than a half mile from here."

Though the wheels and the engines surely raised quite a din, only the ears of a Noble would be able to isolate each individual sound over such a distance.

"Would you mind if I went?" the baron asked, having already risen to his feet.

"Do as you like," D replied.

Although he knew there were no homes in the area before he even spoke, in light of the powers the Nobility possessed, it would be hard not to consider the Hunter's response indifferent . . . or even irresponsible.

Once the baron's blue cape had vanished into the darkness, D pushed his hat down over his eyes and sat back against the roots of a massive tree to sleep.

Racing madly down the road was a white carriage drawn by a pair of horses. It was so elegantly crafted, it was apparent at a glance that it belonged to the Nobility—and up in the driver's seat, a young man was madly working a whip. Yet his visage was as expressionless as a stark white Noh mask, and he didn't so much as raise an eyebrow at the sound of gasoline-powered car engines now less than fifty yards behind him.

As the upright collar of the man's coat was flattened by the force of the wind, the neck that was left exposed bore a pair of swollen and discolored wounds at the nape—punctures undoubtedly left by fangs. Neither human nor Noble, this being was merely a puppet who moved at the commands of the master who'd given him the kiss of the Nobility—a *Cesare*.

Although he'd avoided the post towns, he was spotted by a bunch of rustic youths who'd been out playing too long on the back roads, and they decided to give chase. But whether that troubled the driver's numbed brain or not was difficult to determine.

At that moment, a cold voice linked the youth to the vehicle like a thread.

"Our foes are coming. What in blazes are you doing?!"

With veritable thunder echoing from the wagon wheels, the comment rang in the young man's head as if it had been whispered right into his ear.

"It's beyond my power to make them go any faster," he replied, not seeming particularly agitated. "Mistress, I think perhaps you might—"

"Do you think I would actually sit up there next to a servant and work the reins?" the voice said softly, but she quickly laughed, "Oh, very well. Move over!"

Offering no protests, the young man slid to the right, at which point the roof of the carriage opened smoothly and a figure of pure white appeared in the void. Moonlight gave her the luster of silver.

As the figure moved into the position the driver had previously occupied, the young man reeled backward.

The figure in white—clearly female from the sound of her voice—put one hand to a fresh wound on his neck that had left his head connected by a narrow strip of skin. She was stanching the flow of blood.

Turning her golden brown eyes in a loving glance at the youth who'd been killed instantly, she said, "Now that I no longer have you, I shall have no choice but to do it myself. Hmm . . . I wonder where I shall find my next servant?"

As she pursed her lips, a gunshot rang out behind her. One of her pursuers had fired a conventional rifle. As if on cue, a number of sparks shot from various spots on the carriage.

Without warning, the carriage tilted to the right—the figure in white had suddenly tugged the reins to turn. Though the horses managed the angle, it proved too much for the vehicle. Bolts in the coupler connecting the horses to the carriage blew out automatically, setting the animals free.

The vehicle toppled over. Wagon wheels churned up dust and threw grass from the plains everywhere. Shaking the earth, the vehicle rolled a second time and then a third before settling down.

Less than five seconds later, a quartet of lights came gliding down the highway. Cutting their engines about fifteen feet shy of the carriage, the young men got out of their low-slung motorcars armed with every imaginable weapon.

Their vehicles hardly deserved to be called cars. The bodies were rough frames from easily workable materials like wood and light alloys that'd then been fitted with tires and an engine—in other words, go-karts. Each of them looked well used, with their engine compartments pitch black with soot.

"You figure they're dead?" asked one of the young men.

"No chance. We're dealing with the Nobility here. We can't afford to let our guard down."

"If we can catch it instead of killing it, it could be more useful later. We could bring it to some research center in the Capital, and I hear they'd pay a fortune for it."

Compared to other areas, the western Frontier had been relatively free of trouble with the Nobility after their decline. It was therefore understandable that as generations passed, there were more and more people who didn't know how fearsome the Nobles truly were.

These young men didn't realize that when actually faced with one, their earlier words would count for nothing.

Driven purely by a lust for fame and wealth, the men walked right over to death's door.

The door opened.

With the creak of hinges, the upward-facing carriage door slowly swung in an arc. From it, something like a white glow popped up, then glided down to stand beside the carriage, where it resolved into a young woman with a white dress and flowing black tresses. She had prim little eyebrows like willow leaves, eyes as dark as a holy night, and a nose and lips that were beautifully delicate, with every tiny wrinkle and crease of the latter so sharp they'd burn themselves into the retinas of all who saw them. The girl's entire body was also shrouded in white phosphorescence. You could actually go so far as to call it a white flame.

The unearthly aura that welled from her hypnotized the recklessly courageous young men.

One stepped forward with a longsword in hand. He was their leader, and by far the fiercest of the bunch.

It's just a damn Noble, he told himself, but there was nothing he could do about the tremble in his legs. As if to shake it off, he gave a shout of, "Take that!" and drove his blade into the woman.

They had heard about the Nobility's immortal nature from their mothers and fathers. Although stabbing such a creature anywhere but through the heart wouldn't destroy it, it could still prove fairly effective. They would try and grab her while she was still wincing from being struck in the belly—that's what the leader thought.

Without moving a muscle, the woman took the blade through her svelte abdomen.

"Holy shit!" the young man screamed as he stumbled forward.

Feeling no contact, no physical resistance whatsoever, the longsword sank into the young woman's form up to the hilt, and then the young man himself slipped right through her body.

"Whatever are you doing?"

Slamming nose first into the ground, the young man snorted angrily but quickly got up again as her voice resounded behind him with naked scorn. He turned around in shock.

The woman's form had vanished abruptly, but she now stood about ten feet in front of his compatriots, who'd also turned the same way. In her left hand she cradled the man whose head dangled back on the thin strip of skin connecting it to his neck—her driver. Her right hand kept his gaping neck wound covered all the while.

"You—you stupid bitch!"

"Come to me. This time, I shall be the real thing," she told them, her voice so refreshingly clear, it seemed as if the moon above them had spoken.

Ignorant of what lay behind that tone, all the young men aside from the leader shouldered their rifles. Flames and the booming report of gunfire rocked the night air. Because their ammunition used far more gunpowder than necessary, the heavy rifles kicked their barrels up nearly ninety degrees.

But what shook horribly under the impact of the bullets was the driver's corpse. Even though the young men realized she was using him as a shield, it still looked to them almost as if he'd stepped in front of the gunfire of his own accord. For a second they were blasted by a gale of sheer terror, and their fingers ceased pulling the triggers.

"I desire a substitute," said the voice of the unseen girl. It was as if the headless corpse had spoken. "One of you—for the rest I have no use."

A white blur rose straight up from the corpse's neck. The five fingers that'd capped the wound had been taken away.

But something sparkled brilliantly in the moonlight as it rose in a geyser. As the youths watched, it spread in midair, billowing against them like black gossamer and staining their bodies with something dark. Blood. The blood of the driver.

There was no sense protesting that the heart pumping his blood should've already stopped. The only possible explanation was that it continued working even though his head had been almost completely taken off.

Dyed black, the young men stood paralyzed with disbelief for a while, but each soon gave a dying scream and fell to the ground. The gore that'd rained down on them was no ordinary blood. As a result of coming into contact with the girl's hand, it had been transformed into a drug of sorts that, on entering the youths' body, caused a chemical reaction with their blood that in turn formed an unknown but virulent poison. Even their flesh and bones were dissolving.

Ironically, the only one spared was the first one whose skin had come into contact with the black blood. As his friends' faces and limbs collapsed into piles of offal, the leader could only stare in utter shock.

"Come to me," said the girl, beckoning to him with her hand. Now no longer necessary, the corpse of her driver had been discarded at her feet.

It was the leader's good fortune that the girl's beckoning gesture was done half in jest—she had put no hypnotic power behind it. He still had a means of escape. Pushing his longsword against his neck, he slashed through the carotid artery before the woman's voice or the gleam of her eyes could reach him.

"Of all the nerve," the girl said, her voice carrying the first signs of loathing and agitation. "He won't make much of a servant like that. Now where am I supposed to find another one? But wait—there may be a chance if he's not completely dead yet!"

As if she'd just had a wonderful idea, the girl raced gaily to the prone form of the leader. So long as he hadn't died, it would be possible to give him "the kiss of the Nobility" and transform him into one of the living dead. It would be easy enough to get him to do the trivial duties she had for him.

Easily taking away the longsword he gripped, she grabbed the leader by the scruff of the neck and flipped him over. At the time, she didn't notice the spokes from the broken wagon wheel lying beside him.

The leader opened his eyes a crack.

"How splendid! I hope you shall enjoy serving me."

Her pale and lovely visage slowly moved closer to the nape of his neck, and a heartbeat later, an unearthly scream gushed from the girl's mouth. She was going to suck the blood from a half-dead man who could offer no resistance. But in the end, it was this simple act that'd invited her to drop her guard.

Like a curse on the swell of bosom in her white dress, the wooden spokes that'd supported the rim of the wheel were stuck through the middle of her chest. In his dying seconds, the group's leader had wrung one last bit of strength from himself to drive the jagged chunk of wood into the girl's torso. Though he ceased breathing almost immediately, he must've been satisfied by her screams, because in death his face wore an unsettling grin.

"You bastard! You rotten bastard!" the girl bellowed as she reached for the stake in her chest.

In truth, her wound wasn't that deep. The young man's strength had been spent. And yet the girl couldn't pull it out.

On closer inspection, the wheel had lost its outer rim, and most of the wooden spokes had broken off the hub; a pair was still left sticking out from either side, forming the shape of a cross. A cross-shaped stake.

White smoke poured from the hand that'd grabbed hold of it, and the woman's skin had melted away.

Unable to say a word, she was writhing when her body was abruptly turned over to face upward. Before her surprise could even register, the stake was pulled out.

"Who are you?" the girl asked. Apparently some of the cross's effect still remained, as she was barely able to catch her breath.

"I am Baron Byron Balazs," the figure in the blue cape said, snapping the stake in two and hurling the pieces far away. "What are you doing out here?"

Putting one hand to her chest, where a crimson rose had blossomed, the girl let out an easy breath. She'd recognized him as one of her kind.

Curtsying respectfully, she said, "I am Miska, granddaughter of Duke Cornelius Drake, director of the Southern Frontier Control Committee. And I have certain business that takes me to the village of Krauhausen."

"What are the odds?" the baron muttered, and the girl seemed to read something in his expression.

"Could it be that you're headed there as well? If you don't mind, might I travel in your company?" she asked in a voice that tugged at him with dependency.

"That may prove problematic," the baron said noncommittally. He wasn't exactly traveling alone.

"I can't, then?"

Despair spread across her face like the legs of a black spider, but at that point the girl turned with a start. She'd just noticed that the baron was staring at something.

About thirty feet away, D stood beside a colossal bole.

"And who is this?" the girl—Miska—asked in spite of herself.

His sordid raiment was so mismatched with his elegant features, she couldn't help but ask. He looked like nothing shy of a Noble.

"This is my trusted escort. He's known as D." And after introducing him, the baron asked, "Well?"

He was referring to the matter of Miska.

"D? It can't be," the girl said before the man could respond, shock reshaping her countenance. "Vampire Hunter 'D'—how many times I've heard that name. He's our sworn foe!"

"He's traveling with me. He's my partner, so to speak."

At the baron's words, Miska's expression wavered.

"Is he your servant, then?"

"Regretfully, I haven't laid a finger on him. As I mentioned, he's accompanying me on my journey to the village of Krauhausen to keep me safe."

"Impossible," Miska groaned as she put her fist to her mouth. "A Noble and a Hunter would never travel together . . . I simply can't believe it!"

"Regarding what I just asked you—what do you say?" the baron inquired.

"She'll only be in the way," said D. "We'll do what we can. But if you're taking care of her and find you're unable to keep yourself safe, I don't want to hear any complaints."

"Understood," the baron said with a firm nod.

"You can see how it is," he told Miska. "I'm sorry, but we have no choice but to part ways with you. You would do well to try to reach some remote locale before dawn. You'd best go now."

"Do you mean to tell me you, a Noble, answer to a lowly dhampir?" Miska said in a resolute tone. Glaring at D with wildly blazing eyes, she added, "In that case, allow me to ask something of you. I should like you to see me to a safe location."

Though she made this request without any visible concern, it left the baron in a difficult position. As a Noble, he couldn't very well leave a lady in distress. However, he had a greater purpose, and in order to achieve his ends, D would prove indispensable.

Miska gazed at the baron with a rather angry look.

"Very well, we shall bring you to a safe area," he said.

The vitality returned to Miska's expression—like the stars lighting up the night sky. It embodied what it was to be a Noble.

"However, this is only for tonight," the baron added. "If I may speak candidly, the journey we're on is extremely dangerous. Even with this Hunter along for protection, you would probably still be safer traveling alone. I certainly would never leave you to fend for yourself otherwise. I just want you to understand that."

"Understood," Miska said curtly.

The baron's face clouded at the reaction, though it was exactly what he'd expected.

"I realize your position and your terrible plight," the girl continued. "However, this is unforgivable. If you abandon a frail woman simply because it suits your own convenience, the rest of the Nobility shall surely point at you and jeer till the end of time."

The baron fell silent. Though he'd expected a remark like this, he found her words had far more power over him than he would've dreamt possible. For a few seconds, his thoughts made him want to retch blood.

"We can accompany you for tonight alone. If the code of the Nobility decrees that I'm to be an object of scorn for the rest of my days, then I shall resign myself to that fate."

Once more, Miska's expression changed.

III

After that, the group raced along for about an hour until an especially deep and black forest came into view.

Reattaching the steeds to Miska's carriage and helping her inside, the baron then told her, "Once the dawn comes, we must take our leave."

"Thank you ever so much for going so far out of your way on my account," Miska replied as if she was reading a prepared statement, and then her carriage sank into the abyss of silence.

Wearing a bitter grin, the baron walked over to D, who stood by Balazs's carriage.

"Be they Noble or human, someone must look out for women and children," the baron remarked.

"That girl killed four young men," said D.

"Surely that was their fault."

"I'm not blaming her. Even a Noble has a right to defend herself. But if young Nobles had been doing the same thing, you'd certainly have been capable of turning a blind eye."

"Are you certain we can't bring her with us?"

"She could be an assassin," the Hunter told him.

"Impossible!"

"There's no way to be sure. In this world, anything can happen."

"True enough."

"Did you ask her why she was going to Krauhausen?"

"No," the baron replied with a shake of his head. "Hmm, I suppose that is too much of a coincidence. I imagine going our separate ways truly is the best solution."

But no sooner had he made peace with the idea than there was the creak of hinges. The door to Miska's carriage opened, and a white glow stepped down. It was Miska. Without even glancing at the pair, she headed toward the highway with a gait that made it seem like she was swimming.

"What's that all about?" the baron asked, squinting his eyes.

"Stay here," D told him before heading off after the glowing Miska.

Though she wasn't traveling all that quickly and he soon caught up, it almost looked as if a wind whipped up by D drove her forward as she glided along thirty feet ahead like a soap bubble he was chasing.

In a corner of the forest so overgrown even the moonlight never reached it, she vanished abruptly.

D halted. Though it was so pitch black most people wouldn't see their own hands in front of their faces, his eyes saw the world as if it were in broad daylight.

"I see I was successful in my bid to lure you out, interloper," Miska's voice said from nowhere. "I'm quite sure the only reason that gentleman has treated me so poorly is because you've been filling him with foolish notions. There's no other reason why any upstanding Noble would leave a lady behind in her hour of need. You lowly half-blood impostor—here I'll send you to your maker!"

"So, you're a lady in distress?" D asked softly. "A woman who would hunt a Hunter—I'm sure you must be terribly frail."

"Silence!"

And as if in response to her furious roar—a human figure suddenly glowed just ahead of D. It was Miska. Without even seeming to move her feet, she closed on D.

"Interesting," someone said. It wasn't D, but rather a hoarse voice from the vicinity of his left hip.

D's left hand went into action.

Something knifed through the wind and pierced the trees. There was a woman's gasp, and then it quickly became quiet again. At the same time, the glowing Miska faded.

Bounding to her without making a sound, D took a look at the plain wooden stake stuck in the tree trunk before he spun around. Ahead of him, a black fog had billowed up silently. D's kicking off the ground and the fog's enveloping him were almost simultaneous, and it was a few seconds later that a cry of pain arose from the bushes about fifteen feet away.

"You did a wonderful job of seeing through my little deception, but you can't stop the fog of death. I should've expected as much from Vampire Hunter 'D.' My carelessness has simply made more work for me," said the figure in white who'd appeared from thin air—Miska.

Apparently she'd taken D seeing through her illusion into account all along.

"When my blood enters your body, it'll become poison. Even a Noble can be immobilized for three days by it. But that's nothing compared to what it'll do to a miserable dhampir."

As her feet pattered across the grass to bring her to where D had landed, her right hand clutched an imposing foot-long knife. It was anyone's guess where she'd kept it hidden up until now.

As expected, D fell flat on his back among the roots of the tree.

"I'm sure the baron will be rather cross with me, but I'm prepared to accept that."

The girl raised her knife, and then swung it down. But it was stopped cold in midair.

"It can't be!"

As Miska's eyes bulged in astonishment, the youth far more lovely than her slowly got back on his feet.

"So, are you the real thing?" D asked.

"Why didn't my fog of blood harm you? Do you mean to tell me you're indestructible?"

Of course, Miska had no way of knowing that a faint snicker issued from the part of his left hand that came into contact with her wrist, holding back the deadly blow.

"Kill me," Miska groaned. Both her lips and her voice quaked. Her spell had been broken by a human/Noble half-breed. For a Noble like Miska, the humiliation was a fate worse than death.

The young man wasn't the sort of person to pardon anyone who'd made an attempt on his life. Miska would meet her fate here and now.

D's right hand flashed out as his longsword shot up above his head.

The shadowy figures that'd just leapt down from the tree were bisected before they could cry out, leaving a total of six pieces.

"It's not over yet," Miska said as she watched the dark forms. Shockingly enough, it looked like she was enjoying herself.

D also realized it wasn't over. Even before the half-dozen pieces of the bisected figures sluggishly got up again, he knew there was something wrong from the unusual feel of his blade as it'd gone through them.

"It would appear you have someone else to take care of before you deal with me," Miska said, her eyes turning to the half-dozen pieces.

The figures didn't move. Though they'd returned to life, they'd already tasted D's blade once. But the right hand of each glistened with the cutting edge of a weapon.

Still facing them, D raised his left hand, and then something whistled through the air. Just then, the shadowy figures pounced on him. D's blade struck down only the first figure. The upper and lower halves of the remainder flew through the air, but they then fell to the ground like puppets that'd had their strings cut.

The leaves trembled, shaking off the moonlight. Seconds earlier, D apparently hadn't missed the groan up in the tree. The rough wooden needle had found its mark.

"Done playing with your dolls?" D asked as he looked up.

Miska knit her brow. She didn't understand what D meant.

From the treetop, a mournful voice flowed out, saying, "It figures he'd only hire the best as an escort—you're the first person to ever find me while I was hidden."

"So, you're a puppet master?" said D.

"Aye. Folks call me 'Mario the Puppeteer.' Keep in mind; the ones I just threw at you were merely a test. I wonder whether you'll be able to spot the puppets I use next time," the voice said, laughing as if its pain were already forgotten.

Once more an arrow of light flew from D's right hand, and the stand of trees swayed in response.

"We'll meet again, dashing Hunter! Perhaps next time it'll be in the depths of hell," the same voice called from the grove to D's rear. The treetops rustled noisily before it became quiet again.

D used his hand to bat away what was falling in front of him.

Miska also seemed to notice it, and she said, "Whatever could these strings be for?"

She then looked quickly at the figures lying at her feet and nodded knowingly to herself.

"Say," she called out to D, but then she noticed something that completely altered her expression. D still had a firm grip on her right wrist. One had to wonder how he'd managed to work his sword or hurl the wooden needles under the circumstances.

Their eyes met. His were still ice, unchanged from when he'd told her he would dispose of her.

"Do you still intend to do something . . . to me?" Miska said, backing away a step.

Terror shot through her from the very top of her head down to the tips of her toes. The Hunter had just released her, and she knew what that had to mean.

Glittering, D's blade went into motion.

And then—

"Wait!"

The voice was that of Baron Balazs. Crossing the grass, he said, "I came out here thinking something like this might've happened. Stop, D! I won't allow you to lay a hand on this girl."

"She tried to kill me."

D's reply left the baron at a loss for words. Noticing the black shapes lying at his feet, he'd thought that was what had attacked them.

Quickly turning to Miska, the baron said, "That was a foolish thing to do—you must never do so again."

Miska lowered her eyes at his harsh tone.

D stepped forward.

Somewhat flustered, the baron told him, "Stop it! Dawn will be here soon. Then we part company. Just let her be."

"Out of my way," D replied.

"I'm your employer."

"And what have you employed me for? If you don't have me around, you'll be in danger. She was well aware of that."

"This time, I must ask you to restrain yourself," the baron said coolly. "Besides, as my guard, you committed a major error."

"What error?"

"I was attacked just now. See for yourself."

The left side of the baron's cape was thrown back, revealing a jagged wound to his shoulder. Due to the incredible recuperative powers of the Nobility, the actual wound had half closed already, but the clothing over it was damp and red.

"They struck at the same time. They must've waited for you to leave my side. And as my guard, your failure to realize that was an obvious mistake."

Although the Nobleman may have been exaggerating a bit, D's sword returned to its sheath.

"There won't be a second time," the Hunter stated, but it was unclear if his remark was directed at Miska or the baron. The young Noblewoman's shoulders still dropped in relief.

"We're going back now," D told him.

The baron was captivated by a strange thought, and he followed the Hunter naturally enough. Although he'd agreed to comply with D's instructions for the duration of the journey, a Noble would ordinarily never accept such an arrangement, particularly when it involved an employee whose way of speaking and general hearing were light years away from where they should be. Yet he wasn't at all angry. In fact, he got the impression he could trust the Hunter, and that this was the safest thing to do.

Of course, dhampirs had some Noble blood in them. The empathy that sprang from that connection was actually the biggest reason the Nobility detested dhampirs. A human being with the same regal blood they possessed? Due to these feelings, the highest honor a dhampir could receive was to be treated as a Noble, but for a Noble, the very lowest form of employment was exterminating dhampirs.

At a certain Noble's mansion in the southern Frontier district, a "head market" was held once a year in imitation of the open-air markets in human cities. Of all the countless severed heads on exhibit there from humans and beasts, the cheapest of all were those of dhampirs—which were sold by the mound. Of course, you could say such excessive contempt only served to betray the Nobility's mixed feelings about dhampirs.

And the baron probably wasn't exempt from these emotions. Though he was indispensable where this trip was concerned, taking orders from D the dhampir had to be more than a little humbling to his psyche. Miska's actions were most likely prompted by this unease as well. And yet, the Noble couldn't help but wonder if the young man wasn't something far greater than even he could imagine. The baron had to consciously push back this thought when it suddenly popped into his mind.

"What was your attacker like?" D asked as they were walking.

"Someone made up of flowers."

"Flowers?"

Not long after D had gone off in pursuit of Miska, a golden pollen-like dust had blown in on the wind. Immediately holding his breath, the baron had seen a figure in all the colors of the rainbow standing just beyond the eddying swirls of yellow. The cape that shrouded the tall figure had spread wide. The reason he seemed to have every imaginable hue was because the body beneath that cape was covered with lovely flower petals. The dust—or pollen—flew from one of his blooms.

The baron had taken cover behind his carriage, but a split second later, more madness assailed him from above. He'd narrowly escaped, though his shoulder was rent wide in the process. The only thing that'd allowed him to get off so lightly was the superhuman reflexes he possessed as a member of the Nobility. He'd quickly looked up to the sky, but even with the lyncean eyes of a Noble, he hadn't discerned any more than a shadowy winged figure flying off to the south at incredible speed, and the multicolored assassin had also vanished.

There had been two foes.

"Do you know them?" asked the baron.

"The flower character? Yes."

"Oh, really?"

"He's known as 'Crimson Stitchwort,' and he's a famous Vampire Hunter in the eastern sectors. Mario, whom I ran into, is one of the top three out west. It seems you've got every half-decent Hunter on the Frontier out to get you."

"Do you suppose I have someone spooked?"

"Only you'd know that."

The baron smiled thinly, but didn't say another word all the way back to camp.

Seven Assassins

CHAPTER 2

I

Seeing Miska as far as her carriage, the baron said, "The eastern sky is beginning to brighten. You'd do well to get some rest."

And with that, he kissed her hand.

"I'll thank you to tell that savage not to set fire to my carriage," she replied, glaring at the Hunter.

"Certainly," the grimacing baron replied with a nod. "When you awaken, we shall no longer be here. So this is farewell. Please take care."

"And what will become of me if I should be set upon by those villains from earlier?"

"You must forgive me."

Miska spun about indignantly and disappeared into her carriage.

Looking over his shoulder and seeing what D had in his hands where he stood behind him, the baron furrowed his brow. The dagger with an eight-inch blade had a cold, black gleam to it.

"I'll have to operate on you before you get into your coffin," said D.

"Why?" the baron asked without any particular concern.

"I've heard a bit about the flower person's tricks. Apparently his pollen is absorbed by the body, and flowers bloom in profusion in the blood. 'The blood is the life.'"

"I see. So?"

"Do you know what happens to a Noble when his blood is drained?"

"I'm in your hands, then," the baron said, nodding. "There are operating instruments in my carriage, you know."

"There's no time for that."

"But I—" he began to say, but his voice was abruptly choked off. Clutching his throat and coughing, the baron fell to his knees.

And what did D do? Suddenly seizing the collar of the baron's cape, he pulled him closer.

At precisely that instant, a flash of stark light shot up from the ground . . . and D and the baron were in entirely the wrong spot. A blade more than three feet in length ran deep into the baron's right lung.

"D—" said the baron, his voice echoing with pain and astonishment.

As well it should have. From any vantage point, it seemed as if D had pulled the baron right onto the naked steel that came out of the ground.

One great leap back carried D away from the Noble's caped form.

His foe hadn't fled—the fearsome assassin still remained beneath the black soil. However, even if he had dug a hole, the surface of the ground was still hard. Whoever it was, he wouldn't be able to move freely. Realizing this, the eye D turned toward the earth was that of a man entering a life-or-death struggle.

The sensation from beneath his feet changed without warning.

D took to the air—and a stark flash of light thrust up after him. Spinning nearly one hundred eighty degrees, D countered the attack with his own naked steel. The flashes clashed together, and then one of them snapped off and flew away. Spinning around in a way that beggared belief, the blade that had shattered the attacker's weapon was then thrust halfway into the earth beneath the Hunter's feet.

Not even bothering to feel if it'd made contact, D pulled his steel back out and focused his senses on the ground.

In order to travel through the solid earth, his foe sent out molecular vibrations that turned the soil into sand. Furthermore, once he'd moved, the ground promptly returned to its original state. That was why the enemy's blade had easily been able to pierce the ground, but D's sword had only penetrated it halfway.

While D hadn't been fatally wounded, blood was gushing from his right leg. Would he be able to parry a second attack from his elusive opponent?

For a heartbeat, stillness settled over heaven and earth. Surely D must've noticed what was happening. The air had a touch of blue to it, and in the forest, the birds were stirring in the treetops. In less than twenty minutes, the morning sun would be shining down on the baron. A mere twenty minutes—all the time that stood between life and death for an immortal member of the Nobility. What if his subterranean foe didn't make a move before then?

Five minutes passed. Ten.

The shadow at D's feet was growing ever deeper.

It was then that the carriage door opened.

"Baron!"

Standing motionless in the doorway, Miska seemed to shimmer like a mirage, backlit by the illumination from her carriage. Most likely she'd come out for a look after sensing danger.

A heartbeat later, the ground broke at D's feet. Another blade was thrust up.

D was in the air. Not because he'd sensed the molecules beneath his feet transforming, but because he'd kicked off the ground with Miska's appearance only a few tenths of a second earlier.

As the blade sank back into the earth, the Hunter landed and drove the sword he had raised straight down into the black soil— and all the way to the hilt.

Intense spasms traveled through the ground. Perhaps D even heard the cries of pain from the attacker in his death throes.

Earlier, when his sword had only gone halfway into the ground, it was merely an act he'd staged when he realized his opponent had already moved. The subterranean assassin hadn't comprehended the strength of the dhampir—the fiendish might granted him by his Noble blood. And seeing Miska's arrival as just the thing to divert D's attention, he'd casually drifted up to a dangerous depth . . .

Having determined that the foe whose face he'd never even seen was dead, D raced over to the baron. Miska was already cradling his head.

"D—why?" asked the baron.

He wanted to know the reason the Hunter had put him in front of the oncoming blade. However, his discomfort seemed far less than before, and his breathing was deeper. The wound to his lung wouldn't have caused him great pain, but what had become of his earlier agony?

"From the way you were breathing, I could tell there were flowers blooming in your right lung," said D.

Though Miska was glaring at him, her cheeks flushed unconsciously.

"I could've removed it myself, but the enemy showed up."

The baron's eyes went wide with disbelief.

Even Miska lost all her Noble restraint as her jaw dropped.

"You mean to say you turned his thrust against those flowers? Impossible!" Miska cried.

"You seem to be breathing easier," said D.

Everyone fell silent.

If this were true, then in a split second, D had gauged the speed of the sword shooting up from the ground and the location of the malignant growth in the baron's chest and excised the bizarre flowers with that thrust of the blade. He'd used one of the assassins' attacks to remedy the damage they'd caused earlier . . .

Through the silence, a roseate glow suffused Miska's cheeks.

Suddenly rising to his feet again, the baron used one hand to fend off the sunlight as he turned to D and said, "You're a man of incredible practicality."

"We've got a long road ahead of us," D replied. Rarely did he answer each and every comment made by someone else.

†

After the two Nobles had returned to their respective carriages, D got on his horse. As the mount and rider started off in the watery light, the baron's carriage creaked after them.

When they came to the road leading out of the forest, D didn't even look back. They'd left the white carriage in a clearing no human was likely to visit before nightfall. As the horses meekly continued to wait for further instructions from their slumbering master, their manes sparkled in the sunlight, and occasionally they'd make a movement that made it look like a bolt of white lightning had shot down their backs. No one would disturb them. Even if someone did come along, one look at that carriage would undoubtedly send them packing.

When the woman in the white dress awoke again, the stars would be twinkling forlornly above her. It was a horribly lonesome image.

Although they had to gain as much distance as they could by daylight, their foes' attacks would likely become more intense. D regarded the battle the previous night as a mere test of his strength. The real battle was still to come. At any rate, there was a small village a little over a mile ahead.

On entering the village, D and the blue carriage were the focus of the fearful stares of the inhabitants. A young man of inhuman beauty with a gorgeously luxurious carriage—everyone knew what that meant. Whispers of *Noble, Noble* flooded the morning street, spreading like ripples on a pond. Yet those who looked up at D on his steed got a rosy flush to their cheeks. Irrespective of age or sex, his heavenly beauty was enough to enrapture anyone.

In no time, D and the carriage had pulled into the blacksmith's on the edge of town. In point of fact, the blacksmith had a workshop the size of a small factory. Not only did he produce and repair farm equipment, but he also sold automobiles and basic electronic devices. To conduct the latter sort of business, it was critical to have suppliers in the Capital.

On hearing D's request, the smith's eyes went wide.

"Half of that we can do here, but the other half is impossible. You'd need one of them 'traveling smiths' for dangerous riggings like that."

"How long would you need for the half you can handle?"

"Let me see . . . Roughly two days."

"Kindly do it in one."

"In that case, I'm gonna have to ask you for one hell of a fee," the blacksmith chuckled, a despicable grin plastered to his face.

"How much?"

The amount the smith quoted was five times the going rate.

"Fine," D said with a nod.

As he surveyed the other man's handsome visage, the smith's grin was bisected by a stark flash. His greasy face had been split from the forehead, along the nose, and right down to the tip of his chin. Although only the skin had been broken, it was incredibly painful. Still, the smith couldn't move an inch.

The gorgeous young man before him had been transformed into another creature entirely. And from him an unearthly aura blustered.

"There's your special bonus," said D. "I'll pay you the regular rate right away."

"Ye-yes, sir," the blacksmith stammered weakly. He was stained with red from his face to his chest. "My regular rate will be good enough. I won't charge you a bit more than what I've got coming. I promise you that."

"I'll pay you double," said D.

"Huh?!"

"With you doing two days' work in one day, that's fair compensation."

The blacksmith's expression made it clear he had no idea what was going on. Some time after D had walked off, he finally muttered, "There's just no telling what a guy that good looking is likely to do."

†

The villagers watched with unsettled looks on their faces as showers of sparks and pale electromagnetic discharge shot from the blacksmith's windows all day long.

"They're still at it. Looks like they'll be working through the night," said the man gazing off through the darkness before he returned from the terrace to the room with a thin grin on his face. He was on the second floor of the village's only inn. Though the blacksmith's shop was nearly a mile away, apparently the man had eyes as sharp as a hawk's, and even by the dark of the moonless night he could see as clearly as if it were midday.

There were four other figures in the room. Reclining on the sofa, seated on the floor, or leaning against the wall, they varied widely in dress and appearance, but each had a disturbing air that made it plain they were no ordinary travelers. Each had arrived alone during the past hour.

"What do you suppose they're doing?" asked a tall man wearing a brown cape. He was the one D had called Crimson Stitchwort.

"Rigging up some nasty surprises for the lot of us, I wager. I suppose they're adding something to the carriage," said the man with the darkness-piercing eyes.

To that, another man in priestly vestments remarked, "We'll simply have to ask the blacksmith when we set out tomorrow. However, if we wait, it could prove problematic."

"Should we go toss down the gauntlet before they've had a chance to finish their work, then? But who'll go? They'll be up against the same guy who took out Tunnel," said the man who'd come in from the terrace. His face was strangely narrow, and he was dressed in a needlessly restrained wardrobe of black.

"I want no part of it," said a man who'd been in one corner of the room the whole time staring off into empty space. His right hand was in front of his face and his left was held up by his chest. Though it looked like he was tugging on something, there was nothing to be seen.

"Lost your nerve now that he's seen through your tricks once, Mario?" the man with the narrow face inquired sarcastically.

In response, Mario pulled down the collar of his yellow coat. The nape of his neck had been split more than an inch.

"How did you get that?" asked the man in priestly garb.

None of the others seemed concerned by it. Before taking this job, each of these men had been wounded as badly countless times and had survived far worse injuries.

"I knew he used throwing needles. I even saw his hand go up. Yet I still wound up like this. But that's not the real problem. Watch this," Mario said, spreading his fingers in front of his eyes.

As the others watched, blank looks took over their faces.

"I still don't have complete movement in them. Why do you think that is? His sword cut my puppets in two. And I could feel it *in my hands!*"

Now the men looked at each other. They were all competent Hunters gathered from across the Frontier. However, they were only disquieted for a second before they all smiled thinly.

"In that case, why don't we all hit him at once? All but the cowards, that is," said the man whose eyes pierced the night.

The reaction was unexpected—everyone looked rather perturbed.

"If we do that, we'll have to split the reward, too."

They all nodded at the remark from the man in the vestments.

"If we're going to move against them, then daylight's definitely the time to do it. You said something about throwing down the gauntlet, but that fellow certainly is a force to be reckoned with. Plus, the baron's bound to be up by now."

"So we're just supposed to sit on our hands and let them prepare their countermeasures?"

"No, I'll go give them some trouble."

"What?!" cried one as the eyes of all the others bulged in their sockets.

"You trying to jump to the head of the line? D might be fair game, but I thought we already settled on the order we'd get a crack at the baron," Crimson Stitchwort protested.

The man in the vestments replied softly, "Relax. I'm simply going to make them stop working. Besides, my turn is the one after next.

I would think I'm entitled to at least go and survey the target."

The men in the group exchanged glances. An unsettled air filled the room.

But onto the deathly still waters of that silence plopped a sudden droplet.

"That's fair enough," said the fifth man, drawing the attention of the entire group.

He was the youngest of them all. He didn't appear too different from D or the baron. His countenance was oddly pale—like paraffin. Up until now he hadn't said a word, but had merely leaned back against the wall. The reason he'd been ignored wasn't because he was disagreeable or less than impressive, but because even a vicious mob like them found him somehow unsettling.

"Go, then. But before you do, listen to the next set of instructions."

There were cries in the affirmative as they all turned to face him.

II

It was roughly a month earlier that a strange request had reached these men scattered across the Frontier. A miniature communication disk had told them, *You are to assemble in certain ruins in a southern Frontier sector. I would like you to exterminate a young Nobleman while he's on the road. Details as to your compensation shall be discussed later. In addition to yourself, I am summoning six other Hunters. As proof that this is no fool's errand, you should be receiving sufficient funds to cover your traveling expenses to the ruins at about the same time this disk reaches you.*

Renowned professionals of proven mettle, these men would've normally sneered at the thought of teaming up with anyone else, yet all of them complied with the request because of the almost indescribable regality of the voice on the disk, and because of the sum for traveling expenses that'd surely arrived slightly before or after the message. Even if they were to use the most extravagant means imaginable to travel to the ruins and back, that sum would've been enough to make the trip more than ten times over. To put it in simpler terms, it was basically equivalent to what each of them earned in a year.

At the ruins waited an old man in black who was vaguely reminiscent of an insect. His dried and shriveled lips had issued a request that they assassinate a certain Noble. Neither the reason for the assassination nor the name of their client was made clear. Though they normally might've tried to extort that information from the old man, he had an unearthly air about him that hardly left any of them inclined to do such a thing. The compensation would be enough to buy up half a Frontier sector. As proof that this was no empty promise, the old man had given each of them an ingot of a precious metal the Nobility alone had been able to synthesize.

"That alone is valuable enough to allow you to live in luxury for the rest of your days. You can take it and leave without accepting the job, for all we care. However, it goes without saying that a professional of the very highest order has ambitions that are also of the highest order. I don't imagine any of you are so simple minded you could turn a blind eye to the rest of the reward. It shall be up to you to decide how the work is carried out. Whenever necessary, instructions shall be relayed to one of your number. The target's location and description will be given to you presently. We wish you luck."

And then, as if suddenly remembering something, the old man looked up and said, "Ah, yes, there's one thing I neglected to mention. Although only six of you have gathered here, there is in fact one other. A rather unusual individual and somewhat difficult to reach, but I finally managed to make contact this very day. Though they shall be operating independently, it appears they'll take the job. The name is Shadow. Even I myself don't know their sex. But don't forget that you have an additional colleague."

And then the old man crumbled on the spot. The eyes of the six assassins were met by black clothes filled with pale gray dust and a miniature disk that contained both the whereabouts and a description of the Noble—Baron Balazs.

They promptly went into action.

What would they do? How would they kill him? Would they go after him one at a time, or all at once? Based on their characters, individual strikes would be most likely, but they knew better than anyone that a Noble's power left little margin for error.

They talked the matter over right then and there. While they were all in this together, the flames of hostility were hardly hidden in their fiery discussion. And then an arrangement was reached—they agreed there would be no trying to steal a march on the others, but to avoid the kind of equal split they all despised, they would attack in turns based on a strictly maintained order decided by a drawing. While they were free to attack solo, if the person in question sought and received additional aid, the reward would be split evenly by the attackers in the event of a successful completion.

And having reached this accord, the six Hunters raced off to Baron Balazs's location . . . but the baron wasn't there. What they beheld was naught save the melted ruins of a castle. As a result of an exhaustive search, word had reached them just ten days earlier that the young Nobleman was headed to Krauhausen. What's more, that knowledge was accompanied by frightening information. The Noble had been out looking for D.

D's name was quite familiar to them. Though these murderers had absolute confidence in their own abilities, each of them realized at that moment that they had to hit the Noble before he met up with D, and they began hatching plans to that effect. The results had been disappointing—they were too late. Having allowed the two to meet, Tunnel had taken his turn and was slain quite handily, while Mario—who'd aided him—escaped with minor injuries. And he was afraid to be involved in the next attack.

While it was unclear when the pale man in black had come into possession of the miniature disk player, he pulled it out of his raiment and set it on the table, where it began to play back a hoarse tone familiar to all. It was that of the old man.

It would seem you've been having a difficult time of it, he remarked.

Everyone grew tense at these words.

The voice continued, *Allow me to share his destination with you. It's the village of Krauhausen. Though any number of roads lead there, if you follow him for a while, you'll soon know his route. Lie in wait for him along the way. Some gear that should be of use to you has been left in Shabara Canyon. Very well—good luck.*

His last words were threaded with laughter.

The five conspirators looked at each other. Their expressions were indignant.

"Well, then," the elderly man in priestly garb said to the others, but no one replied.

At the blacksmith's workshop, everyone from the smith to his apprentices was hard at work. And each and every face was marked by awe and surpassing terror.

With the setting of the sun, the door to the blue carriage opened and a caped figure alighted. Without ever seeing his gorgeous features, it was easy enough to imagine his true nature. What's more, the young man who was there to greet him was even more inhumanly beautiful.

"What are they doing?" Baron Balazs asked D as he faced the workshop.

"Rigging up something in case of attacks," D responded coolly.

"So, to protect myself from the blows of lowly humans, I'm forced to enlist the aid of other lowly humans?"

"Arriving safely is the primary concern."

The baron's lips twisted.

The craftsmen all turned to look at him in unison. They'd felt his ghastly aura.

"I believe I'll take a stroll out in the night," the baron remarked as he started to walk toward the door.

"Don't forget your promise," said D.

"You have my word," the baron replied with one hand raised as he stepped out onto the darkened street.

"Still as proud as ever of his Noble blood. Someone like him could cause problems for the humans," a hoarse voice remarked from the vicinity of D's left hip. "You think it's safe to let him go?"

"I don't know."

"Hmm. His foes are nearby, too."

"I realize that. So does he."

"Oh, you mean to tell me this arrangement isn't based on mutual respect? Hmph, that's just great!" the voice said in a sarcastic tone.

D's fingers creaked into a fist that cut off the voice.

But then another voice rang out.

"What the hell do you think you're doing?!" the smith shouted angrily.

Before him, a middle-aged craftsman with a vacant look on his face was cooling a piece of melted iron.

"Well, I was just—"

"You put that in the damn water right now and you'll make air pockets in it. If you can't get the goddamn fundamentals right after ten years working here, I've gotta wonder what you bums—"

Right before the smith's bulging eyes, the craftsman foggily replied, "Well, I just kinda thought that was what I should do."

"What?!" the smith bellowed, wrath on his face as he grabbed the front of the craftsman's shirt. "Listen, I'm not out to help anyone allied with the Nobility. To be honest, I'd just as soon chuck this whole job right out the door. But I've already taken it on, so there's no backing out. We'll do the best we can. I don't care who we're working for, I won't have any slipshod work or screwing around in my shop. And that includes you. You got that?"

Having lambasted the craftsman, he turned to the rest and said, "You're all clear on that, right?"

But the second he spoke, there was a massive burst of electromagnetic sparks from the other side of the workshop, accompanied by a scream.

"You damn fool," the smith said as he rushed over and dragged the injured man away with the help of another craftsman who'd been nearby.

Pale blue lightning had scorched his powerful shoulders and arms.

"How did that happen?" the smith asked the other craftsman.

"This idiot went and turned the voltage up into the danger zone all of a sudden!"

"What?! Why in the hell would you do a stupid thing like that?" he shouted at the man they'd just saved.

His face and chest were horribly charred. His mouth opened a crack, and the thin thread of a voice that he squeezed out said, "Somehow—I thought that was what I should do . . ."

"You, too?! What in the hell—" the smith began to say, but then he froze.

And he wasn't the only one. The other craftsman and even the molten iron seemed to have been transformed into an icy forest.

D was standing beside the smith.

"You, you're . . ."

Ignoring his question, D asked the wounded man, "Why did you think that?"

"I don't know . . . I just thought so . . . I had to obey . . ."

"Obey? Who'd you have to obey?" the smith interrupted.

"I don't know . . . Just someone . . . important . . ."

"Someone important?" the smith said, glancing at D with an expression of utter confusion on his face. "Damned if I know what you're talking about. My wife will patch you up in the back room. We'll have to make do without you."

"Boss, you think maybe I could lie down for a while, too?" asked the first craftsman he'd reprimanded.

"What are you talking about?!"

"Er, I just thought that . . ."

"That you should? What, did the almighty sun order you to? Or was it someone important in heaven above? Well, I don't need any of your crazy talk in my shop. Get the hell out of here. And don't bother coming back!"

"Hey!"

"Shut your hole! Get your ass out of here, and Yama and I will do the rest."

"Boss," Yama called out. "Sorry, but I don't feel up to it, either."

With the veins rising in the smith's forehead, D walked off toward the door. Reaching the street, he looked to either side before advancing at a rapid clip in the same direction that the baron had gone.

For the baron, a nocturnal stroll wasn't necessarily sheer pleasure. The stars shone through crystal-clear darkness to make it bright as day for him. The night air was filled with the perfume of nocturnal blooms and the scents of creatures—odors that goaded the cells of his still partially slumbering brain into action. And yet the baron's expression was stiff, his breathing erratic enough to threaten the stillness of the night. To be precise, he was thirsty for blood.

Perhaps due to the fact that this area had been liberated from the Nobility's control long ago, lights burned in the windows with undrawn curtains in many homes, and laughter spilled out in the streets along with the glow. The form that flitted by one window was that of a woman with long, flowing tresses. It stimulated the baron, stoking the fires of his hunger.

The baron's carriage was stocked with dried plasma. Three times a day he dissolved it in water to fill his empty stomach. Synthesized by the Nobility's science, it didn't differ in the slightest from human blood in scent or taste or nutrients. But it was still no use. For the Nobility, feeding wasn't about ingesting nutrients. It was about sustaining the psyche. Victims cowered like rabbits in the sight of a fierce wolf. There were thrills to be found in chasing prey, pushing her to the ground, and searching out the pale nape of her neck. What a joy it was to see the faint blue of her veins. And the instant the baron's fangs sank in, his mouth would be filled with a sweetness and warmth for which there were no words. When he paid a second iniquitous call on his victim several days later, she would let him into her bedroom and expose her own throat—and then he would taste the rapture of conquest! That was how a Noble fed.

Safe as this region might be, apparently there was no one who ventured out on the streets at night. That, coupled with the promise he'd made D, would serve to keep the baron from drinking any blood.

Just then, a figure appeared before him. It was apparently a young girl from the village. In her right hand she held a basket of flowers. The baron suddenly realized he'd entered an ornamental garden. To either side of the path, pale blossoms reflected the moonlight as a sweet aroma wafted from them.

Spotting the approaching baron, the girl froze in fear. A human could sense a Noble, just as a rabbit always recognized a wolf.

"You . . . you're . . ." the girl stammered, the words falling from her lips unbidden.

"What are you doing?" the baron inquired.

He could think of nothing else to say. An impulse that was difficult to describe seemed to be building in the pit of his stomach. Restraining it, he asked, "Are you picking flowers?"

The girl nodded.

"Tomorrow I'll be leaving the village . . . so I thought I'd give them to my friends as a farewell gift . . ."

Eyeing the white blooms that filled her flower basket, the baron came closer and took one, which he then raised to his lips.

The girl was trembling. Waves of fear and a fragrant aroma emanated from her body. And the pale nape of her neck swayed before the Noble's eyes.

"Such a lovely scent," the baron said as he returned the flower to her basket. "The night is dangerous. Hurry back to your home."

The girl looked up at him dumbfounded.

"Why . . . ?" she asked, her tone dripping with perplexity.

The baron smiled.

"You mean why aren't I going to suck your blood?"

"Yes . . ."

"I would like to do so, but you see, I've made a promise. If I were to break it, I'd be left all alone. In my present situation, that would be problematic."

The girl didn't know what to say.

"Go."

The girl backed her way around the baron, finally turning once she was behind him to run off. The sound of her shoes pounding the ground faded into the distance.

The baron let out a deep sigh. Somehow he seemed to have overcome his urges.

He turned back the way he'd come. His cape whirled out. From within it, a fierce flash of light raced off to assail a figure some sixty feet ahead of him.

"Oh my!" the figure cried out in surprise—and the old man in priestly garb threw himself to the ground.

The flash that sailed over his head didn't vanish into the darkness, but rather spun around and was swallowed by the interior of the baron's cape.

"What's wrong? Get a bit too close?"

At the baron's remark, the aged priest slowly got back up again and sheepishly stroked his bald head.

"Woe is me, it is just as you say. I happened to observe you speaking to that lass from the village, and I'm afraid my zeal to see what would happen next got the better of me. Nice to meet you. My name is Yoputz. I'm one of those that've been sent to do away with you."

"A filthy little Hunter, are we? Well, today is the last day of that for you," the baron said, his eyes pulsing with a chilling light.

With a loud squeal, the elderly priest—Yoputz—turned tail and made a mad dash in a decidedly un-Hunter-like fashion.

From the baron's cape shot a golden glitter that skimmed by Yoputz's neck.

Yoputz didn't stop. After running an additional thirty feet, he fell limply to the ground. Or his headless torso did.

Once more the flash of light returned to the interior of the Noble's cape.

"Fool," the baron spat in a tone as cold as ice. He began to walk toward the corpse, but halted almost immediately.

A darkness deeper and more beautiful than the dark of night took human form and stopped beside Yoputz's remains—by his decapitated corpse. The old man's head lay in the road about fifteen feet closer to the baron.

"For your information, he was a Hunter out to get me," said the baron.

Nodding, D turned around again. He didn't tell the baron to go back. He'd merely followed Yoputz's presence out there.

"So he was after him, just like we thought. But the way he took that clown's head off was something else. I wouldn't wanna tangle with him," a voice remarked from the Hunter's lowered left hand.

There was the sound of footsteps behind him, and then the baron walked to D's left.

"Why don't you continue your stroll?" D suggested.

"No, thank you. I wouldn't call this a particularly pleasant evening," the baron said in a frosty tone, seeming a completely different person from the terrifying butcher he'd been a minute ago.

A short while after the pair walked off, a low voice like that of the dead could be heard down on the dirt road where only the moonlight lay, saying, "Dear me! Chopped in half again, am I? However, I did overhear something interesting in the bargain. My good baron, it's not right to deny yourself!"

III

Early the next morning, D left the village. But before doing so, he parted company with the blacksmith in front of his workshop.

"Good journey to you," the smith said, his face looking every bit as enervated as his voice sounded.

Surprisingly, D said in return, "We're in your debt."

Pulling a little bag out of his breast pocket, he poured the contents into the smith's outstretched palm. The golden flow continued.

"Hold up a second! You've given me too much there," the smith shouted, his scraggly beard jolted by his cries.

The pyramid of gold that'd been built on his palm was twice the sum he'd initially demanded.

"That's to get your workers patched up and to cover your hard work," D said softly.

On returning the previous night with the baron, he'd seen the smith silently continuing solo after all his craftsmen had thrown in the towel. All by himself he'd done a job that four people would've barely been able to finish.

"Okay. Since you put it that way, I'll take you up on your generous offer."

D mounted up in front of the somewhat bashful-looking smith.

As if he'd suddenly remembered it, the smith called out, "Oh, there's something you'll wanna keep in mind. Lately, bandits have been running rampant to the north of the village, and a bunch of travelers have been killed. What's more, even though we know what kind of characters got them because they'd been cut and their valuables were missing, the immediate cause of death has been drowning or being buried alive in mudflows. Come to mention it, there've been a lot of mountain tsunamis, downpours, and thunderstorms lately. I don't see how they could possibly be connected to the bandits, but you'll wanna watch yourself."

D raised one hand lightly. That was his farewell.

"So long. I don't suppose we'll meet again," the blacksmith called out forlornly to the back of the dwindling figure.

But the echoes of his words were soon effaced by the creak of the wheels from the carriage that began to move with D.

†

In about an hour, they reached a mountain pass. It was roughly ten feet wide, and as the road climbed, the left-hand side became narrower, as if the ground had been sheared away. If one were to lean over on his horse, he could glimpse the silvery ribbon running one hundred fifty to two hundred feet below. It was a tributary of the three-hundred-mile-long Mertz River, one of the major rivers in the western Frontier. Though they could've gone around the pass instead, D had chosen this route precisely because it would make it difficult for pursuers to make a move. As rough as the going was for them, it would be just as arduous for anyone following behind. If they were to ride through the night, they would reach a certain location by dawn. For the time being, that was D's goal.

Hearing what sounded like a drumbeat nearby, D gazed up at the sky. A shadow formed on his handsome features.

A black cloud churned and spread like a drop of ink falling into water. Purple lightning streaked from one corner. The roar came later.

It took less than a minute for the whole world to blur as a pelting rain assailed the carriage and D. The raindrops struck with such force they would've left the average person's limbs swollen even through foul-weather gear, but the cyborg horse advanced effortlessly. And on the mount's back, D was completely unaffected, as if he were beneath clear skies on an Indian summer day.

Just then, from the carriage to his rear, a voice said, "Someone's coming." Sounding as if it'd risen from the very depths, the voice was terribly low, yet it pierced the pounding rain to reach D's ears. It was that of the baron.

The vampiric Nobility naturally required physical rest by day. However, there were a few Nobles able to operate almost as they would in the dark so long as they weren't directly exposed to sunlight, though their biorhythms dipped unavoidably. Extremely rare, such individuals were almost invariably members of the clans that had been dubbed the Greater Nobility. The Balazs family was precisely that.

While it was unclear whether the baron's unsettling pronouncement had come as news to D, the Hunter didn't turn around at all but silently advanced on his steed.

It was three minutes later that the white carriage drawn by a pair of horses caught up to them. Naturally there was no driver, and the windows had heavy curtains to block the sunlight.

"Dear me, you seem to be in much less of a hurry than I imagined."

Shadowy though it was, the voice that seeped from the white carriage was also a bit showy. It belonged to Miska.

"Look who we have here," the baron's voice whispered. The way that he spoke made it easy enough to picture his wry smile.

D didn't even bother to look back.

"For your information, I haven't come this way in hopes of traveling with the two of you. Even if the opportunity were to arise, I don't expect I should undertake a lengthy journey requiring mutual trust with the kind of Noble who would leave a frail woman to fend for herself, or with his bodyguard. Therefore, our meeting here is sheer coincidence. You needn't offer me the slightest consideration."

Having said all of this without needing to draw a single breath, and delivering the words so coolly they seemed like a prepared statement, the owner of the white carriage then abruptly fell silent. For a while, the only sounds to be heard were the pounding of the rain and the creak of wooden wheels.

"We've got trouble now," the voice from the blue carriage then whispered in a tone D alone would hear. "Can you do something about her?"

After a short pause, D replied, "Yes, I can."

"What?"

"If she's interfering with my work, I can always do what you hired me for."

The baron's voice fell silent. The implications of the Hunter's words had dawned on him.

"For a guard, you sure are a dangerous customer."

"The woman's a lot more danger to you than I am. Even if she came here by chance, she may cost you your life. This would be the second time one Noble asked me to destroy another, but I don't mind."

Call her a Noble, call her a vampire, the beautiful young flower of womanhood in question still only looked to be sixteen or seventeen. Knowing this, what kind of cruel, cold psyche did the Hunter possess in order to say such a thing?

"It would seem you hate the Nobility, too," a somewhat depressed tone remarked from the blue carriage.

At that moment, the world turned white.

A tree that'd been struck by lightning fell over. Directly beneath it, D gave a kick to his horse's flanks and raced forward.

Perhaps it was the bole's impact that made the ground give way. The earth had already been loose, and after the rain had seeped into it, there must've been more than enough danger of it collapsing.

Tilting wildly to one side, the two carriages didn't right themselves again, but rather slowly fell down the incline along with an avalanche of dirt. And then the mountainous terrain beneath the advancing D went as well, with the Hunter maintaining extraordinary equestrian form as he dropped toward the silvery river below.

What awaited him was a raging torrent. There weren't even banks. Swollen by the sudden downpour, the waters swallowed the shore, covered boulders, and roared like a beast as they continued to rush by. D and his mount quickly vanished from sight, and even the pair of carriages whizzed along like two little arks as they floated away without the slightest resistance.

And when they came to a sharp turn two or three hundred yards later, some sort of net hung down from the rock ledge above and snagged the pair of carriages and their horses. The carriages stopped.

Up on top of the ledge, the other end of the net was attached to a powerful winch, and as the pair of carriages banged repeatedly against the rocky face, they were hoisted up.

There were three men by the winch. Each wore a vicious scowl and had weapons strapped to his back and waist. As one of them operated the winch, the net went slack and the teams pulling the carriages stood up.

Aiming a powerful magnetic pistol at the horses' heads, the third man said, "All right, I've destroyed their control chips."

At that, the other two hopped up into the respective driver's seats.

"Well, this sure is a hell of a thing to have fall into our laps," the man who'd climbed onto the blue carriage said, sounding greatly impressed. "No doubt about it, this here's a Noble's ride. It's probably still inside."

"So long as it's daytime, we're safe enough. The bastard's probably still dreaming about sipping someone's blood," the man on the white carriage replied, giving a shake to the reins.

The horses changed direction to face the rock ledge, where a hole fifteen feet in diameter opened up. It appeared to be the home, or at the very least an outpost, for the men—the bandits.

"What about the other one—the guy on the horse? We just gonna let him slide?" asked the man who'd gone back over to the winch and was peering down at the raging flow of the river.

"The boss would never let something like that go to waste. We've got a net set up just waiting for him a little further downstream. We'll nab whatever he's got on him, take his life . . . and then all that'll be left is a waterlogged corpse," the driver of the blue carriage declared blithely.

The Dragon Fang Trap

CHAPTER 3

I

The back of the rock ledge was a passageway—it was a natural cave that'd been widened further. Marks from blasting and chemical melting still marred the rock face in many places. At the far end of the passage was an almost perfectly circular clearing. It had to be easily six hundred feet in diameter. Surrounded as it was by rocky crags on all sides, no one would ever see it unless they were looking down from the sky, and the bandits could use another natural passage in the southern portion of the mountain to get back to the road.

Actually, the bandits *had* discovered this location from the sky. While searching for a hideout to use for attacks on travelers, one of them had been flying around with a glider pack when he'd made the lucky find. Five huts and a warehouse, all constructed from expandable building materials, formed their domain.

In the center of the clearing, almost a dozen figures surrounded the two carriages. Had they not been blurred by the rain, the heartless countenances of the men would've been enough to make even an adult grow pale—and there were two equally tough-looking women.

"How about shutting off that weather controller, Erde? If we're gonna take down some Nobles, there's no place better to do it than under a blue sky," a giant of a man with an infrared scope over his right eye said to one of the women. He was definitely the boss.

The woman—Erde—tapped her fingers across the remote control strapped to her left forearm.

"It's not responding all that well again. I'm still doing some work on it," she replied. "But whether it's dark or not, the Nobility sleep by day, so relax."

"What are you talking about?! If the river overflows and washes out the road, we'll be shit out of luck. Hurry up and get it fixed. Venice, you help her out."

"Will do," the other woman replied in a gruff voice. She wasn't nearly as good looking as Erde. That may have had something to do with her tone.

Giving a toss of his chin to the carriages, the giant said, "I never seen such luxurious rides before. I'd bet my eyeteeth they're carrying grand old Nobles and a butt-load of treasure. Well, we've gotta bust 'em open before the sun goes down. Get to it!"

And at his command, the men with assorted tools of dismantlement in hand set upon the two carriages like a swarm of black insects. Though these carriages made use of precious metals and rare woods, as belongings of the Nobility, no one save the decadent millionaires in the Capital would be interested in purchasing one. And since transporting one would be such a problem, when this mob got their hands on such a carriage, they quickly stripped it down.

However, these two vehicles were somewhat different from any they'd ever dealt with before.

The guy with the six-thousand-degree laser torch in his hand cried out, "This ain't doing squat!"

The man with the heavy alloy drill that could tear through rock howled, "It broke my freaking bit!"

"Damn, you are one sad-looking bunch! Looks like we got no choice but to rough up the merchandise a bit. Hey, get ready to blast!" the giant ordered.

One of his men asked, "Are you sure that's a good idea? I'm not sure I like the way this is going."

But just as he was offering that objection, the giant pounced. There was a *splat* like something slamming into the mud, and the giant's hand sank into his henchman's solar plexus up to the wrist.

Hurling the man instantly killed by his blow over fifteen feet, the boss held his hand out in the rain to wash the gore off before saying, "Hurry up and get everything ready." His tone, however, was rather low.

Naturally, several of the others hastened to the warehouse.

The slight whir of a motor could be heard emanating from the giant's palm.

Three minutes later, a fuse and two pounds of high explosive had been affixed to the bottom of the blue carriage, and a remote control was used to detonate the charge. Though the carriage flew up off the ground and landed on its side, a trio of long thin shafts came out of the bottom and quickly righted the vehicle again. The mechanism housing the shafts hadn't initially been part of the carriage, but rather had been added later. The fruit of the blacksmith's hard labor had stood up to the explosives.

"Shit! Make it twenty pounds this time!" the boss shouted as vermilion pervaded his face.

"Hold on a second," Venice said to him. Pointing to the wagons, she added, "A traveling blacksmith once told me the Nobility's carriages could stand up to shocks well, but they were comparatively weak to heat. Let's use an incendiary charge, boss."

"Okay, incendiary charges it is!" the giant quickly ordered.

"Just a second, boss," Erde said in a tone that seemed to carry a special significance.

"What is it?"

Throwing Venice a spiteful glance, Erde explained, "Those charges get upwards of twenty thousand degrees. If the carriages get burnt to a crisp, we'll be left with nothing. After we went to all the trouble of wiping out that pass and everything, all our efforts to get the treasure would end up pissed away. There's a smarter way to do this."

"And what would that be?" Venice asked as she took a step forward.

Ignoring the other woman, Erde continued, "We might not be able to stop the downpour, but we can turn it into sunshine. I just finished some repairs, and I could switch it over to sunlight mode and train it into a tight beam. If we keep that focused on them and raise the temperature little by little, we should be able to cook them just right."

"That sounds great," the giant declared with a nod, Venice's idea apparently forgotten completely. "That's our Erde! Do your thing."

"Stand back," the woman said as she began to make adjustments to the device on her left arm.

Several seconds later, a streak of blinding light shot down from the heavens to envelop the pair of carriages. The bare rock beneath them dried instantly, and any rain that touched the light evaporated.

As their faces were buffeted by the steam and the dazzling radiance, the bandits backed away even further.

"Seven thousand degrees," Erde said as she squinted her eyes. "Eight thousand . . . Eight thousand five hundred . . . Nine . . . Are we still okay?"

"Keep at it," the giant bade her.

"Ten thousand . . . It's too dangerous to go any higher. The bedrock is starting to melt."

"I don't give a shit. Keep going. This is about showing 'em what we're made of. I'll be damned if I'll let some has-been bloodsuckers humiliate the human race!"

"Fifteen thousand . . . Twenty . . ."

The carriages appeared to be sinking into the ground . . . and they were. The exposed bedrock melted and the pair of carriages sunk down into the bubbling magma without so much as giving off a little steam.

Just then, there was a telling sound from one of the vehicles. It almost sounded like a door being unlocked.

"Stop!" the giant bellowed, and the gray sky and rain returned.

At the same time, there was a terrific hiss and a cloud of white went up—the work of the rain on the magma. The wheels were half buried in the molten rock—leaving the vehicles resting on their bellies—but the carriages themselves didn't appear to have suffered any damage.

"What in blazes—what did they make these things out of?"

"What the hell was that sound just now?"

And as all of the other henchmen grumbled similar remarks, they heard a *creeeeee*. It was clearly the sound of a door opening. And once the intractable doors of both carriages fully opened, a pair of coffins the same hue as their respective vehicles were then ejected.

Seeing these drifting on top of the magma, the giant exclaimed, "Cool 'em down, Erde. Make it winter, pronto!"

The air suddenly cooled, but it took a full ten minutes for steam to stop hissing from the magma like a dying gasp.

Cautiously approaching the lake of molten rock, one of the men tapped the solidifying mass with the end of his boot, and then touched his hand to it before declaring, "It's okay."

The rest of the men surrounded the coffins. *Finally*, said the greedy glint in their eyes, but the shadow of fear hung there too, as if to eclipse it.

"Why'd they come out?" one of the men muttered.

"The heat was probably more than they could take, so the carriages' protective systems got them out. That's fine. We've still got time. Pry those mothers open and turn those Nobles to dust," Erde said as she fiddled with the device on her left arm.

"Hell yeah!" one of them loudly cried as he brought both of his arms down.

It was a steel sledgehammer that whined through the air toward the blue coffin. A heartbeat later, it bounced back hard, leaving the man who held it reeling wildly.

Letting go of the hammer, the man shook his hands and groaned, "I guess regular strength just ain't gonna cut it."

Turning his bloodshot gaze on the coffin, the giant went over by the man and, with one hand, picked up the hammer his underling had dropped. Shoving a laser-burner-wielding henchman out of the way, he stood beside the coffin and raised the hammer high. Both his arms gave off the whir of motors.

The speed of the hammer's descent and the whistle it made were both ten times what they'd been the first time.

There was a crash that sounded like an explosion.

A cheer went up from the group. The coffin had been dented.

Once again the giant raised the sledgehammer. Both his arms were artificial limbs—high-polymer muscles wrapped around bones of steel. They were controlled by electronic nerve centers in his shoulders, and the motors they contained could put out a thousand horsepower.

When the second blow pushed the coffin's lid in even further, the henchmen were no longer shouting. They were going to get to see the inside of a Noble's coffin. Each of them felt their body being enveloped by an aura of excitement and curiosity the likes of which they'd never experienced.

Aside from those who'd actually experienced the long battle between the Nobility and humanity firsthand, humans regarded the opening of a Noble's coffin as a sin, like breaking some holy writ and intruding on hallowed ground. The act may have even had sexual undertones as well, so elegant and beautiful were the Nobles who slumbered wrapped in artificial fog or flowers. The men were often dressed in black formal wear while the women were usually in dresses, though Noblewomen would occasionally wear just a single sheer garment, or sometimes nothing at all. Only the Nobility's uninhibited nature made this possible.

But if by some chance her coffin should be broken open and she were exposed to vulgar human eyes, the allure of a Noblewoman's physique would be her final defense against the stakes and swords raised against her. They possessed the kind of beauty you could go your whole life without encountering: crimson lips that were half

open and looked damp and ready to moan; full breasts; the sexual magnetism of the region from the slim waist down to the thighs that need not be elaborated; veins that seemed to creep like blue snakes beneath that paraffin-pale skin. These attributes often came as a great shock to the brains of the would-be hunters and stayed their murderous hands. As if enchanted, they would remain motionless, gazing on and on at the lovely vampire. Five minutes became ten, ten minutes became an hour—and before long, the time had flown and the sun had lost its power. Blue twilight would spread across the sky, and the next thing they knew, there was a crimson glow in the face of the Noble that had risen from the coffin. The instant they were drawn anew into those burning eyes, they forgot all human reason and became no more than a blood feast for the Nobility.

The bandits were cognizant of this fearful possibility, thus they all got their broadswords and stakes ready when the coffin was dented. They would open the lid and, without even looking at what it contained, strike without a moment's hesitation. And yet the fact that even now some of these wretches had their eyes open a crack only testified to the powerful and perverse lust they had for what the Noble's coffin contained.

"Come on now!" the giant bellowed, his words practically a cry of rage as he brought the hammer down.

At that very instant, the lid of the coffin popped open. It came as little surprise that even the giant couldn't halt the hammer he'd swung with all his might, and the mass of iron went right into the coffin—or it was about to, when it stopped short.

A hand stretching from a blue topcoat had a tight grip on the head of the mallet. Though it had been brought down with the combined power of two thousand horses, it had easily been halted with one hand—and now the sledgehammer was being driven back! It was pushed away as the shadowy blue form began to rise.

The occupant was coming out. His shoulder appeared first. But even when he rose quickly, putting his whole body into view, the giant didn't let go of his hammer. Confronted by the beauty of this pale aristocrat, he was truly frightened. Even though the sun wasn't out, it was still the middle of the day, and he'd never heard of a Noble coming out of its coffin at a time like this.

His henchmen had actually frozen without a word, and a few of them had even dropped to the ground in abject fear. However, it was clearly the raging fires of hostility that left the giant of a man trembling.

"Hiya," said the giant.

Baron Balazs quietly stared at him with eyes like ice, as if he hadn't had enough sleep yet.

"Dogma is the name. I'm a miserly little bandit. It sure is an honor to meet a Noble at this time of day."

The baron's lips quickly went into action, forming words: "I am Baron Byron Balazs."

At that moment, the giant realized that his hammer was no longer being held. Hurling the sledgehammer as he leapt away, the man drew the broadsword from his hip with all the speed one would expect from the leader of a mob of brigands.

The hammer scored a direct hit on the baron's forehead that left the Noble off balance.

And the second he saw this, the giant kicked off the ground in a mighty bound. The blade he had braced against his hip was aimed at his foe's heart. And surely enough, it pierced it.

The gorgeous face was right in front of him. And the smile it wore was so alluring, and solitary, and cruel.

"Well done."

Even though the Nobleman's words left him dazed, the giant saw the baron raise his right arm and glimpsed the black hammer that he grasped. Reflexively, the bandit leader brought his left arm up to block it. His artificial arm had a thousand horsepower to use in his defense.

The mass of iron fell against his arm. Sparks flew. Muscles burst and bones snapped as electrical fire colored the limb.

The misshapen hammer rose.

The giant hoped to stop it with his right arm, but the time it took him to discard his broadsword kept him from making it.

The wet *splat* that rang out was the sound of his skull being pulverized. Blood and gray matter flew everywhere, delivering a hearty spattering to the henchmen, who were keeping their distance. With this, they all returned to their senses.

"You bastard!"

"Freak!"

Weapons flashed out, and the men were about to make a murderous charge when the baron's cape spread to either side like the wings of a mystic bird and an intense flash of light flew from it, leaving a trail as it weaved through the henchmen. Heads sailed through the air, and seconds later geysers of blood shot up. It was quite some time later that the decapitated bodies fell over.

A short distance away, only the two women were left. For some reason, the baron's murderous light hadn't flown in their direction. Erde and Venice looked at each other's paled faces as the former reached with her right hand for the weather controller on her left arm. She couldn't stop the rain, but she could still bring some sunlight.

The baron turned to her. Before Erde's shriek of terror had ended, he had bounded to stand right in front of her. The woman was beset by dementia. Forgetting all about the controller as she tried to spin around, she felt an iron blade driven through her heart from behind.

"Ve-Venice?" she rasped in disbelief. "I'll take care of this bastard. But you get to go to hell a little bit sooner than he does."

As Venice shoved her erstwhile companion forward, she tore the controller off the woman's arm.

The baron's movements were checked by Erde's body, which hadn't fallen over.

Venice was well versed in how to operate the controller. She'd had to learn how to use it just in case anything ever happened to Erde . . . and something had certainly happened to Erde now.

"All the treasure of the Nobility will be mine! I'll bring it to the Capital and get a fortune for it!"

A beam of sunlight should have speared down between the clouds, but as Venice reached for the switch that would trigger it, her arm was stopped cold. Pale fingers had reached around from behind her to encircle her wrist. She only just remembered that there was a second coffin when a pair of lips that were chill as ice but incredibly soft pressed against the nape of her neck.

"Stop!" the baron shouted. "You won't be able to travel with us any longer."

That was enough to stop her Noble instinct—the craving for blood. "Damnation."

Breaking free of Miska's grip, Venice tumbled forward from the effort. As Miska glared at her, a dazzling light began to fall on her and the baron from above.

II

The two vampires stood immobilized in the sunlight.

"Die! Take that, you fuckers!" Venice exclaimed as her fingers continued to work the controls. "Ashes to ashes, dust to dust!"

This was something humans always said when destroying a member of the Nobility, but no sooner had Venice finished speaking than the control was slashed in two, arm and all, and half of it fell to the ground.

The sunlight faded.

Four figures lived out in that downpour. But in whose favor had the odds increased?

Catching Miska in his arms as she collapsed, the Noble in blue saw the rain-blurred figure in black approaching.

Glancing without the slightest trace of compassion at the female bandit writhing in a lake of blood, D said, "Looks like I'm just in time," as he returned his sword to its sheath.

The trio that stood in the driving rain like heavenly creatures were so lovely, they would've made anyone who saw them completely forget the downpour.

Naturally, the rest of the bandits had attacked D, and the results of that encounter went without saying. Taking one of them alive and forcing him to disclose the location of their hideout, the Hunter had then hastened back. But it wasn't the stomach-turning scene on which D's gaze paused, but rather the lips of the baron and Miska.

Looking then at the bandits who'd splashed up blood and rain when they fell, he didn't have a whit of emotion in his eyes. "Get in your coffin," he said.

"D, there's something I must tell you," said the baron. "She didn't take a drop of—"

"My rate just doubled," D said as he walked toward the two carriages. "Which of you is going to pay the remainder?"

A hue of delight suffused Miska's countenance.

"I will."

"No, I shall pay it."

And with these words, the baron took Miska's shoulder and held her up while he quietly began to trail D.

Even in this gore-splattered world, D could see that the pair of Nobles had withstood the urge to drink human blood.

As the stark white ribbon of road continued on dispassionately through the ocher land, it seemed as if a lone magnificent flower had blossomed. A tent like the arc of a rainbow broken in two was set up by the side of the road—although it was actually little more than an awning. Inside, there stood a tall elderly man in a black tuxedo jacket and a silk hat. More conspicuous than the arrangement of red jewels on his bow tie was the man's beard, which flowed all the way down to his chest.

Though the central highway was normally lightly traveled, because the villages in this area lived relatively close together there were many passersby, and nearly a dozen men and women had gathered around the tent. There were even two or three children.

"Well now, whether you've come here from far away or live close at hand, take a good look. Before you stands the world's greatest prestidigitator—the road is my home, and people have come to call me 'Lord Johann, the Trail Magician.' Now you may enter and witness acts of legerdemain not to be seen in any village or town, nay, not even in the Capital, but only out on the road, and only for the price of one thin dant. Kindly pay the young lady."

Only once he'd given his speech did the people notice the person off to the side indicated by his white-gloved hands.

A rumble churned through the crowd. Had that girl been there before?

She was pretty, and seemed oh-so-sad. As befit a magician's assistant, the young lady wore a gold dress slit high up the side that gave tantalizing peeks of her pale thighs while she moved among the patrons and collected their coins in a second silk hat. The hair that hung all the way down to her waist was a hue of gold even more dazzling than that of her dress.

What was a woman like her doing by the side of the road out on the Frontier, working as the assistant to some petty little magician? That's what the people wondered, but once Johann's sleight of hand began, they were instantly captivated. His long white fingers flashed out, and between them, balls in four different colors appeared. With a single cry, they then transformed into four breathtaking beauties. Before everyone noticed they were the same girl who'd collected the money from them, the bevy of beauties became warriors clad in metal armor, and amid the cheers they then changed into a gigantic reptile that swallowed a nearby spectator whole.

It was all so incredibly real that the patrons were left silent and frozen in place. And at that very moment, the object of their terror vanished without a trace, as if it had never existed, leaving just the people and tent.

It was nearly noon. The heavy rains of the previous day were like a distant dream and the road was bone dry, leaving only the stark sunlight—and the creak of wheels. Almost everyone facing in his direction then caught the young man in black on a chestnut cyborg horse and the pair of carriages following along behind him from the corner of their eyes. The young man's gorgeous features made them forget all about the golden maiden. Even the girl seemed enthralled by him.

"Did you all see that? Did you see that beautiful traveler?" Johann called out, his words accompanied by some exaggerated gestures.

Still facing forward, the young man in black rode off slowly.

Noticing that the pair of carriages trailing behind him apparently belonged to the Nobility, the people began to murmur a few minutes later, not because the impression the young man had left on them had become any weaker, but simply because their attention had veered from his unearthly aura.

As if that were precisely what he'd been waiting for, Lord Johann twisted a lock of his flowing beard as he told the restless spectators, "Well, ladies and gentlemen, do you know the secret to magic? The first thing you have to do is divert the audience's attention away from the trick . . ."

About an hour after passing through a little village, D halted his horse. Ahead of them, the land took an ashen shade, and in scattered places there were glints of silver to be seen, like the tracks of a snail. The black trees crowding either side of the road became scarcer, and their silhouettes were stretched tall and thin like well-worn memories. Perhaps it was due to the miasma that gushed from the earth, but the most unsettling thing of all was the way even the very sunlight was warped, making distant vistas seem close at hand and things nearby so horribly distorted they slipped right out of view. This was a famous spot in this district, a vast swamp that stretched thirty miles east to west and a dozen north to south. It was said that poisonous gas issued from the ground in spots, and that monstrous fish large enough to swallow a grown man whole lurked in its waters.

Off to the left was a wooden pier that jutted out over the swamp. A pair of figures stood by it. D approached them. Without even glimpsing the faces of the rail-thin boy and the plump girl, the Hunter knew that they must be brother and sister. Each looked to be about eleven or twelve. Four battered suitcases rested at their feet. On noticing D, they both donned expressions that suggested they were lost in dreams, and when the Hunter dismounted, it only got worse.

On the wall of the rest house situated to the rear of the pier hung a metal plate with what was apparently a timetable. Though it was fifteen or twenty feet away and the print was so tiny it practically required a magnifying glass, D scanned it for a minute or two and then seemed satisfied.

"Um, excuse me," the chubby girl said to him. Her face was flushed. "Which way are you going?"

Glancing down at her cheeks, which looked like they might fall off at any second from their own weight, D said, "North."

Ordinarily, it was inconceivable that he'd answer a stranger's question so promptly.

"Oh, so are we!" the girl said, fiddling with her hands in front of her chest. Stars glistened in her eyes as she gazed at D. Pattering over to the boy, she pointed to D as she said something, and then folded her hands as the two of them came back.

"That's an awesome sword," the boy commented in true male fashion. "Mister—are you a warrior? Or are you some kind of bodyguard?"

"Wrong on both counts," D replied, his actions once again inexplicable.

"In that case—are you a Hunter?"

D said nothing.

"Holy! He's the genuine article, Sis!"

Now there were two pairs of eyes filled with stars.

"Wow!" they both exclaimed with obvious appreciation as they began to circle around D. To anyone who didn't know how hair-raisingly dangerous their actions actually were, this simply would've looked like a heartwarming scene at the ferry's landing.

"Mister, we're going to the Capital," the boy said, his chest puffed out.

"What do you think we're going to do there?" the girl then asked him.

"I can't imagine," the Hunter replied.

"This!" she exclaimed, her cry curling backward. Still wearing her heavy overcoat, the girl executed a perfect backward somersault.

And over her head flew a lithe figure clutching both legs—the boy. An instant before he landed, they both extended their arms, and the second they touched, the two of them flew up into the air together. Moving in spellbinding arcs as they passed each other, they then flew up higher. Even if there were something inside them that let them defy the laws of conservation of energy, it still would've been a stunning display of acrobatics. It almost seemed as if the siblings would never have to come back to earth again so long as their hands could touch.

Though their acrobatics seemed to be the work of angels, the performance was unexpectedly short. Piercing the mist, a massive hovercraft had appeared from the far reaches of the swamp. The jets of air shooting from the belly of the ship sent muddy water spraying wildly, and the craft's speed was nearly sixty knots.

Coming back to earth without a sound from a height of thirty feet, the siblings raced over to D.

"How was that?"

"How was that?"

Both asked the same question at the same time. They certainly were brother and sister.

"Remarkable," said D.

Although his reaction was far more miraculous than their performance, the children were frankly delighted.

Rolling closer, a white mist enveloped all three of them. The hovercraft—or swamp ferry—had plowed through the dank cloud as it pulled up to the pier. A sizable ship, it was large enough to accommodate up to a hundred people or twenty-five wagons and carriages. Onboard were four or five passengers that looked to be merchants, and as they disembarked, they bid farewell to the elderly ferryman who'd preceded them onto the pier. Their mouths all fell open when they saw D, but the way they paled on seeing the carriages behind him was truly a sight to see.

"All right, now, all aboard! Move along now! We're off again in ten minutes!" the gray-haired ferryman called out in a raspy voice.

III

Less than ten seconds after they began to move, the rocks and pier had vanished behind a white veil. D was all the way at the stern of the ship, and his eyes were turned toward the pilothouse and the two children who were apparently talking to the ferryman.

Are we crossing a pond? a voice from the blue carriage asked him.

"A swamp. Get some rest," D replied.

Shut in his coffin as it rode inside his carriage, the baron still seemed to be aware of the situation. If he were watching through a closed-circuit monitor, he never would've said anything about a pond, so he must've had some Noble extrasensory perception.

There are three other people here . . . and two of them are children.

Seeming to catch something in the baron's tone, D got a hard look on his face as he told his employer, "Don't go back on your word."

I know. You needn't worry, the carriage owner responded. *It may go without saying, but this could be exactly what the enemy wants us to do. One of them flew.*

"I realize that," D replied, but his expectations remained a mystery.

This swamp was so deep in parts as to be practically bottomless, and if they were to fall off the ship, neither the carriages nor the coffins seemed likely to ever surface again. And skilled as D was, the morass surrounded him on all sides, and even he couldn't have any way of combating an enemy who could attack from the air.

Just then, what had looked to be a fallen log floating some thirty feet ahead on their starboard side suddenly stood straight up like a proverbial jack-in-the-box and stretched right toward them.

The brother and sister shrieked with surprise.

Although it had appeared to be nothing more than a tree, it had a suckerlike mouth and a trio of eyes at one end.

"Oh my!" the ferryman shouted as he cut the wheel.

The ship veered to port, showering the creature with sludge in the process.

Which would be faster? The creature's mouth rising over the boy's head, or the ship's turn?

Three figures sprinted into action. The two smaller ones flew back, the one in black moved forward, and then a flash of light surged out.

The creature's severed head crashed against the deck with a booming thud, while its neck thrashed around like a whip. Suddenly, deep red blooms of blood formed in midair, but by the time they fell like an unseasonable winter shower, the ship was already pulling away at full speed, headed back the way it had come.

"What—what in the blue blazes are you kids?" the captain asked as he gripped the steering wheel, and his curiosity was completely understandable.

"We're acrobats, as you can see," the girl replied, spreading both arms wide and bowing in gratitude.

"We were invited to join a full-fledged troupe of performers in the Capital and left the little circus we'd been with up till now," the boy said, putting his hand to his chest and bowing his head.

"The Capital, eh?" Doing a job like his, the old man must've had plenty of courage, so when he expressed his admiration, his tone was back to normal again. "That sure is a heck of a journey for a couple of kids out on the Frontier. What about your folks?"

"They died a long time ago," the boy answered. There wasn't a trace of gloom in his reply.

"Is that a fact? I suppose that wasn't exactly the best thing for me to be asking," the old man said with a grin.

"And you—" he said as he turned to D.

The boy and girl gazed at the Hunter with a look that surpassed mere respect—something that might even be called love.

Before the old man could continue what he was saying, D asked, "Aren't we supposed to be taking a safe route?"

"Well, sure—it's the same one as always. In a manner of speaking, that critter was the one that was off course. Very rare—doesn't happen much at all, so you can put your mind at ease."

"Is there a lair of dangerous creatures out here?"

"Sure. Further to the east. Not to worry, though. They'd never come out this way."

"Is there any danger ahead?"

"Let me see—you mean the *Sturm?*"

"What's that?" asked the Hunter.

"Nothing to be concerned about. We've still got plenty of time—" the old man was saying when his breath was suddenly taken away.

Ahead of them floated fallen black trees . . . and not just one or two. The swamp was filled with them for as far as the eye could see.

"That's plain impossible! Their lair's supposed to be way to the east of here!"

"Back away," D said as he took the children by the hand.

"No time for that. We'll have to pull through real slowly. Don't talk. Don't even breathe."

Naturally that last request was absurd, but the look on the old man's face made it clear he meant every word of it.

Now out in the middle of the black logs—or rather, the herd of long-necked dragons—the ship had cut its air jets and switched over to the low-speed mode of the gasoline engine and floats that jutted from the craft's belly, creeping forward so slowly it wouldn't raise even a ripple on the water's surface.

While D was another matter, it came as no surprise that the children and the ferryman were pale faced and frozen with horror. But the boy and girl were truly people of the Frontier, and as such, they never took their eyes off the objects of their terror. Not even a yard away—their glistening black forms wiggled in the water and muck just a foot from the sides of the ship. Though they didn't move much, occasionally one would twist itself a bit, and a number of others around it would writhe in response, bubbling the mud in a disturbing manner and even splashing some on the ship.

"Nothing ventured, nothing gained," the saying goes, but the only thing they hoped to win with this gamble was a chance to keep living—and this was like playing with marked cards. Not actually sure how much noise or movement it would take to wake the creatures up, the ferryman had the feeling that if the engine growled even a little bit louder or the waves from his vessel got just a tad stronger, the monsters would come down on them en masse.

The ship moved ahead. Their fate rested on the soft purr of the engine and the minor ripples it sent out.

Ten minutes passed . . . then twenty—and then the ferryman let out a faint cry of surprise.

Roughly a hundred yards ahead there weren't any more of the monstrosities. There were only expanses of black muck and silvery water for as far as the eye could see.

The brother and sister hugged each other without saying a word. The hands of both were still clasped by D.

"I'll be damned!" the ferryman remarked, letting another cry of surprise slip out. But this time it had a different ring to it.

At the point where they would exit this unsettling waterway, a lone person was standing on the black mud. It was a man, and from the neck down, his body was hidden beneath a wine-red cape of some sort. His face was horribly gaunt. If the baron had been there instead of in his coffin, he would've seen that his worst fears had been realized. The night D had slain a subterranean foe, the baron had been assailed from the air by this very man.

"Are you an assassin?" D asked.

Though his question certainly seemed to reach the ears of the man up ahead, the siblings merely looked at D with an odd expression, and the ferryman didn't even seem to notice that D had said a word.

"That's right," the man promptly answered. "My name is Hichou. I crossed paths with the owner of the carriage behind you before. This marks the second time—and there won't be a third!"

"Did you have something to do with these creatures?" D asked.

They still had seventy yards to go.

"Right again. See, I left their favorite snack all along the ferry's route. I'm surprised you made it this far. But this is the end of line."

Hichou extended his arms, and his red cape spread out. It was a huge, wine-colored pair of wings.

The instant D saw the glistening cylinder the cape had concealed, he shouted, "Full speed ahead!"

They weren't through the herd of monsters yet. Be that as it may, the ferryman followed his command as if under a spell. The hum of the engine changed, and at the same time it began to operate as a hovercraft again. A blast of air like a jet exhaust lifted the vessel three feet and propelled it forward at a speed of seventy-five knots.

The second the ship sped at the man, flames and white smoke flew from his cylinder.

Missing the ship by a hair's breadth, the missile was swallowed by the water where the craft had been a second earlier, and then there was a roar as a pillar of water shot high into the sky.

An unearthly cry rang out. Raising their snakelike necks into the air one after another, the monsters glared down at their prey.

Hichou didn't have time to get off a second shot.

Not even giving the monsters a chance to lower their heads, the hovercraft sped at Hichou. There was no impact, as a wine-red streak rose into the sky. Because the man had flown off to one side instead of straight ahead, D had drawn just a fraction of a second too slow to hit his mark, and the rough wooden needle he got off a little too late was avoided without any problem. Hichou rose like a veritable bird in flight to some sixty feet off the ground, then halted. Flames and smoke flew from beneath either arm.

"Damn!" the ferryman growled as he worked the wheel, but a tenth of a second later the missile scored a direct hit on the stern of the ship. A section of the handrail was blown away, but that was the extent of damage, due in part to the compact size of the missile and in part to the skill of the ship's captain. However, the pair of carriages tilted wildly, the white one skidding toward the stern.

Seeing that the section of railing that'd been destroyed was wider than the vehicle, the girl managed to cry out, "Oh no!"

D became a bolt of lighting as he bounded over and grabbed the reins of the blue carriage's lead horse. The blue carriage advanced, and the white carriage followed suit. But above them, black snake-like heads and suckermouths were coming down.

Still keeping a grip on the horse, D lashed out with his sword. Despite his predicament, the Vampire Hunter's skill was peerless. Each of the heads fell, with one of them rolling across the ship to the bow. D was about to dash off—and then the stern of the ship dipped appreciably. The carriages moved backward again, and D tried to get the horses to stop—and then he halted.

A scream went up.

The severed head that'd rolled across the ship had popped back up and latched its suckermouth onto the ferryman's right shoulder. As the old man tumbled backward with a loud groan, his face swiftly shriveled like that of a mummy. These monstrosities subsisted off the bodily fluids of other creatures.

A rough wooden needle whizzed through the air and pierced the monster's brain.

As soon as the creature let go of him, the captain fell—and then got back up again. Clinging to the wheel for dear life, he steered it to port. He had no choice but to try and cut through part of the waterway where there were relatively few of the monsters.

The path before them was already barred by a tangle of tapering necks. But due perhaps to the ungodly skill of the ferryman, the ship advanced through the seeming jungle without stopping once, finally escaping the herd.

"You did it!" the boy shouted in a manner that was only fitting.

However, his sister was facing the stern, and she quickly cried in terror, "They're coming after us!"

While it was unclear just what shape their bodies took below the waterline, the creatures had their lengthy necks craned at a sixty-degree angle, and they gave chase at a rate that conceded nothing to the ship's sixty knots.

Perhaps due to its outrageous speed, the ship rocked violently and bounced, and there was little D could do as he steadied the carriages.

"Captain—they're gonna catch us!" the girl shouted.

And at that very moment, the ship's movements changed. But it wasn't the ferryman's doing. Something about the muddy water was different.

"Ohno-ohno-ohno-ohno—" the brother and sister screamed in terror, their cries hardly sounding like anything human.

Ahead of them the swamp was swirling. Three hundred feet in diameter and still expanding, the vortex had at its center a funnel-like depression that kept growing deeper and steeper at the sides. The ship was near the outer edge of the vortex, pinned there by centrifugal force.

Was this it? Was this the *Sturm* that the ferryman had mentioned?

The same sort of massive whirlpool that could be caused in the sea when the tide went out was happening here in the muck. The time it'd taken them to slip through the herd of monsters—and the path they'd chosen to escape—had conspired to send the ship right into the center of that muddy vortex. And it wasn't the ship alone that was threatened. The monstrosities that pursued them felt their black snakelike necks twist together as they struggled and slipped down the muddy incline of the whirlpool and were sucked to the bottom, one after another. As chilling as the scene was, it was also somehow comical.

Laughter rained down on everyone from above.

Looking up, D and the siblings saw a caped figure roughly fifteen feet from the edge of the whirlpool floating about thirty feet above the ship. While it was unclear what kind of power his cape possessed, Hichou hovered in the air without so much as flapping his wings.

"What do you think, D? I set this whole trap myself. I got the monsters all worked up, sent the ship right into them to buy some time, and even spaced the critters out so I could drive you right this way when I fired that missile at you. I want you to remember all my hard work as you sink into the muddy depths. Or will you find some remarkable way out of all of this?"

Hichou doubled over with laughter.

"There's only one way for you folks to get out of there. And that would be for me to fire one of my missiles down into the whirlpool. Unlike the ocean, if the bottom changes, the flow of the mud changes, too. However, my missiles are trained on the lot of you at present."

True to his word, Hichou had a silver cylinder pointed at them. It didn't seem that even D would be able to escape this situation.

Just then, two figures bounded straight into the air. Or rather, because the ship was nailed to the sloping sides of the whirlpool, it's more correct to say they flew up at an angle. One figure made contact with the other in midair, and from there they bounded once again. Hichou never would've dreamed that it was he they were headed toward, because the pair moved with such speed, nor could he have imagined that anyone possessing such skill was on the ship.

For a second, the three figures converged, and the missile spat flames. Its trajectory threw it right into the center of the vortex. A pillar of black water—actually, a pillar of muck—went up, and then the vortex lost momentum at an astonishing rate, its sloping bowl pushing out again and setting the ship back down in the water.

Falling toward the vessel were three silhouettes. D's sword was there to meet them. Without leaving so much as a nick on the brother and sister, the blade sliced Hichou in two at midtorso, and the high-flying assassin scattered fresh blood like red ink as he plummeted headfirst into the sea of mud.

The Talos Arsenal

CHAPTER 4

I

Having escaped the attacks of serpentine beasts and a giant whirlpool, the ferry reached the opposite shore some thirty minutes later.

D prepared to disembark after he was sure that the two carriages and the children were safely ashore. The ferryman remarked, "I'll be telling that story for the rest of my life. But you weren't really the hero who saved the ship and all of us on it . . . though you already knew that."

The ferryman's gaze was concentrated on the two tiny figures who stood dazedly with their bags in hand.

"Now I can't tell you to take 'em all the way to where they're headed, but the least you could do is stick close to those kids until they get on their coach. Brave little tykes, aren't they?"

"I'm in a hurry," D replied, his tone cool.

"Well, their coach won't get here till after dark. Not everyone who comes by between now and then is guaranteed to be an upstanding person. And I've got to turn this thing around and make the trip back."

"Go, then," D told him as he turned his back to the man and stepped across the gangplank to shore.

"You sure are a cold one. You're like a damned Noble," the old man said, his words jabbing at the Hunter like a knife.

Walking over to the brother and sister, D said, "You did great."

Taking his eyes off the children, whose cheeks were flushing deeper by the second, the Hunter got on his horse.

As the young man in black rode down the road with the carriages trailing behind him, the brother and sister silently watched him go. They weren't sad. They didn't have a mother or father—this wasn't the first time they'd had to say goodbye.

"I wonder if we'll ever see him again?" the boy muttered. Although he already knew the answer, he really wasn't looking for it.

"Let's just forget we ever saw him, okay?" the girl said, and her brother nodded. Though he wasn't yet old enough to realize this was a hundred times more painful for his sister, there was nothing else he could do. Still—

"I wonder if he'll turn and look back this way?" the boy mused.

The back of the second carriage finished climbing a gentle rise, and then the young man could be seen no more.

"He's got no connections to anyone. He'd never look back," the girl said, looking at the listing guidepost that stood at the base of the slope. The Capital seemed so terribly far away. And then she looked up at the sky. There was still quite some time until evening. But it felt terribly close.

"Can't you see them any longer?" asked the voice that drifted out of the blue carriage.

"Worried about them?" D said in reply.

"As I dreamt, I saw the battle. It's thanks to the two of them that we reached here safely."

"Well, why don't you go back and thank them?"

"What nonsense!" Miska spat scornfully. "Though the twilight may be upon us, we are still Nobility. I maintain that rather than bow our heads to the lowly humans, we should wring every last drop of blood from them. Ah, a miserable half-breed like yourself could never hope to understand how we feel."

Her voice suddenly became a bloodcurdling scream.

The four horses had frozen in place.

Though things were back to normal in less than a second, no more of Miska's abuse was heard. Surely she'd sensed that just one touch of the reins from D had immobilized her team.

"You'd do well to hold your tongue," the baron said in a sober tone. "His primary duty is to serve me. Not you."

"What a thing to say! Do you intend to side with some ill-bred Hunter instead of with me?"

"I was merely stating a fact. I don't know whose blood flows in his veins, but from his prowess and his state of mind—I don't think it wise to dwell on the subject."

"You're growing soft, aren't you? Using honeyed words with a lowly dhampir."

"Again, merely stating a fact," the baron declared in a firm tone that put an end to the dispute.

And in lieu of their exchange, D said, "Another half mile or so and we'll come to the Talos arsenal."

"You can't possibly be thinking of stopping there, are you?" Miska asked, her voice now rocked by anxiety.

"This area is crawling with monsters. That's the only place we'll be safe," replied D.

"Why don't we just keep going? Is that not why you were hired as a guard in the first place?!"

"The struggle back on the ship has left the horses ready to throw some of their shoes. They'll have to be taken care of. If any greater beasts were to attack us in the meantime, it'd mean trouble."

"Resign yourself to it," the baron said, his voice settling yet another dispute. This time it came from terribly close by—from up in the driver's seat.

"Leave the carriage to me," the pale Nobleman said, taking the reins as he surveyed the scene about him.

"Stay inside," the Hunter told him.

"I've looked forward to the twilight for so long. It's so cramped in there."

"Pretty odd for a Noble," croaked a voice, but of course it wasn't D's.

Coffins were not only the resting place of the Nobility, but they also occasionally served as their homes or escape pods, and great effort was expended to make the time spent in them as enjoyable as possible. Fifty years previously a study had been conducted on part of an old graveyard, and the people marveled at the fact that nearly two hundred of the coffins unearthed were equipped with circuitry that expanded the interior dimensions. Despite the fact that their owners no longer occupied them, a number of these coffins were still operating perfectly. Time wouldn't permit enumerating the number of researchers who'd vanished off the face of the earth because they'd become hopelessly lost in the palatial gardens contained within a coffin or had drowned after falling into the middle of an endless sea. In fact, there were even records of Nobility who went their entire lives without ever setting foot outside their coffins. Although what Baron Balazs's coffin was like was something of a mystery, it was clear that its owner was rather unusual.

Off to the right-hand side of the road, a massive fortification was drawing closer, like clotted darkness. So imposing that even the touch of its shadow made people want to leap out of their skin, it had the power to cow not only those who passed on the road, but even the normally willful monstrosities.

D and the carriages halted before colossal gates studded with iron nails as large as a grown man. As far as the fortifications went, this was merely the main gate that faced the road, while the actual fortress was within the towering mountain of rock to the rear. Looking up, the walls had been scoured by wind and rain, and there was no sign of anyone in the passageways or at the loopholes that resembled vacantly staring eyes. The parabolic antenna vainly scanning the heavens for some voice from the distant Milky Way was the only thing that glittered in the moonlight—the sole respite from this desolation.

"We do the strangest things," the baron muttered as he gazed at the walls. "Why use rotting masonry on the exterior when we've developed metals that can go ten millennia without so much as a flake of rust? It's almost as if we long for decay."

The gorgeous men stayed motionless in the moonlight. The wind was whistling. When would the dawn come?

Getting off his horse, D went over to the control box to one side of the massive gates. Opening the rusted iron lid, he stared at the controls intently, but turned back toward the gates without ever touching them.

"It's no use without a passkey. Why don't we circle around back?" the baron suggested.

"The gates are unlocked."

"It still doesn't matter. They're made of liquid metal and weigh fifty thousand tons. There's no way to force them open from outside."

Ignoring the blunderbuss stored up by the driver's seat, the baron instead took up the short spear that lay beside it. Although he merely seemed to lob it gently, the spear flew off with the speed of a swallow. His missile sank into the nail-studded gate almost up to the very end. It slid into its target like it was going through water, and sure enough, ripples spread across the surface of the gate from where it'd been pierced. In two blinks of an eye, the spear was spat back out again. The liquid metal of which the gates were composed redirected all force back in the opposite direction. All the energy in the world could be thrown at the gates without even scratching them. To the contrary, it would only repair itself.

"You can see what it is you face here. You would do well to abandon this posthaste and find us someplace else to sleep," said Miska, who'd taken a place standing beside her carriage.

Not turning to face her, D picked up the fallen spear and threw it back. The baron effortlessly extended his hand, and the weapon landed perfectly in it.

The two Nobles saw that D had placed his right hand against one colossal door. It sank in up to the wrist.

Miska had a smirk on her face, but her eyes suddenly bugged. Unless her vision deceived her, the tremendous door was slowly being pushed back.

"It can't be . . . It simply can't be . . ." the Noblewoman in white muttered, stunned not that a fifty-thousand-ton door was being opened with one hand, but that D had done it.

And the woman wasn't alone. As he sat there paralyzed in the driver's seat, Baron Balazs couldn't even speak.

When his lips finally did move, he said, "I heard something long ago. In every fortress or mansion of the Nobility, no matter how secure, there was something that would allow certain people to come and go as free as the air. And that only the members of that line knew where it was and how to make it work."

Miska looked up at the baron with fear on her face, for she understood what his words meant.

"It can't be . . ." the proud Noblewoman said once more, as if those were the only words she knew. "An outcast like him . . . related to *him* . . . ?"

Once they'd passed through, the castle gates closed once more, leaving the group surrounded by the air of devastation. Hemmed by rock on three sides, the space was reminiscent of the bandits' hideout. However, looking up at the darkened sky in place of the blue heavens, one found an expansive wall of craggy stone that looked infinitely heavy. Aside from the gates, everything else in the castle had been carved from the rock of the mountain. In addition to the buildings that were distinguishable as generator plants, substations, and energy transformers, there were a number of facilities of unknown purpose. The baron remained calm but curious as he focused his attention on his surroundings.

"So this is the Talos arsenal? I've never been anywhere that was supposed to be cursed before," he remarked before long.

During the height of the Nobles' prosperity, the meaning of those words had been the subject of some debate among humans, but in recent years, they had finally come to see the true extent of the horror. Even those commonly cursed had fearful things upon which they in turn laid curses. For instance, the form of plankton called "the red cloud" that lived above the atmosphere had, one winter's day, suddenly come down with its body covering twenty thousand square miles and absorbed every living thing beneath it. The only thing that saved the Nobility and the humans from that horrible fate was the fact that due to the leisurely pace of the creature's descent, they were able to discern exactly when and where it would touch down and evacuate every form of life—plants and animals included. They then simply had to wait three days. The sight of that enormous cloud leaving called to mind a magnificent sunset, as it were. Having descended in search of food and disappeared with its stomach still empty, how the creature managed to subsist for the next two decades was something even the Nobility's vaunted science had never unraveled.

Another example was the "Nobility-specific maze" that was said to exist somewhere in the eastern section of the Capital. For any humans that entered, it was merely a honeycomb of passages. But when anyone of Noble blood set foot in it, the structure instantly became a labyrinth from which they could never hope to escape. Why did it elect to trap only the Nobility? The reason was unclear.

"I'm cold," Miska mumbled as she hugged her shoulders.

D and the baron could both feel it, too. From the very second they'd set foot inside the stronghold, an unearthly aura had buffeted them.

"What do you think it is?" the baron inquired.

"There's no need to ask," D informed him, his gaze still angling off to their left.

Though the edifice, more massive and bizarre than the rest, melted into the darkness, these three of Noble blood had eyes that could see as clearly as in broad daylight.

"This warrants some investigation, doesn't it?" the baron remarked as he began to walk off. Turning after he'd advanced about ten paces, he said, "Stay close to the lady," and then continued walking.

"Please, take me with you," Miska said as if summoning up her courage. "I am loath to be left in such an eerie place with a lowly dhampir."

"It's still safer than going with me."

"No," she replied in a tone that sounded almost doleful.

Though he was clearly rather disliked, D stood there completely expressionless.

"Very well, then. However, if you become a burden, his first priority will still be to protect me."

"I understand that," she said, glaring cruelly at D.

Miska went next, and D brought up the rear as the group began to walk toward a shared fate. As his guard, D should've stopped the baron. Ordinarily, that's precisely what he would've done. He hadn't simply because he'd decided that they really did need to find out what made the atmosphere so chilling. The air was that unearthly.

In the foyer of a building with hornlike protuberances that seemed to have sprung out with a crazed disregard for spatial relationships, the trio came to a halt. Not surprisingly, there was another liquid metal door. D was about to step forward when the baron stopped him.

"This time, I'll give it a try," the Nobleman said as he stepped to the fore.

As he set his right hand against the somehow limpid silvery surface, it suddenly sank up to the wrist. Almost simultaneously, the door began to slowly recede.

"You are a natural, Baron—very nicely done," Miska called out, even her words seeming to glow. With a heaping load of sarcasm, she added, "Any trick a common half-breed can do comes easily enough to you." With a brief gasp, she said, "Could it be that the Sacred Ancestor was one of your—"

"Regrettably, we're not in the least bit related. The Sacred Ancestor is truly like a god to me," the baron said in a coolly refreshing tone. There wasn't the faintest trace of vanity in his words, and his last remark trembled with boundless fear and respect.

"Follow me," said D.

As this was perfectly natural behavior for a guard, Miska held her tongue even as she remained vexed.

And with that, the young man in black stepped into pitch darkness eddying with an unearthly aura, his steady manner making it seem as if the pair behind him didn't even exist.

II

The trio was greeted by a vast space, perhaps even a void. There was nothing. Not a single thing. They could see only numerous protrusions on the walls, floor, and ceiling that all looked like old lava flows.

"It was melted," Miska said as she looked down at the nearest deformity. "Everything has been melted. And yet it looks completely normal from the outside. Whatever could have happened in here?"

As he surveyed their surroundings, the baron suggested, "A battle? But if that's the case, it's odd that there isn't a single body left, and the way everything's melted has a strange orderliness to it. I get the feeling someone merely intended to destroy the interior."

"It had to be destroyed," D said, taking over the discussion.

Miska looked at him in astonishment. She felt like the gorgeous young man was the one behind the destruction.

Whether or not he knew what she was thinking, D continued, "They didn't want the equipment in this factory to ever be used again. That was as far as their intentions went."

"In other words, they never wanted to make another such weapon. And what kind of weapon was it?"

But the baron's remark wasn't really a question.

This was the arsenal of the Nobility, as they'd mentioned several times. It was not merely a place for storing weapons; a look at the equipment made it clear they'd also manufactured them here. Production had been assisted by androids, but Nobles had been in charge.

The cruel masters of earlier days were haughty fiends who knew no fear. What sort of weapon could they have created that would've made them destroy their equipment so they could never create another?

"At least, this is how I understand it," the baron mumbled, answering his own question. "Naturally, I don't know exactly what kind of creature they created, but development of their weapon took centuries. Each and every attempt in the first two stages of development died off, but in the third attempt they finally achieved success. But I've heard that the instant it was completed, the one in charge gave the order that everything was to be destroyed, and so it was done."

"A Destroyer created merely so that it could be destroyed?" D muttered.

There in the darkness black as spilt ink, the two Nobles were momentarily left speechless.

D steeled his jaw. In this darkness rife with death and destruction, their destination was the wall up ahead.

"That's it."

Nodding, Baron Balazs turned to D and asked, "What are you going to do?"

D advanced as if the other two were forgotten, and on reaching the wall, he placed his hand on its surface. As proof that the same miracle that'd opened the fortress gates was at work again, his arm slipped into the wall up to the elbow. After about five seconds, he turned around and went back to the other two.

"That was a brief trip," said the Noble in blue. "Are you just going to leave it at that?"

"I saw that 'the Destroyer' hadn't been eradicated."

Miska's breath was taken away.

"It's somewhere beyond our reach. And it will never have any effect on the outside world."

"Never?"

D nodded.

"Some things simply can't be understood," said Miska.

The two men looked at this pale flower of a beauty.

"The sense I got was that the eerie aura began shortly after we passed through the gates. Up until that point, these had been mere ruins. Might there not be some reason the Destroyer has been reactivated?" the Noblewoman asked, her eyes turned toward the baron.

"Perhaps. Someone of the Sacred Ancestor's line might be capable of such a thing."

Looking to either side, the baron remarked, "I don't believe we'll be able to rest here very peacefully. Let's go."

On exiting the building, a bird could be heard crying in the distance.

"'Children of the night?'" the baron said as his gaze narrowed. "Even they won't come into this lair of the Nobility."

"Whatever are you talking about?" Miska countered. "'The children of the night' and all those other creatures are our creations. It is awe that keeps them from coming to us."

"Awe becomes simple fear all too easily. And when it does, what does that leave but hatred?"

"So it would seem. But isn't that good enough? It is an honor for the superior to bask in the hatred of the inferior."

"I was taught the very same thing. By my father."

"And a superb father he must be!" Miska replied. She didn't know that the baron was on his way to slay the man.

The bird cried out again.

The baron turned to one side. He'd caught D's voice from off in that direction.

"What is it singing about?" the Hunter had said.

"It is singing praises to the glory of the Nobility," Miska said, her comments clearly directed solely to the baron.

"What do *you* think?" the baron inquired of his beautiful guard.

"To glory and awe," said D.

Miska smirked.

"To extinction."

Though Miska was certain to voice some objection to this, she was stopped by a nod from the baron and another cry from the bird—this one seeming to bid them farewell a second before it flew away. Out with the moonlight, the wind, and the darkness, time was the only thing still moving.

D suddenly realized that he'd been sleeping. He was weary, of course. However, what had drawn him down into the depths of slumber was something unlike any exhaustion he'd ever known, physical or mental. Even his dhampir's sixth sense had unconsciously been swallowed by the darkness.

Pulling away from the carriage he'd been slumped against, the Hunter looked over at the baron. The sight of him just getting up from the ground only served to make this unwanted sleep seem all the more strange.

"Did you hear that?" D asked as he turned toward the factory building.

Although an ordinary person would've heard nothing at all, he'd been awakened by a cry like the leaves of a tree riffled by the wind.

Without any prompting at all, the baron looked in the very same direction. Both men had noticed that there was no sign of Miska. The two of them sprinted ahead, leaving the wind swirling in their wake.

The door was open.

D leapt through it first. His darkness-piercing eyes could clearly discern a circular opening in the wall he'd examined earlier, agape like a screaming mouth. The unearthly aura no longer gusted from it. The interior of this factory ruled by devastation was terribly still. Something fearful lurked there.

"There!" the baron exclaimed as he raced over to the right.

Catching sight of the pale beauty that lay out of the corner of his eye, D then went over to the hole in the wall and stepped through it without the slightest hesitation. It was ten feet high, and it ran straight into the heart of the darkness. Whatever Miska had released had come out of there. More precisely, she had probably been lured by it, and D and the baron put to sleep by it as well. That which had been sealed away had waited thousands of years to foil the efforts of those that'd put it there.

As if to challenge this tremendous stretch of time, D sprinted deep into the darkness.

The gorgeous figure that appeared from the factory was met by the baron. Miska was nowhere to be seen. An hour had passed since D had disappeared into the far reaches of the hole.

"Miska is in her coffin," said the baron. He knew his guard in black would never inquire about the welfare of a Noblewoman with whom he had nothing to do.

"How is she doing?" D asked, easily betraying all the baron's expectations.

"She's terribly weak. Her biorhythms have dropped to extreme levels. The rest is up to the RS."

The RS, or Rebirth System, was an indispensable piece of equipment installed in the coffins of the Nobility. Though the Nobles prided themselves on being ageless and undying, the axes and wooden stakes humans used proved they weren't necessarily indestructible. The Nobility's efforts to counter this were nothing to scoff at, the greatest of which were crypts and coffins that ensured a "blood sleep" in perfect safety. Resting places might be secured by DNA-keyed locks, multilayered psychological defense systems, or perhaps best of all, doors comprised of thousands or even tens of thousands of layers of ultra-dense alloys. Even if human ingenuity managed to get past all of this, the passageway leading to the coffin's resting place might be a false passage or an endless hallway that would usher the intruder into a pocket dimension where brutal mechanical soldiers or robotic beasts no living creature could withstand would be waiting.

However, if a stake of rough wood pierced their heart or their head was lopped off, someone with a Noble's superhuman vitality could manage to pull the stake out or replace the severed head—even incorrectly—on the wound. In that case, before the final embers of the vampire's life force died out, they might be returned to their coffin, where the product of their intellect and foresight—the RS—would do everything in its power to keep them off the road to destruction. The DNA of darkness would be reconstructed and revitalized, and though it might be a week or a year until the true indestructibility of their immortal form could be confirmed, when the coffin's lid opened once again, the fearsome creature supposedly destroyed by humanity would return.

While the reason for Miska's loss of strength was unknown, something as simple could be cured in the course of a night.

"We should dispose of her," D said, making his fearful proclamation in a stoic tone.

"Why is that? Did you see something at the back of the hole?"

"A sealed sanctum."

That was the kind of place where treasures and inventions not meant to see the light of day were locked away. Constructing one required the permission of the Nobility's House of Peers.

"It was buried a mile and a quarter deep in the mountain."

III

What D had seen was a space that extended for several miles in all three dimensions. The sanctum had been lent a religious air by the fifteen-foot-long and six-foot-wide bed that had been set in the center of it, and by the bizarre objects filling its immediate vicinity.

"What did you find?" the baron inquired.

"A library of mobius books, a blood fount, and a multilayered battlefield. Those three things took up most of the sanctum."

"So whatever awakened there had books to read, could slake its eternal thirst for blood, and could exercise its fighting skills in endless battles, eh? That seems like the best conceivable way to keep it contained. And yet the one sealed away inside still wanted to be released."

D must've had the very same thought.

Mobius books had no end, and the volume would be back at the first page without the reader realizing it, except the contents had changed completely so the reader would never become bored—to the contrary, their intellectual curiosity would keep them reading forever. However, there was one chance out of all the infinite possibilities of something going wrong with the print, and it seemed likely that the entire wall full of such books D had seen was to guard against that very occurrence, for the Nobility had feared that one case out of an infinite number of times.

The blood fount was a device to satisfy thirst, and it went without saying that part of the enormous machine would continue to operate and produce an infinite supply of blood from a finite stock of materials. And surely other machinery was in place to maintain that part of the equipment, and still other machines existed to keep those support devices functioning.

However, all the books D had seen had been read and discarded, and the supposedly bottomless blood fount had run dry. In that case, the awakened Destroyer would have nowhere to direct its curiosity but to the last of its creators' redoubts—the multilayered battlefield.

While the Nobility hadn't mastered the secrets of time, they'd narrowly come to control space and had used that knowledge in a number of fields. They were able to transport materials by teleportation, or to put an entire lake or valley into a tiny box.

This knowledge also gave rise to game technology that could spawn limitless amounts of foes. Troops and arms were prepared in a space, and thousands or even tens of thousands of these areas could be stacked one on top of another, until even the most enthusiastic combatant would be satisfied—or could at least go on fighting for all time. Perhaps it was only natural that such a device would be left in the resting place of the ultimate Destroyer even the Nobility had feared.

"You don't mean to tell me the battlefield was malfunctioning, do you?" the baron asked, his question also perfectly natural.

"No," D replied. "Everything in it had been destroyed."

"That's incredible," the baron said, his words carrying boundless awe—and murderous intent.

It was said that the more powerful the opponent one faced, the more an individual burned with cruelty and the urge to fight. This crowning characteristic had dominated the Nobility's civilization.

"There was only one thing left."

D's remark did more to stir up the baron's curiosity than it did to quell the rest of his psyche.

"Oh, and what was that?"

Pulling something from his coat's interior, D held it up before the pale face.

About eight inches long, the crystalline object was a pale purple color, and it had a metallic sphere set within it.

"That's a communication crystal from roughly five thousand years ago. Did you view it?"

"No, part of its decoding system has been damaged. Looks like it could take a while to fix."

"There must be tens of thousands of levels to the battlefield. How did you ever find it?"

"It was held in a subfield. And it had a buoy on it."

"So that the Destroyer wouldn't notice it? There are few even among the Nobility of the lineage that could uncover such a thing. D—what are you?"

"It must be stared," said D. "For blood and for destruction. The passageway I took went on for a mile and a quarter. The whole thing had been filled in with a polymer paving material. And the Destroyer spent five thousand years tunneling back through it."

"But then it took a rest. And that must've been when we came along. Why has it awakened again, D?"

"Miska knows the answer."

"Perhaps the Destroyer was awakened by the aura of another of its kind. D—was it *you?*"

The Hunter said nothing.

"That was probably horrendously rude of me."

"Next time, don't start talking in your sleep until you're actually sleeping," D said, diverting his gaze to the fortification's exit. "There's no indication that it went outside. It's still in here."

"There are other structures out back."

"Stay here," D said, turning around.

Just then, there was the rattle of wooden wheels out beyond the massive gates. A sound that only D and the baron would hear came to a halt in front, and soon the echoes of someone hammering on the doors reached their ears.

"It's a stagecoach," said the baron.

It was probably the coach the children had been waiting for. Running nearly a half day late wasn't an uncommon occurrence on the Frontier. The frantic pounding seemed like a call for help, and the reason for this soon became apparent. The sound of other hooves was drawing closer. As the pair listened to clomping that by all rights they shouldn't have been able to hear, their ears were easily able to tell there were a great many mounts involved.

"I wonder if it's bandits? What should we do?" asked the baron.

"You're the boss. Do as you wish."

"Well, it's hell out there . . . and hell in here, too," the baron muttered as he dashed off toward the colossal gates.

Not waiting for D to get there, he reached out for the controls that opened and closed the doors. While the controls outside were another matter, the ones inside weren't broken.

As soon as the gates opened wide enough, a coach drawn by a team of four raced madly into the fortress.

Once more, the baron's hand touched the controls.

And at that very moment a woman's scream shot up to the darkened heavens. D and the baron weren't the only ones it affected—the foaming team of horses with bloodshot eyes that drew the coach also froze in its tracks.

The scream had come from Miska, but she wasn't outside. In the safest of all places—in her coffin loaded into her carriage—what could've frightened her so?

D saw.

The baron saw it, too.

The battlements that ran from the main gates turned to the right at the edge of the front garden, but a tall figure had casually ducked out from behind that corner. The gigantic figure was ten feet tall—a fitting size for a bed—but even wearing a warrior's helm and breastplate, greaves and gauntlets, he looked much too thin. What the reflections of the scant moonlight made clear was that his armor wasn't made of metal but of synthetic leather, and only the fifteen-foot-long throwing spear in his right hand had the glint of steel. A longsword also dangled from his right hip.

The earth shook.

He opened his hitherto shut eyelids just a crack. His nose and lips looked like halfhearted additions to his face, but his rough countenance underwent a change. As a warm red light began to spill from his eyes, they caught sight of the group of pale, semi-translucent riders rushing through the gates.

The mob was comprised of some of the most vicious and fearsome of all the demonic creatures and foul beasts that inhabited the Frontier—the ghost knights. A few of them had a human form, but there were others who were no more than bleached bones clad in ragged garments. There were beings with two heads, or covered with eyes, or with dozens of squirming arms and legs—and each and every one of them was half-transparent and gave off a white phosphorescence, just like their mounts. It was easy enough to spot them from a great distance, and while it seemed that potential targets would be able to flee before they were victimized, the reason that this wasn't the case soon became clear.

The horses pulling the coach reared up once more. The giant had moved. Not only the coach's team, but the knights' horses backed away as well, though the only one to fall to the ground with a scream was the coach's driver.

"H-h-help me!" he stammered as he spun around in a full circle. He didn't have the faintest idea from whom he should seek help.

A blue light shot out.

A silvery flash crossed it.

Although D's blade moved with unholy skill, the blue light pierced his blade and stabbed through the driver's right eye, going through his goggles and into his brain.

A strange sound shot up to the heavens. The giant had howled. And Miska's scream had been intertwined with it.

Apparently the phantoms had decided that he was their most immediate threat.

Given this gap in the action, D opened the door of the coach and scooped up the brother and sister within. However, hadn't one of the phantom's attacks gone through the Hunter's blade as if his steel were no more than a mirage? Would even D be able to get back with the children when his sword couldn't parry these attacks?

His path was barred by a pair of horsemen. Another pair went for the baron, and the rest charged at the giant. Carrying both children under his left arm, D leapt forward.

Blue darts struck the body of the carriage and ricocheted off.

Twisting his body as he sailed headfirst, D slashed through the forefeet of both steeds. His blade cut thin air. A split second before he was going to slam into the ground, D put down his left elbow and used it to spring back up and take a huge leap back. A blue arrow sped to where he'd been, and it too rebounded.

D's eyes were invested with a crimson glow. It was as if they'd solved the mystery.

"D!" the baron's voice cried out. "Your attacks—you must see they have no effect!"

Blue lights took flight.

D's blade didn't move at all. The streaks that connected with D's neck and the middle of his forehead bounced off him easily and fell to the ground.

Perhaps it could be said that the phantom's attacks were entirely mental. In the midst of battle, a combatant would have to either dodge blows or parry them. If they parried and their foe's attack wasn't too strong for them, it would be deflected. That was simply common sense where physics was concerned, and the person blocking the blows would certainly think so. Or rather than actually *think* it, they'd simply *believe* it subconsciously.

The phantoms' attacks were a reversal of that faith. Arrows that should've been deflected pierced the parrying blade, penetrating armor or iron plate. And as long as one held to the premise that by cutting their foe they would destroy them, they would simply guarantee that their blows wouldn't cut the enemy at all. But if one could see through that, it seemed victory would be easy enough. In other words, attack without thinking you'd cut them, parry without thinking you'd block them—that was all there was to it. But to do so required a change to firmly rooted common sense at a subconscious level. Only a belief that bordered on preoccupation—a faith of unrivaled might—could turn this weakness into a strength and return things to the way they were supposed to be.

If anyone but D had heard the baron's cry, they probably would've instantly met with death without any resistance.

As D bounded, his sword went into action.

A phantom's head was effortlessly removed from its torso, and both it and its horse were reduced to thousands of scattering flecks of phosphorescence that soon disappeared from view.

However, there was another battle taking place within the fortress that bore watching. Blue light flew from the hands of the phantoms surrounding the giant, leaving his massive form looking like a porcupine. The giant howled, but his voice was replaced by the arc of his lengthy spear as he whirled it like a massive water wheel and mowed through the phantoms. Not a single one of them fell, neither rider nor horse, and the pale figures made the giant shudder with fresh arrows of light.

"They're beating the hell out of him," D muttered.

"Not quite," the baron countered.

It was an instant later that their field of view was stained crimson by the glow from the giant's eyes.

The phantoms were also dyed the color of blood. Though their pale phosphorescence seemed to glow more intensely, it was only for a moment, and then they were blown away like a thin fog in the face of a mighty gale. The giant had blasted them with a powerful "death light." It slammed into the gigantic gates directly ahead of him, making the fifty tons of metal buckle almost instantaneously.

When the giant unleashed the blast, his mental state had probably been completely unfocused. Three riders who'd been off the path still remained.

The crimson light was challenged by a bluish hue—the glow of the three riders. The red eyes that turned toward them swiftly lost their light. Perhaps it was merely a question of speed, but the unearthly gaze of the trio was swifter than the giant's death light, and it left him reeling. As the arrows of blue light came to bear on him, the giant began to back away.

The mounted phantoms each extended one arm. One's hand was only bone. And then they beckoned to their foe.

The giant halted. Amazingly enough, he started to head back toward the trio of grim reapers. Their deadly arrows assailed him with their blue glow. Finally, the giant fell to his knees. Slumping to the ground, he looked as awkward as a stuffed animal.

The three riders wheeled their horses around. Perhaps the loathsome wraiths were surprised. In order to guard against the paralyzing effects of their hypnotic gaze, people used dark goggles in areas where they were known to appear. In place of that, the quiet Noble who stood before them like the deep blue sea had both eyes shut tight.

In keeping with the shaken state of the riders, the blue arrows of death were a little late in being launched.

A band of white light spread out further and further, and as if making the most of its freedom as it zipped between them, it decapitated all three.

"Good thing you figured out their weakness," D said to the baron as he lowered the boy and girl to the ground. It was pleasure more than fear that now filled the children's faces. After all, they'd been able to see D again.

"I fought them once, long ago," the baron replied as the children filled his field of view. Their little throats trembled as they swallowed involuntarily. No human could ever mistake the sight of a Noble.

"But you must've realized what it was, too. There's no way they'd get the better of the man the whole Frontier knows as D. Now, about him," the baron said, his gaze directed at the fallen form of the giant. The arrows of blue light had vanished.

Telling the boy and girl, "Wait here," D walked off after the baron.

The giant had given up the ghost.

"Is this what was sealed in the sanctum?" the baron asked, his voice wavering with a somewhat dissatisfied ring.

"Yes, though it's hard to believe. The sensation I felt when he first appeared seemed the same as that in the factory and the sanctum."

The baron had understood that much. But was this the final fate of the Destroyer feared so greatly by its very creators? Was this the end of the "weapon" that had tunneled a mile and a quarter to walk the earth again? Believing in this was like trying to dream by the light of dawn.

"And you think it was Miska that released him?"

"Odds are," D responded. "And it might still survive."

"Then I suppose we'll have to examine her, won't we?" the baron said as he approached the white carriage.

Beauty and the Monstrous Cloud

CHAPTER 5

I

Clear weather spread almost magnanimously across the blue vault of the heavens, but after looking up at it for a while, it seemed to loom over them, so the brother and sister sitting up in the driver's seat quickly turned their eyes forward. For a split second, their vacant gazes rested on the handsome young man in black at the reins of the cyborg horse riding along just to the right of their seat.

It was near noon the next day. The wide central road ran across the major artery to the Capital about twelve miles ahead. And it was there that D and the children would part company.

"Say, mister," the girl said to D.

When the Hunter turned just a bit in her direction, she continued in a low voice, "Those other two—they're Nobility, right? What in the world are you guarding them for?"

It came as little surprise that her tone was both slightly unsettled and somewhat accusatory. To any boy or girl raised on the Frontier, the Nobility were no more than blood-crazed fiends.

"The pay is good," D replied.

Though his response was the sort of thing that would crush a child's dreams, the girl didn't seem to bear him any ill will. For as long as she could remember, she'd known in the marrow of her bones that people did whatever they had to do to survive. She also retuned a bit of humor in D's reply. Apparently he behaved a bit differently than usual when dealing with children.

"You mean to say you'll do anything as long as there's money to be made?" she asked with delight while a flicker of emotion played on D's lips.

"That's right."

"In that case, would you take us as far as the Capital?"

"I'm headed in a different direction."

"We'll wait for you at an inn on the thoroughfare. We'd wait there forever for you if need be—wouldn't we?"

"You said it!" the boy added with an enthusiastic nod. "Anyway, Sis and I have our act. We can make some money there while we wait. So you can go take all the time you need to earn your wages without worrying about us."

"Maybe I will," D replied. Though what emotions were in his heart as he spoke remained a mystery.

"But you know something, Sis? I don't hate that fella in the blue."

"Don't you go calling a Noble 'fella' now!"

"But he's been kind to us, hasn't he? He went and let you and me ride in his carriage. Ordinarily, he'd have just drunk all our blood!"

"Well, he didn't do that because *he's* around," the girl said, her pudgy cheeks inflating even more as she gazed at D in infatuation.

"You might have something there . . ."

"How about the woman then?" the girl snapped.

"Oh, I'm none too keen on her."

They were referring, of course, to Miska.

No matter what D made of the pair's discussion, his expression was devoid of any hint of emotion, as always.

After the giant was slain, the baron and D had gone to check out Miska. They both suspected that one of the many possessing spirits that frequented the Frontier might've taken hold of the Noblewoman. In comparison to his supposed power, the giant had proved incredibly frail in the end. They had to wonder if perhaps the giant had merely been a vessel and that the true form—the spirit—had transferred over to Miska when she opened the wall and set him free. Her mysterious weakening, the mad scream she unleashed when the giant appeared—these might be clues. It was quite plausible that the only reason she'd been unharmed was because something like that had taken place.

Though Miska hadn't fully recovered yet, they took her from her coffin and conducted tests as to her physical and mental state using extremely sensitive equipment carried by the baron's carriage. However, the tests revealed nothing out of the ordinary. The testing equipment wasn't malfunctioning.

"She seems to be okay," said the baron.

"Is that what you think?" D inquired.

"Not quite. This equipment can measure anything down to a quadrillionth of the level of a normal psyche. It's conceivable that this could be something below that."

D was slumped back against a carriage wheel, looking down at Miska. The test had taken place outside.

"What do you say to disposing of her?"

"Occasionally I get the feeling I never should've hired you. Is human blood so cruel?"

"It's not limited to humans."

"Though Nobles may have their differences with their fellow Nobility, the bonds of friendship and respect are usually maintained. I firmly believe that. Your Noble blood couldn't possibly allow you to say such a heartless thing about this young lady."

"It may be that human blood is kinder."

"Preposterous. I pride myself on being something of a student of the human race. I'm fully versed in both their virtues and their vices. And you would be hard pressed to shake my faith in the belief their kind is inferior to us."

"It's a matter of fact, not faith. Had you been more observant in your studies, you might've reached a different conclusion."

The Noble in blue and the Hunter in black—for the first time, something dangerous flowed between them.

"Enough already," Miska said, her pained voice dispelling the tension. "Do not speak of the human race before me . . . At any rate . . . are you satisfied now?"

The baron nodded.

"In that case, would you be a dear . . . and dispose of those filthy swine?"

Her trembling finger was pointing at the brother and sister.

"I can't do that."

"Why ever not?" Miska asked as the eyes in her haggard face became lakes of malice.

"Human or not, we can't just leave these children to shift for themselves. We shall drop them off tomorrow in someplace convenient."

"You mustn't . . . Though you've sworn not to touch them . . . they can't come with us . . . If I were in your position . . . I would leave them right in this very spot."

"Kindly return her to her coffin," the baron told D.

Although Miska's whole body trembled with resistance until the black arms lifted her up, she lost consciousness before D started over to the white carriage.

When D returned, the baron was standing beside the children. Turning and seeing the Hunter, he furrowed his refined brow.

D's coat had black smoke billowing from it.

"Defense systems?" he asked.

D nodded.

The defensive mechanisms incorporated into Miska's coffin had determined that D was something other than a Noble. His whole body had been pierced by laser beams of a hundred thousand degrees.

"You must forgive me for putting you in such a situation. I completely forgot you're a dhampir," the baron apologized. And apparently he meant it.

"Don't worry about it. Only half of them went off," D replied, his words leaving the baron silent.

Fortunately, a hint of blue had begun to mix with the eastern sky. The baron returned to his carriage.

"Once day breaks, we'll be off. Load your baggage into this carriage," D told the children.

"Sure," the boy replied, throwing a look at the Noble in blue before he dashed off for his bags. His eyes had a calm hue to them.

"What did you talk with the Noble about?" D asked as he rode alongside the carriage.

"Nothing important," the boy replied.

Hastily tossing her head from side to side, his sister said, "That's a lie. He asked us where we were born, and where we're going."

"Like I said, nothing important," the boy countered firmly, slightly backing away from the imposing and pudgy face before him.

"He asked if we liked the Nobility."

To a child, that must've seemed an important question.

"I see. And what did you reply?"

"I told him I hate them," the girl answered peevishly. She was in love with D.

"I didn't answer," the boy said rather sheepishly.

"Why didn't you say you hated them?!" his sister exclaimed.

"Well, he's a good-looking guy, and his eyes were so kind."

"Kind eyes, eh?" said D.

"That's right. And kinda sad, too. Like yours, mister."

Beneath the blue sky, a pair of gorgeous young men moved on—one inside a coffin, the other on the back of a horse. Both with sad eyes. But perhaps the real question was whether or not D's eyes were kind.

"Now look what you've gone and done—you had to go and say he was just like a Noble, and now he's clammed up."

"Hey, that hurts!"

The girl had furtively got hold of her brother's thigh and given it a twist, and the boy entered into a mute struggle with her. As they were silently wrestling, they suddenly looked forward.

"Oh, my," the girl gasped, her brother still tugging madly at her cheek. But on noticing that D had grabbed hold of the reins and stopped the carriage, the boy also gasped in surprise.

"Use this," D said, dropping a large rifle across their laps before he galloped forward.

To either side of the road were sandstone plateaus over thirty feet high. On the road a hundred feet ahead, a girl with blond hair stood in a daze. What's more, on her back she had a giant purple toad that was as ugly as sin. Noticing D, the girl took a few unsteady steps forward, then fell like a log. But at that very moment, the toad got off her and scrambled up the nearby rock face, disappearing from sight in no time.

Quickly dismounting, D took the girl's pulse. Her long, thin eyes opened a crack. Her beautiful but anemic countenance looked familiar. She was the same young lady who'd been working with the magician by the side of the road back before they'd crossed the swamp.

"Help . . . me . . ." the girl said, barely wringing the words from her throat. But on seeing D's face, her eyes didn't fail to go wide. Even a patient at death's door would undoubtedly react the same way.

"What's wrong?" asked D. He could tell the girl's condition was merely the result of shock and fatigue.

"That toad . . . has been after me . . . forever . . . Please . . ."

"It's already run off."

This only served to put more dread on the girl's face.

"I can't believe it . . . That it would finally . . . let me go . . ."

Not even asking whether she could stand or not, D lent the girl his shoulder as he put her back on her feet. Placing her in the saddle, he took his horse by the reins and returned to the carriage.

What's going on? the baron asked, the words drifting to D in a tone only he could hear. Apparently the Nobleman must've heard the commotion.

Explaining the situation, D added, "She'll go with us as far as the next inn. Although I would like to put her in your carriage."

That's fine, the baron replied.

However, when D tried to get her into the vehicle, the girl started crying and screaming like she was out of her mind. One glance told her that the carriage belonged to the Nobility.

"Stop! Don't put me in with a Noble—I beg of you!"

Struggling as if for her very life, she certainly appeared to be sincere.

"Okay, you two get in there, then," D told the brother and sister.

Though the girl was quick to voice her complaints, her brother was brimming with curiosity as he said, "Sure thing!"

Eyes sparkling, the boy climbed down out of the driver's seat all by himself.

Left no alternative, his sister followed reluctantly.

Loading the spent girl into the driver's seat, D then started them moving forward again. Although he thought the toad would come leaping out at some point, there wasn't the slightest trace of it anywhere.

Taking a capsule from his saddlebags, the Hunter offered it to the exhausted girl. Staring at it dazedly, she apparently gave up any hope of getting additional aid as she weakly took the capsule in hand, put it in her mouth, and chewed it. With vitamins, minerals, and sedatives among its nine hundred ingredients, the capsule brought life and color back into the girl's face in no time—less than five seconds, to be precise. Though such capsules were expensive, a traveler crossing the Frontier without them might as well be naked.

Letting out a deep breath, the girl straightened herself.

"Thank you," she said with a polite bow.

"Feeling better?"

"Yes."

"Then you can get off at the next inn."

The girl was left at a loss for words. The fact that a gorgeous and muscular young man wouldn't want to look after a woman like herself came like a slap to the face.

"Who . . . who exactly are you?" she managed to ask about five minutes later, with despair and anger still churning in her features.

There was no reply.

"This is a Noble's carriage—so the person guarding it would be . . . But you don't look like that's the case at all . . . By any chance, are you D?"

"Where did you hear my name?"

Caught in his stare, the girl's cheek flushed carmine.

"Through the grapevine. They say there's a beautiful Hunter out on the Frontier. But what would a Vampire Hunter be doing guarding Nobles' carriages?"

"One of them hired me."

"To protect him from humans?"

"In a manner of speaking."

"But isn't that the complete opposite of what you do?"

"Perhaps."

"You don't say much, do you?" the girl said, not realizing that in fact that was quite a lot for him. But it looked as if D had ignored her remark.

"Yesterday, I saw you just outside the village of Shamuni. Not that you'd remember me. I was working as a magician's assistant."

Discussion of the girl's personal situation dissolved into the stark sunlight. At some point the cliffs had vanished, and flat green expanses lined the road ahead. The grass was billowing in waves, thanks to the wind. The creak of the wheels went out like a mumbled song.

And there were those inside the blue carriage who also saw and heard these things. The brother and sister stared at the luxurious coffin secured in the center of the vehicle with a somewhat distressed look on their faces. After all, there was a Noble inside it. Though that much was obvious, the sense of incongruity was stronger than that of fear because the impression left by the occupant when they'd seen him the previous night was one of elegance and kindness, and because D was watching over him. But in the end, when a Noble's resting place was right in front of them, the primeval and almost instinctive fear that'd been hammered into the children from the day they were born couldn't help but rear its ugly head.

"It's kinda creepy, Sis," the boy whined.

"It's broad daylight now, so there's not a chance of him coming out," the girl assured him. "But it's all your fault for going on about what a wonderful fella he is."

"That's got nothing to do with this. It's just that coffins give me the creeps."

"Don't worry. You've got me here, and we've got that guy outside, too."

"Yeah, but still," the boy protested.

Where do the two of you come from? inquired the shady voice that echoed through the siblings' heads.

"What's it matter to you anyway?" the girl shot back. "You try anything funny, and we'll tell that guy outside."

I wouldn't want that, the voice in their heads replied in a tone laced with irony. *I'm not quite sure whether I could beat him or not.*

"Like there's a chance in hell of you ever beating him!" the girl said, inflating her cheeks indignantly.

Jabbing her elbow with his own, her brother said, "Don't be so blunt about it."

Apparently he was more of a realist. Ordinarily women were predisposed to be that way, but it seemed that having taken to the road with such a strong personality at an earlier age, he'd developed his outlook to some degree out of sheer necessity. However, given the dazzling acrobatics he'd unveiled back on the ship in the swamp in their hour of need, he undoubtedly had every bit as much nerve as his sister when the situation called for it.

"I'm just saying . . ."

Getting a tight grip on his sister's hand as her eyes bulged in their sockets, the boy replied, "A town in the western Frontier called Liddell. Ever heard of it?"

Can't say that I have. What kind of place is it?

"You're just full of questions, aren't you, mister? It's just this little town out in the middle of nowhere. It's the safest place thereabouts, but on the other hand, it's also real quiet and boring. There were beautiful plains and a waterfall on the edge of town."

Why did you leave?

"Because our father and mother died," the boy responded in a tone that made it seem as if that were the perfectly natural answer.

If you don't mind my asking, how did they happen to pass away?

"They were out in the swamp catching fang shrimp when a snake dragon did them in. The folks in town told us what happened. One of the village bigwigs took us in, but he worked us like slaves. So we lit out of there and got picked up by a carnival that tours the Frontier. We had the whole acrobatics thing down pat in three years."

That's quite an accomplishment.

"You've never even seen our act, so don't be so quick with the compliments," the boy said, waving his arms at the coffin in a way that was terribly adult. His face alone remained appropriate to his age, with a grimace that was both childish and endearing. Fearless he seemed—but in fact, he had merely learned to use his own cheer to master his fear.

"But enough about us. You're a Noble, aren't you, mister? So how come you let us ride in your carriage without doing anything to us?"

"He'll get around to it—just wait," his sister said with surety.

"If he was gonna, he'd have long since done it."

"He can't do a thing with that tough, handsome guy out there."

You may be right about that.

The girl hadn't intended for her scathing remarks to be overheard, and she slapped a plump hand up over her mouth.

"Where are you headed, mister?" the boy promptly inquired.

The village of Krauhausen.

"That's pretty far off. Know someone there, do you?"

My father is there.

"Your father? Lucky you! I bet you'll get to play and stuff. You sure got it good!"

"Knock it off," his sister told him, and this time it was his turn to get elbowed.

"What was that for?!" the boy said, pursing his lips sourly. Seeing how his sister's face had grown red as the setting sun, he snorted and turned away in disgust.

"I like you, mister, but I don't care too much for that woman in white," the boy said.

Why is that?

"Well, she comes off pretty harsh for a woman, and she doesn't have much by way of charm. If every woman were like that, there wouldn't be any sweetness left in the world."

Well, we couldn't have that.

"And there's something kinda funny about the way she looks at folks. Those are the eyes of a loony."

You think so?

"Yep. I don't know if she's your girlfriend or what, but that's the kind you'd do well to drop as fast as you can. For what it's worth, I'm a pretty mean judge of women."

I'll keep that in mind.

"Think nothing of it," the boy said, his chest puffed out as he looked down at the coffin. He was beaming.

A slap resounded from his cheek. The acrobatic genius probably hadn't been able to dodge it because he'd been distracted, and also because the blow had come from a fellow genius.

"What do you think you're doing?!"

His angry gaze was greeted by a chubby face swelling with an ever more intense wrath.

"What the blazes do you think you're doing, sucking up to the Nobility?!"

"I wasn't sucking up to anyone!"

"You were so!"

"Was not—" the boy protested, his body quivering as he tried to strike back at his sister.

There's no reason why you should like the Nobility, but do you hate us so badly? asked the voice from the coffin.

The girl's body quaked as if from madness. "Oh, I hate you. I hate your guts! You, your kind—"

The girl hiccuped. Though she wasn't exactly sobbing, every time her shoulders shook, a little sound escaped her.

"My mom and dad were   "

"Huh?!!" the boy suddenly cried out in a tone not merely of surprise but of utter disbelief as he stared at his older sister. "That's a lie!"

"No, it's true. It's the truth, I tell you!"

"It can't be. They said Mom and Dad were both killed by a snake dragon."

"That's just the story the villagers told you, but this is the truth. What really happened is that Mom and Dad made it back alive— or at least pretending to still be alive. They both complained about how cold they felt, and they sat in front of the heater without moving a muscle. Not saying a word, just staring into the flames. They didn't even look each other in the face. And they were *never* like that before. Even when they were in different rooms, they were always calling out to each other and making all kinds of racket. I was feeling kinda sad, so I went over and tried talking to them. I said, 'Mom and Dad, what's wrong?' And then—"

Her brother had a bewildered look on his face.

"And then, they told me, 'Get out. Don't look at me.' 'Hurry up and get away from us.' They told me to take you, Hugh, and get out. I wondered what was wrong with them. I knew that muddle mold could mess up someone's head, and I thought maybe that's what had come over them. So then I circled around in front of them. Their faces were stark white. Even with the heater burning there, their faces were as cold and pale as Lake Aida. But there was one thing that was red—crimson, even. Their lips. Both of them had lips so red it looked like blood had welled up to fill them. I realized the truth right away. I don't actually remember what I said then. The next thing I knew, you were still asleep but I held you in my arms and I was outside the house. Sheriff Gidari and a bunch of volunteer deputies were around me and were talking something over, but I couldn't understand what they were saying. I watched the house burn. Our house had always seemed so tiny, and it seemed strange how huge the flames were. Later, Gidari told me Mom and Dad had been attacked by a Noble out in the swamp. Someone had seen it, so they'd all come over to the house. And that was the last time I ever saw them."

The boy was looking out the window. Blotches of shade slid across his pink face. They were the shadows of the trees that adorned that side of the road.

"You're also a Noble, right? Boxed up in your posh coffin, and going out each and every night to drink human blood. To be honest, I never wanted to ride in your carriage. Even now, I'd like nothing better than to put it to the torch."

That would be rather inconvenient, the baron's voice remarked. *I'll have to ask you to refrain from setting that fire for a while. Until I've attended to my business, that is.*

"You mean to tell me I can torch it after that? Ha! There's not a chance of that happening, so stop yanking my chain."

If you come along, I see no reason why you couldn't.

The boy turned and looked at the coffin in amazement.

However, I'll give you an honest fight, too. How does that sound?

The blood drained from the girl's pudgy face. She turned to her younger brother. His expression told her not to do it. That decided it.

"Fine. I'll put you down for sure. You'd better wear an iron plate over your heart if you don't want me to put a stake through it."

That's sound advice. How about you?

The boy needed a few seconds to realize the Noble was addressing him. He was still dumbfounded by his sister's utter recklessness.

"I—"

"Naturally, he wants in on it too. The two of us have nothing but each other. Isn't that right?" the girl said, glaring at her brother with an intensity normally unimaginable.

"Sure," the boy said with a nod.

You seem rather devoted to your sister, the voice from the coffin remarked, and the tone seemed to be tinged with laughter. *Very well. Although the two of you must part company with us soon, no matter where you should happen to go, I will call on you once my business is settled and you shall show me exactly what you're made of.*

"You promise!"

I swear on the name of the Sacred Ancestor. And by the honor of the Nobility, I shall keep my word.

The girl's face flushed crimson with her fighting spirit, and as her brother tilted his head to one side with a less than satisfied look on his face, the carriage suddenly began to slow down. Opening the window and sticking his head out, the boy gasped aloud.

"What is it?" his sister asked, following his lead. "Oh no!" she exclaimed as her eyes went wide.

A purple cloudlike mass floated far off near the horizon, and it was headed in their direction. It might've been three hundred feet high, or then again, it might've stretched up nearly a mile. With a number of massive knobs piled one on top of the other and fused together into shapes that protruded even further, this mass beneath a blue sky that seemed ready to flee was so disturbing it outstripped any thoughts of majesty.

The shadow of the carriage flickered on the ground from countless strands of lightning that tied the purple cloud mass to the earth below.

"It's an electric cloud!" the girl screamed as she so eloquently identified the threat.

Though it was said the number of artificial monstrosities the Nobility had scattered across the world was in the thousands or millions, of them all, the cloud creatures that could cover an area of several hundred square miles and reach almost three miles in height were easily one of the five most dangerous. These gaseous masses imbued with life formed into thirteen different varieties, and while the composition varied, the center was usually an eerie mix of toxic gases, while the exterior typically contained a half-million volts of electrical current, acid rain, and winds that brought death and decay. As a result, after one of these had passed, the land was left dead—literally not a blade of grass standing. The only saving grace where every other living thing was concerned was that these things had a short life span. From the time of its formation, the cloud would vanish again within one day and night's time, as only a composite life form would. To wit—for the twenty-four hours after its creation, it would be death incarnate on a mindless rampage. Toward that end, the Nobility had seeded its gaseous brain with a boundless hatred toward any but its own kind and thoughts of nothing save destruction. As for why they had also given it such a short life span, the clouds and their brutal nature were merely one of their larks—and intended as no more than a brief amusement. The clouds had only been created so they might mock the humans for a while as they ran willy-nilly.

What will we do, D? the baron's voice inquired, ringing in the Hunter's ear as he rode along on his mount.

"We've got no choice but to run for it."

Do you think we'll make it in time?

"That's hard to say."

In that case, get everyone into the carriages. You and the woman should go in Miska's. I've already informed her. And let the horses loose.

D made up his mind in an instant. The second he scooped up the young lady from the driver's seat and loaded her into the white carriage, he slapped the hindquarters of the horses. Already noticeably spooked, the horses raced back down the road they'd come from without a second glance.

The young lady stifled a cry of surprise. Twice as spacious as it appeared from the outside, the vehicle's interior was filled with white blossoms. Ephemeral and nigh translucent, the petals swayed with every movement of the two new occupants.

No sooner had D closed the door than the sun was blotted out. A yellow cloud of dust billowed up from the road, and every last tree bowed in the same direction—an omen that was a mixture of weirdness and silence.

Death is outside, said the voice from within the coffin. Miska's voice. *The Nobility or the human race—which do you think deserves it more, D?*

The blue shadow that filled the vehicle's interior served as D's answer. The trees that lined the road were engulfed in flames, instantly transforming them to fireballs.

"I'm scared," the woman squeaked.

"A hell of a thing this is. Make one mistake and the whole lot of us will be wiped out," another voice that didn't belong to any of them muttered glumly, but no one save D heard it.

"Sis!"

"Hugh!"

The children cried as they clung tightly to each other in the blue carriage.

An impossible darkness covered the world, and to the young siblings it seemed like the unfathomable depths of death itself. In a second, lightning focused on the pair of carriages from all sides. The ionized air made it easy enough for the electrical strikes, and the heat they generated instantaneously fused the ground into glass whenever they came into contact with it. Enveloped by this pale illumination, the horseless carriages themselves looked like some sort of bizarre creatures. Even if a monster more terrible than this cloud were to appear, it didn't seem like it would be able to withstand the same deadly talons that raked the carriages.

II

After the overwhelming curtain of death had passed, nothing remained but savaged terrain. Smoke curled from each and every stand of trees, and here and there the ground glittered with the bright sunlight where heat had fused it into glass. The two carriages were right where they'd started.

Ten minutes after the monster cloud had moved on, the blue door opened and the two children cautiously climbed down to the ground. Scanning their surroundings with eyes alight with fear and curiosity, they quickly exclaimed, "Mister!" and "There you are!" before racing over to the black-coated figure basking in the sunlight.

Gazing suspiciously at the young lady beside him, the boy then said, "I thought we were goners!"

"Me, too!" said his sister.

The cries of both swam with a sparkling vitality.

"I'm surprised we held up all right. Everything around us got burnt to a crisp!"

As the girl listened to her brother's remarks, she looked to the carriages behind them and began to say, "They really are incredible . . ." But then she held her tongue. She'd decided that might be taken as some endorsement of the vehicles' owners.

It was unclear how the Hunter in black viewed the death and devastation surrounding them, or the lively chattering children there in the middle of it who seemed to belong to a whole different world.

"We were saved by the power of the Nobility," D said.

Regardless of whether that was their intent or not, the pair of carriages manufactured by the Nobility had safeguarded the lives of two beings who still had a future.

"You're right. They sure did have awesome science. A long time ago, some scientists came to the village where we were born and explained that it was a waste to simply destroy the Nobility's civilization when we should be making use of it. And I think they were right."

But the girl was quick to counter the opinion of her impressionable younger brother.

"Spare me any more talk about how great they are. The damned cloud that caused this whole mess in the first place was made by the Nobility, wasn't it?"

"Well, that is true, but—"

"And we still owe them for Mom and Dad!"

"I know that. It's just—"

"Just what?!"

Apparently quite scared of his older sister now that she'd bared her teeth, the boy held his tongue.

"By the look of it, the inn up ahead would've been destroyed too," someone stated flatly, the words bringing the brother and sister back to reality. Their eyes came to rest on the young woman who stood there quietly.

"Who are you, miss?" asked Hugh.

"Nice to meet you. Taki is the name. I'm a magician's assistant."

"Wow! So, can you do tricks too?"

"A few, I suppose."

"Great! That'll make the trip a little more fun. I'm Hugh."

"You little dope. The inn's been laid to waste," the girl said to him, before calmly introducing herself to Taki, saying, "Oh, I'm May. Pleasure to make your acquaintance."

"It doesn't look like the cloud will return or do anything else strange. Get back into the carriages," D told them.

As the four of them turned around, the carriages seemed to tower there resolutely, and from off in the distance they could hear the hoofbeats of cyborg horses on their way back, almost as if the animals had caught D's instructions.

As expected, the coach stop by the highway had been reduced to dust. And every village dotting the landscape for several hundred miles had probably met the same fate.

"The next coach to the Capital is at noon tomorrow. Wait here."

At D's instructions, the boy and girl looked at each other.

"But—the stop's weapons and emergency shelter are gone now. If any monsters come, we'll be sitting ducks!"

"We'll leave you with weapons."

"Wouldn't you be good enough to bring us as far as the next village?" asked May. "We could get off there."

"It'd be a lot safer for you to stay here rather than come with us. All the monsters have been burnt up. There won't be a sign of anything for a week."

Although the Hunter's assessment was perfectly accurate, the children didn't know that. The power held by the dark of night was far more real than any spoken promise could ever be.

Why don't we bring them with us?

"Stay out of this."

If you're worried about Miska's desires or my own, then we'll simply stay in our coffins. I swear it.

"Neither of you have any idea how strong a Noble's craving for blood can be," D responded flatly.

Why do you say that?

"Have you ever been starved?"

The pause that followed was like a little explosion.

"Have you ever wanted to drink human blood so badly you clawed at the walls? Has it ever been so hard to bear you had to bite into your own arm? That's what hunger is," D said in a voice the children couldn't hear. And yet, their eyes were riveted to the face of the gorgeous Hunter.

Have you, D? the baron's voice inquired.

"No Noble has ever triumphed over the cravings that come from hunger. All who've tried have failed," D replied.

Among the vampires, there were some who found the taking of a human's lifeblood repulsive, and they endeavored to somehow resist the hateful urge. In the ninth millennium there appeared an individual known as "Gullit the Corrupter" who wrote five hundred volumes on how loathsome he found the act of drinking blood. He tried various means to break himself of the habit, but all attempts ended in failure, and he ultimately disavowed his theories. His writings were subsequently cast on the fire.

For example, what happened to a famished Noble imprisoned somewhere where escape was impossible? Their ageless and indestructible constitution never allowed them to starve to death, so they suffered no physical harm from an exceedingly empty stomach, and their brain didn't even allow an escape into madness as they were tortured by hunger. During the Nobility's so-called Age of Conflict, countless Nobles were divided into allied and enemy camps by the fighting, and the most sadistic punishment the victors could impose on their captives was just such an imprisonment. It wasn't difficult to imagine how cruel it was to be trapped in a heavy-gravity dungeon for centuries while the hunger only grew. When cease-fire treaties were drawn up and the captives were released from the untold depths of the earth, they pounced on their saviors and drained them of their blood.

"You can't change your stripes. No Noble can, so long as they remain a Noble. It's the same as humans taking the lives of their livestock. And people will even eat other people."

How many years had this handsome young man lived, and what had he seen? As D related that terrifying information so stoically, his profile remained stern and diligent.

You are correct, as always. Indeed, I haven't known the hunger of which you speak, said the voice from the coffin. *However, so long as I ride in this carriage, there is no danger of me starving. I won't lay a hand on the children.*

"Please, let's do that," Taki added. The young lady must've come from an area where the Nobility's influence had died out long ago. "Leaving such little children out in the wilderness would be like putting a snack out for some monster. Surely you'll regret it later."

Nothing you can say will matter in the least.

Everyone turned toward the white carriage. The words she'd practically sneered had reached everyone's ears.

It is not I or the baron that he fears. It is himself. Did you know that, little human children? Were you aware that this man you trust above all else is a dhampir? A traitor that sides with you and hunts our kind, even though he possesses the same blood that we do.

Neither D nor Taki could see what kind of expression the brother and sister wore, for the clear sky had turned dark in a matter of seconds. This time ordinary lightning flashed, and the wind buffeted D's face as he looked to the heavens. Even for the plains, the changeability of the weather in this area was particularly fierce.

As clouds of dust eddied away, Miska's voice coursed out triumphantly, saying, *D, were you actually concerned about the baron or myself giving the kiss to them? No, your misgivings are in fact based on your own hunger, are they not? Those children are always around you. You can smell the scent of their bodies. And from it, can you not glean the sweet aroma of their blood? When you do, doesn't the Noble blood run hot in your veins?*

"Get in," D told the children.

Heaven and earth settled into an endless blue haze. It had begun to rain. The sound of the wind became that of the rain beating against the earth, and all three pressed their hands to their heads while D did nothing. The force of the impact was terrific. Perhaps it was only right that it had no effect on a Hunter so callous he could've left children out in such an environment.

Though Taki was about to walk away, the two children didn't move. As they looked up at D, their faces were blurred by the rain. Whatever expressions they wore couldn't be seen.

Once the group was back inside, the carriages sped off at a fantastic clip in keeping with D's handling as he sat up in the driver's seat.

Taki peeked out the window, then her cheeks hardened as she shouted, "We've strayed from the road!"

The brother and sister pressed their faces to the windows, too. Though the downpour shrouded everything like a gas, they could still somehow make out that ahead of them lay a black rise that seemed to be some sort of hill.

"Wh-what's going on?"

Seeing that her brother had turned his gaze to the blue coffin, the girl then nudged his shoulder.

"I'm sure there must be a reason, if *he's* the one doing it," said Taki.

And once they'd raced up a less-than-gentle incline to a height of thirty feet, they knew in an instant what the young woman had meant. In addition to the noise of the rain, there was a low sound like a rumbling from deep in the earth, and it came from the right side of the road.

"It's a flood!"

Although it was water all the same, it looked like a little mountain of gray. Perhaps there were lakes nearby that had overflowed, or maybe it was the work of water sprites, but the surging gushes erased the road and swallowed up the devastated wilderness without the slightest hesitation. The water reached the hill, and the carriages slipped backward a bit.

But that wasn't the only reason the three people inside one vehicle let out a scream. The lid of the coffin had opened. Even though they realized the figure who'd risen from it was the baron, the terror of witnessing a Noble's appearance from his resting place had triggered their basic human instincts.

"Don't get so excited," the Nobleman said in a sober tone, his cape spreading like a deep expanse of sea.

Before the trio he'd left frozen stiff could blink their eyes, the figure in blue was gone, and the door closed again, spraying droplets of rain in abundance.

D could guess who it was that approached him.

Once the baron had taken a seat, the Hunter asked, "What brings you out here?"

"I don't care to be swept away by that flood. The current is strong, and we can't afford any further delays."

"Then get back inside. The sun is still high."

"Fortunately, the water is only halfway up the wheels. If someone were to support the back end, it wouldn't slide."

"That's a good idea."

"At this point, I'd like to remind you of our employer/employee relationship," the baron said with a grin.

D leapt down into the muddy torrent without saying a word. Circling around behind the white carriage without fighting the mighty flow, he braced the vehicle with his shoulder once he was sure of his footing. It stopped moving backward.

The baron lashed out with a whip. Once more, the horses advanced to the crest of the hill.

It was two hours later that the waters receded.

When D came over and stood beneath the driver's seat, the baron told him, "You did a good job."

"I should say the same," D remarked as he looked up. "Please hurry and get back in your coffin. It wouldn't do to have you collapsing up there."

Though the rain continued to fall, it was still midday. For a Noble, it would be even more brutal than it was for D—his flesh would burn and melt, and yet severe chills would run through his whole body. Indeed, the figure in blue staggered a bit.

A pale light resided in D's eyes. The sky to the north was brightening. Golden light was peeking out from between the clouds.

As the Hunter's hand reached over to pull out the stairs, the baron stopped him, saying, "No, it's fine. I've always wondered what the morning light was like—this is a rare opportunity . . ."

His voice crumpled feebly.

Bounding up to the driver's seat, D scooped up the figure in blue and carried him into the carriage. Once the baron had been placed in his coffin, the lid closed by itself.

Without so much as a glance at the three people who sat there with eyes bugged, the Hunter asked, "Did you see it?"

No, a pained voice responded.

Even after D left without saying another word, the three faces brimmed with dissatisfaction while golden light showered in on them as if to chase off the rapidly dwindling patter of the rain.

The Frontier Illusionist

CHAPTER 6

I

An hour had passed since they'd come down from the hill. Savaged by the monster cloud and the flood, nearly half of the landscape had been erased, and it was less than three hours before the group was swallowed by the blue mountain that lay ahead of them. This wasn't to say they were completely out of danger. When traveling out on the Frontier, the plains and mountains could be riddled with fiendish creatures. And yet, in keeping with human nature, the interior of one of the carriages was filled with an air of relief as the vehicles rolled forward in peace for the time being. Needless to say, the cheeriest of all was the boy—Hugh.

"Tell me, miss, where do you hail from?"

At his query, Taki squinted. Sifting through her memories, she soon replied, "I don't know."

"What?" said May, her eyes wide.

"Strange as it is, I truly don't know. Actually, I'd never given it any thought before."

"How'd that happen? What've you been doing up till now?"

"I was a magician's assistant. To a man known as Lord Johann, the Trail Magician."

"Never heard of him. So, why did you run off, miss?" asked the boy.

May winked at Taki, but her younger brother didn't notice.

As the boy continued to badger her, Taki smiled wryly and replied, "My boss was kind of a pain in the neck. He tried to get me to follow in his footsteps."

"Really? But that doesn't sound too bad, being an illusionist."

"Maybe not, if you're making your money honestly."

"Huh? You mean to tell me he was a cheat?"

"That's right. Sleight of hand is his specialty, after all. It was easy enough for him to borrow people's wallets and replace the contents with worthless fakes. But I couldn't bring myself to do that."

"Of course you couldn't. He sure is scum!" the boy said, his eyes ablaze with righteous indignation. "So that's why you hightailed it? Can't say that I blame you. You'd do well to get as far away from him as fast as you can."

"But I'm still worried," said Taki.

"Why is that?"

"My boss is a scary guy. I bet he'll come after me. If I stay here with the rest of you, I'm sure to cause problems for everyone."

"Ha ha ha," the boy laughed with his chest thrown out. "Not to worry, not to worry at all. We've got that guy out there, don't we?"

"Hugh!" the boy's sister snapped, the corners of her eyes rising wrathfully.

"Well, it's true, isn't it? The way he looks and the things he does may seem cold, but he's really a lot kinder than you think. I can tell. It's not in his nature to just desert someone who's in trouble or in pain."

"You shouldn't say that. He—he's a dhampir! There's Noble blood in him," his sister said, and her body quaked with good cause.

"So what if there is? He's half human, isn't he?"

"And half Noble! That's why he's so handsome, and so powerful. The Noble blood in him must be stronger."

"So what if it is?"

"Sooner or later, he's sure to turn his fangs on us."

"That's idiotic!"

"No, you're the idiot! Now that you know he's half Nobility, are you scared of him or not?"

After these words, the girl held her tongue. The expression that'd surfaced on her younger brother's face was beyond description. It was a look she couldn't help but regret having caused.

"You think I'm scared?!" the boy cried out in a loud voice, as if to fend off his own thoughts.

As he pressed his lips closed, something dark ran across his face. A shadow. As if following its path, the boy turned his eyes to the other side of the vehicle—and the window that was set in the door.

No longer in the driver's seat, D looked up from the back of his horse.

He saw a gigantic multiwinged flyer. With two powerful engines equipped on each of its twin pairs of wings, it could carry three hundred passengers. The Nobility's flying machines had made use of antigravity or magnetic fields, while the human race had devised other kinds on their own. Judging by the craft's ungainliness, it was clearly one of the latter. Fifty or sixty years earlier, airfields were completed that linked the Capital and the Frontier, and business flights had begun. In fact, aircraft production hadn't been able to keep up with demand, so those still in the air were dilapidated and had been that way for a good long time. Perhaps that was why the aircraft gliding along off to the left of the carriages seemed to be drawing ever closer to the ground.

It was Hugh that shouted, "It's gonna crash!"

Most likely the pilot had done all he could do to choose this plain. The craft had too much speed. The massive canvas-covered body tilted downward a bit, and the bottom wing on the left side was the first thing that made contact. It effortlessly snapped off at the base, due to the fact that the wings didn't run clear through the body of the craft, but rather each one had been independently welded to it. The upper-left wing followed the lower's example, and, bouncing high into the air, the body of the aircraft rolled to the left in compliance with some unknown principle of physics. Since the forward momentum still remained, these two forces combined to throw the aircraft in an unfathomable angle, and, skidding noisily against the ground, it slid off diagonally into the woods to the group's left.

Even after the rumbling of the earth subsided, D didn't halt the vehicles.

"Mister—stop the carriage!" Hugh exclaimed as he hung out the open window. "The flyer crashed! Look, you can see the smoke from it. We've gotta go help them before it explodes."

"There's a village nearby," D responded coolly. "I'm sure a rescue party will race out here. We're in a hurry."

"You've gotta be kidding! That had a lot of people onboard. They could be dying. We've gotta help them. If you can't be bothered to, mister, then I'm going! Stop the carriage, you big coward!"

Before D could turn in that direction, the door opened.

"Hugh!" his sister cried.

"Stop it!" Taki added.

However, the cries of the two girls only seemed to propel him forward as his diminutive form shot out of the vehicle. Landing with a spectacular roll, he stood up and shouted, "You go on ahead. I'm gonna wait here for the rescue party!"

While it wasn't clear who that cry was intended for, that was all he left them with before dashing straight into the black forest.

"Hugh!" May cried, and she would've gone after him if Taki hadn't held her back. "Let go of me! I'm going, too. Wait for me, Hugh! Let me go already!"

But even as D listened to the girl disgorging these words like she was spitting up blood, he swatted his mount's hindquarters with the flat of his hand.

Hugh was close enough to see the remains of the aircraft, but no explosion occurred. He wondered if it'd run out of fuel and had to make an emergency landing.

The body of the aircraft was badly battered. It looked like some sort of monster that'd been butchered for its meat. The outer skin was torn as if it'd blown free, and through the rips, the infrastructure jutted out in all directions just like real bones. There was no sign of anyone moving.

"Gotta hurry and get them out of there fast. If the fire spreads, that'll be the end of them."

If carnivorous monsters were to catch the odor of burning flesh and converge on the site, the boy could well envision the hellish frenzy that would ensue. Checking to see if anyone had been thrown free, Hugh approached the aircraft. He peered into it through the nearest rip.

"Holy!" he groaned in disgust, the word coming out on its own.

Although he hadn't been able to see anything from the outside, the interior of the craft was a mound of corpses. Most were still belted in and had slumped forward, apparently killed by internal injuries.

"Is there someone—anyone—still alive?" Hugh shouted out before checking.

There was no reply.

Climbing into the aircraft just to be sure, he certainly was a courageous child.

Going over to the nearest body, he put his hand on its shoulder and shook it.

"Huh?!" he exclaimed at the strange way it felt. "Holy smokes!"

As Hugh froze in amazement, the grisly scene around him changed completely.

He was outside. The body of the aircraft was right in front of him. However, it was only a model of a biplane that couldn't have been more than three feet long.

"What in the world . . ." the boy muttered as he fearfully picked up the plane and folded back the tattered cloth. He wished he were back in the carriage.

The inside of the model was just what Hugh had seen. The passengers were all slumped forward. But each was a wire figure less than half an inch tall. A thin cotton thread tied each wire figure into its cloth seat.

"You mean to tell me what I saw—was *this*?!"

"Very astute," said a cheerful voice that caused the boy to jump.

Turning, Hugh found an old man in a black silk hat and tuxedo grinning right in front of him.

"Mister— are you Lord Johann?"

The words came out reflexively, and made the old man bug his eyes in surprise.

"Taki told you about me, did she? It's a pleasure to meet you," he said with an exaggerated bow before offering his right hand.

Given the cordial atmosphere, Hugh looked back and forth between the man's drawn face and his hand before extending his own.

"Do you know why I've done such a thing?" asked Lord Johann.

The hand that clasped Hugh's had all the gentleness of someone dealing with a child.

"I—"

"It was actually my wish that another person would come. Well, I wouldn't exactly say a *person*. A dhampir."

"You mean Mister D?"

"Yes, indeed I do."

"Well, he won't. He's not coming at all."

"You're right. If an aircraft were to crash, any normal person would rush to the rescue. However, it appears I'm a poor judge of character. He truly is a hard man."

Hugh tried to pull his hand away, but it wouldn't budge at all. The magician's hand remained as soft and powerful as ever.

"But I was fortunate. At least one person couldn't ignore others in their hour of need and ran out here. How good of you it was to come! You really must stay a while."

"No! Let me go!" Hugh cried, taking an unexpected step forward.

In Lord Johann's fist, the little wrist twisted forward with a pop, and a heartbeat later, the dislocated wrist easily pulled free of the confines of the magician's fingers.

"Why, you little—" Johann growled as he reached for the boy, but Hugh spun once, then a second time, flying away with a series of graceful somersaults.

"I just knew you had to be a bad guy. I'm gonna go tell Mister D right away!" the boy shouted, and he was just about to run back the way he'd come when his body suddenly rebounded with a thud.

"Ooooh," Hugh groaned, bright blood gushing out between the hands he'd brought to his face. Tripping over his own feet, he fell flat on his back.

Looking with satisfaction at the path—and the boulder that'd suddenly appeared to bar what had been a straight run back to the road—Lord Johann toyed with the flowing beard he was so proud of as he expounded, "The secret of sleight of hand is to focus concentration solely on that which should be seen."

II

It took two hours to reach the next inn. After halting the carriages in front of the sheriff's office, it went without saying that D was met by the wrathful gaze of May when he opened the door.

"I'm gonna go look for him," the girl declared resolutely.

"The sun's going down," was all D said, but it froze her tiny form.

It would be no exaggeration to say that for anyone who lived out on the Frontier, the movements of the sun meant the difference between life and death. Dawn brought life, and twilight invited death.

"Yeah? Well, what's gonna happen to Hugh, then?"

D glanced over at one of the carriages. At some point the door had opened, and beside it stood a figure in cobalt. The deep ocean blue of his raiment was truly suited to the twilight that tinged the Frontier.

"You should go for him," said the Nobleman. "Or that *would* be my suggestion, but you aren't about to trust us by night. I should be glad to accompany you, but that would still leave Miska. Even I can see there's something wrong with her condition. You should keep an eye on her."

"What?" Taki said, her mouth dropping open as she stood beside May.

"I shall go in search of her brother," the baron said softly.

The fact that the half-crazed May had her mouth agape at that and even D knit his brow only went to show just what a shocking pronouncement it was.

"I'll be damned," another voice muttered, and a beat later Taki gasped and looked around, but she didn't see anyone who could have made the remark. The voice had been hoarse.

Turning to D, the baron said, "I won't break our agreement. Rest assured."

"Fine," D responded, consenting easily.

"No! Not on your life!" May protested. "You can't let a Noble go out there. He'll drink Hugh's blood!"

"What did you just say?"

Although they'd noticed the door to the sheriff's office opening, no one had ever imagined that the lawman himself would come walking out with a rivet gun in hand.

Seeing the group lined up on the street and realizing that they had some unbelievable intruders, he discarded his rivet gun and shouted, "Hey, Calco! Get my stake gun!"

A deputy came flying out and handed him a rifle with a magazine of thick stakes projecting from its underside, then quickly ducked back into the building.

"Gutless wonder," the lawman snarled, his face as red as a devil's as he held the rifle at the ready. The undisguised hue of terror on his face notwithstanding, he certainly had pluck.

"We only came to drop these two off. We'll be leaving right away. A large aircraft crashed on the plains about two hours by carriage to the west of here. You should go help," D said, but that wasn't the right thing to say.

The sheriff's eyes were filled with the image of Miska, who'd just opened the door to the white carriage and stepped out. By her side stood Baron Balazs. It wasn't the sheriff's fault he got the wrong impression about just who the two being dropped off were.

As soon as he had the weapon against his shoulder, he pulled the trigger. Since the stake gun utilized a powerful spring, its force was most effectively displayed at close range. The stake had an instantaneous speed that was seven-tenths the speed of sound. No god or demon could protect itself from the projectile.

Two blinding streaks of light flashed out like bolts from the blue.

Sliced into three pieces, the remnants of the stake spun harmlessly through the air.

One of the two streaks of light resolved into D's longsword, which was now pressed against the base of the sheriff's throat.

The sheriff was already as pale as a corpse when D whispered into his ear, "Don't interfere with us in any way. We'll leave the girls here and go."

But why did the lawman's cheeks seem to flush?

"Okay," the sheriff said with a nod of his sweat-slicked face. "But you'd best give up the notion of leaving the women here. Take a look—the whole town's watching! Even if I tried to protect them, they'd get torn to ribbons just for traveling with the Nobility."

D quickly nodded. "I see. We'll take them with us. But see to it there's no more funny business."

Though the sheriff's teeth were chattering, he did manage to say, "I swear it. No one here wants to end up a damned slave to the Nobility."

As soon as D stepped away from him, the sheriff slumped to the ground. It was then that the Hunter in black realized the baron was nowhere to be seen.

"He's flown the coop," said a low voice no one else could hear. "But, I tell you, he sure is a piece of work. From the Nobility's point of view, he might be a weakling and a human lover, but when he was cutting down that stake just now—he was faster than you!"

It was an hour later that the baron arrived at the crash scene. Granted, it was now night, but the fact that he'd covered a distance that'd taken the carriages two hours in half that time had to be attributed to something other than just the powerful legs of a Noble. Needless to say, there was no one there. There weren't even any fragments of the aircraft.

"An illusion? But who would've staged it?" the baron mused, having seen through the deception on the spot.

He went on to thoroughly investigate the area where the aircraft seemed to have fallen, not that he'd expected to find Hugh when he raced out there. Since the boy hadn't been headed toward town, he was either hiding somewhere or he'd been killed. In either case, at least some trace of him should've remained. The baron was conscious of how clever the child was.

After a few minutes, the baron halted. He seemed to have found something, and it was actually at this very spot that Hugh had—

A tremendously chilling aura enveloped the figure whose cape remained blue even through the darkness. Someone with special eyes would've undoubtedly seen the demon fires blazing up.

The air whistled sharply.

Before the baron even had time to turn and look, black steel had gone right through his chest. Staggering, he fell flat on his back.

The weapon that'd pierced him could be described as a short spear. Roughly two feet in length, about half of it was taken up by the flat spearhead. But who in the world had hurled it?

Although it seemed like the baron had been killed instantly, at that point a second spear sank into his solar plexus with a dull *thunk!* The baron didn't so much as twitch.

A dozen seconds or so passed—and then, from the depths of the darkness where not even the birds sang, a human figure suddenly drifted to the fore. A man dressed in black. The face illuminated by the moonlight looked horribly pale, and it had nothing to do with the source of the light.

"I finally got my turn. Never thought it'd be this easy, though," a voice entirely lacking in vigor muttered as a man approached with a gait equally devoid of vitality.

When he'd come within ten feet of the baron, the figure in blue sat up with lightning speed and hurled the short spear that'd pierced his chest. Blazing through the air, the spear went right through the man's heart, just as intended, leaving him standing stock still.

"Oh, so you're still alive?" the baron said as he got up, pulling the other spear from his abdomen before approaching the man with long strides. "You almost had me there for a second, sir. I should like your name."

There was no stain on the chest of the Nobleman's blue garments, for the baron had caught the deadly short spear in flight and cradled it in his armpit.

"Vince," the man replied, and a mysterious odor began to fill the air simultaneously.

Just then, something strange, or rather very unusual, happened. The baron slowly put his fangs into the neck of the man—Vince—and drank his blood. While this wasn't at all abnormal for a member of the Nobility, it was something that never should've happened in a place like this.

Several seconds passed—and then a cry of agony rose to the night sky.

"Your blood . . . It's acid . . ." the baron gasped, bringing his hand to his throat and backing away while white smoke rose from his mouth. His lips, mouth, and tongue were all burning.

Smirking at the foe who'd pierced his heart, the man said, "Precisely. It's also loaded with garlic extract. The first smell was something I was finally able to synthesize—something that would attract vampires alone. You wanted to drink blood so badly, you brought about your own demise."

"Why . . . won't you die?" the baron said, his mouth disgorging both the words and a large quantity of blood. The acid had begun to dissolve his internal organs.

"I introduced myself, didn't I? My name is Vince. As in 'invincible.' No mere spear is going to kill me. That's why I'm able to synthesize poisons in my own body."

"How informative."

Saying this, the baron spat out a mass of blood at his feet. When he turned toward the astonished Vince, the Noble's face was still just as pale, but it was filled with a much greater vitality than before.

"Impossible! You mean to tell me the garlic extract had no effect on you?"

"No, it had an effect. But at present the situation's not quite so favorable. I'm out of my mind with rage now. And that's far more powerful than your poisons."

There in the darkness, a pair of lights began to glow like flames— the eyes of the baron.

"This is simply unforgivable. If you are invincible, as you boasted, none of my attacks should have any effect on you."

An amber flash of light shot out at the young man from the interior of the blue cape. Without time to dodge it, his head was separated from his body and went sailing through the night air. At the same time, iridescent smoke rose straight up out of the stump of his neck, smothering the moonlight.

Unable to remain upright this time, Vince's body tumbled to the ground, and shortly thereafter the baron fell to his knees. The poisonous smoke had taken its toll. But only briefly, as the baron soon staggered back to his feet. Considering the potency of the poisonous smoke, he exhibited physical and mental strength that would've caused even other Nobles to marvel.

"Where did he go?" the baron muttered. He was referring to young Hugh, of course. "The scent of blood remains. What happened here?"

This was indeed the spot where the boy had slammed into a boulder he didn't see and fallen to the ground. Although catching the scent of blood that'd seeped into the ground hours earlier was one of the Nobility's preternatural abilities, it was curiosity about the fate of the missing boy that'd stirred the baron's ire and made him weather Vince's attacks.

"I'll find him if it's the last thing I do . . . even if it's just his remains."

Not long after the baron vanished into the darkness, from the direction Vince's head had disappeared, a vacant voice distinctly lacking in vigor could be heard to say, "I can see now why one of his own kind would want to murder a Noble like that—this'll take more than ordinary measures. Of course, I'm not all that easy to kill myself . . ."

✝

D and the three women set up camp in the woods on the outskirts of town. All the lights in the post town had gone out, and not even the cries of the night-singing birds could be heard.

Consoled by Taki, May had finally calmed down a bit, but from time to time, she looked at D with inexpugnable traces of sadness and anger in her eyes. The flames from a fire built with branches they'd collected illuminated her face.

As he leaned back against the blue carriage a short distance away, D stared off into the darkness before him. Though his lips didn't move at all, that didn't mean he wasn't having a conversation.

"Not exactly the most comfortable place to be, is it?" a hoarse voice from the vicinity of his left hand said in a mocking tone. "Even if you finish this job, it's gonna be a pretty painful one. I mean, it's not like you're not worried about the kid, and on top of that—"

Cutting off the voice, D said, "Where are you going?"

His question was directed at the figure who'd just opened the door to the white carriage and stepped down to the ground.

"That's my own business. Or so I should like to say, but I don't imagine that would suffice for you, would it? If I told you I was going for a walk, would you give me permission?" Miska said, turning away indignantly. Her right hand carried a fairly large box. The jewels that studded it glittered in the moonlight.

"Don't go anywhere near the town."

"I understand that," the woman in the white dress said before her form dwindled into the depths of the moonlit forest.

"There are no houses over that way. Must just be an ordinary stroll. After all, for them, it's like the middle of the day," his left hand remarked. "But all that aside, there is one thing that has me wondering."

"I know," D responded.

"That guy back at the arsenal—he got taken out much too easily. I mean, any way you look at it, it doesn't seem like the kind of monster that'd be feared even by the Nobles who created it."

There was no reaction from D.

Miska maintained her pace for about ten minutes before stopping.

She was in the middle of the forest. Although devious shapes and crimson eyes moved through the branches and behind the trees, none of them approached the pale woman who seemed like some sort of forest nymph. No matter how great her beauty, they could tell she was a Noble.

The place where Miska halted was a circular clearing. Mere coincidence hadn't formed it. Judging from the faces of what looked to be stone sculptures poking from the ground here and there, it had apparently been a place for rituals of some sort in ancient times.

Standing in the middle of the clearing, Miska looked up at the heavens. As she took a deep breath, the crisp night air and the perfume of nocturnal blooming flowers flowed into her.

"It's a nice night," the woman in the white dress said, setting the box she carried down on the ground and gently opening its lid. Extending both hands, she pulled out a single golden disk. The box was a player.

The antique platter seemed like it must have been several millennia old, and Miska gazed at it dolefully as she put it into the player. The three seconds it took before the fifty-thousand-micron memory particles began to play back were by far the most melancholy for this Noblewoman.

A burst of noise enveloped Miska. The pensive melody of a violin rang in her ears. Why did the accompaniment of a waltz always have to be that way? The aroma of an understated perfume filled her nostrils, and the next thing Miska knew, the eyelids she'd held closed had opened quite naturally.

"Hello there!" Daron Krolock said, one hand raised in greeting.

Though he had the avian slimness of a crane, his razor-sharp nails could have killed an armored beast instantly. There was no one more learned in the field of Humanity in the Middle Ages.

Behind him, the couple Mircalla and Adam Karnstein chatted away. Apparently they'd just come back from a trip through the stratosphere in an ion ship shaped like a swan. After another five centuries or so, the two of them were talking about having their coffins put into orbit around the earth.

So many figures glided elegantly above Miska, for the ball had already begun. White dresses and black formalwear spun in graceful circles as blue lighting rained down, and the flowers that adorned the crystal tables swayed in the breeze blowing through the hall.

A handsome young man stood in front of Miska and bowed. It was a son of the Zollern clan. The high, straight line of his nose was to Miska's liking. Both the way he slipped his fingers into hers and his steps on the dance floor were impeccable. What followed was the sweet strains of a waltz and blue light.

In the distance, there was a woman's voice. *Why is it that we cast no shadow? Glasses, marble pillars, and carriages all throw a shadow on the ground, so why not our kind?*

You're drunk, a different voice said soothingly.

That is the very proof that we are Nobility, yet another voice asserted.

In the blue light, a dance for the people of the night went on and on. They lived outside the passage of time, knowing no springtime of youth and no decay.

Miska turned around suddenly. Quickly pulling the player closed, her left hand hit the old-fashioned kill switch. The shrill notes faded. The hall faded, too. Even the people faded away.

In the clearing in the night woods, Miska stood alone. But not really—in front of the thicket to her left stood a trio of figures. D and the two girls.

"What do you want?" Miska asked softly.

A hot mass was rising from the pit of the Noblewoman's stomach. Whether it was anger or something else, even she couldn't say. This wasn't something to be seen by humans. That was why she'd come out here.

D didn't answer her.

"He invited us to come out here with him," said May.

"What is the meaning of this? Did you follow me out here knowing I'd come to relive dreams of long ago?"

If D had thought Miska was going to be in danger, he'd never have brought the girls with him.

"I saw the player," D replied.

Miska first knit her brow, then laughed haughtily.

"Kindly refrain from your jests. This is a priceless item bestowed upon my grandfather by the Sacred Ancestor. There's no way the likes of you would know anything about it . . ." she said, but her voice petered out and her eyes quickly opened as wide as they could go.

Left as horribly shocked as if she'd taken a blow to the head, Miska stared at the gorgeous Hunter.

"Is this truly the same player? Why don't you tell me the name it was given?"

Miska's field of view was occupied not only by D, but by the two girls as well. And by the look they gave her. It was one of sympathy and understanding. However, that was precisely what invited Miska's fury.

"Answer me! What was this possession of the Sacred Ancestor called?"

The madness that gripped her was something she herself couldn't fathom, and it caused her fangs to poke out over her crimson lips.

D put his hands on the two girls' shoulders. As the three of them turned, the Noblewoman was just about to call out to them—

"It's 'Shin-ai,'" a hoarse voice said, stopping Miska from shouting anything further.

That was the correct answer.

"Shin-ai   " Miska said, rolling the word around in her mouth. It was bitter as a pill, and sweet as molasses.

Just before they vanished behind a stand of trees, Miska saw the little girl turn and look at her as clear as day. She had the same look in her eye again.

"Shin-ai—how ridiculous!" the Noblewoman spat with rage.

In the language of a country that'd long since been destroyed, that name had meant 'beloved.'

III

"Has he finally gone?" a tree whispered in the darkness sixty feet above the earth. On a large branch near the top of the tree, a pair of figures stood blended with the shadows. "Even watching him from way up here is enough to give me goose bumps. You sure are lucky to have fought him and lived to tell the tale."

It was Mario.

"Yeah, I just realized that myself. I thought that if he got in the way when we tried to grab that Noble, we'd just take him on, but then I suddenly didn't feel like coming down out of the tree."

Wiping the sweat from his face with the edge of his brown cape was the man D had referred to as Crimson Stitchwort. From what he'd just said, they had planned to abduct Miska and had apparently hidden up on a branch toward that end. But the real question was how they'd made it out here.

Actually, they'd circled ahead. Back before Hichou was slain in the swamp, they'd used the same kind of flight pack he had to cross the swamp, and then waited for his return. Instead, it was D and his group that'd arrived. The death of their compatriot had angered them, but the fiends had exchanged unsettling grins. Any danger of Hichou earning the whole reward for himself had passed.

Knowing D's fearful strength, they refrained from launching a massed attack on his party and simply watched them go, so that they could learn their route and head them off. When they'd confirmed that the party had entered the Talos arsenal, they'd clucked their tongues and thought that would be the end of it, but when they saw everyone leave again without harm, their fear of this formidable foe only increased. They knew in the marrow of their bones that any haphazard attacks would be futile. The only thing that would slay the Nobles and D was an exhaustively detailed plan with an assault that was swift and precise. And having reached that conclusion, the assassins had hastened to the next post town to buy themselves enough time to come up with a strategy. That was how they'd managed to avoid becoming embroiled with the monstrous cloud and the great flood D and his group had encountered.

On the other hand, they also didn't realize that D's party was going to be late, so the pale young man whose turn it was to attack next had grown impatient and gone out to scout for them. Though he'd taken the main road, D had elected to use a riskier but comparatively shorter back road. And that had been so he could drop Taki and May off in town.

Of course, the other three who'd remained at the inn knew that D and his group had paid the town a visit. And from the trip so far, they could well imagine where the Hunter would stop for the night. Then Crimson Stitchwort and Mario had watched the group camping out from the top of a big tree. The preparations had been made. Though their plans were upset when the baron doubled back on the road they'd taken there, it still looked like the assassins could slay D and the Noblewoman.

However, the elderly priest who was supposed to be the next attacker—Yoputz—had suddenly vanished, and that only further complicated their plans.

And that wasn't all. While they continued their surveillance, they couldn't believe how harsh D's unearthly aura felt as he drew closer. Filling with chills, they made excuses about how it wouldn't be right for them to skip Yoputz's turn while he was gone, and then decided they should just remain observers.

And then the female Noble had left D and gone deep into the forest. Given this perfect opportunity, they'd followed after her, but D and the girls had soon appeared, and it seemed that their attack on the Noblewoman wasn't meant to be. However, D had soon left.

The pair's conversation continued.

"Are we gonna do it?"

"Of course."

"Well, Yoputz is gonna be pissed. He'll be all over us for going out of order," said Crimson Stitchwort.

"The Noblewoman's of no consequence. From the very start, she wasn't covered by our contract, so anyone can do whatever they like to her. It's a hell of a lot less trouble than trying to have a go at D. Besides, when our turn comes up next, it'll be a lot easier to handle D and the Noble in blue if we've got a hostage."

Oh, so these two were saying they intended to abduct the female Noble?

Far below the pair's gaze, Miska stood alone, her mind in a haze.

"Well, let's get to it. We'd better act fast, before D gets wise to us," Mario said, and with that, he sat down cross-legged on the branch and closed his eyes. Apparently focusing his will on something, he looked as sublime as a monk earnestly endeavoring to grasp the truths of the universe.

Around Miska, black forms came into view less than a second later. Needless to say, they were dolls under Mario's control. Ordinarily, they would serve as a distraction so the real Mario could attack and slay his opponent. However, even when the shadowy figures approached, Miska stood in a daze, not even bothering to look at them. Although someone clucked his tongue in the distant treetop, that sound didn't reach Miska, of course.

The next instant, a foglike mass drifted out in the moonlight. Settling neatly over Miska's pale figure from above, it was clearly a net made of a fine line that was nigh invisible. In less than the time it took to draw a breath, Miska had been hauled into the air.

Once he'd pulled Miska all the way up to the branch, Crimson Stitchwort secured her like an insect in a cocoon.

"She can't talk now, right?" he asked Mario, just to be sure.

"Yep," the puppet master said with a nod, his meditative state already broken. "That net's woven from the same string that controls my dolls. The instant it wraps around something, it sinks right into the flesh and keeps them from even breathing. The woman should be out cold."

"We're dealing with a Noble here."

"I'm well aware of that," he declared in a tone brimming with confidence. However, suddenly crinkling his brow, he added, "But to be honest, it was just too easy. She wasn't surprised at all by my dolls."

The pair's plan had been to throw her off guard and then release the net, and the results had been satisfactory. However, there was still something they couldn't understand.

"It looks like she's Balazs's mistress. With her as a hostage, it'll be child's play to lure the baron out. He'll probably walk right into a trap for the honor of the Nobility and all that crap," Mario said, looking down at the woman and laughing. "But from where I'm sitting, she sure is one fine-looking lady. Hey, you ever had a piece of a Noblewoman?"

Crimson Stitchwort was stupefied, exclaiming, "Come on—you can't be serious!"

"She's out cold, after all. Plus, we wouldn't have to take the net off her. Even if we let her loose from the waist down, she still won't be able to do anything."

"Count me out."

"Okay, have it your way. But it wouldn't be easy for me to do my thing with you looking over my shoulder. Make yourself scarce, will you?"

"I'm not trying to be a pain. Just don't do this."

"Stay out of this, okay?!"

For the briefest instant, the two assassins on the branch glared at each other. But Crimson Stitchwort was the first to turn his face away indignantly, saying, "Do what you like, then. I'm going on ahead. Don't call out for me."

The next instant, the branch dipped straight down and he was swallowed by the darkness below.

"Sheesh, what a pansy!" Mario remarked spitefully.

Hauling Miska up, he reached over to paw at her body with his right hand—and had his breath taken away.

In the moonlight, the net glowed like some weird fog, and within it, Miska's body was bound tight by nigh-invisible threads, just as Mario had said. Her right shoulder and breast were half exposed and the left side of her dress had risen greatly, leaving her pale and alluring thigh exposed almost to the waist. But more seductive than anything was the way her face was twisted with pain. She was a veritable work of forbidden sculpture that would never be seen by human eyes except here, deep in the forest on a moonlit night.

The second his eyes saw her damp red lips make an O and his ears heard the faintest moan that O allowed to escape, Mario lost his last fragment of rational thought. One swipe of his nails easily severed the strings, and her pale and damp thighs spilled out onto the branch.

"I wonder what happens when Noble blood and human blood mix? Eh?"

Holding both her slim ankles, the puppet master spread her legs far apart.

What happened then, the moon alone knew.

What D heard was an explosion that sounded like a great hole opening in the heavens. As the girls jumped back up, D commanded, "Get in the carriage."

Shutting the door, he then raced off with the wind whirling in his wake.

When he arrived at the clearing, there was no need for him to look up above. Miska was standing in the center of the clearing. There was no sign of Mario.

"What happened?" asked the Hunter.

D's senses told him there'd been no change at all in the sky or on the earth. The wind had been stirred, but that was all. After an explosion, such stillness was difficult to comprehend.

"Nothing," Miska mumbled, and then she collapsed on the spot.

As D gazed down at her, his face was palely illuminated by the moon. Hard beyond words, his expression still made it clear that even he feared this kind of bizarre development.

Pale Fallen Angel

PART TWO

The Magician's Kingdom

CHAPTER 1

I

Dawn came without either the baron or Hugh returning.
After laying the still-disoriented Miska into her carriage and leaving Taki and May in the baron's vehicle, D announced that he was going to head back to where the aircraft had crashed.

"I wanna go, too," May said, clinging to the Hunter like a shadow. If Taki hadn't stopped her, she probably would've gone right after him.

"Leave this to me," Taki said.

With her words hovering behind him, D rode off on his horse.

Along the way, his left hand inquired in a hoarse voice, "You think she'll be okay?"

"Which one?"

"Taki. Because if she starts acting crazy, May will be in danger, too. Did you leave her behind because you think she's still okay?"

"No, because she'd be in the way."

"I suspected as much. What's more, we've got that vampiress—that's even dicier. There's definitely something possessing her."

"We checked her."

"Then it must be something we wouldn't find that way. What comes to mind is—"

"We'll find out eventually. Very soon, I'd say."

"Hmm, I suppose that's true. But you know, I've got a really bad feeling."

Without replying, D rode all the way to the crash site in silence.

A bizarre scene awaited him there in the sunlight. No matter where he looked, there was no sign of the aircraft. Of course, D hadn't actually seen it crash in the first place. All he could do was guess at the area based on the speed of the aircraft and the angle of its descent.

As he sat on his mount with eyes gleaming, D seemed to find something. Dismounting, he walked over to one corner of the clearing. What he picked up there was a thin shred of cloth. It wasn't old. And it was stuck to a clump of brush.

"Looks like this was the end of the line for the airplane," said his left hand.

Indeed it was.

Putting the scrap into his pocket, D turned his gaze to the shadowy depths of a grove of trees. While Hugh might be another matter, the baron would probably be lying in there somewhere where the sunlight couldn't penetrate the branches and leaves. This was probably the last thing in the world a Vampire Hunter should be doing, but at any rate, the person in question was his employer.

Just as D was about to head in that direction, the wind whispered to him.

The forest is . . . dangerous.

The thread-thin voice was that of Baron Balazs.

"Where are you?"

Can't really be sure . . . of your position . . . but there's a large rock . . . on the south end of the clearing.

Turning his head ever so slightly, D saw it.

There's a fissure under it. That's where I am.

"What are you doing?"

What do you think I'm doing—listening to music? The sun came up before I could head back.

"You were searching for Hugh all this time?"

There was no answer. He wasn't the sort of man that needed to reply.

"Stay there for the time being. I'll look for him."

I ran into an odd character. Vince was his name, and he didn't die even after I put a spear through him. He can turn all the blood in his body to poison. I'm sure I separated his head from his body, but when I came back after searching another area, the corpse had vanished. Apparently, "Vince" stands for "invincible."

"One of the Hunters?"

Yes.

As if he had no further interest in the matter, D wheeled his horse around. Regardless of what he may have thought of this new foe, nothing could be gleaned from his gorgeous but expressionless visage.

These woods are strange, the wind told D in the baron's voice. *Though there's been no change from what I saw last night, they seem completely different.*

That being the case, he had no choice but to enter them—that's what it meant to be the young man named D.

"I'll say it's strange," a gleeful voice remarked from the vicinity of the Hunter's left hand the second he rode in among the trees.

Midday darkness enveloped the rider and his mount. Shadows of the countless branches interlaced on either side of him. The scant light and crushing darkness cast a hazy patchwork on D's handsome features.

The forest was deep, but nevertheless, a number of narrow paths ran through it. Though most were game trails, the wider ones had surely been left by humans who'd come hunting and gathering. Mixed in among the verdant grass and moss were pretty colors like something out of an artist's sketch—probably wildflowers. Occasionally there was the beating of wings as a black silhouette flew by overhead.

While D looked to be advancing on his steed as if there were no problem at all, every fiber of his being was focused through his five senses. Needless to say, at present he could isolate each sound and find the source of not only every cry from the birds and the beasts, but also the scratching of the bugs burrowing down into the moss and the rustle of grass and leaves swaying with the breeze.

Off to the left-hand side of the trail towered a massive tree that was a good thirty feet in diameter. Its bark made one wonder how many millennia it'd seen, giving way to countless crevices and knots and emitting a dull glow here and there. The glow came from lumina moss, which was said to grow only on trees of considerable age. It could be boiled to make a tea that proved highly effective in treating lymphatic disorders.

From behind the great tree came a pair of figures. Hugh—and an old man in a black tuxedo and silk hat. The pointed tails of his coat nicely complemented his flowing beard. The jewels encrusting his bow tie put a red glow in D's eyes.

"Nice to meet you . . . although technically that's not correct. We met once by the side of the road. I am Lord Johann—but people call me the Trail Magician."

Though the old man waited a bit, D made no move, so with a shrug of his shoulders he continued, "Can't be bothered to introduce yourself? D, isn't it? My assistant is imposing on your hospitality."

D's mouth finally opened as he said, "Release the child."

Perhaps sensing something in that quiet tone, the magician shrank back.

"And if I don't—there'll be violent deeds in place of words? I don't know which of us would prove the victor."

Twisting his lengthy beard, he smirked. The teeth exposed by his thin lips were pointed like a carnivore's.

"However, I shan't let you have this boy. If you want him back— well, now, why don't you throw down that sword for a start and show me where I might find the baron?"

Though the magician's face wore a smile, his eyes were cruel as could be.

D's right hand went for the sword on his back. He made no fuss about doing as he was told—or so Lord Johann must've thought as a grin split his face, but at that moment, he reeled backward wildly, his body spinning around two or three times. Something long and thin was jutting from his right eye—a needle of rough wood. The hand reaching for the sword had drawn it from a hiding place on the sheath and hurled it with lightning speed, though no one who'd witnessed it would've ever believed it.

"You—you son of a bitch! You have some nerve!"

Lord Johann's face paled as the sound of hoofbeats rolled over him. Without giving the man time to get back on his feet, D raced toward him on his horse.

A flash of light shot out from the man on horseback.

With the sword that'd cleaved Lord Johann's head still in hand, D turned his mount around. In the meantime, the magician ran unsteadily for the cover of the gigantic tree. Though D's blade seemingly split not only the man's silk hat but the head beneath it, it sent an odd sensation into the Hunter's right hand.

At the end of the blade's graceful curve hung a hat—and not the magician's top hat, but a bowler. Or so it appeared for a second before it melted into a black tar that then covered the entire sword.

Not even glancing at the boy on the road—ensuring that there were no foes nearby came first—D leapt off his horse's back at Lord Johann, who was attempting to circle around behind the massive tree. D was a beautiful black wind in flight. The horizontal swipe of his blade narrowly missed the magician's head, biting into the tree trunk instead. But who would've ever thought it'd bounce off?

Furrowing his brow only for an instant, D then chased after Lord Johann, circling around the trunk himself. But the magician was gone. Not even a trace of his presence remained. D's ultra-keen senses confirmed that he'd neither risen up into the heavens nor burrowed into the earth.

Giving no further chase, D looked at his blade. Apparently the melted bowler hat was meant to dull the edge it coated.

The Hunter returned to the road.

Hugh stood in a daze in the same spot as before. The only thing different now was the length of rope that hung down to his hands. He wasn't holding it up. Rather, it hung down from the sky.

D looked up.

The sunlit gaps between the branches opened into a round canopy. The rope ran right up into the center of an opening in the trees.

Even after Hugh took hold of the rope with one hand, D still didn't move. Perhaps not realizing D was there, the boy began to climb the gently swaying line as if he were a monkey. After he'd climbed about fifteen feet, a needle of white wood flew from the Hunter's right hand. Just as it was about to strike, the rope twisted as if possessing a will of its own and batted the needle back down. And the writhing didn't stop there. As if to guard against D's next attack, the rope swiftly began to rise along with the still frantically climbing boy, and in no time at all they had vanished into the heavens.

D got back on his horse. He looked up high. But he didn't find the heavens he sought.

Something resembling a black cloud had descended from the sky, and what spattered against the ground was fresh blood. Striking with such force that it tore at the earth, it must've fallen from an incredible height. As he watched, a mass the same color whizzed right by his eyes. Warping the ground and bouncing back up again were the pair of arms that'd been taken off at the boy's shoulder. A bloody spray went out. The arms were followed by a pair of legs. There was a loud thud. A torso sunk into the black earth. Taking the shock from the bottom up, the organs sprayed up through the stump where his head had once been. The last part splattered like a rotten tomato.

From the back of his horse, D gazed at what had once been a human body. Each piece still had clothing attached—Hugh's clothes. Even the horribly mangled head seemed to retain the features of the brave young boy.

"What's all this?" a voice asked from the vicinity of the Hunter's left hand.

"It's a fake," said D.

Although it seemed the Hunter had been right out in the middle of the bloody rain, his nigh-translucent skin wasn't marred by even a drop of vermilion.

"Oh, I see. Not a bad job. But it's not a synthetic form. It's a real human body. That bastard—he grabbed another kid just to put a scare into you."

And the magician had apparently butchered him in cold blood as well. While the child had looked exactly like Hugh, D's eyes had undoubtedly found discrepancies in the severed limbs.

"What are you gonna do?" the voice asked in a leaden tone, but the Hunter's gorgeous features remained like an icy blossom as he didn't so much as arch an eyebrow.

Based on that image, it would've been difficult to imagine him then sending his coat whirling out as he dismounted. Once he'd gotten down and taken a single step, the corpse suddenly moved. The twisted pair of arms slid over to the torso that was stuck in the earth, planting their palms against the ground to lift themselves up and press their stumps to the gaping wounds at either shoulder. The fingers moved. Almost seeming at a loss, at first the digits of one hand and then the other twitched, but finally growing more accustomed, all ten fingers worked together, curling and bending before they began to twist the opposing wrist. After this continued for about twenty seconds, the arms finally put their palms flat against the earth, and after many attempts at straightening their elbows, they lifted the torso out of the hole in the ground once more. The pair of legs rolled over and attached themselves to the lower body. Accustomed to standing, the legs straightened, and the figure rose.

By anyone's estimation, it was a perfectly good body—well, perhaps not quite. All the limbs had been left twisted by the shock of striking the ground, and bones jutted out by the right elbow and left knee. A pulpy mess from the chest up, the torso was covered with blood, and it lacked a head as well.

"He sliced it to pieces and yet he can still push it around? Must be one hell of a magician," the hoarse voice said in apparent amazement, but the corpse showed no sign of stopping at its words, and now misshapen hands reached for the pulverized head on the ground.

D quickly stepped forward.

Beneath his blade, the diminutive torso was sliced in two. The manipulated corpse collapsed without ever witnessing the final act of misery.

"I thought your sword wouldn't be up to doing any cutting—nicely done," the hoarse voice cooed in admiration.

Cutting with a blade that shouldn't be able to cut—D had the power to surpass mere physical phenomena.

D went back to his horse. Wheeling the animal around, he slowly headed back the way he'd come.

"*The going is easy, easy*—or that's what the song used to say," said the voice that trailed after him. "How did the rest go? *It's the trip back that's scary* . . . We're headed in the opposite direction."

As if he'd already known this, D asked, "What happens if we keep going this way?"

"There'll be a trap, I suppose. After all, this is the magician's kingdom."

The horse's gait didn't change at all—D chose to ride right into the lion's den. Perhaps he thought that if he played into the enemy's hands, it would bring him into contact with the one responsible.

Unexpectedly, his horse came to a dead halt. The animal then reared up on its hind legs for dear life. Though D tugged at the reins, the cyborg horse didn't respond. Its rear quarters went back a step and, unable to bear it any longer, the front legs came down again. But there was no ground beneath them. Where the earth was supposed to be, D saw a great void. The wind swirled behind them as they fell.

It was a hallucination, something that couldn't exist in the world. However, the way the wind snarled in his ear, how his hair and the hem of his coat streamed up behind him, and more than anything, the feeling that he was dropping at a velocity of nearly two hundred miles per hour didn't seem to be a lie.

"A hell of stroll this turned out to be," remarked a wind-tattered voice. "If we slam into the ground at this speed, we really will be smashed flat as a pancake. Tell yourself none of this is real. Eep!"

Returning his balled fist to the reins, D continued to fall.

The black earth grew closer. They were falling at more than three hundred miles per hour toward the ground.

D was suddenly standing on the road in the forest in the same spot where he'd started. He surveyed his surroundings. Something that wasn't quite blood and not quite oil had been splashed all over the road and the bushes. The fragments spread far and wide in all directions were pieces of his cyborg horse. His mount hadn't been able to escape his foe's psychological attack.

D started to walk without saying a word. Before he'd gone a hundred yards, his surroundings were enveloped by white light. The fact that the light wasn't artificial became clear when D was involuntarily driven to his knees. Natural light—yet it shone with a hundred times the brilliance of the sun at high noon.

"A land of light in the forest of darkness—now this is the very essence of Lord Johann's magic," a malice-choked voice called down from the heavens. The old man's ragged breathing was a vivid testament to the gravity of the wound D had dealt him.

"The Noble blood that flows in a dhampir won't allow him to escape the light. How will you get out of this, Vampire Hunter?" the voice said from the direction of the light.

Although D sent a needle of rough wood flying in that direction, the only result was a burst of scornful laughter.

"At a loss, Hunter? If that's the best you can do, it'll be my turn now. Here!"

The ring of dazzling light took on an added glint. Countless steel arrows assailed D, and were in turn sent flying by his longsword. However, every last one of them turned into an arrow-shaped scrap of paper. Actually, the scraps of paper had been fluttering down gently, but Lord Johann's fearsome art had made it seem to D that they moved with the speed of real arrows.

An instant later, D was pierced through the back and out the solar plexus by a short spear. Roasting in the sunlight and with all his nerves focused on the false attack, the Hunter hadn't been able to fend off that blow.

"The secret of magic is to draw their attention with a deception in the right hand while the real trick is being done with the left," Lord Johann said with a mighty laugh. "Can you see through my grand trick, Hunter?"

His laughter was cut short by the sound of something knifing through the wind. A streak of black lightning had shot to the sky from D's right hand. Extracting the short spear that impaled him in a flash, he'd hurled it in the direction opposite the voice—into the treetops off to his right. The leaves shook with the crash of breaking glass, and a cry of surprise rang out. Simultaneously, the prison of light that'd restricted D's movements suddenly disappeared.

"Can you see through Lord Johann's magic, D?"

A needle of unfinished wood flew off toward where that shout had originated, and once again, a scream of pain was heard. Glittering fragments rained down from the treetops, and deep red blood dripped down on their glassy surface.

D raised his sword with his right hand. His foe hadn't been fatally wounded yet.

The mechanical groan that was heard next only proved the accuracy of the Hunter's assessment. From the region where the short spear and wooden needle had vanished, a flying machine descended like a bird with wings spread, and at its center—through the round glass window of what was apparently the cockpit—Lord Johann and his flowing beard could be seen. He had a black handkerchief pressed to one eye.

"We shall meet again, my fearsome Hunter. I have to repay you for what you've done to my eye. Remember that."

The black wings beat clumsily and the device began to rise, disappearing between the branches with a speed unimaginable from its stocky form. There was the sound of trees breaking, and after a few branches dropped like parting gifts, all other noise ceased.

Sheathing his blade, D turned his gaze toward the countless glittering bits spread out a short distance from him before leaving. Not merely shards of glass, they reflected the stand of trees as sharply as a mirror. It must've been how the magician had magnified the scant sunlight to restrict D's movements, and made scraps of paper seem like arrows to the Hunter. Although it was said that the simpler the trick, the more effective it was, the effects Lord Johann was able to achieve bordered on sorcery.

Before walking back out of the forest, D wiped his lips with one hand. As he rubbed the blood from the back of his hand off on his coat, his eyes burned red. The blood that flowed back into his lungs from the short spear wound had given the dhampir the strength he needed to escape the mysterious bonds of sunlight.

D returned to the boulder that concealed Baron Balazs.

Your spirit is in disarray, the wind said in the baron's voice. *I take it from that you were less than successful.*

"I'll go back first. You can come once the sun has set."

D began to walk away.

They've taken a hostage. I'm sure they'll be in touch soon. However, I'd like you to hold off on taking any action until I've returned.

"Very well," the beautiful black shadow said as he walked away in the sunlight.

On top of a hill quite some distance away, the black insectlike flyer came down for a landing.

In the shadow cast by the craft, a youthful voice said, "The attacker became the attacked, as expected." The tone was one of both understanding and contempt.

"He truly is something," Lord Johann replied. "Exposed to sunlight like that and impaled by a spear, and he still lived. I'm sure he'll recover quickly, too. However, my eye will never see again, and the wound to my abdomen shall take some time. It would seem the price was too dear."

"Which is exactly why I offered to help you. Last night, you were the one that approached me."

"I wanted to see what D was capable of with my own eyes. No matter how skilled an opponent he might prove, I was confident I would come back unharmed and dispose of him later. To be honest, it was my intention to enlist your aid at that time. This isn't something that can be done by conventional means, you know. He is neither a regular Vampire Hunter nor your average dhampir."

"Certainly not. And Baron Balazs is also formidable."

"I'll get right on coming up with the next plan. This time, I'll take special care to see to it I don't fail. You go back and join the others."

"I'd have done that anyway. But when you contact me, do so secretly, Lord Johann."

"Not to worry. And for your part, see to it no one learns that you've joined forces with me."

"Nothing to worry about there. The mere thought of how great the reward will be without them getting a cut is enough to keep me from allowing even the tiniest slip-up. All so that we can dispose of that meddling Hunter and get rid of Baron Balazs."

And then one portion of the shadows broke away from the rest and left the wind swirling in its wake as it dashed down the hill.

When D returned without the boy, a small storm of panic blew through the camp.

"Where's Hugh?" May muttered absentmindedly.

"He was abducted," D told her bluntly. He wasn't the sort of man to offer a softened explanation of the facts.

The girl's eyes swam with tears.

"Why—why didn't you go look for him? Who took him?"

"I know who it was. I'll get him back."

"What if . . . they kill him first?"

"No one abducts someone just to kill them," the Hunter replied.

Suddenly, May launched herself at D. Her hands pounded relentlessly against his broad chest.

"You left Hugh back there! He's my one and only brother! My mother and father were both killed because of the Nobility, and Hugh'll be killed, too! The Nobility are our enemy! They're murderers! Half of your blood is the same as theirs. That's why you could leave him out there to die!"

Her little fists struck his coat time and again, bouncing off it each time. But even though her fists sprung back, May kept hitting him. It was as if making this gorgeous young man feel pain would somehow bring Hugh back to her. She didn't care if her hands broke; she wouldn't quit. Her breathing was ragged, her hands weak as she raised them. Nevertheless, she went on pummeling him. As her swollen hands relayed the dull pain, May's face twisted in agony.

Fingers like steel took hold of her wrists, and it finally dawned on the girl what an incredibly foolish thing she'd done.

"Hit me any more and we'll be looking at some broken bones. Namely, mine."

The instant she met the gorgeous visage peering down at her like an icy blossom with dark eyes, May rapidly lost all her strength. She knew she couldn't do anything to D. She also knew that D's words were a lie. And she understood for exactly whose benefit he'd feigned this weakness.

The next thing to hit D's chest was May's upper body. Both arms hanging by her sides as she leaned against that powerful physique, the girl did the last thing she could for her younger brother. She began to cry in a loud voice. Her voice traveled around the clearing only to be swallowed by the stands of trees and sunlight, but still she kept crying.

And then May unexpectedly pulled away from the Hunter and ran off into the trees without a backward glance.

As D quietly watched her go, a teasing voice asked him, "Are you not going to follow her?"

The voice drifted from the white carriage to D's rear—from Miska.

"No, there's no point in chasing her," the Noblewoman continued. "The girl's heart seethes with hatred for you and thoughts of her brother. You'd best take care she doesn't slit your throat while you slumber. Noble and human—and held in disdain by both races because of the two kinds of blood that flow in your veins—that is a fitting fate for the half-breeds we call dhampirs. Oh, I do believe I'm beginning to grow a bit fond of that lass—"

The Noblewoman's words ceased there.

As if frightened by something, her team of white horses reared up on their hind legs and whinnied fiercely. The horses and carriage had been enveloped by a ghastly aura that defied description.

The one emitting that aura had a hard gaze trained in the direction May had disappeared, but he suddenly turned to the right.

Taki had just come out of the woods. Apparently preparing to make camp, she had a huge pile of dead wood in her arms. The reason she'd frozen in place before he even saw her was undoubtedly because Taki had been baptized by his unearthly aura.

Perhaps deducing the situation, the young woman said, "You didn't find Hugh, did you?"

"No. May's in the woods over that way."

"I see. I'll go find her."

Dropping the firewood at her feet and dusting herself off, she then took two or three steps before she turned around again. It took a while for the firm, straight bar of her lips to open.

"D—If something happens to Hugh, I know it won't be your fault, but I'm sure I'll hate you for it too. You and those two Nobles."

After Taki dashed away, only the young man in black was left in the clearing that swam in the white sunlight. His stern face was beautiful to the point of violence, looking as if solitude and

all other worldly matters and every human emotion from grief on down had no bearing on him.

II

Soon after the sun went down the baron returned.

"So, you haven't found the child?" he asked.

May and Taki were by the side of the campfire, gazing vacantly into the flames.

"We're setting out," D said from where he leaned back against a tree. A cyborg horse was by his side. He'd gone back to town to procure it.

"This is a rather abrupt departure," the baron said, turning a pained gaze in May's direction. "Let's take another day to search for the child."

Neither Taki nor even May could keep the surprise from showing on their faces as they stared at the Noble who'd just shattered their preconceptions.

"There are no objections to that, I take it?" he said as he turned to D, and then there was the dry whistle of dead wood and a white needle stuck in the ground at the Nobleman's feet. There was a note of some sort attached to it.

Pulling it off, the baron read it.

Continue your journey. The child will show up along the way.

"Who left this, and when?"

"A white rabbit carried it here around noontime."

The speechless baron gazed at D.

"It's true," said Taki. "It stuck it on the door of the carriage—and stood up on two legs to do it! When D put a needle through it, it exploded."

"I suppose you can't have a magician without rabbits," the baron remarked with a wry smile. "In that case, we had best proceed. But before we do—"

Perhaps the baron noticed the swish of fabric to his rear. Miska's white dress had a hazy glow, as if it were a thin fog that shrouded her.

"Have you had any problems?"

"You needn't worry on my account. I am the very picture of health," the beautiful woman said with a smile. Even a human out for her blood would've been left disarmed by her allure.

Although her air was the same as always, the baron's brow crinkled slightly, as if he sensed something.

"That's fine, then. What I said still stands. We leave immediately."

"For the child's sake?" Miska asked, eyes wide with feigned disbelief. "Is your travel itinerary to be determined by the life of a human child?"

"Do you have a problem with that?"

"Don't be absurd. I owe you my life. I wouldn't think for a moment of questioning your wisdom."

"Then return to your carriage. A journey by night can be a pleasure, too."

"One thing first," said the Hunter.

His remark paralyzed everyone—and even made the flames seem to freeze.

"What is it?"

The baron looked at D, and then quickly stared at Miska. He was following D's gaze.

"Last night, there was a sizable explosion," D said, his gaze still locked on Miska. "And you alone were on the scene. The surrounding air hadn't been disturbed in the least. Such a phenomenon is impossible. What did you see?"

Miska laid the four fingers of one hand across her lips to hide a silent laugh, replying, "Is this somewhere where impossible phenomena occur? Spare me your foolish chatter. I shall overlook it as the nonsensical ramblings of a half-breed."

As she turned to walk back to her carriage, her sensuous figure froze as if nailed to the ground.

Everyone felt the swirling vortex of unearthly and overwhelming energy that bound the Noblewoman and the gorgeous Vampire Hunter. The vortex would consume one of them . . . and what would happen then? Would it be D or Miska? The unsettling aura narrowed and tightened. At that moment, it was neither density nor intensity the aura required of them. It was will—pure, crystallized focus. The vortex grew taut between D and Miska.

Just then, the baron's blue cape spread out as he shouted, "Stop it!"

The torrent of ghastly energy was sent flying by his cry.

Somewhere, insects chirped.

"If you take this any further, one of you will get hurt," the baron said as he looked at one, then the other. "As a fellow Noble, I can't very well allow a lady to be harmed. And I would be in quite a predicament if I were to lose such an excellent bodyguard. Allow me to intercede."

"From what I saw, your fate may depend on this too," said D. Needless to say, he was talking to the baron. "Nothing could be more dangerous than traveling with someone who's become part of some unknown entity."

"I don't believe the degree of danger is something I've been too worried about in my journeys. And I don't suppose you have, either," the baron said with a smile. "If I were to insist that she accompany me, would you quit?"

"You're the boss."

"In that case, I believe I'll exercise that privilege. Both of you return to the carriages. We'll address D's concerns at another time," the baron declared in a firm tone.

The dark of night was split by the wind.

The road wasn't exactly flat. With D speeding ahead on horseback, the two carriages were jostled up and down, throwing up dark earth and dust. But inside, they remained perfectly tranquil.

"Do you think Miska's been possessed by something?" the baron asked in a low voice from the driver's seat.

"Probably, back at the Talos arsenal. Maybe by the Destroyer," D replied.

While the echo of hoofbeats and wheels obliterated the pair's conversation, the words reached their ears softly and clearly.

"We checked her out."

"We have no way of knowing what knowledge they possessed in ancient times."

"It certainly is dangerous beyond all measure. And yet knowing that, you'll accompany us, Vampire Hunter 'D'? You certainly appear confident."

"This is my job."

"Do you know no fear?"

There was no reply to that. Instead, the Hunter said, "At this rate, we'll reach the village of Diemli in less than three hours. It's a ghost town, so we'll blow right through it. We'll probably see the village of Corma by dawn."

"Which of them will have our foes?"

"Both."

A daring smile skimmed across the baron's lips.

"Although we haven't discussed it, another problem remains. The young lady."

He was referring to Taki.

"She said she was Lord Johann's assistant. Is she friend or foe?"

"Foe," D said, not an iota of ambiguity in his reply. Yet the fact that he'd left May in her care when he went off in search of the baron and Hugh showed that he had nerves of steel.

"As I feared," was all the baron said, being equally reluctant to voice any more unsettling opinions.

He had been fully aware of the danger when he undertook this journey, and though this was tantamount to making off with a baby fire dragon while a rope tethered it to its mother's neck, the Nobleman didn't seem the least bit disquieted. Perhaps he was even grateful to have someone to baby-sit the children.

"I wonder how many foes remain," the baron said absentmindedly.

And the Hunter immediately replied, "At least five, counting Lord Johann."

"How do you know?"

"That's the number I came up with by dividing the distance you have to travel by the number of times they've attacked. Each is given one attack—there may be slightly more, but I think that just about covers it."

"Remarkable," the baron said, and in his heart he was truly impressed. Though he didn't know if that was the actual number, it agreed exactly with the figure he'd imagined. Although he'd hired this man because he'd heard he was the greatest Vampire Hunter in history, D's power and abilities far exceeded even the baron's conjecture—the young man was truly worthy of being dubbed a gorgeous demon prince.

On the other hand, there may have been some things about the young Nobleman D couldn't fathom either.

In all their lengthy history, there were very few examples of the Nobility comprehending humanity, and that comprehension only extended as far as concrete measures such as reducing the humans' labors or keeping them from being pillaged by other Nobles. The quintessential act of inhumanity—the drinking of blood—had never been done away with. Even Nobles who'd displayed boundless compassion for human beings while sated would sink their fangs into the throat of a girl whose head they'd patted lovingly should their hunger take root. There was no record of any Noble lasting three days alongside humans. In that sense, you could say that Baron Balazs deserved a place in history.

"Do you find it odd, D?" the Noble asked as if he'd read the Hunter's mind, and D looked over at him in the driver's seat.

"Do you know how to use telepathy?"

Long ago, the same ability had been a paranormal skill called "mind-reading." It was probably that same talent that had allowed the baron to confer with D from the distant cover of a boulder.

"A little, you could say," the baron responded. "To be honest, I can't say I don't feel a hopeless longing when I'm with the three of them. After sating my hunger with artificial blood, all the dreams I have in my coffin are of their pale throats. No doubt it's the same with Miska. Come now, don't give me that look! I'm still your employer, as it were. Rest assured. Even if you weren't around, I could restrain myself until I reached my destination."

D's eyes gleamed as he asked, "Why is that?"

More than the question, it was unclear if the baron could fully comprehend the mindset of the one who posed it.

"My mother underwent a certain procedure while I was in her womb," said the baron.

The wind snarled, and the wooden wheels broke the ground.

Perhaps the clouds that swirled in the darkened sky were calling up a storm. Lightning flashed.

D asked, "Who performed the procedure?"

The flash of light bleached both their faces, and then the thunder roared.

Due to its distance, the baron's voice could still be heard distinctly as he replied, "The Sacred Ancestor."

The Hunter's horse galloped. The carriages raced along as well.

"Is that the reason you're going to Krauhausen?"

"I suppose so," the baron said, turning his eyes forward. "My mother pleaded with the Sacred Ancestor time and again not to do the procedure. But it was Vlad Balazs that insisted it continue."

D said nothing.

"Do you know what the result was, D? Strangely enough, I get the feeling you'd understand."

The baron raised his right hand. The back of his blue glove was covered by a piece of armor the same hue. When one of his five fingers made a sound like a motor, the armor plate slid back, glove and all, exposing the hand below, starting with the split finger.

There was a cry.

"What's the matter?" Taki asked as she shook the girl awake.

May was terribly hot, her pink cheeks covered with tears and sweat. The girl's eyelids seemed sewn shut as they trembled, and when they finally opened, her eyes were etched with a look of stark terror.

Looking up at Taki until her fear faded, May then buried her face against the woman's chest.

"You're okay now. You're safe. Had a nightmare, did you?" Taki said as she stroked the girl's shoulder, and the violence of the quaking she could feel made the young woman a captive of her mournful thoughts.

"It was Hugh . . . He was . . . His whole body just melted," May cried as if her sobs had just been transformed into words. "It was scary . . . so scary . . . what happened to his body . . ."

"It was a dream. Just a bad dream," Taki said as she stroked the girl's hair gently. "I'm sure you'll have better dreams now. Bad dreams don't come true, you know."

And then she softly shut her eyes and added in a tone May wouldn't hear, "Neither do the good ones."

Village of Death

CHAPTER 2

I

Though they intended to go right through the ghost town, the group had been pelted by torrential downpours for an hour and a half, so D decided that they'd take shelter instead.

"But as soon as the rain lets up, we move out again, even if it's the middle of the night. Keep that in mind," the Hunter told them all once they'd entered a brick building that seemed to be a meetinghouse almost at the center of town.

Aside from the dust and the thick fog of spider webs, the room had suffered almost no damage, and once the atomic lanterns had been lit, Taki and May used a leather sofa as a bed. Outside, the rain echoed like the beating of a war drum, and the girl anxiously fiddled with the front of her blouse.

"It's really coming down," Taki said with fear in her voice.

"There's a river not far from the village, I believe. I wonder if there's any danger of it overflowing?"

D responded to the baron's query, saying, "I'll go have a look."

His black form was quickly swallowed by a darkness of the same hue.

Taki averted her gaze from the two Nobles out of instinctive fear and hatred.

"Scared?" Miska asked with a mocking laugh after a few minutes of naught but the sound of the rain. "Two Nobles and two humans—

as numbers go, a perfect match. When you think of it, it would be strange if *nothing* happened."

As the white figure got up off another sofa, something suddenly seemed to slice through the air. Before the little rock could hit the far wall, Miska saw that the one who'd thrown it—May—was fighting her way free of Taki's grasp to stand up.

"So, my little pebble of an opponent uses a stone to throw the gauntlet, does she?"

Though the girl was even more reckless than her brother, her features hardened at the grim spectacle of the white fangs that peeked from those grinning vermilion lips, but May's malice promptly came to the fore as she spat, "You think I'm scared of you? Sooner or later, we'll destroy both of you. If I were frightened, your kind would still be running the show now. You're an extinct breed, thrown out of our world and with no place else to go. Come on! I'll take you out right now! I'll make you pay for what happened to my mother and father!"

"Oh, now this is something I hadn't heard before. Your father and mother fell into our hands?" the pale woman said, her eyes burning with a cruel delight that spilled over into her next remarks. "How fascinating! I'm sure they must've been overjoyed. Very well, I shall send you now to join them."

May's body trembled, but not from fear. She shook with a rage she couldn't contain.

"Stop it!" the figure in blue said as he leapt out in front of Taki, who had taken up a position shielding the girl.

"You're interfering," Miska snapped angrily as she stared at the baron. "Why would you protect these wretched humans?"

"I made a promise to D."

"A filthy half-breed like him—"

"He's more important to my journey than anyone—even you," the baron stated, his words carrying more than enough force to shake the bloodthirsty Noblewoman.

Taking advantage of the situation, the baron said, "A stroll on a rainy night might be nice, don't you think?"

And with that, he reached out and took Miska by the hand.

The Noblewoman wasn't the only one to have confusion rise on her face. Taki and May looked at each other with astonished expressions.

Water—particularly flowing water—could have fatal effects on the vampiric Nobility. The biorhythms of Nobles soaked by the rain dropped to the nadir, and in the process, their actions became unusually sluggish and their thoughts unfocused. And it was for this reason that even now a Noble's grave was often soaked with hoses or buckets of water before it was pried open. There were a number of examples of travelers who'd been attacked but had saved themselves by running out into the rain, and many carried a pot of water with them when they took to the road.

Opening a case he'd unloaded from the carriage, the baron handed Taki a plasma rifle and told her, "In case of emergency. We'll be right back."

And then he stepped outside with Miska. The outlines of the pair turned white from the spray of the rain, and then even that faded away.

Right in front of D, the black water raced by with a deafening roar. The Hunter's eyes could see through the darkness as clearly as if it were broad daylight, and even in a torrential downpour, he could tell in an instant that fording this muddy flow anytime soon would be impossible. The waterway was a good hundred yards wide—some might even call it a major river. Once strong wooden bridges had spanned it, opening trade routes with other villages, but after the villagers left, they'd rotted and had been washed away, leaving the group no choice but to cross at a rope bridge much further upstream or use a ferry a great distance downstream. What's more, perhaps due to the dark clouds hovering overhead, the black expanse of water grew as the Hunter watched, to the point where it was about to overflow its banks.

Just then, D did something strange as he watched the flow. He put the blade of the sword he'd drawn against the palm of his left hand.

"Not gonna be able to do it right away," said a voice that mixed with the sound of the rain.

"When will you be back?" asked the Hunter.

"In an hour or two at the earliest. In the meantime, you'll have to find another weapon. I'm sure you could cut down the average monster with this thing, but our foes this time are pretty tough—"

"Leave that to me," D said as the water that'd already climbed the banks suddenly jumped from his ankles to his knees.

A second later, D's body flew lightly into the air as he leapt back fifteen feet to an enormous tree and landed on a branch about the same distance from the ground. If not for the pounding rain, it would've been clear that neither the branch nor its leaves stirred in the slightest. However, descending from Noble blood or not, it was a rather exaggerated effort to flee from the running water.

The reason for his actions became clear from the way D concentrated his gaze on the muddy black flow.

A number of figures had risen from the water that'd covered the banks. The shapes that showed through the semi-translucent gelatinous substance coating them from the top of their heads to the tips of their toes made it clear they were human. But who were they? There was only one thing that could bring them to the ghost town this rainy night—and from the way they'd made their appearance, getting shelter from the rain wasn't their aim.

D did nothing, and as his silent vigil continued, the foremost form raised one hand to give a signal. The figures dove in one after another, the jelly around them turning the same color as the water before every bump and contour melted away in a mere foot or two of the flow and they drifted off.

"More assassins, you suppose?"

Without responding, D leapt to the next closest tree to the village.

"Hold up a second. I wanna see what they can do," the hoarse voice said.

†

When the rain wasn't actually falling on them, the sound of it was a comforting melody. The baron and Miska stood under the eaves of a shrine a short distance from the meetinghouse.

"What was this?" Miska asked as she turned to look up at the shrine and its lofty tower.

"This was where the villagers worshiped their gods, I imagine."

"Gods—what nonsense! We are the only gods the human race needed. I wonder if the administration bureau in this district did nothing to suppress these practices."

"Even in the Capital they had their holy places. Force probably couldn't do anything to change that. They believe in something greater."

"You seem rather well informed regarding humans," Miska said with a sarcastic smile. "I wonder if that might be the reason you let those children do whatever they wish."

"Are you keeping yourself in check?"

The baron's question shook Miska. It had just dawned on her that at some point, the desire to drink blood had completely left her.

"I got a slight sense of it from your attitude and the way you look at them—in which case, it's a rather intriguing development," the baron remarked.

"What is?"

"We may be the first Nobles to successfully control our urge to drink blood in the presence of humans."

Miska stiffened as if a jolt of electricity had just passed through her, then quickly tilted her head back on her pale neck and laughed.

"Baron Balazs, that's the most ridiculous thing I've ever heard. The only reason I have left them alone is to honor your wishes. If you were but to give me your blessing, I would return posthaste and you should see me clamp onto their throats."

The baron turned his thoughtful countenance in another direction. Black water was streaming down the street.

"Have the banks overflowed? The way it's raining—" he muttered as the black current promptly covered the steps. From the way it was going, it only seemed a matter of time before the interior of the buildings would be flooded as well.

Tension filled the baron and Miska at essentially the same time the black blobs flew up out of the water.

"Ah!" Miska cried as she covered her face. A jet of black liquid had shot from the face of the shadowy figure to plaster her eyes.

The amphibious attacker croaked out a froglike laugh, but a heartbeat later, his face was split lengthwise. He probably couldn't believe it, because the same viscous mass that'd robbed Miska of her vision had been launched at the baron as well. Just before he was reduced to a corpse and fell back into the black water, he'd seen that the baron had one hand up shielding his eyes . . . and the viscous mass clung to the back of the Nobleman's hand.

"Are you okay?" the baron asked as he raced over to Miska.

"I can't see," she said in a composed tone.

"Does it hurt?"

"No. But it's not coming off easily. Who could these characters be?"

"I have some idea," the baron said gravely. "Let's go back. The meetinghouse might be under attack."

"Once again, thinking of the lowly humans."

Though her voice was choked with malice, Miska had lost some of her forcefulness along with her sight, and the baron took her by the hand and began to walk away.

It was at just that moment that the earth sank. Was it the power of the muddy flow? No, insistent as that was, it didn't have that sort of force. The houses here had also been built to withstand it.

To the rear of the unexpectedly reeling baron, a trio of figures leapt up from a depth of water that ordinarily never could've concealed anything their size.

His left hand still holding onto Miska's, the baron latched onto a column supporting the porch with his right. Now he didn't have use of either hand.

Behind him, sharp gleams came from the hands of his foes—metallic claws. They were eight inches long. Apparently believing their chances of victory good, the attackers pounced, bringing their claws down artlessly in midair at the backs of the Nobles.

At that instant, a single flash of light mowed through the torsos of the trio. They probably never even realized it'd come from under the baron's cape.

The shadowy figures sprayed a liquid darker than the black waters as they fell, but the baron didn't even bother to turn and look at them as he made a hard pull on his left hand. Wrapping his arm around Miska's waist as she flew up easily, he then swung both feet upward. A black hole opened in the porch roof, a product of a mighty kick—or rather, the strength of the Noble's legs. His feet kept going right through the hole, and through some maneuver or other, the baron's body followed suit as he and Miska went out through the ceiling.

"Do you think this sinking is their doing?" Miska asked, easily maintaining her balance on the pitched roof.

"Without a doubt," the baron said, handing Miska a handkerchief blue as the twilight and telling her to use it to shield herself from the rain.

The flash that had dispatched the trio of assassins had already returned to the interior of his cape. With such speed, power, and control, the baron's secret weapon could cover him against attacks from all three hundred sixty degrees, and any opponent trying to take him by surprise would find themselves dead and buried before they even got off a single attack. Perhaps even D.

"Let's go," the baron said, his arm still wrapped around Miska's waist.

A particularly strong gust of wind-driven rain blurred the two outlines as it passed. And once it died down, the pair of Nobles was no longer there.

II

"Water!" Taki turned and shouted after standing in the doorway looking outside. "The river's overflowed. Head upstairs!"

But by the time Taki had finished speaking, the girl was already speeding toward the staircase, accompanied by a dazzling light. With only the atomic lantern and what baggage she could carry, May was truly a person of the Frontier.

When Taki reached the stairs, the tarlike water swelled under the door, spreading across the floor like a cloud of black smoke. Less than a foot deep, it split open as a pair of figures leapt from it to land right in front of May, who was only one step from the top of the staircase.

There was a shriek, and Taki whirled around in its direction with the plasma rifle. Though her finger was on the trigger, she stopped just a heartbeat short of firing it.

One of the two figures with froglike heads and bodies had reached out with a hand full of strangely sharp claws and scooped up May.

A second later, a searing pain shot down Taki's spine and she tumbled backward. A shadowy figure who'd leapt up from the water without making a sound had brought his claws down on her. As she lost her balance, she fell into a pair of clammy arms.

Thick lips opened like a crevice, and the dark figure said, "The kid we'll take hostage."

His voice was exactly what one would expect if a frog were capable of human speech.

"This other one—you can dispose of."

From the feel of Taki's body as it went limp, it looked like she had no strength to fight them, and the creature raised his clawlike weapon to strike the fatal blow. And he did so slowly.

"Sorry, but it's better to give than to receive," Taki said just as the claws suddenly stopped and her bloodied form spun around.

Her right elbow shot up at an angle, slamming into the batrachian's face with peerless precision. As he lurched away with a groan of pain, she used her own weight to slam him face first into the wall, and when she leapt clear of him, she already had the plasma rifle braced against her shoulder.

The compatriots that'd been holding May sprang at Taki from up on the staircase. As they plummeted toward her, they were greeted by flashes of crimson light. Hit directly in the base of the neck, both the top and bottom halves of their bodies were reduced to vapor.

As Taki dashed up a few stairs, a froggy voice called down to her, "I'll kill the brat!"

From below, another called out, "Drop it!"

The latter was bellowed angrily by the one she'd nailed in the face, but since his face had been broad and flat from the start and he wasn't bleeding, the only way to judge how badly he'd been hurt was by the sound of his voice.

No matter what she did, it was clear that Taki, with foes to either side of her, was caught in a deadly bind. If she let go of her plasma rifle, they would most likely carve out her heart with their cruel clawed weapons.

"Taki!" May cried, her voice stabbing the young woman's eardrums like a knife. Perhaps they were hurting her, because it sounded like something was clogging her throat.

"Don't you lay a hand on that girl or I'll shoot!"

"Drop it," the other voice countered.

But the coup de grace was when May stammered, "T-Taki . . ."

The pain became an unfathomable weight that hung on the end of Taki's plasma rifle.

Seeing the barrel of the weapon sink, the frog man below croaked out a laugh.

And just as he did, there was what sounded like an explosion as a window facing the second-floor hallway shattered. As the froglike man turned in amazement, it came as little surprise he used May as a shield. A heartbeat later, one of his eyes was pierced by a rough wooden needle.

What happened in the next instant even D probably couldn't have imagined as he kicked off the floor. May's body slipped easily from the grasp of the reeling foe and she executed a beautiful somersault, then went on to bring a kick up under her opponent's jaw that laid him out on his back.

The instant he saw a blast from the plasma rifle down on the staircase cut the villain's body in half, D reversed his sword in midair and turned it into a bolt of lightning.

The frog man who was about to pounce on Taki from behind had the Hunter's blade protruding from his belly. Slain instantly by the powerful thrust, the amphibious humanoid made no effort to remove himself from the blade, but flipped over the handrail and fell into the black water below.

"Have a look at her," D told Taki, who was still frozen partway up the staircase, as he leapt over the handrail to reclaim his sword. Pulling his blade out of the potbellied villain who'd sunk into the water, he then returned to the second floor, where Taki had the trembling girl hugged to her bosom.

"She's not hurt," Taki informed him as she rubbed the girl's head. "She's so strong. She didn't cry or anything."

Without replying, D looked at the young woman and told her, "You did well."

Letting out a sigh, Taki said, "You choose the damnedest times to show up, you know." She sounded angry. This was a result of a psychological swing brought about by her sudden feelings of relief.

By the time D had raced back to them by leaping from tree to tree, the black water had already inundated the meetinghouse. After landing on the roof, D had seen the situation through a skylight and narrowly managed to intervene.

Turning his gaze to the blackish figure that lay a short distance away, he asked Taki, "Ever seen them before?"

"Of course I haven't."

"You sure they're not some of Lord Johann's tricks?"

"I've never laid eyes on them. But they could be something he was saving for a special occasion."

D circled around behind Taki without another word. Just below her right shoulder, a pair of gashes ran all the way down to her waist. If they'd been a half inch closer to her backbone, her spinal column would've been irreparably damaged. Needless to say, she was covered with blood.

"Don't move," D said as he put the palm of his left hand to the gash on the right.

"Don't touch it!"

"This is just first aid."

As his hand slid lower, lazy wisps of white smoke rose from where he came into contact with her wound. The rent flesh closed miraculously.

Treating the other gash, D then straightened up again and said, "You'll be fully healed in two days' time."

Tossing her head lightly, Taki asked, "What are you?"

"Never mind me. You should be asking who *they* are," D replied.

"You should ask me," someone else said.

Baron Balazs and Miska stood in the doorway to the hall.

Taking his eyes off the opponent D had slain, the baron said, "They are assassins sent by my father."

Leaving the two girls in an empty room that'd been prepared for them, D went into a room across the hallway. The baron and Miska were waiting there.

Apparently once a committee room of some sort, the chamber, some five or six hundred square feet, was littered with an assortment of rustic desks and chairs.

"Have they gone to sleep?" asked the baron.

"Yeah."

"It doesn't look like the rain will let up. After we've had about an hour's rest, I'd like to set out again."

"That shouldn't be a problem."

"Why don't we leave immediately?" Miska asked after turning from the window that'd allowed her to gaze outside.

"The humans need to rest during normal human hours. You'll just have to bear with us for a while."

"In that case, let them sleep all they like. However, we can't do that here if you wish to depart before those assassins' compatriots arrive. No matter how you look at it, leaving immediately is the best course of action. My dear baron, you're putting your head into the noose. And all because of that baggage. Leave them here!"

The Noblewoman's eyes looked like fire would erupt from them, but they were met by a deep gaze.

"I can't do that. What's more, that's not to say we can't wait. I will take full responsibility for seeing you safely to your destination."

"They were synthetic life forms," D said, changing the subject. He was referring to the froglike assassins. "Do you know everything your father has up his sleeve? It will be problematic if there are more things lying in wait for us up ahead."

"Some of them I know. Some of them I don't," the baron replied stoically.

He was out to take his own father's life, and his father had designs on taking the young Nobleman's as well. His expression made clear that he knew perfectly well the gravity of the situation.

He then said, "Foes before us and foes to the rear—things are getting a bit tricky, aren't they, D?"

"Is your father aware of your abilities?"

"Yes, he's known for quite some time," the baron replied, a fitting response for an immortal Noble.

"Can we get rid of the carriages?" D asked him.

"I have no objection."

"According to the map, there's an airfield nearby. It's been out of use for a long time, but I heard ages ago that there were still aircraft left there."

"Oh really?" said the baron, his eyes glittering. "In that case, it'd be but a short flight. But just how long ago was this?"

"Quite some time."

"Perhaps nothing remains now of these flying machines but the stories," the baron remarked with a wry grin. "However, it still may be worth going for a look. So long as we're not chasing a phantom."

There was no reply. D seemed to have his ears focused on the sound of the rain.

The baron followed his example.

A strange rhythm—that was the only way to describe the beautiful melody that drifted through the room.

"Why, that's the sound of a harp," Miska said, her eyes still shut. She, too, had been listening intently.

"A water harp, to be precise," the baron said as he gazed out the window. "Let's get going, D."

"What's a water harp?" asked D.

"Strings stretched either through the water at the base of a waterfall or out in the rain. They make a beautiful sound when they come into contact with water, and if any living creature touches them, they wrap around it and choke the life from it. Those who approach it—" the baron said, and he'd already started walking.

Slipping through the doorway, the Nobleman stepped out into the hall. Confirming that there was no one out there, he then opened the door across from them.

A pale figure had one leg resting on the sill of the open window and her upper body leaning out. Flying effortlessly through the air, the baron caught Taki around the waist and pulled her back in. Held tightly by his arms of steel, the young woman waved her arms about, trying to move forward again. The utter lack of expression on her face was disturbing.

D then went over to the window and peered out through the opening that had allowed May to escape.

"They weren't intended as hostages," said the Hunter.

"Precisely. You and I can withstand this because of who we are. But even among the Nobility there are few who can resist the sound of the water harp. We must find the girl."

Before the baron had finished speaking, D stepped out of the room. Going back to the first room, he quickly returned again. The Nobleman might've done something special, because Taki was now snoring away on the bed.

"What of Miska?" the baron inquired.

"Apparently she was called away."

D stepped closer to the window. The tune of the water harp played on.

"Two blocks south of here there's a house of worship. Let's move over there."

By that, the Hunter must've meant that the enemy was already wise to their location.

"Very well," the baron said with a nod, but the beautiful figure in black didn't even wait for this reply before melding with the darkness.

As he turned a melancholy profile to the notes splashed out on the harp by raindrops, the Nobleman said, "I'm counting on you, D."

And with those words, the baron gently lifted the sleeping girl.

III

A muddy black stream appeared to have melted the road, and D could see it as clearly as if it were midday. Though it wasn't as strong as it'd been immediately after overflowing the banks, the water that clung to him almost to the knee still had a current powerful enough to keep anyone from moving with perfect freedom. Undoubtedly both May and Miska had walked down the elevated planks of the roofed sidewalks as they'd left . . . or as they were spirited away. The strings of the harps seemed to have been strung everywhere, as their haunting echoes grew neither closer nor farther away.

Going from roof to roof, D continued north. The rain pouring down from the heavens, the water rushing across the ground, and the sounds of the harp that tied them both together—each of the three made a different noise, but the Hunter could sense the slightest added disturbance in each.

His foes were moving underwater. They could normally move undetected even by D, perhaps maneuvering around the wires strung everywhere. The added disturbance to the sounds of the water was no doubt due to the fact they had Miska and May with them. In a sense, these hostages were their greatest weakness.

Coming to the end of a row of houses, D leapt into the air without ever breaking his stride. A gorgeous darkness crossed through the dim night, landing again on a massive branch of a tree nearly thirty feet away. Astonishingly enough, not so much as a single leaf stirred.

Needless to say, D had elected to move through the air to avoid fighting his foes in the water—their home territory.

Even the ageless and immortal Nobility had a number of weaknesses, and water was one of them. When Nobles came into direct contact with the rain, their metabolic functions dropped to half their normal levels, and if submerged, they became like statues, barely able to move their arms or legs at all. The sight of this gorgeous dhampir effortlessly traveling from tree to tree under such unfavorable conditions was nothing short of miraculous.

Poised to leap down to the ground from the last of the trees, D suddenly halted.

He was at the edge of the village. Part of the outer palisade was completely missing, as if something had taken a bite out of it. Miska and May had probably been taken out this way.

D's attention remained focused on the darkness. A white line ran from the branch on which he stood to a grove of trees—the water harp had been strung here as well. Ordinarily, D would've had no trouble at all finding it. But the effects of the rain might mean the difference between life and death.

D became a black wind as he slipped around the right end of the line.

A rough slap echoed from his body. With exquisite timing the wind had lashed him with rain.

Still, D didn't break form as he sailed toward his intended grove, but when he came down on a branch slick with water, it was truly unforeseen that one of his feet should slip out from under him. As he tried to regain his balance, his swaying form was once again blasted by wind and rain, and his left hand went for one of the harp strings.

The jolt to the taut line traveled through the grove, and then raced across the ground. Dozens of lines that'd been set up God-only-knows-where let go, flying at D up on the branch a heartbeat later.

And what became of those who'd plucked at the harp's strings? The strings that struck the tree trunk sank halfway into it, and the massive branch was lopped off like a piece of straw.

If all of the attacks had originated from the same point of the ground, D might've been able to fend them off. But the strings assailed him from all directions.

The rain stopped. Or rather, it was cut short—cut down by a stark blade slashing through the darkness. On the ground, on the branch, and above both—the scattered raindrops carried pieces of the wires with them.

Having sliced through each and every one of the slender instruments of death flying at him, D then launched himself at the next stand of trees.

Miska was conscious. Those mesmerized by the strains of the water harp usually hastened to the source of the sounds, as numbed as a sleepwalker. But surely the reason Miska was aware of her surroundings was because of the extraordinary senses she possessed as a Noble.

After slipping out of her room, the first thing she'd done was to go down into the street where the water flowed. And when she did, something caught hold of both of her ankles and began to pull her against the flow. She knifed through the water at a speed that rivaled a motorboat, propelled by a force she couldn't comprehend—a force that defied normal physics.

In less than five minutes' time Miska had left the village and even crossed the river with consummate ease before being sucked into the enormous whirlpool that opened at the roots of the colossal tree towering over the northern forest. And all the while, her speed never dropped for an instant.

The reason the colossal bole had been put to various uses over several centuries was its absolutely preposterous size. At the base it was thick enough that a hundred people would need to join hands just to encompass it, and it rose haughtily to the heavens, dwarfing the surrounding trees with its height of over three thousand feet. When people learned there were natural cavities in it—and the ownership of the land had changed several times—they made use of the spaces and carved new passages wherever it suited them, making rooms large and small, then stocked the tree with vast amounts of goods which were then protected by the people and weapons they posted there. At times the colossal tree could be a watchtower beyond compare, a control tower for an airfield, or an evacuation center during disasters, and it was also the ideal storehouse.

And now, you could say it was being put to a somewhat more peculiar use.

What awaited Miska inside the massive tree, with its twisting maze of stairs and passageways and both small rooms and structures two or three stories tall was May—who'd been abducted just shortly before her—and about a dozen black figures. At a glance it was clear that the shadowy figures croaking like amphibians were synthetic life forms, but among them there was one who looked like a normal human, and he stepped to the fore.

"Ah, just what I would expect from a Noble! You may have lost mastery of your body, but the control of your brain seems to be another matter," he said.

Beneath the night-vision goggles set in his helmet, his right eye alone seemed to give off a fierce gleam—he only had the use of one eye. From the nose down, the rest of his face was concealed from prying eyes by a shield of black metal. But that shield was apparently equipped with an amplifier for his voice. Every time the man drew a breath, it was accompanied by a rasping whistle.

"However, that is unfortunate for you," he continued. "Now that you're before me and I see that you're a Noble, I can't let you have an easy death. Soak her in the vat!"

Apparently Miska knew what the result of this torture would be, and her beautiful countenance—ordinarily the very epitome of haughtiness—grew pale, as if the blood had drained from it.

Without further ado, pulleys clanged from the darkened region of the ceiling and a container that would easily accommodate five or six people was lowered. Several of those who stood behind the leader quickly raced over and steadied it on the floor. Water filled it to the very brim.

"I've heard that if you soak them for a full day, even a Noble will be headed for the next life. Is that true? Well, I have a different punishment to try with you." Turning to the others, he said, "At any rate, get her in the water."

A number of arms lifted Miska like a mannequin and put her in the vat.

"Add the acid!"

One of the man's subordinates appeared from somewhere carrying another container and began to transfer its contents into Miska's vat with a wooden ladle. When the semitransparent liquid came into contact with the water, white smoke went up like steam from a geyser.

An unvoiced scream split the Noblewoman's seductive lips. The acid-laced water—or the water-laced acid—burned Miska's skin, dissolving the very flesh.

"This acid was especially made for torturing the Nobility. But truth be told, it was a Noble that came up with it," the leader remarked with visible amusement. "Although it won't destroy you completely, it'll torment the hell out of you. There's really no difference between what humans and Nobles will do, is there?"

"Who—who are you?" Miska heard herself ask.

The pain was so great she'd regained the use of her vocal chords. Yet her body remained immobilized.

"Why not simply run me through the heart . . . Your halfhearted games . . . will be repaid a thousandfold in pain . . ."

Her voice then became an agonized squeak. More acid had been added.

"That's enough. But don't let it get any weaker, either," the leader told the subordinate holding the ladle, and then he turned to May, who stood in a daze beside him. When he placed his right hand on the crown of her head, a single spasm went through May's body, and then the life returned to her eyes.

"Notice anything?" the leader inquired as the girl backed away from him reflexively.

"Never fear. We won't do anything to you for the time being," the leader said, his voice tinged with mirth. "We'd intended to use you as a hostage, but the Noblewoman came along, too. We can make better use of her. Just stay here and behave yourself for a while."

He gave May a frightening glance that froze her on the spot.

"What will you do with her?" the girl asked when she saw the vat that contained Miska.

"That should be obvious. We're going to use her as a hostage instead of you. Luck was with you."

"She looks like she's in terrible pain. What did you do to her?"

"We're soaking her in a special acid that dissolves Nobles' flesh. Though it can't destroy them, I'm sure it must hurt terribly."

"How could you do such a thing? Please, stop it! Save her!"

"What?!"

The leader's reaction was the very peak of astonishment, but Miska herself must've been even more dumbfounded. Her agonized expression quickly turned to face the girl.

The leader fixed May with a hard stare.

"You mean . . . When I heard they were traveling with human children, I thought you were their snack, but you still look normal enough. Why would a human stick up for a Noble?"

The information he had on May must've been supplied by the first group of assassins the group had encountered.

"I'm not sticking up for her at all," the girl replied clearly. "But when you do something that horrible, it makes us just as bad as the Nobility."

The eyes of the leader opened even wider.

"Could it be you've been brainwashed? It wouldn't be beyond them."

"It's not like that. I'm fine. That's why I know what you're doing isn't right."

"We're talking about a Noble here. These are the same creatures that tortured and killed us like insects for many long years. In a manner of speaking, we're just paying them back."

"You mean you're human, too?"

At her grave question the leader laughed out loud.

"Indeed I am. Although thanks to the Nobility you would protect, I was given my current condition."

"So—they did something to you?"

The leader said nothing.

A voice that seemed to rise from the bowels of the earth made the two of them turn around.

"Why would a Noble choose to use a human?" Miska asked as she glared at them with glittering eyes from the bubbling vat. "You must be one of the assassins dispatched by the baron's father. Oh, it makes my sides ache that you should choose to call us your foe. Do the Nobility's trained dogs forget their place and stand on two legs when they see a human?"

"You've let your mouth run a bit too far, princess," the leader said as he walked over to Miska and grabbed her left earlobe. Drawing the hefty broadsword that hung from his hip, he put it against the back of her ear.

"Don't—"

Before May's scream had finished, he sliced one of the Noblewoman's ears clean off. Red droplets dripped into the vat of boiling acid, quickly mixing with the liquid.

"Next I'll shave off your nose and carve out your eyes. But don't die on me. I have a million interesting ideas of what to do to you!"

"I won't die."

Miska's reply froze May.

"Do you think this is all it takes to destroy a Noble? You said we treated you like insects, but I happen to be quite fond of insects. After I was done ripping others of your kind to shreds, I always gave them to the insects to eat. The fact of the matter is, you were lower than worms."

She tried to laugh, but her face was pulled to one side. The leader grabbed a fistful of her golden hair and yanked it right out of her head. Half the beauty's face—or rather, her whole face by this point—was stained with vermilion, but as shocking as this was, it was the sight of her half-denuded head that made May hide her face in her hands.

Dropping the bloodied ear and clump of hair on the floor, the leader stuck his hand in the acid.

"Oh, your face is a mess now. I suppose we'll have to disinfect that wound, won't we?"

He let the water he'd scooped up fall directly into the wound. The flesh dissolved, and a cry split Miska's lips.

"Have some more," he said, water trailing from his hand as he raised it, but then a black shape hit his arm.

In a bound, May had sailed over the leader, delivering a kick to his wrist with one foot in the process. The water splashed on the leader's coat, which gave off white smoke.

A number of figures surrounded May when she landed.

"Don't touch her," the leader reprimanded them. "Being human, I should think even the most upstanding of people would be overjoyed to see a Noble in torment. Put the Noblewoman in a cell, and bring the girl to my room."

The man actually sounded rather intrigued.

"Mister Galil, sir," one of his subordinates said in a froglike voice.

"What is it?"

"Part of the water harp has been broken. It seems a foe has slipped in through the break."

"Let them come. Whether our foe is the baron or his bodyguard, we should be more than enough to handle either of them."

The Tiger and the Wolf

CHAPTER 3

I

D reached the colossal tree about thirty minutes after he first began following the tracks. After carving his way through the harp strings that'd assailed him like so many tributaries running to a common stream, he'd been able to advance through the rain. And in the vast and well-lit hollow in the tree he found the leader waiting alone to meet him.

"Rumors of your beauty can't do you credit—you're D, I take it. I am Galil, leader of Lord Balazs's Dark Water Forces."

"Where are the two women?" D asked, keeping his question short and sweet. There was no murderous intent in him now. But when it came out, only his dead and buried foes could say what fate lay in store for his opponent.

"Not to worry. We haven't laid a finger on the girl. But whether or not that continues to be the case will depend on discussions between you and myself."

"Where's the other one?"

"If you mean the Noblewoman, we put her in a cell after having a bit of fun with her. We couldn't destroy her, but she's in no condition to escape." With a cruel smile the leader—Galil—added, "If you wish, I can show you to her at any time. But first, I have two or three things to ask you. Why would a Vampire Hunter, of all people, take a job guarding a Noble?"

"Because his aim is to slay a Noble."

"How about the Noblewoman, then?"

"She stays per orders of my employer."

"I'm amazed that humans have been traveling with Nobles without anything happening to them. But they'll bare their fangs sooner or later. D, which side are you on?"

A naked blade pressed right against the base of Galil's neck. And no one there had even seen D draw it.

"I'll give you five seconds," said the Hunter. "Bring the women. If I have to wait a minute, I'll take your ears off. At two minutes, it'll be your nose, and after three, I'll carve your eyes out."

"Are you out of your mind? If you do any of that to me, they'll do the same to those two," Galil countered, but his eyes were certainly swimming with terror.

"Five," D counted off coolly. "Four . . . Three . . . Two . . ."

There was neither a lethal intent nor an unearthly air about him. Anyone who didn't know the Hunter would've sworn he had the blade out in jest.

"One," he finally said.

"Okay," Galil said gravely, raising his right hand.

Without the slightest delay, the sound of pulleys echoed from the ceiling and two basketlike objects were lowered. The gigantic birdcages and the thick iron bars that surrounded them were red with rust. And sure enough, May and Miska were inside them. Once they'd reached the floor, the doors opened naturally and the two of them stumbled out. Without a second thought they took shelter behind D.

"Take them and go," said Galil.

"No, not yet," D replied.

It was at that moment the eyes of the Dark Water Forces' commander lit up with true fear. As he leapt back, a flash of white light pursued him.

D's blow was true, and his sword bisected Galil's torso. But what did the Hunter make of the mysterious sensation his blade met?

When Galil's torso landed ten feet away, it had indeed been sliced straight through just below the chest.

"Do you find this strange, D?" he asked, trying to laugh or smile, but his lips were too stiff for either. He had, after all, just taken a stroke from D's sword.

"So, he's a water warrior?" said a voice from D's left hand that he alone heard. "He's one of those liquid humans they say the Nobility made to supervise their synthetic soldiers in battle. There weren't many—maybe a dozen every thousand years—but I hear they were the death of ten million of their foes. This could be . . . bad."

"Not even your sword can cut me," said Galil. "This is the body I was given when I became the Nobility's pet, so I might destroy Nobles. D, it's still not too late. Join forces with me. Go back to being a real Hunter. Together, the two of us can destroy Baron Balazs and the woman."

Without a sound, a writhing blackness spilled from the entrance to the chamber and inched toward D's feet—water. Galil had referred to them as the Dark Water Forces. Rising from a flow that couldn't have been more than a fraction of an inch deep, a number of lumps flowed determinedly toward D.

Leaving the two women there, D kicked off the ground. His coat sailed out like a pair of wings.

While it was unclear what he made of the Hunter hanging there like a supernatural bird about to descend on its prey, Galil commanded his men, "Get him!"

A number of the shadowy figures bounded to D's rear. In the time it took them to bring down their axes, a far swifter and more dazzling light zipped through them.

D landed some fifteen feet from Galil's subordinates.

"The three of them have also been given 'water warrior' abilities. Although not as perfected as myself, I dare say mere steel can't cut them down," Galil laughed snidely. His subordinates stood there arrogantly—the man had witnessed D's blade mowing through their torsos.

Without so much as looking at the opponents that surrounded him, D stepped forward. The trio was poised to follow after him. And at that moment, something incredible happened. Black water spurted out of the torso of each in all directions and the trio quickly lost their forms, reduced to a mysterious liquid that spread across the floor.

"My water warriors—have you cut down my water warriors, D?!"

D's blade slipped into the face of Galil, who was now as still as death, but the resistance it met only felt like water.

"You're wasting your time," Galil sneered, but he quickly abandoned this attitude.

Pressing his right hand to his face, Galil reeled backward. Black water was dripping through his fingers.

D's sword had sliced the impervious body of the liquid human.

Sensing another blow about to descend on him from above, Galil exclaimed, "Look behind you!"

The young man wasn't the kind to turn around at such a remark from an opponent. What stopped him in his tracks and stayed his blade was May's cramped cry of, "D!"

Both women had been seized by the head from behind, and the sharp blade of an ax rested against the throat of May and the heart of Miska.

May had been returned to a room in the old board-covered jail—a tower that hung out in the middle of the hollow—about twenty minutes after Galil summoned her to his room. The cells were side by side. While the Dark Water Forces member who'd brought her there was busy opening an antiquated lock, May took a look at Miska. The Noblewoman was slumped against the wall with her back to the girl.

"Are you okay?" May asked.

The acid may have only had an effect on the flesh of the Nobility, as there was no change in the clothes Miska wore.

She soon got her reply.

"What . . . what did you tell them?"

The way her voice tapered off at the end like someone dying terrified May.

"Nothing at all."

"You're lying . . . Surely you told them all about myself and the baron . . . you little traitor! Human beings . . . especially ones like you . . . are nothing but vulgar cretins . . ."

"No! I just listened to what the guy who caught us had to say—that man Galil."

"Galil . . . So, that's his name?"

The second May heard the Noblewoman's voice, she backed away.

"At present, my body is melted, and regeneration will take quite some time. However, when that has come to pass, I shall tear off his arms and legs and head with my own two hands."

"Stop it! If you do that—if you just keep the hate going back and forth, nothing will ever get any better!"

Once she'd spoken, the door to May's cell was opened.

The synthetic person quickly left again.

May tried desperately to get Miska to talk to her. Though she went over to the bars to make her entreaties, there was no reply. Muttering and pounding the wall, she'd already given up when one of the bricks her little fists hit seemed to slide back into the wall. On closer examination, she found that it could be removed without disturbing the mortar around it, and once the brick had been put back in place, no one would ever notice it. No doubt long ago, some prisoner confined to this cell had used it as a means of communicating with a friend in the adjacent cell, or had started it as part of an escape attempt.

"Are you okay? Are you in pain?" the girl inquired in a low voice so as not to be heard by the guards wherever they might be, but there was no reply.

Removing her locket and clutching it in one hand, May crept across the ground. The hole left by the removable brick was down at the same level as the floor. Her hand barely fit through it. Just for good measure, she put her arm in up to the elbow.

Suddenly something latched onto her wrist. More than the viselike pressure, it was the bone-chilling cold of those fingers that horrified May.

"That hurts . . . let go!"

"Such a warm hand you have," Miska remarked, a shadowy echo to her voice.

"So, you can still talk. That's good," the girl said with relief, and at the same time she got the feeling that the pressure on her wrist eased.

"What have we here?"

"There's medicine inside it. Hugh and I put it on when we take a spill doing our acrobatics. I don't know whether it'll work on your wounds or not—but that's all I have on me."

Silence descended.

A short while later, Miska said, "Do you not hate the Nobility?"

"Of course I do! My mother and father were both killed by your kind. It's only natural that I would."

"That being the case, is this medicine a poison?"

The Noblewoman's jeering tone enraged the girl.

"You'll find out just as soon as you put some on! I'm not the sort who could let a hurt and crying human—er, person—no, that's not right either . . . Anyway, I couldn't just stand back doing nothing. When a Noble finds one of their own kind in pain, I suppose they run right over and drain them of blood. But human beings aren't like that!"

Her wrist was gripped so painfully tight it seemed her hand would be torn off. But before she could let out a scream, the pressure vanished, and May reflexively drew her right hand back.

As if following it, the locket also slid across the floor.

Anger made her forget all about her pain.

"I'm only trying to help out, you stubborn goat! Just take it already," the girl said as she slid it back through.

It came right back.

"I can't believe this!" May said, and she slapped it through again.

It was a bizarre game being played through the wall.

"You're a stubborn little snip of a girl, aren't you?"

This time, it was a laugh that came through rather than the pendant making yet another trip.

"Hell, you're a lot more pigheaded than I am."

"Then I think perhaps I shall simply discard it over on this side," Miska said, her voice the very embodiment of cruelty.

"Do whatever you like, you idiot!" the girl shouted in a vexed tone, turning her face away. "You're wounded pretty badly. If you don't do anything about it, I'm sure it's gonna hurt, Noble or not. Why would you throw medicine away?" May said with a sudden sob as she wiped at her tears with one hand.

Just then, there was the sound of approaching footsteps.

Madly scrambling to put the brick back in place, the girl then leaned back against the wall and tried to look natural. And it was just in time, as several figures stood on the other side of the bars. The door was unlocked. Having heard the same sound from the next cell, May knew they must be calling on Miska as well.

"Wh—what do you want?" the girl asked, instinctively bracing herself while before her, a pair of Galil's froglike subordinates stepped to either side. The one on the right reached out to the left, the one on the left in turn reached out to the right, and a grayish membrane spread between their outstretched arms. Across its glistening wet surface crept a streak of watery fluid.

"Don't try anything funny with me. Just let me out of here!" the girl bellowed at them, though it seemed like even her words were going to be swallowed by the spreading grayness that approached her—but a split second before that could happen, the diminutive figure vaulted right over the thin membrane with unbelievable litheness. By the time the two subordinates had turned, she was already out through the cell door.

May turned left. Even at this point, she was still thinking about saving Miska.

A wall of black rose before her very eyes, and something came down with an intense strength on both the backpedaling girl's shoulders, stopping her dead.

"What a busy little heroine you are."

Looking up at the source of the words raining down on her, May felt all the strength drain from her body.

"Be still for a while. We merely need to take a mold of the two of you," Galil said calmly, the breath rasping noisily from his throat.

II

Glancing at the blades poised against the two women, D lashed out to the rear with his left hand.

Pierced through the wrist and eye by needles of unfinished wood, the water warriors reeled backward. Even Miska had been run through the heart!

"Have you lost your mind, Hunter?" Galil bellowed, his words like a curse, while May made a mad dash over to D. In her right hand she held a weapon that had belonged to their foes.

"D!"

Two streaks of light whizzed through the air, crossing paths.

May was split from the head to the crotch. Naturally, the Vampire Hunter knew that her blade had been aimed right at his back.

"How—how did you know?" Galil groaned as he retreated to the far side of the chamber.

There was no reply. But if D had answered him, it probably would've gone something like this: No Noble still physically intact would ever stand there like a statue, even in the grip of a water warrior. The reason D had left May for later was because he had not been able to tell whether she was the real thing or not. But once his opponent had shown her true colors, sneak attack or not, she was no match for D with his sword already drawn.

Galil's scheme had failed miserably.

"Come here, D!" Galil called out, his voice inviting the Hunter into the back room. "I have an opponent in here just for you."

The floor all around the Hunter was already covered by black water. The figure that leapt up from it to attack him was cut in half without so much as a sideward glance as D dashed along soundlessly.

His senses alerted him to a strange reaction. His blood flow was swiftly stagnating, and his limbs were growing heavier. Bubbles were rising from his gorgeous lips. Although nothing had visibly changed, D's surroundings had suddenly been transformed into water.

In his swaying field of view, there writhed a whitish shape. Some might've called it a gigantic jellyfish. Beneath an essentially flat umbrella was a blob of a body, and from that, hundreds or even thousands of threadlike tentacles swayed and wriggled as if in search of something.

"No matter how outstanding a Hunter you may be, being part Nobility, your offensive and defensive capabilities will come down a notch underwater," Galil's voice laughed aloud, though the man was nowhere to be seen. "This synthetic creature is able to alter any environment into the one that suits it best—water! You would do well to remember the name of the Kenlark. Say, if you don't hurry to the surface, you'll drown. This creature was originally developed with the baron in mind, but it would seem equally useful against dhampirs."

The tentacles reached out. Blue streaks ran through the creature's white, semitransparent core. Veins or nerves, dozens of them floated up like threads as they were severed by D's blade.

Through a painfully slow process, D finally worked his way under the Kenlark. The tentacles were roughly forty-five feet long, with the entire creature measuring over sixty feet in all.

The Hunter kicked off the floor hard. As he rose, it was just like he was floating to the surface.

Without warning, the resistance from the water vanished. The Kenlark had turned the area around D alone back into normal space.

Stopping for a second, D began to fall, but his hand caught hold of a tentacle.

"That's not good!" the same hand shouted.

In the blink of an eye, the hand let go.

The fall back to the floor should've been graceful, but his whole body twisted into a strange shape. Or rather, it was compacted. D got right back up again, but his proportions were strangely off.

"Can you keep hold of it?" he asked his left hand, but it wasn't clear exactly what he meant.

"Oh yeah," it replied, but before the reply had even finished, D jerked down with his left hand.

"Oh yeah!" the hand exclaimed once more, this time with astonishment.

Above D's head, the monster was pale and quivering like a veritable full moon beneath the sea, but its tentacles dropped off its torso with a rubbery snap.

Avoiding the falling tentacles without seeming to dodge them at all, D then heard someone call his name. Turning, he saw a tiny face peering down at him from the top of a lengthy spiral staircase.

"Up here! Come this way!"

A number of shadowy figures leapt at May from the black water, but struck by the rough wooden needles flying from D's left hand, they fell back into the depths from which they'd come.

Hurrying to the foot of the stairs, D raced up to where May was.

The Kenlark's head and torso were vanishing into the upper part of the chamber.

"Mr. D!" the girl cried, trying to give him a warm hug before he stopped her.

"Where's Miska?" he asked in a strangely heavy tone.

"Over there!" the girl replied, her cute little finger indicating one of the towers that hung in space like some sort of gourd or melon. "She's been burned and melted all over. Save her!"

"You'd better come with me," said the Hunter.

The two of them reached Miska's prison without any of their foes giving chase.

The door to May's cell was ajar.

"How did you get it open?" D inquired. This was rare for him.

"Earlier, when they were taking some weird kind of mold of me, I pretended to put up a struggle and lifted the keys off the guy that had them," May told him, her chest puffed with pride.

Though the keys were used to open the cell doors, they automatically locked again when closed. So it stood to reason that as they were leaving, her captors never even noticed the keys had been stolen.

"Oh, that's right. I got wrapped up in this odd membrane thingy. When I finally freed myself, there was a perfect impression of me left inside it. I don't know what they're gonna use it for, but be careful."

The copies of May and Miska created from that membrane had already fallen to D's blade.

D put his left hand to the iron bars—this prison was intended to hold humans. Miska had been put in it because Galil reasoned the horrible torture had left her with neither the physical strength nor the will to escape, and they must've planned on moving her to some other prison or destroying her later. As soon as the Hunter pulled with his left hand, the door flew off. The flying screws hit a distant wall, making a number of melodious sounds.

"Let's get out of here," said D.

Miska had her back to them, but she quickly got to her feet. She covered her face from the nose down with the sleeve of her dress. Even with the regenerative powers of the Nobility, her recovery would take a long time.

"Let's go!" May said, taking hold of her wrist.

The Noblewoman's hand was melted and misshapen with keloid-like scarring.

Miska batted away the girl's hand, snarling, "Unhand me, you filthy little beast!"

"Okay, you pigheaded jerk! I'll never bother saving you again." Face swollen indignantly, May then turned to D and said, "Let's go."

With D leading the way, the trio ran toward the stairs. It was only a second later that a roar echoed up below their feet.

Taking a peek out the door, D gauged the situation. The lower sections of the massive spiral staircase had broken off and fallen into the black water. The twisted wreckage was reminiscent of a gargantuan skeleton.

"Up!" D said, placing one foot on the remaining portion of the staircase. It was sixty feet down to the bottom. That wasn't too far to climb back down carrying two women. Not for D, anyway.

May shrieked, her cry flowing downward.

The floor of the prison undulated like a liquid, and the girl's legs sunk into it up to the knees.

Reaching out with his left hand to grab the girl's arm and pull her back up, the Hunter told her, "We've got to hurry."

D started to dash up the stairs. Although it was unclear just how old this staircase was, it ran up through the cavernous chamber in the tree, hanging from ceilings and walls, and with skinny passageways and rope bridges running off it.

"I can't do this anymore," May said, slumping back against the handrail after they'd climbed about three hundred feet.

"She's little more than a burden. I say leave her here, unless you fancy carrying her on your back," Miska spat.

Ordinarily, that's what D would've done. Instead, he asked her, "Can you stand?"

"Let me rest a bit. All I need is a minute," May replied, her answer broken by heavy breaths.

Looking down, Miska said, "Everything is rapidly turning into water. At this rate, we shall only have another thirty seconds."

She sounded amused. After all, she was indestructible.

"Okay. Let's go, then."

May stepped away from the railing—and stumbled. D was right by her side. She reached out for him, but as her hand touched his hip, it sank all the way into his solar plexus.

"Huh?!" May exclaimed, pulling her hand back a bit too forcefully. Once again she fell back against the handrail, but then there was the loud crash of something breaking, and her body suddenly sank.

That section of the antiquated handrail hadn't been able to bear the impact.

A cry rose from her—and was quickly cut short.

Grabbing the girl's belt to hoist her back up, D set her back down on the stairs.

"This is intriguing. It would appear you've been turned into water," Miska commented as she stared at D with blazing eyes.

So, the gorgeous Hunter's battle with the Kenlark had had fearsome consequences. Perhaps the secret of how the Kenlark could transform its surroundings into water lay in the tentacles D had seized. Surely the only thing that allowed D to retain his human shape was the Noble blood that flowed in his veins.

"But you were able to carry that brat with your left hand. Why is that?"

Ignoring Miska as she knit her delicate brow, D turned to May and gave a toss of his chin in the direction of the staircase leading upward.

Swaying weakly all the while, the girl began to climb the stairs. Although it had only been a brief rest, her steps were steadier than would be expected due to the way her acrobatic training had strengthened her heart and lungs. However, her feet had already turned to lead, and her heart was forgetting to beat. Before May had climbed another sixty feet, she threw in the towel.

"Oh . . . I can't do this anymore. Leave me . . . and go."

True to form, D neither replied to that nor offered her any encouragement, but he looked from the girl at his feet to a nearby catwalk.

At the other end of the walkway was a three-story building that jutted from the interior wall of the tree. So weathered that it seemed to have become part of the wall, the wooden door had a sign above it written in what appeared to be ancient symbols.

"We'll go in there," D said, making not only May's eyes go wide, but Miska's as well.

"What, are you kidding?!" the girl began to say, but the figure in black had already started across the catwalk.

Crafted of thin planks laid across a collection of logs, the walkway creaked disturbingly. Something that was either dust or sand rained from the bottom of it.

Halfway across, D turned to the women and said, "All three of us can't do this together. Once I'm across, you two can come."

And with that he took another step, but at that very instant there was the snap of a board breaking.

"Ah!" May gasped, but it was unclear whether it was a cry of disappointment at the way the walkway had broken in two, or one of admiration at the way the gorgeous figure had flown to the building's entrance like a black wind.

Breaking the door in with his left hand, D called out, "Head up, and I'll be right behind you," before he vanished into the darkness.

"You worthless cretin—saving your own skin," Miska snarled, her body quaking with rage.

"He wouldn't do that. Let's get going," May said as she looked up at the giant spiral that continued above them.

D must've found some definite form of salvation for them in that building. If not, he'd risk his own life defending them. When the catwalk gave way, he'd have undoubtedly sprung back to them instead of over to the building.

Unexpectedly grabbed about the waist, May found herself hoisted into the air.

"What are you—"

"What a nuisance you are! By rights, I should probably drop you to your death right now."

With the girl's face reflected in eyes ablaze with hate all the while, Miska began to climb the vast staircase with the light step of a Noble. And the stair her feet had just left collapsed into a shapeless mass.

III

Once D had left, the Nobleman had relocated as per his instructions, and another ten minutes after that, Taki had regained consciousness.

The baron had taken a sound-dampening fluid from his carriage and squirted it into her ears, as the sounds of the water harp continued.

"I was just—what happened to me?" Taki asked as she lay on a blanket that'd also come from the blue carriage.

The baron explained to her about the water harp and where D was. He then added, "It was me that our foes sought. I'm sure they'll come again. And I don't imagine merely changing our location will be enough to give them the slip."

"Are you talking about the same enemies that've been after you all along?"

"Yes. Assassins sent by my father."

"Your own father?!" Taki said, the breath knocked out of her. "How could he do such a thing?"

"Because I'm on my way to kill him."

Taki was at a loss for words.

"Get some rest. If there's any problem, give this a squeeze," the baron said as he handed her a cylindrical ultrasonic transmitter, and then he headed out of the room.

The second he closed the door, ultrasonic waves pierced his eardrums like a needle. Flying into the room in amazement, he found Taki standing bolt upright in front of the bed.

Eyeing the transmitter in her hand, he said, "Triggered it by mistake, did you?" and was about to leave again.

"No," Taki told him in a brooding tone.

The baron turned around.

"Then you did it on purpose?"

"Yes."

"There may be those among my enemies who can hear ultrasonic waves. No more playing around."

"I wasn't playing. I want to speak with you."

"With me?"

"You're not like any Noble I've ever heard of. Mr. D is a dhampir. However, you're pure Nobility. And yet, you try to defend the weak and the small, almost like you were human. I find that very puzzling."

"Wouldn't your fellow humans do the same?"

"No. I mean, you're trying to save a *human* child. We don't go around defending bugs."

"In that case, I suppose it would mean the Nobility truly created a higher civilization."

"What they needed wasn't ships capable of interstellar travel, element-converting contraptions, or buildings with half a million floors. It was something much simpler—a heart," Taki asserted, and then she wet her lips with her tongue. She was horribly thirsty. "The Nobility face an inevitable decline. If they'd had, say, thirty thousand more people like you, it might've been avoided."

The baron remained silent and motionless. From the window, the melody of the water harp could be heard.

"What'll you do next? After you've killed your father, I mean. Or perhaps you'll be the one who's destroyed," Taki said in a feverish tone while staring into the baron's eyes, as if both he and herself were melting in them.

The baron was just about to say something when the young woman's warm body was thrown against his chest with unexpected speed.

"I don't want you to die. Don't die, for my sake!"

"For your sake?"

The baron stared at the pale nape of Taki's neck, then raised one hand and touched his fingertips to the left side of her throat.

"Ah . . ." Taki gasped, her body trembling slightly.

"Though I may defend human children, I am still a Noble. I am no different from the other bloodsuckers your kind abhors. Do you know what kind of temptation I battle now just having you here before me?"

The Noble's fingertip was as cold as ice against her skin, and it made Taki fearful for the first time.

"The thought has crossed my mind before. Perhaps it would've been easier had I been an ordinary Noble. Why did I have to be this way?"

Taki said nothing. Her body had suddenly constricted—the baron's breath had fallen on her. And it was every bit as frigid as his finger.

"Your throat is so warm," said the baron.

When the Noble's lips pressed to her flesh, Taki fainted. Easily supporting the woman's form with one hand as all the strength drained from her, the baron took his lips away. Taki's throat didn't have a single mark on it.

There was a doleful cast to the baron's expression as he said softly, "I'm not to drink human blood. And on account of that, my father banished my mother and myself. If possible, I would've liked to have been an ordinary Noble."

Scooping Taki up in his arms and putting her back down on her bed on the floor, the baron then heard a knock at the front door.

Travelers? he thought. *My foes wouldn't have made a sound.*

It wouldn't have been unusual for travelers to take refuge in this house of worship until the downpour had stopped. But they posed a serious problem nonetheless.

A heavy bolt was across the door. In two or three minutes' time, they'd probably give up and leave.

The Nobleman's expectations proved correct. The shades were drawn on the windows. There was no need to worry about any light leaking out.

Checking to see that Taki was still sleeping, the baron was just about to leave the room when his ears caught another sound coming from a different direction. From above.

The house of worship was a three-story building. On the first and second floors, the windows were covered by iron bars to keep out the Nobility. But the uppermost floor had none. After all, no Noble would go to all the trouble of flying into the air to get to the aged priest who would've been the building's sole caretaker by night.

For upstanding travelers, this would also be an odd method of getting inside.

Partway up the staircase to the third floor, the baron halted. A man's voice echoed across the hallway above.

"Everyone's supposed to have fled this village. There shouldn't be anyone to bar the door from inside. So there's definitely gotta be someone in here."

"It sure would be nice if it was dancing girls out on tour or something like that. They could give us a topless show tonight," another man replied with a vulgar laugh, but it was suddenly cut short. The baron had shown himself, and no human could fail to recognize a Noble.

"No—Noble!" one of them shouted. The man's face and body were both quite angular.

The other was the exact opposite, flabby and round.

Both were covered from head to toe by vinyl rain gear, and they had knapsacklike devices strapped to their backs. They were individual flight packs—a means of transport even humans who lived in the Capital didn't see every day. Various types were available, such as jet engines, rockets, or ion-powered fliers, but from the look of things, the ones these two wore worked on magnetic force.

"Where did you come from?" the baron asked, and as soon as he did, the men both reached for their hips.

Once you came face to face with a Noble, no amount of running would help you get away. The only way for humans to defend their dignity was to fight and slay their opponent or to take their own lives. This rule of the Frontier lived in the hearts of the two men.

Looking at the fear-stricken faces and the sizable muzzles pointed in his direction, the baron said to them gently, "I'm not going to do anything."

His field of view was stained a burning-hot crimson. The two men had simultaneously discharged the contents of those muzzles— homemade firebombs. Right in the baron's face.

With one hand shielding his eyes, the Nobleman was instantly transformed into a man-shaped inferno. Based on kerosene and petroleum jelly supplemented by a number of chemical fuels, the firebombs sent seamless sheets of flames across the corridor and the wall.

The baron took a step forward. His blue cape spread like the wings of some demonic bird and struck a window. There was a loud explosion, and then the majority of the flames vanished without a trace.

Not surprisingly, the baron still had black smoke and little flames rising from various spots on him as he closed in on the two men, seized them by their throats, and hoisted them off the floor.

"Good Lo —"

"S-S-Save me!"

Lacquered with a mixture of despair, fear and cold sweat, their faces were only inches from the baron's when his charred visage swiftly reclaimed its beauty and the luster of the night.

"I believe I said I wasn't going to do anything. Those flight packs—where did you get them?"

In an instant, the life returned to the men's utterly hopeless expressions—they'd been reminded of the power of the mechanisms they wore on their backs. The remote-control switch was set in the right side of the harness.

It was as if the bodies of all three had lost all weight as they floated up to the ceiling.

"Split up!" the man on the right shouted.

By doing so, they'd leave the baron no choice but to let go of them. If he didn't, his arms would be ripped from his shoulders.

Thin smiles rose on the men's lips.

Who would've suspected the Noble would jerk both men back as they were about to go in different directions?

Fire seemed to shoot from the Noble's eyes. Slamming the backs of the men's heads together with terrific force to render them unconscious in midair, the baron then quickly snatched their remote controls and made a graceful landing.

On more intense questioning, the two explained that they'd come from the air terminal to the north of the village. The taking of the departure and arrival terminal had been the decisive blow in getting the Lesser Nobility that'd overseen the area to flee, and because of this, leaders at the revolutionary army's headquarters had ordered that nearby villages make an inspection and maintenance call on the facility once a year. This year, it was their village's turn, and after a month out on the job, today they were finally on their way home.

Constructed by the Nobility, the terminal continued to be automatically inspected and maintained, so their job consisted of merely checking to make sure the systems were still operating. There were even aircraft still stored in the hangars, and according to the machines that checked them, they were in perfect shape. If the group were to take to the skies, they could reach their destination far faster than by traveling overland.

With rain blowing in through the window as he gazed out at the darkness, the baron had a faraway look in his eye as he muttered, "Hurry back, D."

Those That Soar the Heavens

CHAPTER 4

I

Miska halted.

"What is it?" May inquired in spite of herself.

Less than ten minutes had passed since the Noblewoman had taken the girl under her arm and started to move. In lieu of a reply, Miska dropped May on the stairs. Truly a professional acrobat, the girl managed an effortless landing before a cry of despair slipped from her.

Roughly thirty feet ahead, the staircase broke off. As her eyes slid further up, they found that the stairs continued on again about sixty feet beyond that. Even for Miska the distance was probably too great. As an expert in the field of leaps and bounds, May understood that much at least.

"What should we do?" the girl said as she looked around. At this point, it was astounding that she didn't ask, "What are *you* gonna do?" But she wouldn't simply rely on Miska—this was how the girl had always lived.

Though they still had a bit of a lead on the liquefying staircase, it would only last a minute or two. While it wouldn't have been unusual to collapse into madness at this point, the girl said, "Look!"

Her cheery tone made Miska turn. There were ropes or vines hanging down from the ceiling in the direction May was pointing.

And the girl had noticed that one of them was some distance from the main cluster, hanging down by the stairway.

"I'm gonna jump over onto that. I'm sure that on your own you'll be able to reach the other side. That's the plan!"

"What foolishness!" Miska spat. "Indeed, I shall be able to make it. However, I have to wonder if your legs will carry *you* as far as the vine. It must be thirty feet."

"I can just barely make it," May said with a nod after eyeing the distance.

"What's more, that vine appears rather old and decrepit. Even supposing you were to reach it, it couldn't possibly support your full weight."

"Is that a fact? I'll have you know I'm an acrobat! And if I don't make it, at least you won't have to look at me anymore—isn't that right?" the girl said, feeling much better after getting that last dig in at the end.

May dropped all the way back to the wall. Even with a running start, she'd be cutting it close, but it didn't seem like she had enough room. If she were to really reach out her hands, she might barely get the vine. But if it were to snap right off at that point, there'd be no saving herself.

"Well, see you."

It was unclear whether the girl's remark was directed at Miska or at the gorgeous Hunter who hadn't made it there in time.

After the girl had dashed with all her might, her body was caught in midair, and a grunt escaped May from the tight grip around her waist as she whistled off in a different direction.

"Why?" she asked, her question unveiled in midair.

The reply came in midair, too.

"Be silent!"

While it was common knowledge that the power of a Noble by night far outstripped that of a human, there was of course some difference between Noblemen and Noblewomen. Sixty feet—such a distance would be tricky for a man, but Miska flew across it like a great white blossom. Her right hand caught hold of the handrail, and her feet came down on the edge of the stair—which collapsed completely!

May let out a shriek that was swallowed by the pit— but in mid-scream it stopped out of shock. The right hand that'd latched onto the railing was supporting the two of them. There was relief—and then May's ears caught the sound of the handrail cracking.

"Let go of me! We'll both fall!" the girl shouted, although even she didn't know why she'd said it. "Let go of me! Let go!"

"Be quiet for a moment," Miska said, her tone horribly calm.

Strength surged into her hand.

"Oof!" Miska groaned from the effort, though no one would've ever imagined the prim and proper Noblewoman was capable of making such a sound.

Every ounce of her strength was concentrated in her right hand.

The two bodies swung gracefully into the air, this time landing in a safe spot on the stairs.

"Oh my!" May exclaimed, collapsing in exhaustion on the spot.

Miska had released her.

What should the girl say? Was she surprised by all this? Or was she filled with admiration?

Training a fierce look of scorn on the girl, Miska sneered, "Do you now see the difference between human beings and the Nobility? Well, on your feet, then! Be quick about—"

The change in the Noblewoman's tone made May look up. And it came as little surprise that a gasp escaped her.

From the distant reaches of the spiral staircase, a creature that beggared description had descended. A spider. A tremendous arachnid more than fifteen feet long. Its ash-gray bristles stood out like needles, and its eight legs seemed to grow more animated as it spied the two of them. Perhaps it was the master of this colossal tree, as it had a number of broken spears and longsword blades stuck in its back and sides.

A rasping sound reached the two women's ears—the sound of breathing.

Out of the frying pan and into the fire—although it seemed they'd leapt into something a hundred times worse than any conflagration.

Miska stepped to the fore.

"What are you gonna do?"

May didn't ask what *they* would do this time. Not even the acrobat could think of anything she might do against this monstrosity.

Miska stared without a trace of fear into the unsettling eyes of the spider as it closed on the most delectable of prey, and when the creature had come to within fifteen feet of the women, the Noble raised her right hand high.

"Back!" she said in a high-spirited tone.

May watched dazedly as the spider's movements halted.

The Nobility could command wild beasts. Not that such creatures understood their words, but rather the communication came from a kind of telepathy.

"Stay just as you are," the Noblewoman commanded it, and then she told May, "Come with me."

She didn't even turn to look at the girl as she said it and then climbed the next step. Her pace was understandably swift, but she stood straight and tall, as one would expect of a Noblewoman. It was as if she didn't fear the massive arachnid at all. However, in her heart of hearts, Miska was actually terrified.

Although it was said the Nobility could command the lower beasts, that didn't necessary apply to every creature in creation. Upon sensing the slightest disruption in the will of a Noble, in many cases a vicious beast might suddenly break free of their control and bare its fangs. The woman's haughty demeanor now was purely a product of her Noble pride and nothing more.

They came before the spider. Its high arching legs were nearly thirty feet long, and they covered the staircase from side to side.

"You mustn't step on them," Miska said as she came to the side of the spider's head. Its reddish-brown eyes were focused intently on her. Though she had confidence that the spider's mind was under her control, Miska realized that her heart was racing wildly. Right in front of her, a shaggy leg arched high into the air. Merely touching even a single hair on it might bring the spider back to its senses.

The problem would be the space between the body and the legs. The spider's legs were bent in three or four places to form easy arcs, so the width wasn't a problem, but the height was low. Getting through them would necessitate bending down far, and if the women lost their balance, that would be the end of them. There were four legs on each side. Two-thirds of the staircase was covered by the spider's body.

Every nerve in the Noblewoman's body was focused on the tips of her toes. The tension made her movements stiff. She didn't want May behind her to see her moving so clumsily.

Miska's foot sank unexpectedly—part of the dilapidated staircase had given way under her weight. Her body was so tense, her nerves had never relayed the signs of danger.

Without thinking, Miska reached out for something to support her and found one of the spider's legs. But just as her fingers were about to touch it, Miska was bodily pulled back.

"Of all the—" May said, her plump face full of anger when the Noblewoman turned and looked at her. "Pull yourself together! Can't you even manage to climb a flight of stairs? This time, I'll go first."

Miska was speechless.

"I may not look it, but I'm an acrobat. I've done backflips on a wire strung over a nest of man-eating ants before. And the wire was covered with grease."

Crouching down low, the girl got in front of Miska, and true to her word, proceeded to slip right through the spider's legs.

Miska moved ahead at the same pace. She was desperate. No human being could surpass the Nobility. Slipping past the last leg, it took her no time at all to reach the tail end of the spider.

"Hey, not bad for a Noble!" May said, folding her arms as she gave an appreciative nod.

Miska looked down at her with utter loathing and said, "That's the last smart remark I shall take from you. Climb!"

"Yes, ma'am!" the girl said, doing a somersault. But that was where she got sloppy. When both her feet hit the floor, it gave way once more. Letting out a shriek as she twisted her body, she instinctively sought a safer spot on the opposite side of the staircase—and landed on the spider's back. It was a moment to chill her blood. May froze, forgetting that she should get off the creature as fast as possible.

A hand swiped out from one side to snatch the girl away and toss her down on the stairs.

Unable to even offer any protest, May stared up at the enormous arachnid. Its legs rustled with movement.

Miska brought one hand up to the base of her throat. She was fighting back a scream.

However, the creature's legs stabilized in their new positions, and it moved no more.

The two women let out long sighs in unison.

"Hurry—let's go."

May didn't give the Noblewoman any argument, but got right to her feet.

"Stupid human," Miska spat, and then a tiny spider dropped down from the ceiling and landed on her shoulder. "What in the—?!"

Put off balance by her frantic efforts to dislodge it, Miska brushed the gigantic spider's torso with one hand. That alone probably wouldn't have been enough to rouse the spider. But what Miska's hand came in contact with was the handle of a broken spear that was still lodged in the spider's body.

The spider leapt up—it sprang a good fifteen feet in the air with that one bound. Changing direction in midair, it brought its mandibles together as it touched back down. And caught in their viselike grip was Miska's torso.

Reeling backward without saying a word, the Noblewoman struck the beast with her fist, but its steely jaws didn't give an inch. Beneath them, a cavernous maw gaped blackly.

May kicked off the ground, soaring like a swallow in flight. Landing on top of the spider, she used both hands to seize the same spear Miska had just hit, driving it inward as hard as she could.

Now it was the spider's turn to taste hellish pain. Loosing a screech that was like steel raked across glass, it pulled in its legs.

As Miska fell to the ground, May shouted to her, "Run for it!"

Two of the spider's legs were dropping down at them from above. The monstrosity had hooked its limbs in directions they shouldn't have been able to turn. Latching onto May and raising her up, the creature brought her toward its mouth.

Miska didn't get up. Bright blood was seeping from her waist.

Out of the corner of her eye, May saw the black mandibles closing on her—and then they stopped abruptly.

Suddenly freed, May's body did a turn in midair before landing on the stairs.

The spider was twitching. A figure in black suddenly stood on top of it.

"D?!"

May could tell for sure it wasn't the liquefied D of a short while earlier, but rather the powerful Vampire Hunter she had known.

As D stood there in his longcoat with his sword planted in the creature's back, a whitish haze suddenly hid his form. The back of the spider had sent up thousands of threads. Changing direction in midair, they drifted down again, aiming directly for D. A number of strands adhered to the wall, which gave off white smoke and melted away. Apparently the threads had powerful adhesive and dissolving properties.

"D!" May shouted, but her cry was effaced by a whistling roar. The sound of wind.

Each and every one of the threads rose up, and a silvery flash shot through their base. May watched in amazement as the now-severed threads jumbled like thousands of white worms, spinning in a whirlwind as they vanished into the far reaches of space.

Perhaps its strength was spent, for the tremendous spider slumped down on the stairs and moved no more. May thought the

figure climbing down from its back looked like an angel in black.
How beautiful his face was.

"D—how did you get here?" the girl asked as she fought back tears.
"Are you okay?"

"Yeah."

"I was under the impression you had run off all alone. But it would
seem you've mistaken up for down," Miska said as she remained
lying there. Her white dress was stained with bright blood, and the
skirt portion had been ripped when the spider's mandibles released
her, leaving her pale thighs exposed in all their breathtaking allure.

D looked out into the cavernous gap in the tree. More specifically,
he was looking at the same vine May had targeted for her jump.

"So, you climbed that all the way up here. And you're back to
normal, I see," Miska remarked. Apparently she, too, found this
strange. As she concealed her lovely legs, she continued, "How
did you change back?"

Without reply, D extended his hand to Miska.

"Don't touch me!"

"We don't have any time. Look," D said as he turned around.
"The walls are melting."

The same power that had liquefied the staircase had now extended
to the walls, and it seemed it would turn the whole titanic bole into
water. D had been able to avoid that fate because, just as the sign
over the door had said, the room below had been a storehouse for
dirt and compost. In the room, D's left hand had consumed earth,
and then caused such a gust of wind that it lit up like a nuclear
reactor. Earth, wind, fire, and water—all that remained was water,
which D himself had become. The immortal energy his left hand
created was easily able to return D to his former state, and going
from a cable in that room to another rope, the Hunter had then
gone from the rope to the vine, barely arriving in time to rescue
the two women from danger.

"Everything down below has most likely dissolved already. Even
if we make it up higher, it will all change into water sooner or later.

What shall we do?" Miska asked with apparent delight, as if she wanted to lay bare D's dilemma.

The Noblewoman found her body rising effortlessly into the air. D had scooped her up in his arms.

"What are you doing?!"

"We're going up," D said, adding, "You were saved by a little human girl. How did that feel?"

A beastly growl started to rise from the depths of her throat, but Miska made no reply.

II

It was three hours later that they reached the top of the massive tree.

As they'd climbed, they'd been set upon by one bizarre life form after another. Gaseous creatures that each consisted of a vortex of countless gold flecks, two-headed monster birds, gigantic lightning-generating cats—each and every one of these ended up a stain on D's blade, although a surprise attack by baglike creatures that spewed toxic gas had felled Miska and May, so that when they finally did reach the tree's summit, D was carrying both women on his back.

The top of the tree had a domelike lid someone had constructed, yet it was still large enough to allow three or four people to pass at the same time. As the Hunter pushed the lid open, a cry of pain escaped Miska.

The air was tinged with blue, and a watery light was spreading across the eastern sky, and the morning breezes tousled the hair of the trio. They were up more than three thousand feet. The rain had abated. Both the forest below and the distant hills and plains were still sunken in darkness.

"We can't go any higher," Miska said from his back. Being a Noble, she was already recovering from the poisonous fumes.

"In that case, we have no choice but to get down," D said softly.

"That's fine for the two of us, but what about the girl?"

"Are you concerned?"

"Bite your tongue!" Miska replied, but as she did, she got the feeling she caught a bit of hoarse laughter. And it came from incredibly close at hand.

D quickly stood at the very edge of the treetop. The lower portions—everything up to three feet below them—had been transformed to water, and the massive bole swayed unsteadily.

"Grab hold of me," said D.

Apparently the whole purpose of climbing to the top of the tree was to get outside. However, while he and Miska could take a fall from a height of over three thousand feet, how would D ensure May's safety?

D threw himself over the edge. And the three of them dropped like a stone.

The wind snarled in D's ears as their velocity increased.

"Quite a ride," Miska remarked, one hand pressed to the cheek that faced east.

Immortal member of the Nobility or not, the woman still seemed to have nerves of steel. This was the kind of conversation only a Noble would engage in while whistling through the air.

"We shall reach the ground soon. What will you do about the girl?"

"Hold on tight," the Hunter told her.

The woods were drawing closer.

Miska shut her eyes.

The next instant, a terrific shock sent the trio flying upward.

Shooting up through branches and leaves, they flew out of the forest, and then were pulled back down again. Miska heard the sound of a tree trunk snapping. One of her arms was wound around D's neck, the other carried May like a bundle of firewood.

At the very least, the force of the impact should've been enough to crush the life out of D a thousand times over. When they finally stopped bouncing up and down, the Hunter's body listed to the right. They were falling in the same direction as the tree trunk—or so it seemed for a second—then D made a graceful turn and the trio landed on a bough in another massive tree.

Catching her breath on D's back, Miska then climbed down onto the branch.

"What did you use?" she asked. As her field of view was filled by the tree trunk that'd been knocked over as all its branches were snapped, she continued, "Did you wrap something around that tree to stop us?"

D raised his left hand. From it protruded the end of a thread so thin as to be almost invisible to the naked eye.

"And what is that?"

"The water harp."

Taking it in hand for closer scrutiny, the Noblewoman remarked, "This? Well, I warrant something like this wouldn't break even from that velocity. You certainly take the most absurd chances, leaping from a height of three thousand feet."

As Miska looked back and forth between the thread and the gigantic tree, not knowing that the former had also been used to slice through the water-transforming Kenlark's body, D told her, "The sun's coming up. We'll have to hurry back."

It was two hours later that the carriages left the deserted village. Although the ground was still wet beneath an unbelievably clear sky, D surmised that since the enemy commander Galil had been dealt a harsh blow, the danger had passed for the time being. Their destination was the airfield to the north. By the time D returned with Miska and May, the pair from the arrival terminal was no longer there. The baron explained that they'd run off hale and hearty.

That's not to say the inhabitants of their village won't come and attack us. The faster we can set out, the better, he urged D from inside his coffin.

The village of Krauhausen was still a long way off, and a new foe had appeared, but as D sat on his horse, his eyes were cool and clear.

Soon after passing through the village outskirts, they hit the main road. Up in the driver's seat of the baron's carriage, May had her face buried in Taki's chest. The whole dramatic rescue of the past night had wrought serious damage on the girl, both physically and mentally. When May—as if waking from a nightmare—opened her eyes wide from her stupor, Taki looked down at her with sadness in her gaze. On meeting the girl's frightened eyes, she gave her a kind nod.

"I wonder if maybe Hugh's never coming back," May finally said weakly after they'd driven on under the blue sky for nearly two hours without her saying a word.

"I'm sure he's perfectly safe."

"How do you know?"

"I just do," Taki said firmly.

Her tone made it seem more than just a theory, and that put May at ease.

"Yeah, I'm sure you're right. He's always been a lucky one. And I'm sure he is now, too."

"Of course. You're exhausted. Try to get some rest."

But after saying this, the young woman noticed that May's gaze wasn't directed at her. Beside the driver's seat rode a young man so gorgeous he left people fumbling for words despite themselves. And even Taki knew what that look had to mean. The girl sought the assurance of someone strong.

"Say, D. May here is worried about Hugh. Tell her he'll be fine."

There was no reply. Not because he didn't know what Hugh's fate was, but because the brother and sister had no bearing on D—if anything, you could say they were simply trouble.

Taki let out a sigh tinged with a fair amount of anger. "Oh, that's right. Last night, you didn't go out to rescue this girl, but to get the Noblewoman who'd been abducted. Isn't that right?"

She said that because that much she understood. The dashing young man was not her or the girl's bodyguard.

Moving north after leaving the village, they'd come to a stretch of reinforced plastic pavement after about a mile and a quarter. The melted areas that dotted it were no doubt the remains of human destruction. Apparently quite some time had passed since the automatic repair systems had ceased functioning. D had his mount galloping at full speed. Their foes would be waiting somewhere with glittering eyes.

Though the gates to the airfield were secured, their electronic locks opened with a key the baron had taken from the men the previous night.

Upon entering the site, Taki looked around as if in a daze.

"Dear lord," she exclaimed, her eyes going wide.

The vastness of the place was astounding to a human being. It didn't seem like this could simply be an arrival and departure terminal. As the existing land alone had been insufficient for the enormous structure, mountains to both the east and the west were also carved open. Tracks for super-high-speed linear motor transports ran the length and breadth of the place, yet still didn't seem to be an impediment to the oversized aircraft looming here and there. But Taki simply couldn't understand the control tower and something resembling a radar array, both of which were a blur in the distance.

Climbing back into the driver's seat with a firmed resolve, the young woman said to D as they headed for the nearest aircraft, "I wonder why they built such a huge complex?"

It sounded more like she was thinking out loud. For she was afraid she wouldn't receive a reply.

Unexpectedly, she did indeed get an answer.

"It's a reflection of their minds. From the time they began to see the decline of their race, the Nobility moved toward making their buildings so large it defied common sense. It might be best to call it the death throes of their collective psyche."

"So this was their last grab at glory—something like that?"

"I suppose it was," the young man said. His tone made Taki think of ice, and she sensed a weariness in it that took her breath away.

Realizing they were on the road to extinction, the Nobility strove to construct enormous buildings to stave off their decline—as if to make them forget their own fate. A number of new interstellar routes had opened, and explorers had set out on voyages beyond our own galaxy. When the Nobility dragged part of an extremely ancient sunken continent out of the sea, no doubt some of their kind must've believed their twilight had been pushed far off into the distance. However, there was at present no sign of any living creature at the vast arrival terminal as the automated maintenance systems alone mutely continued their labors. The Travelers Center into which they stepped was devoid of people or even so much as a speck of dust, its cleanliness a testament to long years of futility.

So, the party's over, is it, D? the baron inquired. It wasn't clear whether this was merely conjecture or if he could actually see it.

Giving no reply, D got down off his horse when the carriages reached the center of a tremendous hall.

"Wait a second," the Hunter told them as he headed for a door toward the back.

"I'm going too," Taki said as she got out of the driver's seat.

May was sleeping soundly. And there was nothing to fear from the baron or Miska.

The second they stepped through the door and into the structure, the two of them were enveloped by darkness. Simultaneously, the lights came on. Taki felt like she was out in the middle of the night.

"What happened?"

"The main computer has produced an artificial night for its guests. Originally, it probably maintained these settings day and night, but to conserve energy, the circuits only kick in when there are visitors."

"You don't say! I wonder how many years it's been?"

There was no reply.

Staring at D's profile as she thought about rephrasing the question, Taki held her tongue. It was easy enough to glimpse the pain and sadness in the shadows that carved his stunningly handsome features. But it was their depth that had kept Taki from speaking.

"D—are you troubled by the Nobility's decline?"

Having said that, the young woman then thought her heart might freeze solid, yet D made no reply as he climbed into the vehicle at the end of the corridor.

"This is the control center," he told her.

"Identification card please," a mechanical voice chimed. "This is the most critical area of the complex. Even terminal VIPs cannot enter without a card."

Taki gazed at D.

D pressed the palm of his left hand against the entry slot on the control panel.

"Qualified VIP status acknowledged. Please forgive my impertinence."

Taki's eyes bulged with disbelief.

Just a few seconds after the vehicle rushed into motion, the voice informed them, "This is the center. Five hundredth floor."

Once again the young woman's eyes bugged.

Whether ordered by D without Taki realizing it or through the power of his mysterious left hand, the vehicle glided down the corridors of the vast center and was swallowed by a white door. Aside from the white light, Taki couldn't discern anything. Even D's form beside her melted into the glow.

"Welcome to the main control room," a crisp female voice called to them from nowhere in particular. It was computer synthesized.

Taki envisioned a cold and intelligent beauty scrutinizing them from somewhere.

"You are the first guests I've had in five thousand and one years, two hundred and ninety-eight days. And such a regal visitor; I must prostrate myself before you. Kindly convey your every wish to me."

"I'd like you to calculate the gross weight of those in the carriages in the main hall plus the two of us and prepare a suitable aircraft. Posthaste."

"Understood."

"One thing more. A cyborg horse of the highest grade."

"Understood. Please return to the hall. All shall be prepared in accordance with your instructions."

As they were headed back to the transport, Taki called out somewhat impatiently, "D—who or what are you? You get the run of the place in an area where even VIPs can't go. The main computer obeys your every command without so much as an 'if' or a 'but.' No ordinary Noble could do that."

Not saying a word, D gestured to the transport.

Obviously the motion indicated she should get in, but Taki wouldn't move. Her visions of D's true nature had even made her forget how afraid she should be of disobeying him.

"Dhampirs have a Noble as one parent . . . D, could it be that your parent was—"

"Get in," the Hunter said, his tone of ice and snow crushing Taki's will to pieces.

III

When the pair returned to the hall, they were greeted by the baron and Miska. Ordinarily, when the actual time was day, Nobles couldn't even move around in darkened places. Although it was clear the baron was somewhat special in that regard, Miska may have been aided by the power of the Destroyer.

Taking a peek into the other carriage, Miska saw that May wasn't there.

"Before I came out, she said she was going to have a look around and got out of the carriage," said the baron.

"That's not good. I'll have to go look for her," said an apprehensive-looking Taki.

To which Miska remarked with loathing, "What pleasure could a lowly human find in exploring the Nobility's complex? Either she shall soon be back, or else she's lost her way and is blubbering somewhere. Why don't you go find her so the two of you can enjoy a good cry together?"

Taki was glaring indignantly at the pale beauty when a female voice from above inquired, "How may I assist you?"

Lowering his left hand, D said, "A human girl has wandered off in the complex. Do you know where she is?"

"She is in the outer terminal. Go outside and proceed north for approximately fifteen hundred feet and you should find her headed in the same direction."

"Thank you for your help."

"Don't be absurd. Please feel free to call on me for whatever you require."

The voice faded, leaving only astonishment in the hall.

"This is quite a surprise," the baron said with great relish. "That was the voice of a special class-A computer. They have as much pride as any person. She'd never be so subservient to ordinary Nobility. D—who are you?"

Naturally, there was no reply, and even Miska could only stare at D in an absent-minded daze.

D went outside without saying a word. In a landing space about three hundred feet ahead of him, a silver craft lay on its side. Although its stocky exterior could never be described as sleek, the ion engines slung beneath the little wings jutting from the craft spoke volumes about its flight capabilities.

D headed north on foot. And he did indeed see May about fifteen hundred feet ahead of him. The only thing that didn't jibe with the computer's description was the fact that she wasn't moving. She was rooted in place, and before her stood a figure in black. A bit larger than D and a head taller—you could say it was a giant.

Sprinting forward, D left the wind churning in his wake.

May was quickly scooped up. In the giant's hands, the girl's form looked heartbreakingly tiny and frail.

D halted about six feet shy of the towering figure.

There was no murderous intent. Nor was there any tension. Between the two of them lay a void immeasurable to anyone else.

"It can't be . . ." a hoarse voice muttered, but whether that reached the ears of the pair was open to debate. "Could it be . . . *him* . . . here?"

The voice streamed in a gentle arc before stopping. D had raised his left hand and extended it to May.

The gigantic figure didn't react immediately. The almost imperceptible wind rustled his wild jungle of hair and tore mercilessly at the sleeves of the black coat that nestled May, exposing the garment's red lining. Looming over D like some tremendous mountain, the figure seemed rooted to the expanse of concrete.

The giant's upper body trembled slightly, and then May was resting in the crook of D's left arm.

At that moment, D heard footsteps behind him.

"D! What's the matter?!" Taki asked the Hunter as she halted beside him and caught her breath. She'd come out in search of May.

Taking his eyes off the endless expanse of the arrival terminal, D passed May to the young woman. There was a melancholy to the young man that anyone who knew his usual demeanor would've found unimaginable.

"D, the baron's—" she started to say.

"You go on ahead," said D. His voice held a flat rejection in it. He didn't even seem conscious of his own words as his beautiful eyes remained concentrated intently on the spot where the massive figure had been before it disappeared.

Taki left without saying another word.

After they'd gone about fifty yards, she asked May what, if anything, had happened.

"This big person picked me up! And then Mr. D came."

"Was it a Noble?" Taki asked, the color swiftly draining from her countenance. If there were more Nobility at the terminal than just the baron and Miska . . .

"I don't know. But he was really big! And I wasn't the least bit scared."

"In that case . . . I guess he must've been something else."

Just as Taki turned to look at D despite herself, the girl blurted out the strangest thing. And after saying it, it was May herself who was surely the most upset. This was a result of Taki's expression and tone of voice when she turned to face the girl again.

"What did you just say?"

The young woman's voice had a ring to it that made it seem like she, too, had been transformed into a Noble, and it frightened the girl.

What May had said was, "I couldn't see his face, and he wasn't the same type at all—but somehow, he seemed just like D."

And there was one more thing that left Taki terrified as well.

When the two girls returned to the hall, there was no sign of the carriages, the baron, or Miska. They'd suddenly disappeared.

Soon after the two girls had gone, D's left hand asked, "Was it *him?*"

"Probably."

"Probably? You mean to tell me you don't know your own—"

The voice was cut off there.

His left hand still balled in a tight fist, D asked, "Where did that man go to just now?"

The reply came immediately.

"Whomever could you mean?"

"Do even the computers here play games?"

"Pardon me, but I cannot comprehend your question."

Saying nothing further, D returned to the hall. And there he found that everyone—Taki and May included—had vanished.

"Where did they go?" he asked, but there was no reply. "Answer me!"

"I cannot disobey that order. I shall give you an answer. They've been imprisoned in a given location," the computer replied, the adoring tone of the voice making the information it conveyed all the more shocking.

"Why?"

"In order to keep you here in this terminal."

"How long?"

"Forever."

"If I'll stay, will you let the rest go?"

"I promise."

"Tell me why."

"Actually—" the female voice said, the words vanishing into space. She hadn't decided against finishing the reply, but rather it had been cut off by an impossible swell of emotion. She was moved.

D noticed someone approaching from the depths of the hall. It was the same gigantic figure again. Disheveled was the best way to describe his hair, and as always, it fluttered in the wind. It almost looked as if the winds were generated by the violent emotions the giant kept in check. Lips that seemed lacquered with darkness opened. And surely enough it was darkness that packed his maw.

D appeared to be waiting for the words that would spill from it.

The wind howled. The giant had just expelled the air from his lungs.

Like someone speaking for the first time in his life, the giant coughed. It was a short time more before a creak of a voice escaped him.

"D . . . D . . ."

When D bounded, it looked as if it were out of anger at having his name said that way.

"Wait!" said a voice that belonged to neither of the men, and the giant leapt back a good fifteen feet without making a sound, his cape spreading wide in the process.

D crouched reflexively, the blade he'd just brought down now held out perfectly straight in front of him. Around them, the walls and doors collapsed like something out of a dream. The winds whipped up by that cape had the power to corrode anything. Just before the wind could hit the Hunter it was hewn in two by his blade, while D waited for the moment the giant's cape stopped moving to hurl a rough wooden needle. While the giant caught it in one hand, D leapt forward with his sword, and this time he split the other man from the top of his head to the end of his chin. Astonishingly enough, this seemed to be enough to destroy the behemoth. His form distorted, twisting, and by the time it hit the floor it no longer resembled anything human, transformed instead into an amalgamation of countless substances.

"Synthetic proteins, reconstructed muscle—the internal organs are all artificial, too. I'm surprised this thing was able to dodge your first blow," a hoarse voice remarked with amazement.

"Not so surprising for *him*," D replied.

The hoarse voice's silence signaled its agreement, for the source of that voice was also well acquainted with the man they referred to only as "him."

Sheathing his blade, D asked, "So, do you have any more of *him*?"

There was silence.

"Answer me. Where are the others?"

His face was bleached white—the false night had been lost. The lighting faded, and the true sunlight threw a lengthy shadow of D across the floor.

"Lousy computer!" the hoarse voice snapped. "Looks like it's cut its own circuits, eh? You know the saying, dead men tell no tales."

"Do you know where it is?"

"In the main control room, I suppose. You know, five hundred stories up."

Ignoring the sarcastic tone, D walked toward the door in the back.

"That was just a cheap copy of him," the voice continued without flinching. "But it wasn't the same one you ran into the first time. Watch yourself. Seems there are more of him around."

"Why are they after me?" D muttered as he halted in front of the elevator.

The voice fell silent at that, as if dumbfounded. "Why, that's easy—because you're—"

Here it took a deep breath.

"But wait—You know, come to think of it, he's never made a move against you. And then to go to all the trouble of making them look just like himself, it's really—"

D's left hand was crushed against the power circuits for the elevator system, for which D had found and opened the compartment. Pale blue sparks flew, and the infusion of this external power made the elevator control system ignore its instructions from the computer and go back into operation.

Several seconds later, D got off on the five hundredth floor.

IV

The room that had been swimming in light was now submerged in a feeble darkness. Looking around from the doorway, D then proceeded to the center of the room. Apparently he could discern the layout of the control center at a glance.

The end of a four-inch cylinder was set in the middle of the floor.

"Can you do it?" asked D.

"You got dirt?"

Taking black earth from his coat pocket, D piled it in the palm of his left hand. The soil was quickly inhaled, and the tiny mouth that appeared from below it let a satisfied belch escape.

"Next comes the water, you know."

Raising the hand that had both eyes and a nose, D put his index finger against his right wrist and pulled. The fresh blood that spouted from him was sucked up to the very last drop.

"Not much we can do about fire and wind. But I suppose I'll manage somehow."

Before the dissatisfied voice had finished speaking, D pressed his left hand to the end of the cylinder. In about two seconds there was light.

"Okay! The circuits are connected. Now to check out the plans of the place."

A pale blue tint mixed with the white light. It came from the wall to the right.

Staring at the map rendered there by luminous lines and dots, the Hunter said, "I see. Break out the schematics of the computer's circuitry."

"Aren't you the slave driver."

At the same time as his left hand made its remark, the diagram changed. The circuitry schematics seemed like they'd be indecipherable even to a computer, but after scanning them for a few more seconds, the Hunter said, "Link the North 289450772 and the South QB lines both to D-XII, D-XX, and D-Z04."

"Aye aye!"

The lights flashed unexpectedly.

Poised with his left hand still pressed to the floor, D turned and looked at the door.

The flickering lights made the giant stand out starkly and melt into the darkness by turns.

"It would appear the computer's playing tricks on us," said the baron.

Beside him and looking up at the heavens, Miska nodded, while May and Taki glanced at each other. Even their horses and carriages were there.

The whole group was sealed away inside a cylinder of light. Though it was bright, the glow that illuminated both the earth below and the heavens above was gentle, never harsh enough to hurt their eyes.

All the lighting in the hall had gone out at once, and the floor beneath them had seemed to shake ever so slightly, and then they were here. First had been the baron and Miska, while Taki and May had joined them twenty minutes later.

Another thirty minutes had passed, and after trying a number of things, they'd come to understand their prison for the most part. When they touched the light, it would push far back. And it wasn't merely one section of the wall that stretched, but rather the entire space grew in a perfectly circular fashion. In theory, if the space kept expanding the further they went, then sooner or later they should be able to get out. And that's precisely what they thought. When Taki touched it, the glowing wall expanded as if fleeing from her. However, the young woman returned again after about ten minutes. There was no end to it. The baron then got into his carriage and raced off, only to learn the same thing.

"It seems we've been imprisoned in an omnidirectional pocket. The glowing wall forms a three-dimensional space and prevents us from being sucked into that multidimensional region. In a manner of speaking, it's not so much a wall to keep us in as it is a stronghold to protect us."

"There must be some way out, is there not?" Miska asked, adding, "And who on earth would do such a thing?"

Her eyes glowed with malevolence.

The answer to that question was the same thing the baron had said a short time earlier.

"What leads you to believe this?" asked the Noblewoman.

"Who aside from us would want to do such a thing? If it wasn't D, then there's only one other thing around here that possesses a will of its own. And though it may belong to a machine, it is a consciousness just the same."

"So you mean to say we shall be stuck for as long as it suits the computer?"

"I'm afraid so," the baron said with an impassive nod. "But I'm not out on a leisurely excursion where I can just sit here and wait for help to come. We must escape."

"How shall you do that?"

The baron looked up at the ceiling. His face was bleached by the light that poured down.

"Even when the borders expand, the center remains the same. Let's try focusing our energy on that point."

"You mean that of the carriages, do you not?"

"No. While they may have power, it doesn't have the right quality. What we need is the energy of the Nobility. That alone can cause a computer built by the Nobility to capitulate. However, in order to do that—"

When the baron's eyes slid past Miska to focus on Taki and May, the two girls backed away without saying a word.

For it was their throats that drew the baron's gaze.

†

"Ah, D!" the giant in black called out. His pronunciation of the name was far crisper than that of the one the Hunter had destroyed.

"What are you?" D inquired softly. This was the tone of voice he used with a foe he'd never seen before.

"Why have you—awakened me?"

"Me?" D replied, seeming to find the question strange.

"I should have slumbered here forever. And yet—"

"What are you?"

The giant had no reply to that.

"Who made you? The computer?"

"D!" the giant shouted, kicking off the ground. His cape spread like wings, making him look like some enormous black bird out of the underworld.

D's blade made an effortless slice through his foe's body. However, D didn't even turn to see what became of the giant as he touched down behind him, and a red mist enveloped the Hunter. It was bright blood spraying from every pore on his body.

The giant took a smooth step forward to prepare for another leap, and D spun around. His left hand was still set against the floor. His pose left him at a terrible disadvantage.

"Stop it," a female voice cried from nowhere in particular. It belonged to the computer. However, it wasn't the same female voice as before.

The giant came to a standstill, and even D stopped for a second.

"That's the voice of—" D's left hand was heard to say in a tone some might even call fearful.

"Please, stop it, both of you," the voice continued.

But D's body took to the air, every bit as much a supernatural bird as the giant's. And a horizontal swipe of his sword removed the larger man's head. No gory spray went up as the massive form fell, the head bouncing once before landing on top of the corpse, and then both parts crumbled like dried clay.

Planting his sword on the floor and using it to prop himself up, D got back to his feet.

"What a thing to do . . . You're even more frightening than I thought," said a doleful voice that made D look up.

"Was that your voice?" he inquired, his tone the same steely one as always.

The female voice had gone back to the earlier version.

"No, I merely reproduced it with help from the great one."

The Hunter said nothing.

"Five thousand years ago, he honored us with his presence," said the computer.

He'd only remained there a few hours. For him, this had been no more than the place where he would begin a journey to the next continent. However, not even he could've predicted the haunting results of that visit—the arrival and departure terminal's computer had fallen in love with him during the few short hours he was there.

"Though I knew there was much to be feared, I wanted to learn everything about him, such as the voice you just heard and various other things as well. I may have been mistaken. The data input was gleaned from the memories of that great man I was never to see again, and I ultimately undertook a horrible course of action."

In other words, it had re-created him.

"Needless to say, it was impossible to make an exact copy. But I wanted to make it as much like him as I could. That's the reason why you've seen two of them here."

And for five millennia, the computer had remained nestled close to the one it loved.

And then D had come.

"He said that I woke him up."

"I tried my best to accurately reproduce the great man himself. Perhaps it was a result of that. He had also told me about you. That being the case, it wouldn't be at all strange if the great men

that I created were to detect your feelings and be roused by them. Your feelings of hatred, that is."

D stood there quietly.

After a while, the Hunter asked in a voice more suited to darkness than light, "Why did you try to keep me here?"

"Don't you see?" the female voice said, sounding so sad. "You and he are so—"

A metallic sound mixed with the words.

"Please, go. Quickly! Your colleagues have escaped. Their methods, it would seem, were a bit rough. They made a tunnel in the omnidirectional field that has reversed the flow of the imprisoning energies. To be precise, in another fifty-nine seconds, this terminal will be utterly destroyed."

This wasn't enough time to make use of any of the aircraft.

"Outside, there's another of the great ones I created. However, there's one thing you mustn't forget. It was you, D, that brought them back to life."

D left the room without making a sound and returned to the hall via the transport.

The giant's cape fluttered in the breeze. It was tousled by the winds of destruction. Had he, too, been summoned by D?

"This one's the closest of all to *him*," said the voice from the Hunter's left hand.

In both power and abilities, it seemed.

There was a sword in D's hand.

The lights flickered madly. They were replaced by interlacing darkness and light. The moment of truth had come for the departure and arrival terminal.

"D! Come with me!" the giant shouted—and then he turned.

It looked as if the figure in blue had always been standing there with the carriages behind him in the strobing lights of the hall.

The giant twisted his body, his cape spinning out.

In response, a streak of light shot from the baron's cape. The light that split the giant lengthwise quickly grew thicker, knocking the enormous form in black to the floor.

"Even you couldn't drop him with one shot, yet he—" the Hunter's left hand remarked in a dazed tone.

"Go back to your carriage," D said as he walked over to the new cyborg horse beside the baron.

As they galloped away at full speed through the sunlight, D turned and looked back at the terminal. A dome-shaped light was swallowing everything in its glow. Looking to be several miles high, the massive bowl maintained a surprisingly gentle glow, and just as D and the others were about to make a turn in the road, it suddenly vanished. D made the turn, never to know what remained behind.

Once they'd returned to the normal road, D had a question for the baron as he lay in his coffin.

"How did you escape?"

"By drinking blood. Now, don't do anything rash," the Nobleman added quickly. "It was my own blood, you see. I believe that's in keeping with our agreement."

D said nothing as he gave a kick to his horse's flanks. A burst of speed put him out ahead of the carriages.

Up in the driver's seat, Taki and May looked completely spent.

Horsemen of the Apocalypse

CHAPTER 5

I

The group raced on without respite until nearly noon.

The forest scenery to either side of them suddenly changed—a vast expanse of earth and sky that greeted their eyes. If one looked hard enough, a number of brownish dust clouds could be seen in the distance, but like heat shimmers, they would waver and fade.

It was dark. Even though the sun was shining, it was somehow gloomy.

"I bet this is an ancient OSB battlefield," Taki muttered, her tone seeming shadowy.

Looking around from the driver's seat, it was easy enough to find harshly glinting spots here and there in the yellow earth. These days, there weren't many travelers that knew those were places that'd been struck by heat rays in excess of a million degrees and fused into glass.

As the carriage advanced, bizarre remnants appeared like mirages in scattered places across the vast landscape. A structure with ramparts and towers on the brink of collapse. A robotic figure with titanic arms that looked like they could easily level entire mountains. Some sort of aircraft that had obviously gone up in flames.

Even dozing May opened her eyes wide at these sights, staring at them without moving a muscle. From time to time, a purplish light glowed in the recesses of her eyes. Streaks of lightning linked heaven and earth.

"What are those?" asked the young woman.

"OSB groundsweepers. By the look of it, they're still alive after five thousand years."

From D's tone, it was easy enough for even Taki to get an idea of how mind-numbingly long that actually was.

It may well have been fortunate for the human race that when the OSB—Outer Space Beings—came to invade, the planet was under the Nobility's rule. Fueled by a super-science some would only term sorcery, the conflict covered the entire face of the planet—land and sea alike—and it was said that this was one remote cause of the Nobility's decline. The OSB offensive grew fiercer in the latter half of the fifth millennium, their attacks founded on a science entirely unlike that of the Nobility, and due to that they proved extremely effective. A number of continents sank into the sea, and Noble bases across the solar system were reduced to ash. Following that, the Nobility began a thousand-year counteroffensive, and after another millennium of stalemate, the OSB then suddenly left the galaxy. "The reason for this is unclear," said the Nobility's historical accounts. The surface of the world was left with the ruins of an atomic war and the remnants of great mountain chains, but in time those were buried by wind and sand. This plain was one of only a few such spots that remained. Even many among the Nobility didn't know of those locations.

The girl shuddered in Taki's arms.

"It's horrible, just horrible!" said May. "I wonder if they're gonna come and attack us."

"It's okay. They're all just remnants of the past. Just stuff that rotted away ages ago."

But even as Taki tried to console her, the girl continued to quake.

D, the baron said, his voice resounding in the Hunter's brain. *Be careful. This plain is dangerous. They're still alive.*

"I realize that," D replied.

As usual, neither Taki nor May was privy to their singular conversation.

Ultimately, we never did learn the reason for the battle between the OSB and the ancient Nobility. Until they pulled out of our galaxy, the fight went on out of pure malice

"And now malice alone remains. For all eternity," D said as he looked up.

High in the blue sky—judging from the size, it must've been up about a thousand feet—a bi-wing aircraft flew at a leisurely pace.

"You see that?" D asked.

I see it, the baron replied, his answer every bit as astounding as the Hunter's question was bold.

D noticed that it was exactly the same design as the phantom aircraft the magician had used to lure away Hugh. The assassin must've decided to let his wounds heal from his battles with D and the baron and race on ahead instead.

"Why, that's—that's Lord Johann!" Taki exclaimed.

She'd noticed the aircraft as well after following D's gaze. From the bottom of her field of view, a flash of blue light shot up. Before she could even gasp, the aircraft had been run through and was quickly engulfed by flames, its nose dipping badly as it began to come down.

A pillar of flames went up from a spot that couldn't have been much more than half a mile from the road.

Ordering Taki and May to get in the carriage, D wheeled his mount around.

As the horse and rider departed, Taki watched in silence. She was sure D wasn't headed off out of concern for Hugh's safety. He would see whether or not Lord Johann had survived, and if the old man still lived, the Hunter intended to rectify that situation.

"That scares me . . ." the young woman muttered.

D arrived at the ruins of an enormous installation—what seemed to be the remains of a factory. Ages had passed since its decay. The wind that blew by told him so. It was impossible to say if the pillars tilting off at angles and pointing to the sky had originally been round or square. And from D's position, there was no telling how long they were—three thousand feet at the very least.

Half of the aircraft that'd fallen in the valley formed by these enormous columns had already burned up.

Up on his mount, D looked out in all directions. Aside from the wind, there was no sound at all. D closed his eyes. He had no choice now but to try to sense some presence.

Something moved off in the distance on the left-hand side. At the base of one of the columns, a circular maw gaped. It was a good fifteen feet high, and darkness filled its interior. From there to a spot about fifteen feet away the ground was littered with black spots. The pilot had fled even though he was bleeding. The reason for this went without saying. He feared his pursuer.

D rode his horse into the darkness.

What sort of twisted psyche had made this nightmare? Although it was clearly a piece of machinery, at the same time, it was also a creature that had expired.

The perfect fusion of organs and machinery in a living being— this was how the Nobility had responded to their foes from the stars. They created a superior life form imbued with both their own indestructibility and the power of a machine.

Who would've believed that the transparent tube that ran across the wall some fifteen hundred feet ahead of D was actually a human blood vessel? Made of dozens of three-foot-wide tubes woven together, it served the same purpose now that it had in the distant past, a little dusty but otherwise unharmed. The tube ran horizontally for fifteen hundred feet before it suddenly became a hard pipe. The way the two were connected without a joint was a secret of the Nobility's science. One theory had it that in their laboratories, there were even human beings who had white blood corpuscles in their body that'd been fused with the molecules of diamonds.

But D didn't spare the mind-numbing machinery so much as a glance. All he sought was the blood trail on the sand- and dust-covered floor. It led D through the mechanism fifteen hundred feet ahead.

Lord Johann lay before a great mountain of a machine that seemed to be some sort of quantum transformer. He was quite a sight, his outfit and the flesh beneath it charred, his right arm torn off at the shoulder, and his left knee twisted nearly eighty degrees. Certain death was spreading its wings across his face, which had a lifeless, waxy hue.

As he saw D approaching, the magician said, "You came . . . did you?"

His voice was an odd mixture of surprise and resignation.

"I'm already dying . . . D . . . You wouldn't cut down an old man . . . with death right before him . . . would you?"

The cyborg horse halted right in front of the magician. As D looked down at the ruthless old man from the back of his mount, he was so stern, and so beautiful.

While Lord Johann begged for his life without any thought of reputation or shame, even his eyes melted with rapture.

Still gripping the reins and making no move to dismount, D inquired, "Where is Hugh?"

"He . . . he was inside . . . the aircraft . . . Poor thing . . . I'm sure he must've burned to death."

No sooner was there a flash of white light than Lord Johann's left ear fell to the floor. Such brutality toward someone who was already as good as dead.

"Next, it'll be your right ear, followed by your left arm."

Lord Johann might've been telling the truth from the very start. The Hunter had no basis for making this threat. And it was the cruelest threat imaginable.

"One of the bounty hunters . . . that's after you . . . will be coming along later . . . I went on ahead to get the jump on you . . . and *this* is what it got me . . . I beg you . . . please don't cut me."

"What's the name of this bounty hunter, and what can he do?"

"I believe it was . . . Vince. And his power . . . he can't be killed . . ."

Without saying a word, D split the aged magician's head open down to the chin. Not bothering to look back at the body as it fell and spewed brains everywhere, he went back out through the entrance.

Fresh death and destruction reigned over the interior as the bizarre mechanism settled once more into silence.

Twenty or thirty minutes passed.

A faint sound was heard. If human actions could be mapped into a machine, it would've been like a yawn on awakening from a long sleep. Another followed right on its heels. And then a light came on in the supposedly dead mechanism. Its massive blood vessel was quivering. Joyfully. But what was the vermilion liquid flowing sluggishly through it? Was it blood?

The ceiling couldn't be seen. Perhaps it ran up straight through the three-thousand-foot-high tower. From somewhere above, blue lightning came down to tie heaven and earth together.

Lord Johann's corpse was on the ground. As his remains were pierced by the light, they twitched a bit. That wasn't an uncommon occurrence in a body that hadn't been dead long. However, the army of silver cords that stretched from nowhere in particular and tapped into every inch of the old man with ends that were neither plugs nor needles was no trick of death. Even now fresh blood surged noisily through the gigantic blood vessel, carrying life back to all manner of machinery.

The cords pierced Lord Johann's body without respite, their numbers in the thousands as they buried the magician's torso within a twisting silver serpent.

What was happening? What could be driving the cords? Who had brought the machinery back to life?

Something still lived in this wasteland.

Another three hours went by.

Somewhere, a special switch was thrown in the electromagnetic circuits. If it were a human voice, it might've said, *Finished!*

Death came suddenly. The lights, the electromagnetic waves, the blood flow—all activity ceased instantly and in unison with a complete disregard for momentum or inertia. Once more the crushing weight of silence filled the air.

In the murk, something rose unsteadily. It was the army of lifeless cords. A storm was unleashed at its center. Thousands of cords were knocked loose with a single blow. And in their center, standing like an angry god, was black steel in human form. The person retained his original shape—scrawny, burned, arm missing and leg twisted, veins standing out on his forearm, a long, flowing beard—only now all of it was steel. Black and glistening. And his face—it was clearly that of Lord Johann, his head still split open.

What's the matter? the baron asked.

"I may have made a mistake," D replied from horseback, adding, "How can you tell?"

It's not that I read your mind or anything. I just get a sense. Are you referring to Lord Johann?

"You said those ruins almost seemed alive, didn't you? From sheer hatred."

Exactly. A machine can feel neither anger nor hate. A living machine, however, is another matter. But did you know that what could be called the ultimate mechanism in those ruins never really went into operation?

"No."

The Nobility actually defeated the OSB in battle. It's theorized that the OSB suddenly pulled out after contemplating the damage that would be done if that weapon were put to use. And the only ones capable of operating that device were a few individuals of the Sacred Ancestor's bloodline, or something to that effect.

"That's good," the Hunter remarked, the wind that struck him broadside deflected by his handsome features.

It was just then that a low rumble spread across the plain.

Wheeling his horse around, D raced over to Miska's carriage. As his eyes peered in through the window, they reflected her quaking coffin.

Was Miska trying to get out, or was it something else? Whatever the case, something was clearly out of the ordinary. Unlike the baron, the woman was supposed to sleep by day.

"What is it?" D asked.

I can't tell. I'm trying to talk to her, but she's in a frenzy. Surely she must've had some portent of danger.

Something that would prevent a Noble from sleeping by day.

The ground rocked again.

D asked, "Is it actually Miska that's responding?"

Silence descended.

After a short time, the baron replied, *No, it's whatever is inside her. I thought she was acting strangely after she got back last night, but whatever didn't awaken while she was with us might be active now—the Destroyer, perhaps?*

"Do you think she's up to controlling it?"

The baron fell silent once more. Not that he didn't know the answer to the question. It was D's mindset that left him at a loss.

I don't know.

"Well, if she can't keep it in check, the best thing to do is dispose of her right now. If whatever's coming out of the ruins is another one of the Nobility's creations, there's a chance it might join forces with the Destroyer."

Then they'd face twice as many foes . . . and foes of the most extreme nature at that.

The far reaches of the plain had a bluish glow that came from a spot where there was some sort of facility. Never fading, the light spread further, becoming an impossibly large canopy of cerulean.

"Something just bought it. It's started now," D said as he hit his mount's flanks.

Perhaps already having caught something with its animal senses, the cyborg horse instantly started to gallop at full speed.

As he raced along, D looked back.

From the distant reaches of the road, a pair of glittering spheres headed in the Hunter's direction. The air was swiftly ionizing. The spheres were glowing balls of plasma.

Grabbing hold of the lead horse's harness, D gave a hard pull to the right. The madly dashing team turned out onto the plain. As Miska's horses followed suit, one of the spheres was absorbed by the road. It looked as if light were gushing up from the bowels of the earth. A section of terrain roughly one hundred fifty feet in diameter sank into the ground.

D jumped over to the driver's seat. His eyes had an intense light to them, and the horses' speed quickly exceeded all their limits, as if the animals were possessed.

"I'm scared," May said, gnawing her lip inside the carriage.

"It's okay," was all Taki could say. But she wasn't the only one.

"It's okay," a crisp, clear voice declared as the two girls saw the coffin's lid open.

A pure-blooded Noble couldn't possibly be coming out in broad daylight.

"Look after the girl."

All Taki saw then was a figure in blue being sucked out through the ceiling.

"I'm heading over to Miska's carriage!"

And saying this, the baron launched himself from the roof of his vehicle toward the carriage behind his.

Such recklessness! Though his arms were clad in long blue gloves and they in turn shielded his face, the Noble experienced white-hot pain merely by exposing himself to sunlight. The flesh beneath his clothes would've already started to melt.

Not even looking at the other glowing sphere that was closing in on them, the baron took a silver sphere from the lining of his cape and hurled it to the rear.

The earth was tinted blue.

The ring of light closed in on the back end of the carriage . . . and was intercepted by an unseen wall! The light rebounded, pressing forward once more, but by the time it finally shattered the force

field, nothing could be seen of the two carriages but a distant blur
through a cloud of dust.

II

Up ahead, the ruins were like a shadowy blur, and D aimed the carriage
straight for them. Though incredibly vast, the ruins were less than
thirty feet high. This facility had surely been meant to accommodate
some device that covered a large area. Inside, both the ceiling and
the floor had the gleam of crystal. The holes that had been blown in
various spots actually ended up looking like minor accents.

Climbing down from the driver's seat, D called out to the baron,
"Get back in your coffin."

"I'm afraid I can't do that. This time, I think it would be best if both
of us were around."

Jumping down from the other carriage, the baron staggered. A
chop from D's hand had raced down at the base of his neck, but it
bounced back again with a heavy thud. The baron had raised one
hand to easily fend off the blow.

"You needn't show any undue concern for me," the Nobleman said.
"If it becomes absolutely necessary, I'll get back into my coffin on my
own. You should try to act the part of the employee a bit more."

"In that case, hold down the fort here," D said, now having taken
the exact opposite tack. His flexibility was a frightful thing.

"And where will you be?"

"Up top," said D.

The building had no higher levels. However, D's gaze was indeed
turned toward the sky.

The baron began setting out cylinders in a row some distance
from the carriages. The alacrity was gone from his movements.

Climbing out of the carriage, Taki covered her mouth with her
hand and let out a cry of surprise. It looked as if the baron's body
was shrouded in a white mist. Actually it was white smoke pouring
out of his cuffs and collar.

"You should stay in the carriage," the baron turned and said.

"But your body's . . ."

"I can still handle it," he told her before he called out, "The enemy is coming, D!"

When the baron twisted around, there was no sign of the Vampire Hunter. Not even bothering to ask where he might've gone, the baron turned instead toward the entrance as the wind buffeted his face. His blue cape spread, and his hair fluttered out.

Taki was lying flat on the ground.

What had entered the room was a black iron statue encapsulated in a glowing sphere—it was easy enough to make out Lord Johann's features on its face. Within the sphere, iridescent bands of light eddied. One such streak shot at the baron. Deflected a foot shy of him, the streak changed its target to the ceiling. Without making a sound, it opened a gaping hole there roughly thirty feet across. Not even a speck of dust remained. The material had been broken down to its constituent atoms.

The baron took one of the cylinders that sat at his feet and knocked it toward the magician. From the end of it, green flecks of light sped at the magician's brow. The second they struck him right between the eyes, countless points of light winked on in every pore on his body.

The magician's iron face formed a toothy grin.

In the blink of an eye, the points of light vanished. Only two remained—one between his eyes and the other in the vicinity of his heart—and when the light on his chest went out, the one on his forehead began to drift aimlessly across the surface of his body.

In a manner of speaking, the cylinder was a sensor for detecting vital points. The luminous dot was a scanning device that traveled across a target's body in search of weaknesses and crucial areas, which it would then relay back to the assault components in the cylinder itself. However, this time it had failed to find any vital points, or even any defenseless spots. In response to this lack of communication from the scanning system, the main computer elected to engage free attack mode, selecting the most likely vulnerabilities from its existing store of humanoid data and connecting to extradimensional power circuits.

A particle beam surged out at the speed of light, and the green spot that had formed between Lord Johann's eyes took on a blinding glow. Lord Johann's smile grew wider as the luminous point quickly faded in hue, and then unexpectedly vanished. Not a single mark was left on the glossy blackness of the magician's brow.

With Taki taking shelter behind him, the baron backed away. To his rear, he heard a scream.

Having turned to face the carriages, Taki had found a woman in white standing right in front of her. Though Miska was out in the sunlight, nothing at all had changed about her pale skin. There was only a piercing golden light to her eyes.

This was what D had been talking about—they might have made foes of two threats created by the ancient Nobility.

Miska opened her mouth. The sigh that spilled from that maw called to mind the chill of some frozen hell.

There was no sign of D, and formidable as Baron Balazs was, it didn't seem the least bit possible that he could take on these two horsemen of the apocalypse and win. And yet as the baron kept Taki safely behind himself, his eyes were so tranquil they would've taken the breath from any who saw them.

The upper portion of the sphere surrounding the magician glowed with all the colors of the rainbow. Its bands of light were sinking into Miska.

As she reeled backward with them piercing her chest, Miska opened her mouth. With a loud gurgle a semitransparent sphere rose from her. It was an enormous bubble filled with water.

It wasn't until the iridescent band pierced the bubble that a look of terror spread across Lord Johann's black countenance. Giving off a tremendous amount of steam all the while, the watery bubble went on to envelop the magician's entire body without slowing in the least.

Lord Johann shouted something. But the words weren't from any human language.

"So, he was an OSB?" the baron said, finally realizing the truth.

Lord Johann's transformation hadn't been effected by the ancient Nobility—it was the work of OSB machinery meant to make warriors to combat the Nobility. It had probably remained there in the ruins as something the Nobility had confiscated from the OSB. D had also mentioned something—the malice alone would live on eternally. The enmity that remained in that device had been enough to take Lord Johann and make him one of their own.

However, that same malicious aura had also been sensed by the Nobility's ultimate tool of death and destruction—the Destroyer. And that was why the baron muttered as he watched the pair's eerie battle, "It's just as we thought, then."

Inside the bubble, the sphere protecting Lord Johann's form melted away pitifully, leaving the magician trapped in the water. And water was the very thing he feared.

The OSB had no concept of fluids. Their species' fatal flaw was the relative ease with which their minds succumbed to "the fear of the unknown." The Nobility had been able to hold the high ground for quite a long time once they managed to discover a number of the aliens' fears.

Lord Johann went mad.

The iridescent band that surrounded the magician spun wildly in the bubble of water, losing more and more of its color all the time. Then it shone. A sizzle rang out like a drop of water falling on a hot skillet, and the watery mass vanished.

As the magician glared at Miska and the baron, his eyes were all white and his whole body trembled. Every hair on him stood on end, and his muscles and veins bulged. Leaning back wildly and pitching forward again, he disgorged phlegm. His target was the baron.

The figure in the blue cape dodged, the phlegm sailing over his head to fall at Miska's feet. With his cape shielding his face, the baron collapsed. Light had bleached his form white. Miska had both hands out in front of her face.

Now *this* was truly one of the OSB's deadliest weapons. There could be no disputing that what the phlegm on the floor gave off was sunlight.

The vampiric Nobility could move about freely under artificial sunlight. What they feared was natural light alone. So what would happen if they were to be exposed to sunlight on another celestial body—say, the surface of the moon? They would have no problem at all with it there. Whether there was some psychological or even spiritual force at work in that regard remained unclear even now. Even with all of the scientific might they possessed, the Nobility didn't understand why exposure to sunlight would reduce them to dust only on Earth. But the OSB's unusual science had solved that riddle. They had more or less artificially manufactured natural light. The phlegm that'd fallen to the ground had given birth to a sun.

The baron had already lost consciousness, and Miska was driven to her knees. And the light that fell on them continued to shine remorselessly.

"Ha ha ha!" the old man suddenly began to laugh aloud. It was crazed, mindless laughter. But seeing the condition of the baron and Miska, it wasn't difficult to imagine that his insane mirth came from the joy of victory.

The iridescent light stabbed into the far wall, reducing it to nothingness. This ultrawarrior created by the OSB—the same aliens who'd plagued the ancient Nobility for so long—had begun to run amok. And it seemed as if he wouldn't stop until these ruins—or perhaps even the whole planet—had been completely destroyed.

Something suddenly blocked the light, and the sun on the floor lost its color. Though the light shining in through holes in the wall was as bright as ever, darkness had begun to slowly cover the region.

As Lord Johann looked to all sides, a heavier darkness spread above him. Or so it seemed, and then it took the shape of a gorgeous young man who split Lord Johann's iron head in half lengthwise. Despite this, the magician raised his right hand. The iridescent band that sprang from his shoulder seemed to twine around his right arm as it assailed D.

A flash of white light bisected the magician's torso. The glint reversed directions, making a second pass through his upper body as it slowly came free of the lower half, sending his head flying.

By the time D rose from a near squat and returned the same blade that had first split the magician's head to its sheath, the baron had also gotten up. Miska alone had gone from being on her knees to being slumped across the floor.

"You certainly took your time," said a voice in the darkness.

Gleaming above their heads like a silver platter was the sunlight now held at bay. D looked up without saying a word.

"Could it be that this was the control room for the entire installation?" the baron asked.

"I suppose you could say that."

Were the control systems set in some space that couldn't be seen from this floor? And had D entered that space and created this? Created darkness?

"The OSB's secret weapon against the Nobility was natural light they could manufacture. So, did the ancient Nobility create natural darkness to counter it?"

"They did indeed," the Hunter replied.

"But there's no record of anything like this ever being used in battle."

"That's because it was locked away," D said as if it didn't mean anything at all.

"By whom?"

"Perhaps by the one your kind holds in such esteem."

"The Sacred Ancestor? But why?"

Before the astonished young Nobleman, D looked up into the void. Darkness filled the light, while here and there the light tinted the darkness like droplets of paint spreading through the water.

"Darkness or light—which of them won the battle?"

To the baron, D's question sounded worlds away.

After a bit, D said, "Go on out ahead. I'll be out once I get rid of this darkness."

"Get rid of it?"

"Don't you see? It's still spreading. Within a year, this whole planet will be enveloped by artificial night. If nothing were done, it would blanket the entire universe."

"Is that a fact? So, is that why the Sacred Ancestor . . . why the exalted one was loath to use this darkness?"

The Nobleman sensed D moving away.

"Who or what are you?" the baron asked, but there was no one there to answer him. "You brought forth the great darkness sealed away by the Sacred Ancestor, and now you say you'll get rid of it. Wouldn't that be the work of the Sacred Ancestor's blood? D—who are you?"

As the pair of carriages raced down the main road a dozen minutes later, the crystal control center behind them flickered like a mirage and was obliterated. Inside their vehicle, Taki and May couldn't help but look out at the young horseman riding along beside them with newfound awe and fear. For they had overheard the baron's question.

III

As D and the others reached the end of the great plains and the blue of twilight had begun to color the air, a lone man sat wistfully on a boulder in the Shabara Canyon. He was one of the surviving members of the group that'd already lost three of their number to D and the baron—Crimson Stitchwort. Though this man had come out of countless perilous scrapes before, he now did nothing to conceal the childlike fear and impatience that surfaced on his face. Above him, a sheer rock wall loomed like a great canopy that hid the heavens, while below, there was the incessant sound of a steady flow of water. If he were to look down, he probably would've even been able to make out the bits of white where water dashed against the rocks in the vast river three hundred feet or more below.

This eighteen-hundred-square-foot outcropping of rock halfway up the cliff was the very place where the disk with their employer's voice told them they would find "interesting devices." Ordinarily, Crimson Stitchwort would've been only too happy to look for the items in question. Though a good number of his colleagues had died, he undoubtedly reassured himself that his own share would be all the greater. However, he was scared . . . but not of dying. When he'd chosen this line of work, he'd basically thrown his life away. And yet, he was still scared. After attacking a woman called Miska in a white dress back in the forest, Mario had never come back, and Vince had also fallen out of contact. Yoputz the priest had made himself scarce, and there'd been no news from him. Of course, the death of his compatriots only boded well for him. That was why when he'd rushed here all alone, his spirits had been high.

But when no amount of searching had located said devices, a certain anxious feeling began to rear its ugly head. After a full hour of looking, he'd given up ten minutes earlier, and although he'd intended to take only a short break, he was so exhausted that an all-encompassing fear overtook him, leaving him with no desire to do anything. The air in the canyon grew cold faster than that on level ground. The sound of the water tempted him with sleep and a mysterious sense of relief. Suddenly, he wanted to die. For no particular reason, he thought about leaping to his death. Getting to his feet somewhat unsteadily, he walked to the edge of the cliff. Without any hesitation at all, he put one foot out into space.

Something grabbed him by the scruff of the neck. In the blink of an eye, the cruelest of Hunters was left rolling on the ground unceremoniously.

"You?!"

The old man looking down at him was the same person who'd met with the group to explain the terms of their employment and their remuneration in place of their actual employer.

"I imagined this might happen, but it's a little too early to be turning on each other. You'd better show yourself too," the old man said to the rock face behind him.

After a while, the priest appeared from behind a pile of odd-shaped stones.

Crimson Stitchwort then realized what had happened.

"Yoputz—you son of a bitch!"

As the man got up with a wrathful visage, the old man checked him, saying, "You two are it, you know."

"Oh, then all the rest are—"

The old man shook his head at Crimson Stitchwort's words.

"There's one other who chooses not to come. Now, let's get those devices ready."

"What do you mean, get them ready? There's no sign of them anywhere, and I've checked everywhere. And it looks like that asshole was probably spying on me the whole time!"

As Crimson Stitchwort's search had ended in failure, Yoputz saw him as no longer being of any use and had utilized his powers to throw him into a nihilistic frame of mind.

The old man looked like something of a philosopher, and there wasn't a trace of emotion on his face as he said, "They don't appear until the appropriate number of people have assembled. That's the way it's set up."

The old man gave a toss of his jaw, indicating the center of the outcropping.

It seemed impossible that they'd appear in such a manner. But what fell from the sky was a wooden box that wasn't very large at all. As it slammed against the ground, the box was smashed to bits. Since this sent chunks of wood flying that the two assassins had to dodge but the old man didn't, the box must've been thrown from quite some height.

Though Crimson Stitchwort and Yoputz both looked up, they saw no one at the top of the cliff.

"They shall be entering the canyon soon. Use these to finish them off," the old man said as if making a declaration.

As the two Hunters looked at him, their eyes weren't exactly filled with endearment.

"What the hell is all this?!" Crimson Stitchwort said, his gaze trained on the contents of the box. "I don't get it at all. They've gotta come with some sort of directions, right?"

"If you need any sort of instruction, I'm sure each item will supply it to you itself. Now fight, and destroy the baron. That's what you've been hired for, is it not?"

Completely disregarding the old man, who vanished as soon as he'd finished speaking, the two turned to one another. Having seen something so incomprehensible, the look on their faces was sheer bewilderment.

Before entering the canyon, D halted the carriages.

"What is it?" asked the baron. The darkness was already heavy, and he could be seen up in the driver's seat.

"This is a perfect place for an ambush. Essentially, once we get through here, it's less than thirty miles to Krauhausen. You could say this is the last redoubt for our foes. An attack will be coming."

"I realize that."

"Wait here," said the Hunter. "I'm going to go see what the enemy is up to."

"I see. Please do."

On this matter, the two men were in perfect agreement.

D rode his cyborg horse into a bottleneck formed by the cliffs that jabbed up at the sky to either side.

Beside the road the Hunter took there flowed a wide river. Though the water was clear, it ran deep and dark. A person's head popped up right in the middle of it, and the sturdy figure that then arose with water dripping from every inch of him was none other than the Dark Water Forces commander Galil. Needless to say, the countless blobs that surfaced from the fluid coursing slowly around him wore the faces of his subordinates. It appeared they'd been lying in wait here for D. Though the bottoms of Galil's feet rested on the water's surface as he stood there defiantly, there was no white spray around them, and he didn't move a muscle.

"Our master Vlad will not tolerate another failure. This is a do-or-die situation for us. Our preparations have been made. D! Baron! This time, you shall find your opposition a bit more of a threat."

And then he seemed to melt as he became one with the water.

If the flow of the stream was considered as a kind of network, then the water it contained could share any information with every location almost simultaneously. Galil had already passed D and was undoubtedly preparing to catch him in an attack. What's more, Crimson Stitchwort and the weird priest Yoputz had bizarre new weapons as they lay in wait for the group. How would D and the baron fight them? How could they defend themselves?

In order to get a view of the entire canyon, one would have to go to a height of at least six thousand feet. At that altitude floated a cylindrical tube about a foot and a half long. As it manipulated a quartet of thin wings to ride the air currents and maintain its position, a "macro eye" set on the bottom surveyed the entirety of the canyon while simultaneously zooming in to capture ultra-close-up images—in other words, the device was a highly maneuverable three-dimensional camera.

As he watched the images it relayed to a thin membranelike monitor, Crimson Stitchwort knit his brow and said, "Looks like we've got some strange company. But I don't care who it is, we'll take out anyone who gets in our way. Before we go after D and the baron, should we wipe them out first?"

"That doesn't sound like a bad idea," Yoputz replied, his deeply creased lips shaking as if with a palsy. "I'll leave that part to you. After all, we've got all this equipment. It should be child's play."

"What's that you say?!" Crimson Stitchwort snapped back.

But the priest didn't even seem to catch the venom in his voice, saying, "Lend me your ear. I've got an idea of my own. It came to me back in that village when I got cut in half. It goes something like this—"

Bringing his mouth closer, he whispered for a while.

"I like it!" Crimson Stitchwort said, readily consenting.

But what kind of bizarre plan could Yoputz have that would unity this acrimonious pair in the blink of an eye?

After the Hunter had followed the river for over a mile, his attention was drawn to the cliffs ahead and a strange item hanging from them. It was an iron chain covered with rust. Formed from metal four inches thick, each link was a good three feet long. Like the summit of the cliff, the end of the chain couldn't be seen.

For D on his mount's back, it wouldn't be terribly difficult to catch hold of the lowest iron link. Raising his arm just a bit, he easily reached the link, and a second later, he was sailing through the air. When he landed smartly without making a sound, it was on the nearly vertical face. He was standing perpendicular to the cliff and parallel to the flowing water.

What was he trying to do?

Grabbing the link with both hands, he gave it a powerful tug. What resulted was a sound wave that rippled out like its more liquid kin. On striking jagged rocks much taller than D that rose like little hills, the sound wave then came bouncing back up with tremendous force.

What was the chain? And what did D want to do with it?

From far, far up in the sky there came a dull roar like thunder. This somewhat subsonic wave fell like rain on the ground, on the surface of the water, beating down, creeping into caves and filling the space between stones like a gas. And while this was happening, D clung to the chain with his left hand, motionless. For the sound waves would bounce off every living thing in the valley, coming back to the chain like some kind of sonar. D could hear the buzz of a drifting insect the size of a molecule of air. The breathing of massive armored beasts that lay all over the canyon, the beating of a butterfly's prismatic wings, and the whispers of lovely poisonous mushrooms that were a pale shade of purple all reached his eardrums. And that wasn't all.

"The main threats are a pair and one other—and that one's got followers with him. Like, thirty of them," D's left hand explained. "The pair would probably be the surviving Hunters, while the other would be Galil with his Dark Water Forces flunkies. From what I've seen, these jerks aren't in cahoots. Well, I can hardly wait to see who tries what!"

D said nothing as he reached his left hand around to his back.

"Hey, what the hell are you doing?!"

The instant that panicked cry was heard, the left hand was severed at the wrist, left clinging to the link of the chain in true agitation.

"What've you done to me?!"

"Deal with it," the Hunter replied, the blade his right hand had held already back in its sheath. Pulling what looked like a ball of woolly black thread from an inner pocket of his coat, D took hold of one end of it. There was a sharp fishhook tied to it.

"Hey, you'd better knock this off!" his left hand cried, still protesting vehemently as the hook sank ruthlessly into its open wound.

IV

Where the team of D and the baron differed from the normal employer/bodyguard relationship was that both of them were highly capable—the one being protected was every bit as powerful as his defender. Due to this, there was no reason for the bodyguard to constantly stick to the baron; instead, he was free to leave his employer when he wished to seek out his foes and destroy them. No bodyguard in the world did a better job of embodying the expression, "A strong offense is the best defense."

After letting go of the chain that stretched up to the heavens, D rode his horse up onto a steep stone staircase that was another six hundred feet away. While it was unclear who had fashioned these stone stairs in the distant past, the cyborg horse finished climbing the ten thousand steps in about twenty minutes.

They came to an open space that seemed to have been carved from the side of the mountain. It was with good reason that the first human explorers to discover this place were so awestruck that they couldn't move for three days or three nights, until they ultimately dried out like mummies.

At the far side of the carved-out mountainside, more than a hundred stone statues over three hundred feet high had been sculpted. Was it gods the mason had tried to carve with his chisel in days of yore, or something else? Some of them glared down at the earth, others scowled at the sky, their hands with fingers curled as if to seize something, or balled in fists, or laid flat to deliver a chop. Their looks were fearsome. The impact they had was far beyond the scope of good and evil, robbing those who saw them of their will and tearing away their minds.

At the feet of the foremost sculpture D could make out the form of Crimson Stitchwort.

"Glad you could make it, D!" the most atrocious of Hunters said as he blinked his eyes.

As intimidating as D was, his beauty was almost enough to make the other man utterly collapse.

Mustering his strength, the assassin said, "However, don't delude yourself that you made it all this way without being noticed. I've got an eye in the sky."

The brief upward glimpse made by D's eyes left Crimson Stitchwort satisfied.

"One of the Nobility's toys?" D muttered. "Where did the other guy go?"

Crimson Stitchwort was shaken.

"How did you know about Yoputz? Well, I don't suppose it matters. It's only fitting that you take on the toys. You can go to your grave being happy to have made it this far. The baron and the woman should be joining you shortly."

He had a strange object by his side—rolled-up parchment scrolls etched with some unknown designs. Drawing one of them from the bunch with his right hand, he shook it up in front of his face. There was a crisp snap, and the parchment unrolled like a wall hanging. Veinlike lines ran across its surface. Suddenly, one of the squiggles glowed with a blue light.

At the same time, the vanguard of the stone statues threw its chest out powerfully. Its stony biceps swelled, and its abdominal muscles rippled. What manner of technology had been used to give it such flexibility? The earth shook as if from a thunderclap. The stone statue had taken a step forward.

At its feet, the figure in black was replaced by the sound of iron-shod hooves at a gallop. Hadn't the Hunter been at all surprised by this?

"Holy shit!" Crimson Stitchwort shouted as he leapt out of the way.

Whether he was just fast or had intended to do so from the very start, D made a horizontal swipe of his blade that was accompanied by the harsh sound of breaking stone.

The stone statue staggered. A colossus three hundred feet high, its ankle had been split by that one blow from D. And at that point, all of its weight had been resting on that leg. Both hands clutching at thin air, the colossus bowed to the laws of physics.

As its body was falling back against the ground, D galloped right under the statue to close on Crimson Stitchwort.

"Hey, keep away from me!" the assassin shouted as another light sparked to life on the surface of a parchment he held.

The second D bounded into the air, something that could only be described as titanic pierced his cyborg horse through the back and out through the belly. The beast was pinned to the ground by a stone arrow more than a hundred and twenty feet in length. It was also more than three feet thick. The power born of the projectile's size and velocity instantly tore the cyborg horse to pieces.

At the far edge of the clearing, a stone statue was readying a second arrow. From midair, D lobbed a silvery cylinder at its feet. It emitted a ruby red light that enveloped the lower half of the statue—it was a Stein atomic grenade the baron had given him.

In the crimson flames, the statue's ankles, knees, and thighs all collapsed like feeble clay, and then the upper body was consumed as well, bow and arrow still in hand.

Part of the flames landed on the ground midway between the airborne D and the earthbound Crimson Stitchwort. D came down in the midst of the flaming mass, but a second later, it was Crimson Stitchwort who cried out. As D was hemmed in by the fire, his sword had taken the other Hunter's right arm off at the elbow. One more swipe of his blade and the number of pursuers would most definitely be decreased.

However, at that point, D audibly heard a hoarse voice tell him, "I sense someone moving toward where the carriages are parked. Someone tough."

Crimson Stitchwort narrowly managed to leap out of the path of the sword while his opponent's concentration was broken.

Instead of giving chase, D spun around. The words "someone tough" prompted him to dash to the edge of the cliff. Now without a horse, he couldn't spare the time it would take to run back down the stairs. But he couldn't possibly be thinking of throwing himself from a height of nearly fifteen hundred feet. Below, the river flowed like a thread.

His coat billowing out around him, the figure in black dropped toward the water's surface like a magical bird.

As D confronted Crimson Stitchwort, the baron was checking on Miska. Her coffin had been transformed into a stylish bed, and the beauty that lay on it in a white dress stared off into space. In the process of coming to the surface, the Destroyer entity within Miska had forced her ego deep into her subconscious. The shock of that still lingered.

As the baron turned his back to her without offering any words of solace, Miska called out, "What—what do you think I am? I know now," she continued. "Inside my body, nay, inside my psyche there is this entity called the Destroyer."

"That's—"

"It shall take control of my body again at some point, and there is nothing I can do to stop it! It will rain destruction on every last thing in this world. Even on you."

"There *is* a way to deal with this."

The baron's reply made Miska knit her brow.

"Is there truly?"

"In the village of Krauhausen is a physician who served the Frontier's Central Controller. His name is Jean de Carriole. I'm sure he of all people could cure you."

Miska was at a loss for words.

"This man received his instruction in the field of magical surgery directly from the Sacred Ancestor. And he delivered me when my mother was pregnant."

"He delivered you, Baron?"

Miska had never seen this tragic cast to the baron's features. She was moved.

A strong hand touched her cheek.

"It may be that I am no longer a Noble. Can you understand what that means?"

"And is it to learn this that you go to Krauhausen?"

"The night is passing swiftly. If you're feeling up to it, why don't you step outside for a bit? The canyon is brimming with moonlight and life."

And leaving her with that, the baron stepped out of the carriage. Above him, the moon glowed. The sharp look he gave to the far reaches of the valley was the complete opposite of the gaze that had rested on Miska. Even back here, the ultra-keen senses of the Nobility had allowed him to catch the sound made by the chain. He alone knew of D's deadly battle.

A scent utterly unbecoming the stillness assailed his nostrils. Covering his mouth and nose with his cape, the baron turned his eyes toward a spot in the darkness. He couldn't sense anyone. Suddenly all the strength left his body. More accurately, he'd actually lost the way will from which that strength sprang. A feeling of ineffable futility filled his being. His cape came down.

The next thing the baron knew, he was a slave to a desire that made his flesh tremble. He wanted to drink. To suck the warm blood from a human. The baron fought desperately to restrain the longing that swelled within him. But the vortex quickly pulled him in, sucking him down. Putting one hand to his forehead, the baron sat up. And as he was doing so, the scent of blood that hung in the air only grew that much heavier.

"No!" he groaned. His whole body shook.

Reason reclaimed what had been a somewhat perverse expression. His mental faculties were wrestling with the craving that set his blood ablaze. He then lowered his face.

A minute passed. Then two.

There was the sound of a door opening back at the carriages. Having glimpsed the baron through the window, Taki had noticed he was acting strangely and opened the door. While the Nobility had a special knack for sensing the aroma of blood filling the air, Taki didn't have the slightest inkling about it. She took a step toward the Nobleman, and then another.

"Stay back!" the baron told her, his words stopping the young woman in her tracks.

Assailed by an instinctive fear, she turned to go back to the carriage.

"No, come to me," the baron said. He had turned in Taki's direction.

"No!" Taki cried, shaking her head.

"Turn and look at me," he told her in the same mannered tone he always used.

A cold wind struck the nape of Taki's neck.

You can't turn around, she thought. *You absolutely mustn't do it!*

Slowly she turned.

The baron was on his feet, his cape covering his mouth. As the breath was knocked out of the girl, the baron's face approached the nape of her neck. His cape had come away from it.

Letting out a scream, Taki fainted.

His face still pressed to the girl's pale neck, the baron held the senseless form for some time, and then laid her gently on the ground after a short while.

Somewhere in the heavens there was a sharp clang.

When D raced back, the wind swirling in his wake, the baron stood slumped back against the carriage, and a thicker aroma of blood hung in the air. Halting, D stared down at the baron's feet. Two figures lay there. Taki and May.

Walking over and examining their necks, D said, "We had a deal." His tone was soft.

A shadow suddenly scudded across the moon.

He'd plunged fifteen hundred feet into the river and then run all the way there. Yet due to his incredible strength, the young man wasn't even breathing hard. He was gorgeous. Simply gorgeous.

"What happened to your left hand?" asked the baron.

Only a stump protruded from D's left sleeve.

The baron made a mighty leap backward. Just a heartbeat later, D's blade mowed through the darkness. The baron limned a graceful arc to the left, and D raced right after him.

The baron's cape expelled a flash of white light.

Batting it away with one stroke, D made a bound. His blade sank deep into the left side of the baron's chest, coming out through his back. The baron's body collapsed, and the blade remained in D's hand as it naturally slid out again.

"What are you doing?" Miska was heard to say from the vicinity of the white carriage.

Apparently the Noblewoman had just been coming out, with one of her feet resting on the ground and the other still on the steps. Her pale and beautiful visage was warped by surprise.

"Baron!" she cried as she dashed over to him, and after looking down at his death mask, she soon stared at D. Her eyes glowed with red tears. Tears of blood. Her elegant expression instantly began to change into that of the devil himself. From hatred—and the scent of blood.

"You shall pay for that, D! I can't believe you would do this to him!"

Standing tall in her white dress, the Noblewoman looked so alluring, so elegant.

"Now the Destroyer wishes to come out. Do you want me to set it free?"

Saying nothing, D readied his sword in the low position.

Taki was dead, May had been slain, and the baron was destroyed, leaving only D and Miska out of the whole group. With the two of them now locked in deadly combat, the utter annihilation of their party wasn't inconceivable.

The moon remained hidden by dark clouds even now, and the sounds of the water were so distant as to be of no comfort.

Could D take on the Destroyer and win?

Canyon of Blood

CHAPTER 6

I

Something strange suddenly occurred at the scene of the deadly conflict. All of the strength rapidly drained from Miska's body. No, not her strength, but rather the will that created that strength. As the stupefied Noblewoman drew back, the blade of D's sword slid in between her breasts far too easily.

Miska fell . . . and she wasn't the only one. D had also been driven to one knee. Struck by a powerful loss of psyche—they'd been robbed of their drive.

A different voice drifted out in the moonlight, saying, "I was going to have the woman slay you, but when I cast my spell on both of you, it turned out you resisted it better than she. Well, that's not a problem. By now, you should be finding it bothersome to even draw breath. You're in no position to feel any hostility toward this humble holy man."

D looked up dazedly toward the source of the voice. On the roof of a black carriage a shape the same hue was moving. A man in priestly garb rose from the carriage. It went without saying that the old man who'd suddenly stood up was Yoputz.

"Surely both you and the baron were searching for some sign of me. But it was no use. Before you is a man who was but one short step from attaining the highest level in a secret faith. The power to replace one's body with nothingness is something not even the senses of the Nobility could see through," the old man said, his stony face crumpling. He'd just smiled.

And then he jumped easily to the ground. Looking at the baron's corpse, he said, "It occurred to me to try this approach after he had to fight the urge to drink the blood of a village girl due to his agreement with you. No matter how powerful his will might've been, he was still a Noble, and after being inundated by the scent of blood, this was the only thing that could happen with two hot-blooded girls so close at hand. D, you did well to fight the urge. Dhampir though you are, I'm impressed. Ouf!"

The cause of that cry at the end was a plain wooden needle that had sprouted from Yoputz's left shoulder. It looked like the reason that this shot aimed for his heart had missed the mark was because even the great D was still to some degree suffering from the effects of Yoputz's spell.

Before D could get to his feet, Yoputz moved smoothly to the entrance to the canyon, where he once again let out a scream of pain as he toppled backward. A flash of light had split open his right side—it had shot out of the baron's cape.

"You . . . you bastard! You're still alive? Oh . . . so it was all an act, was it?"

"Precisely," Baron Balazs replied with a nod as he slowly got to his feet again. "I dealt a blow to each of the girls to knock them out, but I didn't suck their blood. D's eyes were sure to note the absence of teeth marks at the base of their necks. He narrowly missed my heart in order to lure you out, since we couldn't tell where you were. Due to my wound, I may have been wide of the mark just now, but that won't happen this time."

His cape released a flash of light. It went right through Yoputz's body and hit the boulder behind him before flying back.

Yoputz had suddenly vanished.

As the baron's body stiffened with tension, behind him D dashed over to the boulder on his left and drove his blade into its rocky surface. A beastly moan of pain rang out, and as the moon peeked between the clouds, it palely illuminated the form of Yoputz as he appeared on the surface of the rock.

"How . . . did you . . . know?" the old man sputtered, a mass of blood spilling from his mouth as he reached for the blade that pierced the base of his throat. And then his head lolled to one side limply.

Pulling his sword back out, D went back to the carriages.

As he scooped Miska up in his arms, the baron said, "That was an impressive thrust. She's unconscious, but otherwise unharmed. But I would like to know the same thing. How did you know where the old man was?"

"The chain rang out," D replied as he walked over to Taki and May.

Not even the baron noticed the incredibly fine thread that hung from the Hunter's left arm and ran off deep into the canyon.

The pair of carriages traveled through a canyon lit solely by moonlight. Strange as it was, those who owned the vehicles, male and female, could see right through the dark of night. The carriages raced down the road alongside the river that cut through the canyon.

"That just leaves one individual and one group," the baron up in the driver's seat said to D, who rode right next to the carriage.

"Don't get careless," said D. "As long as one of those is in the water, and the other is somewhere in the canyon, they are forces to be reckoned with."

"I'm well aware of that," the baron replied, now fully recovered from their deadly encounter with Yoputz.

Here was a man who'd not only kept from sinking his fangs into Taki and May while the stench of blood surrounded him, but had even had the presence of mind to pretend he was feeding on them. He was made of sterner stuff than the average Noble.

"Are you wondering about that?" the baron asked out of the blue.

D merely shifted his eyes to look at him.

"No, you wouldn't have an interest in anyone else's personal affairs or their motivations, I suppose. To the contrary, it is I that am curious. You are no ordinary dhampir."

"Rumor has it that Vlad Balazs was happy to receive the Sacred Ancestor," D said, changing the subject. "With the help of Jean de Carriole, a doctor the Sacred Ancestor took under his wing, it is said they conducted mysterious experiments night and day. Their subjects were said to be very young girls and infants."

The baron said nothing.

"I can imagine what sort of experiments they must've conducted. So, was one of their results you?"

"Don't be ridiculous," the baron replied, his denial vehement. "But coming from you, I don't find the conjecture that hard to accept. I have met other dhampirs—one or two rather skilled individuals out on the Frontier. But their intellect, their strength, their skill with weapons—none of them were even close to you. You're in a completely different class. D—weren't you the result the Sacred Ancestor was after?"

"Once we're through the canyon, it's just two more days to Krauhausen," said D. "Are you prepared to slay your father?"

"Yes, and I have been ever since I decided to make this journey."

Something suddenly occurred to the baron, and the musings of his heart became speech.

"Miska, what have you come all this way for?" he muttered to himself.

After they'd gone about a mile and a quarter, the road came to an incline. The running water that had D and the baron most concerned was quickly sinking further and further below them.

"Now one of your fears has been laid to rest," Miska called out from her carriage.

When the baron turned to look, the Noblewoman in white was sitting in the driver's seat

Ordinarily, anyone would've agreed with what she'd said, but the two men said nothing. They knew exactly how powerful the Dark Water Forces were.

Just then, a strange susurration reached the ears of all three of them, the sound doubling over itself time and again as if it'd bounced off every single rock in the valley. It was the sound of a water droplet falling.

At that, the trio grew so tense and acted so decisively that it actually seemed quite strange.

The whips cracked in both the baron's and Miska's hands. The hooves of the horses tore at the soil roughly.

D brought up the rear. The horse he rode was one that had been pulling the baron's carriage.

The sound drew closer. Though actually quite lovely, it wasn't just a single sound. Hundreds, perhaps thousands of them pursued the two vehicles.

"Get in your carriages," D ordered them.

The Hunter was slowing down. Suddenly, his horse's stride was broken, and the same was true for the animals drawing the carriages. Partway up this steep slope, the horses bent their legs, lay down where they were, and began to snore quite comfortably. Of course, the carriages had come to a dead stop.

D swiftly got off of his horse and went over to the baron and Miska, saying, "Put these in your ears."

They were earplugs fashioned from hardened wax. Although the baron took a pair and promptly put them in his ears, Miska's fell from her hand. Slumping over the driver's-seat railing, the Noblewoman had fallen into a deep sleep.

"Used the water, did they?" D mused as he got Miska down out of the driver's seat and put her into her carriage.

Basically, the sound of falling water droplets tended to induce sleep. And the Dark Water Forces had taken this simple phenomenon and applied it on an enormous scale throughout the entire canyon. While the reverberations that surrounded the two men sounded rather discordant to their ears, there was actually an extremely refined rhythm to them.

"Well, we can't move now. What will they try next?" the baron asked as he looked down the incline.

In the depths of his ears, the rhythm changed.

An aura of murderous intent enveloped every inch of the two men like a fall frost.

Just then, the horses that seemed to have fallen into a deep sleep rose in unison, twisting around before they began a mad gallop back down to the base of the cliff.

The sound of the water could do more than simply entice someone to sleep—it was a form of hypnotism that could even gain control of the minds of animals.

Caught off guard by the horses' swift and spirited flight, the two men didn't even have time to leap back on, and they could only watch as the carriages dwindled in the distance.

"I'll go after them," the baron said with a glance at D.

"Stay here," said D. Though it was for the protection of his employer, his manner was rather blunt, but the baron didn't seem to take exception to it in the least.

"There's no point in staying. If I were to remain here alone and be attacked and injured, it would be your fault."

"There's Lady Miska to worry about, too."

"If I were in danger, I'm sure you'd say that to get me to flee. And once you'd brought me to a safe location, you'd no doubt return to the battle alone."

"If you're not going to listen to what I tell you, then I'll nullify our agreement. Stay here," D said, his tone as quiet as ever—and like steel.

While It was unclear what the baron made of him as he gazed intently at the Hunter's face, he then raised his right hand and said, "Very well, then. I leave it entirely to you. Good luck."

D spun around.

As he watched horse and rider gallop off for the bottom of the valley like a black wind, the baron muttered, "I'm counting on you."

Counting on D to save whom? Miska? Or someone else?

II

Taki and May were awake from the very start. They'd had plenty of time to sleep and, shut in the carriage as they were, the sound of the droplets hadn't even reached them. Although they noticed the horses galloping out of control, there was nothing the two of them could do but stare at the darkness flying by outside their windows.

When the carriages reached the bottom of the canyon, they raced along the riverside for some time before a full roar began to draw nearer.

Out in the flow, bumps rose by a sandbar like the backbone of some giant monster. Sending up a silvery spray, the carriages rode over them and began to fight the current.

The roar grew louder, until it began to shake the very air. Covering the rocky road, it also coated the trees and grass with its dampness.

After about ten minutes, cliffs suddenly sprang up on either side of them. The flow here was wider and wilder than the actual river, and it raised a steady snarl. But even the clamor of those tumultuous waves was put in its place by the sound of water coursing over a sheer six-hundred-foot drop. A waterfall.

The width of the curtain of water was more than sixty feet, and the top of the falls must've been up more than a thousand feet. The spray that fell where the carriages had stopped was a mere mist, but another thirty feet ahead were actual droplets of water. If you were to approach the bottom of the falls any closer than that, it would've felt like standing in a downpour.

The road before the carriages gleamed damply in the moonlight, but no sooner had a few black blobs formed on its surface than they swiftly rose and took human form. Nothing could've risen from the thin film of water coating the rocks but the warriors of the Dark Water Forces.

"Don't go out there!" Taki said as she held May tight. D had told them that as long as they remained in the carriage, they'd be safe.

The shadowy figures stood still in the moonlight, staring at the carriage without saying a word or coming any closer, and then they unexpectedly sank back down into the rocks.

As the two girls swung between relief and anxiety, their ears caught a knock at the door. The face that hung outside the square of glass like a pale bloom was that of Miska. Although she wasn't exactly the ideal person to make them feel at ease, she was better than the Dark Water Forces, and the two girls put their hands to their hearts with relief.

"Open the door," they heard Miska say. The girls weren't sure if there was some sort of microphone out there known only to the Nobility.

May reached for the doorknob, but Taki stopped her.

"No, not until the baron or D gets here."

"But those other guys took off. It must've been because Miska came out!"

"But I—"

The two of them hadn't seen Miska fall asleep. And Taki for one couldn't fathom why she alone would've come with them.

"Open up. You're safe now," the Noblewoman said with a rap on the window. "We can't wait here for the good baron to arrive. Let's head back to him. If we don't, there's no telling when those villains might come. You shall have to turn your horses around yourself."

That last remark won Taki's confidence.

"Gladly," the young woman said as she opened the door.

Damp night air blustered in. Leaning out the door, Taki grabbed hold of a special handrail and climbed up into the driver's seat. Both the handrail and the seat were soaking wet.

The young woman took up the reins. While working as Lord Johann's assistant she'd learned how to handle horses. But the horses weren't at all inclined to turn back the way they'd come. The road was quite narrow.

"That looks tough. Allow me to help," someone said as a black glove reached over from beside Taki and took the reins.

"Huh?!"

The name Galil didn't immediately spring to mind.

The young woman instinctively looked down at the carriage door. It was open—a pale hand held it that way.

Turning in the young woman's direction and twisting her vermilion lips into a nasty grin, Miska still had the vacant look of someone utterly lacking in free will glazing her eyes.

Instead of hearing the breath being taken from Taki, the sound of a chain's impact rang out in the distance.

After his black subordinates had led Taki and May away, Galil walked over to where Miska stood like a pale blossom and ripped the front of her dress wide open. The breasts that spilled out were even fuller and smoother than they'd appeared through her clothing. Even when his black-gloved hands insolently gripped her, fingers sinking into her flesh from the force, Miska remained expressionless. For the haughty young woman's will was completely under the sway of Galil and his spell.

"We have a use of sorts for those other two. Not that I'm terribly taken with using women and children like that. But when it comes to Nobles, I'm more than happy to get just as rough as it takes!"

Galil then turned to the base of the waterfall.

"Neither D nor the baron will know about this place. Prepare an attack to welcome them with the utmost speed," he ordered in a stern tone.

Twenty minutes later, a gigantic star shone in the night sky over the valley. A flare to lure D and the baron.

Needless to say, the two girls were aces up the sleeve of the Dark Water Forces. And what had they done with them? Incredibly enough, the pair was hanging upside down partway up the waterfall—at a height of roughly three hundred feet. The rope around their legs was held by a member of the Dark Water Forces who was hidden in the cataract, the powerful curtain of water posing no obstacle at all to his kind. While the two girls hung outside the actual falls, they were naturally subjected to its spray. In order that they might continue breathing, Galil had wrapped them from head to toe in a thin transparent membrane. Not a drop of water would penetrate it, but they could still breathe freely. While it may have seemed an unnecessary and even bizarre bit of concern on his part, it was clear that his true motivation wasn't merely an evil desire to keep his prisoners from dying too quickly.

And so they waited. Some of the warriors concealed themselves in the pool at the base of the waterfall; others took cover behind damp boulders with weapons in hand while a deadly determination churned with the roar of the cataract.

And finally, the time came.

The first to notice was the one in the curtain of water who held up Taki and May. The instant he sensed something other than water not quite behind himself but rather in the deafening torrent that fell from above, he took a terrific blow to the head before he could alert his compatriots, and his unconscious form was caught and held fast by a pair of arms like steel.

As the water battered their backs, Taki and May twisted around and saw a hazy but gorgeous countenance peering out at them from the dark torrents. There was scarcely enough moonlight to make out who it was.

"D!" they cried in unison, but thank heavens for small favors—the sound wasn't heard by anyone due to the membrane that surrounded them.

After making sure that they were fine, D then slowly began to climb the falls with the rope in one hand. The group below didn't notice. It was beyond their comprehension that the hand of deliverance would reach down from so incredibly high overhead—from thousands of feet above!

D had indeed come for them, and once he had rescued the pair he made a sure and powerful climb to the top. However, even a little consideration made it clear what an incredible amount of strength this labor entailed. It wasn't just the two girls he was carrying—over one shoulder he also had the Dark Water Forces member who'd held the rope around the girls' ankles. The man hadn't been slain to guard against his blood spilling into the pool at the base of the waterfall, but he added greatly to the load. What's more, there was the force of the water dropping from so high above to consider—it felt hard as steel when it struck.

After climbing about a thousand feet, D sensed something odd off to the right. A rock jutted out roughly into the water. Ordinarily, water would chisel and smooth the rock walls flat over the ages. This rock was an impossible occurrence. Perhaps D had noticed it on his way down the falls, because it was there that he set down the two girls and the unconscious Dark Water Forces member. It was more than wide enough to accommodate them all.

Without cutting through the membrane, D wrapped the thin rope he held in his hand around the outcropping and told them, "Stay here."

The reason went without saying. He intended to finish off the Dark Water Forces.

But how had he gotten there in the first place? Without a horse, it would've taken D a few hours just to reach the top of the falls. Had he discovered some other trick from antiquity like the chain? Or had he known something?

"Well, I'm off."

And with no more apparent concern for the two girls, D took his foe under his arm and dove toward the pool at the base of the waterfall. He plummeted twelve hundred feet. With several tons of water falling per second, no one could distinguish the presence of the Hunter or the Dark Water Forces member he had with him.

Allowing the water to carry him where it would, D then struck out with his blade whenever he came into contact with his foes. In no time at all the dozen opponents who'd concealed themselves in the basin and flow had been slain, each dying instantly, and by the time the soldiers by the wet boulders noticed their losses, D had already leapt up onto the rocky surface to the left and cut into wet stone—or rather, he cut the film of water that covered the boulders. A number of shadowy figures fell without so much as a groan, tumbling backward and sinking once more into the stony ground.

The Hunter attacked almost as if he knew where every last one of them was hidden, even killing the foes who appeared from the looming rock wall with a single blow each, until finally D faced Galil, who stood at the edge of the basin.

"Just what I should've expected from you, D!" the commander of the Dark Water Forces said with admiration, his pearly teeth bared. Taking a quick glance at the falls behind him, he added, "It would appear I've lost my hostages as well. Are they still alive?"

D nodded.

"Good. If there's one thing I didn't like about all this, it's what I had to do to those girls," Galil remarked, the smile on his face horribly serene. "But I'm afraid the other woman was a completely different matter. See for yourself."

Galil raised his right hand and gestured to the black water at his feet. Although the spray fell like a heavy downpour where the two of them were positioned on the outer rim of the waterfall basin, the pair of strange black boulders that loomed to either side of

Galil formed a perfect shelter from the rain. What he pointed to was a spot where the rock had been worn down deep to form a small pool with a placid surface. Something pale drifted into view like a specter. Miska.

"The baron's companion. I don't know whether she's a client of yours or not, but it seemed like she'd serve as a hostage. That makes it a little more difficult to fight, doesn't it, D?"

The blade of the sword D held in his right hand glittered in the moonlight.

"Before we do battle, there's something I'd like to know. Did you come from the top of the falls?"

"Yes," he said, though it was rare for this young man to reply to a question from his foes.

"And the way you dispatched my men—it was almost as if you knew precisely where we were all positioned. Did you get someone to tell you?"

"This canyon was home to a race of people in greatest antiquity whose rule rivaled that of the Nobility," said D. "They hung a chain from the rock face in order to determine the number in their tribe or to uncover invaders. It's said that when it strikes the rock wall, the chain sends a very special sound wave out across the canyon that makes the number and position of every living thing clear. It even reaches into caves in the rocks or the flowing water."

"I see. I wasn't aware of that. So, would that be the echoes I heard? Though in terms of the timing, I don't see how you could've been the one ringing it."

D raised his left hand.

Seeing that the Hunter was missing everything from the wrist down, Galil then squinted his eyes.

"My hand rang the chain. And that's enough talk."

"Not quite. How did you manage to get to the top of the falls without us noticing?"

"I took the elevator."

As Galil's brow crinkled, a silvery flash of light sank into his face. D's stroke split open the very same place he'd cut in the past, sending the man reeling backward.

Galil's right hand stroked the mark where the blade had run from the top of his head down to his chin. The line vanished.

"Last time, I let my guard down. I'm much better prepared tonight."

Galil's finger pointed toward the submerged Noblewoman, and then a tiny spark flew from between his fingers and hit Miska's right shoulder. Her pale shoulder burst out from the inside. The spark had been an ultra-compact missile.

"That's a strange weapon for the commander of the Dark Water Forces to be using," D remarked.

"Lay down your sword, D. Join us."

Once again, the sound of water droplets began to ring out.

"With you and her under our control, slaying even the offspring of Lord Balazs would be a simple task. D—drop the blade."

The simple yet deep melody might've sounded like a lullaby to the Hunter. D's knees buckled. He didn't have anything plugging his ears now.

Galil succumbed to a grin, but it was summarily wiped from his lips. He'd seen a caped figure gracefully closing from behind D, moving in the moonlight with a blueness reminiscent of the bottom of the sea.

"Milord Baron Byron Balazs," Galil called out to him.

III

"I'm—"

"—a filthy assassin sent by my father. And that's all I need to know," the baron said in a tone that called to mind ice.

The sound of the droplets persisted. But with his ears plugged, the baron was reading Galil's lips.

"If you insist."

"Will you destroy me, or will you and yours die?"

"I must accomplish what I was sent here to do."

"Is my father well?" the baron inquired.

"He is the very picture of health."

"I should've liked to talk with him at length at least once more, but that's no longer possible. As soon as I arrive, I shall slay him."

"No—I can't allow that."

"I suppose even now my mother's grave never wants for flowers, does it?"

Galil said nothing.

"What's wrong? Answer me."

"Lord Balazs had it destroyed."

Despite the darkness, the man could see how the baron's complexion had changed.

"He feels the need to defile even the dead, does he?" the Nobleman muttered.

Galil backed away, driven by a fear greater than any even D had inspired in him.

"My dear baron—if you move, her life will be forfeit," Galil said, indicating Miska with his right hand.

"Nonsense," the baron laughed. "Nobles are dead from the very beginning."

The light that flashed from the hem of his cape caught Galil between the legs and shot up through him. As it flew out through the top of his head, the line it'd left in him vanished.

"My father always did have an eye for talent. How about this, then?"

The flash of light changed direction.

Blasting a missile into Miska as he went, Galil leapt for the enormous boulder to his right.

In midair, the light bisected his torso. Such an attack would be ineffectual against flowing water, but the streak of light that entered the man's torso grew thicker for an instant. The liquid cells that were about to join and close the wound were blown asunder by the sheer force of that light. Unable to rejoin, Galil's body was reduced to a pair of bizarre objects that fell into the same dark pool as Miska.

A column of water shot up.

Swiftly throwing himself into the pool, the baron pulled Miska out. The flesh around her shoulder and heart was torn open from the blast of the missiles.

"D—" the baron began, but seeing how the beautiful Hunter stood there silently with sword in hand, he decided against saying anything more.

The sound of the water droplets continued.

"Were you lulled into taking a nap? Or did you just want to see what I could do?" asked the baron.

Without a word, D turned his gaze to Miska.

Perhaps taking this as concern, the baron told him, "She'll be fine. After all, she harbors the Destroyer."

The Nobleman's face suddenly turned to the heavens.

D was already looking up at the sky.

What both of them had felt was a quaking—a grave tremor that seemed to rumble from the very deepest bowels of the earth.

"Get in the carriage," D said as he pointed in that direction.

Now the rocks and the falls—in fact, the whole canyon—were shaking. This must've been Galil's final contingency. Capable of putting even the Nobility to sleep, the rhythm of the droplets had shifted to sonic waves resonating in a destructive range, and the canyon had begun to collapse as a result.

As the baron ran with Miska cradled in his arms, chunks of the rock face fell and rebounded all around him, while the disturbance they caused in the flow of the water sent angry waves crashing over D. Turning and looking back as he opened the carriage door, the baron saw the waterfall writhing like a serpent and the blackness of the shattered precipice, which made it seem as if the very sky were falling.

After about three minutes of this energy running amok, the great canyon that had witnessed tens of thousands of years of history was destroyed, and order returned. Now only a few dribbles of water fell from the rock walls, which were adorned by the dull gleam of metal. With the rocks that had covered it now gone, the true nature of the cliff was finally laid bare. It was a massive metallic rampart. Most of the fortress had been lost in antiquity, leaving this section alone. Ultra-ancient technology had triumphed over the contemporary forces of destruction.

The ramparts hadn't been the least bit rattled by the power that had brought about the collapse, and on what appeared to be a radar site protruding from the lower region of the wall, the two girls remained safe and sound. Seeing the gorgeous man in black far below them in the wreckage of what had once been the waterfall's basin, they waved.

The light of morning had begun to take stock of the world.

"That was a hell of a racket," a hoarse voice called out from D's feet as the Hunter made his way over to an entrance to the rear of the ramparts, where he could take a high-speed elevator up to retrieve the girls.

Bending over and picking up the severed limb, D then put it against his left wrist. And in the blink of an eye, his left hand was reconnected.

D had tossed the needle and extremely fine thread down at his feet before reattaching his hand. Even with the swift reflexes of a dhampir, it must've been quite an undertaking to wind up more than three miles of thread.

The left hand had interpreted the supersonic waves released when the chain struck the cliff and conveyed the number and location of the Dark Water Forces members to D—and knowing that this thread had acted as a go-between, D's action might've been described as ungrateful. The only way he could've known where the bizarre priest Yoputz was hidden was through that very thread.

Somewhere off in the distance, there were signs of movement. Apparently the baron and Miska—and their carriages and horses—had survived.

"Brawling in an ancient battlefield, smashing a whole canyon to bits—this sure has been a lively trip!" the voice said with exasperation. "That takes care of all the assassins that've been after Balazs till now, but there's still time. New trouble may come looking for us. Don't get sloppy."

D walked off toward the ramparts without addressing the remark. And as he did, the air of solitude that hung about him seemed perfectly complemented by the frigid light of dawn.

Postscript

I've been to Transylvania twice. The first time was in 1987 on a personal trip for sightseeing purposes, and the second time was in 1996 for the production of a documentary program for NHK (Japanese public television). Between the first and second visit lay nine long years. And that's just another name for change.

The first time I visited Romania's capital, Bucharest, all the buildings and everyone's clothes were the same color, with the occasional garment in red seeming to glow in contrast. Needless to say, there must've been other colors as well, but that's the only one I can recall now. The president in that time was Ceausescu—the very same person who, along with his wife, was later executed by a firing squad of his own soldiers. Growing tired of steak and salad and carbonated drinks, I went to a Chinese restaurant I'd learned about from a guidebook. They didn't take our order there, but rather pointed to just two of the countless items on the menu while informing us that this was all they had. On seeing a long line of people, I was curious as to what was going on and went over for a closer look, where I saw a small vehicle selling sherbet. I believe each person's serving was smaller than the yolk of a fried egg.

On my second visit, a shifty-looking guy was out in front of Bucharest Station distributing little handbills, which turned out to be promoting a nude show. People's clothing had become colorful, and there was even a Japanese restaurant. Only the poster prominently displayed in the shop's window stated in large print that the menu consisted of curry and spaghetti. This was the state even after substantial changes to the administration, and apparently there was no organized crime in Romania. There was no business—no money to be made. I was to learn this all too well through a certain incident the first day I was in Bulgaria.

I felt the passage of time most markedly when I once again visited the mountain stronghold of Dracula/Vlad Tepes, which looms at the top of a Transylvanian mountain. This is the same fortress that Tepes's wife is shown throwing herself from when she receives false news of his death from the Turkish army in the opening of Francis Ford Coppola's *Dracula*. Now it's known as Poienari Castle. Although there was equipment for illumination and a hut there when I first visited, they had already been abandoned and anyone could come or go as they pleased. But on my second trip, what should I find right in front of the bridge to cross over to the castle but some old guy from the nearby village reading a newspaper and making people buy tickets. And yet, there was no sign that any improvements had been made to the castle or grounds, and even the guideposts that had been set in the ground had disappeared. So the service had gotten worse and now they charged you for it— neither Castle Dracula nor Transylvania could buck the tides of international commerce.

Furthermore, the place where Dracula first appears before Englishman Jonathan Harker in the guise of a coachman—the accursed Borgo Pass—is the complete opposite of the way the book describes it. With a clear view for three hundred sixty degrees, naked men and women enjoy sunbathing in the woods there, while further in is what can only be taken as the beacon of commercialism in this country—the towering Dracula Hotel.

And yet, these things aside, the land and sky of Transylvania certainly evoke Stoker's work. Lightning that races right across the ground, forests dark and deep, the remains of ancient castles, decrepit churches and homes, and women who come down the road before dawn with lit lanterns in hand in a ceremony to call back the dead. No doubt all of these things still live and breathe somewhere in the pages of *Pale Fallen Angel*.

Hideyuki Kikuchi
April 15, 2008
while watching *Dracula Has Risen from the Grave* (1968)

And now, a preview of the next book in the
Vampire Hunter D series

VAMPIRE HUNTER D
VOLUME 12
PALE FALLEN ANGEL PARTS THREE AND FOUR

Written by
Hideyuki Kikuchi

Illustrations by
Yoshitaka Amano

English translation by
Kevin Leahy

Coming in March 2009
from Dark Horse Books and Digital Manga Publishing

Pale Fallen Angel

PART THREE

A Foggy Road Through the Rocks

I

The fog rolled in just after noon. With the sinuous moves of an alluring dancer, the milky-white water particles clung to the driverless carriages and D, who rode beside them.

Hemmed in on either side by great craggy chunks of rock, the road ran on like a slender ribbon. You couldn't really call it a path through the bottom of a valley—it was quite literally a road weaving between the rocks. And as it was usually easier and easier to stray from the road the thicker the fog grew, it was obvious the stone bulwarks would come in handy.

It was nearly noon. Once they traversed this pass and spent another half day crossing the plains, their destination of Krauhausen would be waiting for them at twilight.

They were finally there. But how many people harbored this emotion in their heart? Naturally, there were no voices from the coffins sealed away in the carriages, and D sat astride his mount with a cold clear expression from which no hint of emotion could be gleaned.

It was about thirty minutes after they started down the foggy road that the Hunter's eyes took on a faint gleam. Stopping his horse and doubling back, he then rapped lightly on the carriage door.

What is it? the baron asked in a voice no one save D could hear.

"Don't you know?" asked D. His voice could likewise be heard by the baron's ears alone.

No. What's happened?

"This isn't the right road. We seem to have lost our way."

The road had vanished at some point without their even realizing it.

That's not like you. Although I must add that I didn't sense anything, either. Is it due to the fog?

The Nobleman was apparently cognizant of that, at least.

"Probably," D replied.

Even with his ultra-keen senses, the fog seemed like nothing more than ordinary water particles.

"What do you make of it?" the Hunter inquired, but not of Balazs.

"It's just plain old fog. Even I don't have a clue why we've lost our way."

At that response from his left hand, D ran his gaze over the rocky mounds to either side of them.

"Those rocks are real enough," the hoarse voice continued. "You fixing to wait here until the fog lifts?"

"No."

"I get you," D's left hand said as he raised it up high.

In the palm of it, human eyes and a nose swiftly took shape. Its mouth opened.

The *whooosh* that resounded wasn't the sound of it drawing breath, but was rather the groan of the wind. The fog eddied as it coursed into the palm of the hand.

Ten seconds passed. Twenty seconds.

And then, when the trailing edge of the milky whiteness had been swallowed, someone exclaimed in astonishment, "Well, I'll be damned!"

The voice came from the very same mouth that had devoured the fog.

But even before it had said a word, D had noticed the same thing.

They were on the very same road as before. With great chunks of stone lining either side, the road ran straight for another hundred and fifty feet before breaking to the right.

Something strange is going on, the baron's voice was heard to say.

"We're back in the same spot again," D replied before turning around. "While we were lost, the amount of ground we covered was roughly a hundred feet. I have to assume that something was done to us during that time."

A mere hundred feet. Though that didn't seem like much, getting both D and the baron to advance down that otherworldly road for such a distance before noticing anything was miraculous.

"Know anything about this?"

The Hunter's query pertained to who might've set this up.

Dr. de Carriole could manage it.

"Do you know what moves he's likely to make?"

A number of them. He was my tutor in my infancy.

"Then I'll need you to keep your eyes peeled."

And with these words, D flicked the reins of the horses drawing the carriage. Accompanied by the creak of wooden wheels, the horses stepped forward. They approached the turn in the rocks.

D took the turn first.

Thirty feet up ahead, there lay a dark figure. Lying face down, the person was dressed in black garments, and wore a coat in the same hue.

Like D.

It certainly looked as if the attack had already started.

D dismounted.

Stop, the baron ordered him. *It's obviously a trap. Don't go near him.*

However, they couldn't very well leave a person lying there across the whole road.

White clouds floated in the blue sky. To either side of the path, flowers swayed in ivory beauty. And on the road lay a corpse.

Perhaps D intended to accept this invitation. Going over to the remains, the Hunter bent down.

It was just then that the corpse turned over.

A pale face looked up at D . . . with the face of D himself.

For just a second the two exchanged looks, but then D swiftly stood back up and drew his sword. There was a flash of stark light from his blade, and the head of the figure on the ground was removed from its body.

"It's a doll," said D.

At that point, he felt like something was softly pulling away from his own face.

Sure enough, wood was visible where the head had been severed from the figure at his feet.

What a strange thing to do, the baron said, his voice wavering with perplexity. *If that was the work of Dr. de Carriole, I don't recall him having any such ability. D, do you sense anything out of the ordinary?*

"Not a thing," D replied succinctly as he tossed the wooden remains to one side of the road and got back on his horse. But one thing gnawed at the heart beneath those black garments.

The two carriages passed by in silence, and the only one out in the white sunlight to hear the dwindling creak of the wheels was the severed head of the doll. But as it lay exposed to the sun, the smooth, polished wood of its face was now flat and utterly featureless. The countenance of the gorgeous Vampire Hunter had vanished without a trace.

Though it was daytime, the room was hemmed in by a thick darkness. The darkness jelled even further, forming two figures that were darker still—a stooped old man, and a young man who stood bolt upright and completely motionless behind him. The old man was draped in gold brocade, and he wore a long robe. The unusually lengthy garment fell across the floor behind him like a shadow.

Suddenly putting his right hand to his ear, the old man said, "It's finished!"

"And you think that'll take care of the Hunter?" the young man asked.

Apparently the old man had succeeded in something, and while the other man seemed to be his apprentice or at least his subordinate, the young man didn't seem at all delighted by this. To the contrary, he sounded quite skeptical.

"The spell has been cast. There can be no doubt of that. However—"

"However what?"

"There is one thing that troubles me," the old man said, his expression horribly intense as he slowly turned toward the young man.

Needless to say, while there were other reasons why the darkness of the chamber was fraught with tension, if one were to claim it all sprang from the old man's look, no one would ever doubt it. Hidden beneath age spots and wrinkles and a hoary goatee, his face was like that of an ancient mummy, his thread-thin eyes brimming with a yellow light, while tremendous intellect, evil, and willpower all spilled from his green irises.

"The mask you made of him, Zanus—is it perfect?"

"Do you doubt me?" the young man—Zanus—asked in a hard tone.

"Not at all. I recognize your skill. After all, your 'transference' hex proved effective," the old man said with a nod before turning back the way he'd faced originally.

"Then I shall proceed according to schedule," the young man told him, bowing as he prepared to take his leave.

"Our foe is the same man who slew the water warriors. You mustn't let your guard down. Be on your toes," the old man said, his voice trailing after the young man.

Once Zanus had left, the old man didn't move for a while, but eventually he took a seat on a nearby sofa and mumbled introspectively, "Baron Byron Balazs . . . I wonder if you remember me? Do you still recall the name of the hopeful tutor who saw in you the salvation of your race?"

"Dr. de Carriole," a voice called out from somewhere in the darkness.

As the old man spun around reflexively, his expression was awash with a respect and fear that made it clear he'd guessed who it was that addressed him.

"Oh, my—when did you get here?" the old man—Dr. de Carriole—said with head hung low, while in his heart he chided himself. His laboratory was equipped with warning systems that should've been able to detect even the slightest difference in the makeup of the air.

"I am always around you. It wouldn't do to have you using the fruits of your strange research against me, now would it!"

"Surely you jest," de Carriole replied, but to himself he thought, *That was a century and a half ago.*

That one time alone the old man had tried to put up some resistance. To this day, even he himself didn't know what the result had been, for although he'd tried, nothing had changed at all. The assassins he'd sent had vanished without a trace, and the source of the voice had appeared before the doctor just as always. And from that day to this, de Carriole had gone without a single soul ever censuring him or accusing him of any wrongdoing. Because after that, he'd sworn allegiance to the source of the voice in the darkness.

"Is my son coming?"

From this question, the voice could belong to none other than Vlad Balazs.

"Indeed he is. He'll be here in half a day," de Carriole replied.

"So, even with all your power, you still didn't manage to slay him? That comes as little surprise, given that he has that Hunter for a bodyguard."

De Carriole turned with a start toward the depths of the darkness. He could see through the gloom as clear as day. They both could. Yet his eyes found nothing save blackness.

"Are you familiar with 'D,' then, sire?" he asked.

"No."

The doctor was at a loss for words.

"I don't know D," the voice continued. "Or, at least, any manhunter by that name. However, he does bear a distinct resemblance to another great personage whose name I do know. Or so it would appear."

"A great personage . . ." de Carriole began before breaking off.

It must've been centuries since he'd been surprised twice in a single day. His skin, which had died ages ago and had only been reinvigorated by reanimating drugs, now rose in goose bumps.

The voice mentioned "a great personage." To the best of the doctor's knowledge, there was only one person on earth he would refer to as such. However, from the way he spoke, it seemed it had to be someone else. In which case—

Memories swirled and flowed. One by one, his brain cells were lanced by the point of a needle. Active cells and slumbering cells alike. Cells that had long ago fallen into disuse and ancient brain cells that his own brain had even forgotten existed. And in one of them—he found it! However, it gave off only a momentary flash before fading into eternal darkness. Freezing the flash would be impossible. However, he tried to comprehend it. Forgetting all about his surroundings, de Carriole focused his entire consciousness on that one point. The actual memory of the concrete information took shape for only an instant—and then it quickly slipped away. De Carriole's concentration pursued it, and a split second before it was swallowed by the nothingness, he brushed the tail end of it.

"Now I remember . . ." he mumbled, not because the information he'd wrested from his brain needed to be spoken, but because it threatened to leave him again. "That great personage . . . did indeed have . . . just one . . . But . . . it couldn't be . . . It's simply not possible . . . that a filthy ghoul . . . a Hunter of the Nobility . . . could be *his* . . ."

"Perhaps that is the case. But then, perhaps it is not," the voice said gravely. It was as much a confession that he himself couldn't judge or comprehend the situation. "If the latter is true, then to us, he is merely Byron's cohort, and we shall have no choice but to eradicate him. But if the opposite is the case, there's much to be feared."

And saying this, the voice gave a low laugh.

Is he prepared to bare his teeth even against the great one's very own— de Carriole thought, terrified by the concept. In a manner of speaking, he would be making a foe of the great one himself—the Nobility as a whole were bound by that great personage's regard for his family like no other rule.

"Make ready, doctor! Make ready!" he was told by a voice that echoed both high and low from the darkness. "Before they enter my lands or after makes no difference. Use every means at your disposal if you must, but slay them."

"Kindly leave it to me. You can rest easy while de Carriole handles everything."

It was just then that a voice like a long, long sob was heard from nowhere in particular.

II

It was a woman, and no doubt she was incredibly distraught. Her grief was so great it'd driven her mad, yet still she couldn't help but lament. That was the impression anyone would've gotten.

"Aside from yourself, there is one other who understands that my son is approaching. But I have to wonder, why is it that what should be a song of triumph is instead a wail such as would greet the dead?"

The voice was tinged with laughter.

"Dr. de Carriole!" it added.

"Milord!" the robed figure exclaimed, visibly shaken.

"You had best go. Not surprisingly, that's enough to rend even my heart. I would not have anyone else hear that voice."

"I understand," the old man said as he bowed his head, and at that point he realized that the source of the voice was no longer with him.

"I understand," he repeated to himself. "But who are *you* to speak of how it rends your heart?"

And once he'd spoken, a chill surely ran down the old man's spine, but no bolt of lightning fell from the heavens to strike him down.

A few minutes later, de Carriole descended a lengthy spiral staircase to a depth even he was unsure of toward a certain chamber. In scattered places on the stone walls atomic flames burned with a blue light, casting flickering shadows on the steps and walls.

His descent ended abruptly, as always. As he stood in a vast hall paved in stone, guards sheathed in armor closed on him from either side. All of them were synthetic humans. Weighing over a ton each thanks to the heavy alloys, their footfalls didn't even make a sound. Their long spears came to bear on the doctor, the tips glowing red.

"Out of my way!"

Before the doctor had finished speaking, red glows extended from the ends of the spears to his chest and exited through his back. The rock wall behind him turned red hot, and in no time at all holes two inches in diameter had been bored into it.

When these guards were imbued with life, the first thing they'd been set to do was to slaughter absolutely anyone who happened to come here.

"Idiots! You know nothing of the world. Out of my way!"

As the doctor took a step forward, a blinding band of light shot from the sleeve of his robe and mowed through the guards. And when the light returned to his sleeve once more, the old man walked over to the door that lay before him.

The remaining guards couldn't move a muscle, their spears at the ready but otherwise frozen in place. Though the volume of light was sufficient, there was something frosty about this subterranean illumination that gave all beneath it the doleful aspect of lifeless sculptures.

Halting before a door, the old man put his right index finger to his mouth and bit the tip of it slightly. The drop of blood that welled up so quickly fell into a hole that opened in front of the lock, and less than a second later, the sound of the lock being undone rang out.

Taking the golden doorknob in hand, de Carriole trembled. He had just reflected on the person he was about to see and what would transpire. While heaving a deep sigh, he pushed open the door. It took just as long for the door to open as it did for his sigh to end.

And then the voice that sounded like some despondent lost soul once again reached the ancient sorcerer's ears. Who was this woman who wept in the untold depths of the earth, surrounded by guards who would slay any who drew near?

In scattered places along the lengthy corridor were set doors that seemed to be of bronze. To either side of these doors atomic fires burned.

Casting vague shadows on the floor as he advanced, the old mummy of a man looked as if he were guided by the woman's plaintive cries.

In no time, a door appeared ahead of him, as enormous as a castle gate. The voice was spilling from behind it. However, it seemed utterly impossible that those echoes—thread thin and low and full of grief—could make it through the great door that towered before him.

When he reached the foot of the door, de Carriole put his blood into this lock as he had done with the last. Extracting his DNA, memory circuits within the lock then matched it against the list of people who were authorized for access before giving the okay for the door to unlock. It took but a millisecond.

Splitting down the middle, the door opened to either side. It was fifteen feet thick, and once de Carriole had gone through it, he looked up at the ceiling. It must've been over thirty feet high. He was greeted by light that was like that of the evening.

There was water as far as the eye could see. As proof that there wasn't even a ripple from the wind, the dead-calm surface of the water displayed no tendency to cling to the light as it spread in a placid expanse. There was no end to it. No matter how hard you looked, you simply couldn't see beyond it.

The floor at de Carriole's feet formed a stone staircase with about ten steps, and the lowest one was underwater. At the bottom of the staircase there floated a boat made of bronze. The reason it wasn't moored was because there was no movement of the water.

The woman's voice continued to wail, rustling across the water.

Like some investigator who'd sought that voice for a century, de Carriole climbed into the boat, took the oars that were stored in it, and began to paddle through the water. The ripples spread. It had been a long time since this expanse of water had known any kind of wave.

After rowing for about ten minutes, de Carriole then ceased and listened intently. His eardrums confirmed that the woman's voice was coming from right below the starboard bulwark. Leaning out, he peered through the surface of the water.

Just below the boat, a woman drifted with threads of blood flowing from her body. No, that wasn't entirely correct. The woman was trapped in a single spot for all eternity. Her long black tresses didn't drift, or sink, or float at all, but rather stayed twined around her body and the white dress that she wore, while eyes the same hue as her hair peered up with a quiet emptiness. The smooth line of her nose left an impression that carried over to the rest of her body, right down to the tips of her fingers, causing the old man to wonder for the first time in years if perhaps the water hadn't washed all possible hardness out of her. And the woman's lips. Bloodless and paler than even her skin, he had to wonder why they alone seemed to stand out. It was because they were moving. And through their sensuous and heartbreaking trembling, the voice was produced.

"Milady," he called out to her after a short time had passed. "Milady, it is I—de Carriole. I've come because there's something I must tell you."

It took time to penetrate the water that separated the two, speaker and listener.

"Thank you for coming, de Carriole," she said, her heartbroken tone becoming emotionless as she greeted him.

The old man prostrated himself.

"Have you responded to my voice? To my cries of deepest woe?"

"Indeed I have. Milady has been privy to things even I myself do not know."

"Being underwater, I can hear the sound of the stars moving and the world turning. The sound of coffins opening, the baying of wolves, the wailing of the sun as it sinks beyond the horizon and the jubilant cries of the darkness."

"Incredible."

"My child has returned, hasn't he?" the woman's voice inquired.

"Indeed he has. He is now but a half day from the castle."

"And what of *him*?"

"He seems rather agitated."

"I should think so."

"Although this is merely my own interpretation, I would say that Lord Byron has returned after acquiring power surpassing his father's."

"And he knows it, too. How splendid," she said with a laugh, her voice buoyant even underwater. "Then I take it you are in charge of the efforts to hinder him, are you not?"

"Yes, milady," he replied without any hesitation.

"And I'm sure my child will make it through."

"No," de Carriole responded flatly. "I won't allow that. Lord Byron's life will surely be taken before he enters this land."

"You mean to suggest that a member of the Nobility would fall to humans?" the woman said, chuckling once again.

"Zanus has already gone out to meet him."

The woman's laughter ceased.

"Zanus has?"

"Indeed."

"So, that's who's gone, is it? I see . . . Perhaps Byron *will* be slain."

"It is as you say, milady. And the Hunter acting as his bodyguard is already under our control."

"This is merely the prelude, de Carriole. Merely the prelude."

"Yes, milady. The next person you lay eyes on shall be Lord Byron or myself—and the other one shall never look upon you again."

"It was so good of you to inform me of this, de Carriole. You have my thanks."

"Think nothing of it."

And then, without any further words of parting, de Carriole began to row the boat away again. But his vessel came to a dead stop just as the stone staircase and the doorway began to take shape.

"Milady," he muttered.

He was working the oars. He could even feel them digging into the water. And yet the boat didn't move an inch. And he also saw something calmly reach up for the gunwale from the surface of the water. It didn't take him any time at all to realize he was sinking.

"Am I to take it that you don't wish me to lay a hand on Lord Byron? Very well then."

Rising, he held his right hand out parallel to the water's surface. Water had already begun to creep into the boat over the gunwales.

From the sleeve of his robe something like a silver thread shot out with a trail behind it, but it mixed with the water and quickly diffused.

As the water rose to his ankles, de Carriole set one foot out of the boat and onto the water's surface. He didn't sink. The other leg followed—but even after he'd put his entire weight onto the water, its surface supported him as if the soles of his shoes were resting on a stone floor.

He watched coolly as the bronze boat sank like a petal off a flower. The shore was still quite some distance away. Letting out a single sigh, the aged scientist slowly began to walk back on the path he'd created across the surface of the water.

III

While they still had about an hour to go before leaving the rocks, one of the cyborg horses twisted an ankle. Inspecting it, D discovered that an artificial ligament in its heel had snapped. He decided to take a rest so that he could repair it. The condition of the other horses would also need to be checked.

"Once we're through here, we'll hit the plains," D said as if addressing someone. "For your foes, that'll be the last redoubt. They'll be coming at us in full force."

Not necessarily, Baron Balazs countered. *No, they may come at us, but they won't play their trumps until after we're in the village. I'm sure that's how Dr. de Carriole would do it.*

"I see. Do you know the names of the most powerful opposition in Krauhausen?" D inquired.

First of all, there's Zanus, the voice replied. *Though he's Dr. de Carriole's star pupil, I don't know all that much about him. Only that while the doctor continues to grow older and older, Zanus still seems to stay just around twenty. If he's not a Noble, he'd have to be a synthetic human. Ordinarily he serves as the doctor's assistant, but it's said that he can act autonomously when the need arises. As for his ability—I really don't know. From all that I've heard, he's a fearsome opponent—that's all they say.*

"Who's next?"

Chlomo the Makeup Lover, the baron replied, a ring of distaste to his voice. *He's the captain of my father's personal guards, and from morning till night the man plays with cosmetics. And he applies them not only to himself, but to others as well. Although I don't know exactly what that accomplishes, one theory has it that the person he applies them to takes on a personality befitting that makeup.*

"And the third?"

Sai Fung of the Thousand Limbs. He's a martial-arts genius. They say that using only his bare hands he can beat opponents armed with ranged weapons. It seems that the brutalized remains of his enemies look as if they've been pummeled by a thousand people. And those are our three greatest foes. In addition, there are their underlings. They are also formidable. Each is probably worth about ten ordinary soldiers.

"Yet they haven't come out to meet us."

Once he finished inspecting his cyborg horse, D settled into a hollow in a nearby rock. No matter how exceptional he might be as a Vampire Hunter, so long as he had Noble blood in him, he would find it far more exhausting than a human being to labor out in the sun. By nature dhampirs sought darkness in the daylight, yet at the same time, their recuperative powers transcended those of ordinary people.

With the carriages parked out in the sun and D melded with the darkness formed by the rock, the road through the boulders was visited by an ancient stillness that early afternoon.

It was perhaps a few seconds later that the horses whinnied.

D came out of the hollow.

Cut free of the carriages with a flash of his sword, the cyborg horses galloped forward. They and D alone had noticed the flapping of wings closing on them from beyond the rocks. It wasn't a sound that human hearing could easily detect—it was a hum even fainter than the buzz of a mosquito.

Perhaps whatever was approaching sensed something out of the ordinary, but as a noisy trio came around one of the rocks to close swiftly on D, a stark flash of light blazed from behind the Hunter. All but one of the sounds were lost, but as the streak of light was drawn back into the carriage, strange ripples passed across the black surface of the last noisy invader. Most likely it was some kind of vibration.

The flapping of its wings was replaced by a groan as the object collided with a rock on the opposite side of the road—and exploded. More than the explosion itself, it was the sight of the fireball that devastated the rock wall that made it clear it'd been some kind of incendiary bomb.

The fireball swiftly spread, assailing D and the carriages as the Hunter rolled over. A shock wave accompanied the hundred-thousand-degree flames. The pair of carriages were easily knocked on their sides and slammed against the rock face. Even now, blistering winds beat against the vehicles.

A few seconds passed—after the flames had raced away down the rocky road, only the tempestuous wind was left in their wake.

Are you okay, D? the baron's voice inquired.

The road belched white smoke like some burnt and twisted caldera, while out in the middle of it sat a black shape that hadn't been there before. Flames swayed here and there and black smoke poured from the shape as it rose gracefully. It had taken on human form. That of the most gorgeous young man in black.

"Are you okay?" the Hunter replied, the baron's question apparently having served to prove that the Nobleman still lived.

D said nothing more as he struck the shoulders and chest of his coat to extinguish the flames. No one there noticed the crude belch of satisfaction that escaped from his left hand. With a coat made of special fibers——heat resistant, cold resistant, and impact resistant—and a left hand that could gobble up flames, D had safely emerged from the fiery inferno.

In the far reaches of the plains, a steam-powered coach was parked. The steam engine at its rear looked like a cylinder crowned with a bell, and on top of it a man sat cross-legged.

"Look, a fire's broken out," he muttered, adding, "but—"

With one hand he held a pair of binoculars to his eyes. As for the other hand, it had been engaged for quite some time now in scratching roughly at his back through a fishnet garment. He was reaching over one shoulder to get at his back—but astonishingly enough, his hand hung all the way down to his waist.

"—I don't think that's all it'll take to finish off Lord Byron. Especially not with the man called D as his bodyguard."

His tone was that of a casual conversation.

The reply came from inside the coach.

"I realize that. The firebombs were simply a test. I checked into something I wanted to know."

"That's good. So, what exactly did you cook up?"

"A face transference."

"You can't be serious!" he exclaimed as the hand stopped scratching away at his waist. "You went and—If you screw this up, Zanus, you'll be—"

"I'm ninety-nine percent confident."

"You could be ninety-nine point nine nine nine percent sure and it'd still be a far cry from perfect. Who were you gunning for, anyway?"

"D."

"Holy shit!" the man cried, reeling backward.

His momentum had him just about to fall off the engine, or rather, he actually dropped about three feet, and then stopped there. His long right leg was braced against the bell-shaped head.

"What complete madness! That pretty boy's not of this world, you know. I don't care how damn good you're supposed to be at making masks, that's just plain suicide!"

"No, it's not," Zanus countered in a voice brimming with self-confidence. "As I believe I just told you, the results have been verified. As a success, I might add."

"Is that a fact? I find that hard to swallow . . . even for that son of a bitch Chlomo."

Like a water strider skipping across the surface of a pond, the man lithely hopped back to the very end of the engine, where he let out a great laugh.

"Don't let me hear any more of your idiotic guffawing, Sai Fung!" Zanus said, his voice charged with wrath.

"Okay, dammit, okay! But that son of a bitch Chlomo—"

But once he'd spoken, his mouth hung open in apparent surprise as he cautiously peered around in all directions with a look of fear that was not an act. What was more, he sensed a chilling air from inside the coach that was normally unthinkable.

"Don't talk about him," Zanus ordered him.

"I read you."

Standing up gracefully on top of the engine, the man—Sai Fung of the Thousand Limbs—brought the binoculars up to his eyes once again.

"Hot damn! Now this is something! Let's hurry up and get the hell out of here. The whole damn neighborhood's waking up!" he exclaimed.

Presently, there was a sound from inside the cylinder like a robot or some set of gears going into action, and with a keen whistle white smoke shot out in all directions from exhaust vents around the joint of the bell-shaped head. This unconventional vehicle that didn't rely on horses turned around at a good clip and began speeding back to the village of Krauhausen, which lay a quarter of a day's trip away.

But what did Zanus mean by a success? And who was this third man named by the baron as one of the three greatest warriors in Krauhausen and so feared by the other two—Chlomo the Makeup Lover?

Before they had come out of the rocks, D noticed the wall of smoke rising high into the heavens.

"Looks like a brush fire," said his left hand. "Those flames earlier probably started it. The wind's blowing toward the village. Our best bet is to just wait here."

From where D sat, that seemed like the wisest plan, too.

Flames shot up from the grass, and the gusting wind only served to fan the fire. Everything in their field of view was tinged with voracious hues of orange and black.

Just then—the earth shook terribly. The rocks to either side of the group creaked, and sparks flew where they banged together. The instant a diagonal crack opened across a massive boulder that looked to weigh a hundred tons, D had already doubled back and whipped the hindquarters of the horses hitched to the lead carriage. After sending the second carriage—Miska's—on its way as well, the Hunter was about to take off when the ground sprang up as if something incredibly huge was wriggling below.

The rock went flying. Both D and his horse flew into the air, too—almost straight up. After rising nearly thirty feet they halted, and as the mount and rider dropped straight back to earth, that hundred-ton boulder came right down on top of them.

Literally escaping by a hair's breadth, the figure in black leapt from the back of the horse as it was quickly crushed into an unrecognizable pile of meat, electronic parts, and steel framework, and he then flew like an arrow toward the exit from the rock-lined road. The way he curled into a ball and shot from the exit, it seemed as if he were riding the shock waves of the massive boulder that'd fallen behind him.

Out in the middle of the flames a good sixty feet from the rocks, D tried to see where the carriages had gone, but even with eyes that could see through the black smoke as if it weren't there, he could find no trace of the two vehicles anywhere.

"Oh, that baron should do just fine, I'm sure. Even if he can't get out of his carriage by day."

Flames blew into the left hand as it spoke.

"The village is on the other side of this," the left hand continued. "If we don't hurry up and go, the fire will spread here, too. There's no telling when the wind might change."

A mass of flame shot up by D's side.

"Oh, looks like there's a nest of firebugs or something down there. One false step onto that baby and that'll be the end of the story."

The voice was moving forward. Stepping right through the flames, D broke into a run. The ground was spitting up fire, and the air shimmered in places from the heat. A mass of flames went up. The hem of the Hunter's coat flashed out, and the flames dispersed feebly in all directions.

"Wow! I thought without a horse you'd be in a bad way, but it doesn't look like it makes any difference at all on flat ground. You're something else!" the hoarse voice remarked.

As D ran, he turned and looked back. There were footsteps following him. And more than just one set. The quaking of the earth testified to that.

A terrific force struck the ground, echoing like a tremor.

D's eyes caught a shadowy group rolling forward like a fog beyond the flames. It was spearheaded by a massive swarm of giant black caterpillars covered by needlelike bristles. Behind them was a pack of ten-foot-long plains rats, followed in turn by three-headed boars and burrowing pythons—and this mob of plains-dwelling creatures stretched as far as the horizon in a wild stampede. Fearing fire, they raced off in search of someplace safe, and if caught in their path, even a fire dragon would have been crushed by the hoard. One giant black caterpillar already engulfed by the flames couldn't help but slow down, but in a heartbeat it was caught up in the stampede and crushed underfoot before it even had time to let out a scream.

It was only another three hundred feet to D. Even he didn't possess the speed necessary to outrun them. There was only one thing to do.

"You've got no choice but to get up on their backs," said his left hand.

Two hundred feet.

A hundred fifty.

However, when they had closed to within a hundred feet, the strangest thing occurred. Perhaps it was something they saw, perhaps something they sensed, but the caterpillars in the foremost rank tried to halt en masse. Sparks flew madly, but of course they couldn't stop the stampede. The force of those behind them surging forward promptly crushed those in the vanguard, and what should happen but those responsible then tumbled forward.

D leapt backward. From midair he saw it.

Between himself and the rampaging beasts, the earth had split open in a straight line. The sight of the creatures falling one after another into that black abyss resembled nothing so much as the dead being swallowed by hell. The chasm continued to grow. It even stretched to where D would land.

"This is incredible!" the left hand exclaimed with misplaced admiration as D drifted, right toward the black and bottomless abyss.

To be continued in

VAMPIRE HUNTER D
VOLUME 12
PALE FALLEN ANGEL PARTS THREE AND FOUR

About the Author

Hideyuki Kikuchi was born in Chiba, Japan, in 1949. He attended the prestigious Aoyama University and wrote his first novel, *Demon City Shinjuku*, in 1982. Over the past two decades, Kikuchi has written numerous horror novels, and is one of Japan's leading horror masters, working in the tradition of occidental horror writers like Fritz Leiber, Robert Bloch, H. P. Lovecraft, and Stephen King. As of 2004, there are seventeen novels in his hugely popular ongoing Vampire Hunter D series. Many live-action and anime movies of the 1980s and 1990s have been based on Kikuchi's novels.

About the Illustrator

Yoshitaka Amano was born in Shizuoka, Japan. He is well known as a manga and anime artist, and is the famed designer for the Final Fantasy game series. Amano took part in designing characters for many of Tatsunoko Productions' greatest cartoons, including *Gatchaman* (released in the U.S. as *G-Force* and *Battle of the Planets*). Amano became a freelancer at the age of thirty and has collaborated with numerous writers, creating nearly twenty illustrated books that have sold millions of copies. Since the late 1990s, Amano has worked with several American comics publishers, including DC Comics on the illustrated Sandman novel *Sandman: The Dream Hunters* with Neil Gaiman, and Marvel Comics on *Elektra and Wolverine: The Redeemer* with best-selling author Greg Rucka.